PETERBOROUGH LIBRARIES

24 Hour renewal line 08458 505606

This book is to be returned on or before the latest date shown above, but may be renewed up to three times if the book is not in demand. Ask at your local library for details.

Please note that charges are made on overdue books

D1340568

60000 0000 84674

Published in Great Britain 2013
Mills & Boon, an imprint of Harlequin (UK) Limited,
Eton House, 18-24 Paradise Road, Richmond, Surrey TW9 1SR

LOVE'S REVENGE © Harlequin Enterprises II B.V./S.à.r.l. 2013

The Italian's Revenge © Michelle Reid 2000
A Passionate Marriage © Michelle Reid 2002
The Brazilian's Blackmailed Bride © Michelle Reid 2005

ISBN: 978 0 263 90586 1

026-0613

Harlequin (UK) policy is to use papers that are natural, renewable and recyclable products and made from wood grown in sustainable forests. The logging and manufacturing processes conform to the legal environmental regulations of the country of origin.

Printed and bound
by CPI Group (UK) Ltd, Croydon, CR0 4YY

Michelle Reid grew up on the southern edges of Manchester, the youngest in a family of five lively children. Now she lives in the beautiful county of Cheshire, with her busy executive husband and two grown-up daughters. She loves reading, the ballet and playing tennis when she gets the chance. She hates cooking, cleaning and despises ironing! Sleep she can do without and produces some of her best written work during the early hours of the morning.

THE
MICHELLE REID
COLLECTION

February 2013

March 2013

April 2013

May 2013

June 2013

July 2013

THE ITALIAN'S REVENGE
MICHELLE REID

CHAPTER ONE

STEPPING out of her son's bedroom, Catherine closed the door just as quietly as she could, then wilted wearily back against it. Santo had gone to sleep at last, but she could still hear the heart-wrenching little sniffles that were shaking his five-year-old frame.

It really could not go on, she decided heavily. The tears and tantrums had been getting worse each time they erupted. And the way she had been burying her head in the sand in the vague hopes that his problem would eventually sort itself out had only managed to exacerbate the situation.

It was time—more than time—that she did something about it, even if the prospect filled her with untold dread.

And if she was going to act, then it had to be now. Luisa was due to catch the early commuter flight out of Naples in the morning, and if she was to be stopped then it must be tonight, before it caused her mother-in-law too much inconvenience.

'Damn,' she breathed as she levered herself away from her son's bedroom door and made her way down the stairs. The mere prospect of putting through such a sensitive call was enough to set the tension singing inside her.

For what did she say? she asked herself as she stepped into the sitting room and quietly closed that door behind her.

The straightforward approach seemed the most logical answer, where she just picked up the phone and told Luisa bluntly that her grandson was refusing to go back to Naples with her tomorrow and why. But that kind of approach did not take into consideration the fragile sensibilities of the recipient. Or the backlash of hostility that was going to rebound on her, most of which would be labelling her the troublemaker.

She sighed fretfully, caught a glimpse of herself in the mirror as she did it, then just stood staring at her own reflection.

Good grief, but she looked a mess, though in truth it didn't particularly surprise her. The battles with Santo had been getting worse by the day as this week had drawn to a close. Now her face was showing the results of too many emotion-draining tussles and too many restless nights while she lay awake worrying about them. Her eyes were bruised and her skin looked so pale that if it hadn't been for the natural flashes of copper firing up her golden hair then she would probably resemble some hollow-eyed little ghost.

Not so much of the little, she then mocked herself on an unexpected burst of rueful humour. For there was nothing *little* about her five-feet-eight-inch frame. Slender—yes, she conceded. Too slender for some people's tastes.

Vito's tastes.

The humour died as suddenly as it had erupted, banished by the one person who could turn laughter into bitterness without even having to try.

Vittorio Adriano Lucio Giordani—to give him his full and impressive title. Man of means. Man of might. Man at the root of her son's problems.

Once she had loved him; now she hated him. But then that was surely Vito. Man of dynamic contrasts. Stunning to look at. Arrogant to a fault. Exquisitely versed in the art of loving. Deadly to love.

She shuddered, her arms coming up to wrap around her as if in self-protection as she turned away from that face in the mirror rather than having to watch it alter from tired to bitter, which was what it usually did when she let herself think about Vito.

Because not only did she hate him but she hated even thinking about him. He was the skeleton in her past, linked to her present by an invisible thread that went directly from her heart, straight through the heart of their son and then into Vito's heart.

In fact Vito's only saving grace, in Catherine's view, was his open adoration of their five-year-old son. Now it seemed that even that fragile connection was under threat—though Vito didn't know it yet.

'I hate you! And I hate Papà! I don't want to love you any more!'

She winced painfully as the echo of that angrily emotive cry pierced her like a knife in the chest. Santo had meant those words; he had felt them deeply. Too deeply for a confused and vulnerable little boy to have to cope with.

Which brought her rather neatly back to where she had started when she walked into this room, she grimly concluded. Namely, doing something about Santo's distress and anger.

A point that sent her eyes drifting over to where the telephone sat on the small table by the sofa, looking perfectly innocent when in actual fact it was a time bomb set to explode the moment she so much as touched it.

Because she never rang Naples—never. Had not done so once since she had left there three years ago. Any communicating went on via lawyers or by letters sent to and from Santo's grandmother Luisa. So this phone call was so unique it was likely to cause major ructions in the Giordani household. And that was *before* she gave her reason for calling!

Therefore it was with reluctance that she went to sit down beside the telephone table. And with her bare toes curling tensely into the carpet, she gritted her teeth, took a couple of deep breaths, then reached out for the receiver.

By the time she had punched in the required set of digits she was sitting there with her eyes pressed tight shut, half praying that no one would be home.

Coward, she mocked herself.

And why not? she then countered. With their track record it paid to be cowardly around Vito. She just hoped that Luisa would answer. At least with Luisa she could relax some of the tension out of her body and *try* to sound normal before she attempted to break the news to her.

No chance. *'Si?'* a deeply smooth and seductively accented voice suddenly drawled into her ear.

Catherine jumped, her eyes flicking open as instant recognition turned her grey eyes green.

Vito.

Damn, it was Vito. A sudden hot flush went chasing through her. A thick lump formed across her throat. She tried to speak but found she couldn't. Instead her eyes drifted shut again and suddenly she was seeing him as clearly as if he was standing here directly in front of her. Seeing the blackness of his hair, the darkness of his skin, and the long, lean, tightly muscled posture of his supremely arrogant stance.

He was wearing a dinner suit, she saw, because it was Sunday and coming up to dinnertime there in Naples, and the Giordani family always dressed formally for the evening meal on a Sunday. So the suit would be black and the shirt white, with an accompanying black bow tie.

And she could see the disturbing honeyed-gold colour of his eyes, with their long, thick, curling lashes, which could so polarise attention that it was impossible to think of anything else when you let yourself look into them. So she didn't. Instead she moved on to his mouth and let her mind's eye drift across its smooth, firm, sensual contours, knowing exactly what to expect when another telling little shudder hit her system.

For this was the mouth of a born lover. A beautiful mouth, a seductive mouth, a disturbingly expressive mouth that could grin and mock and snarl and kiss like no other mouth, and lie like no other, and hate like no—

'Who is there, please?' his deep voice demanded in terse Italian.

Catherine jumped again, then tensely sat forward, her fingers tightly gripping the telephone receiver as she forced her locked up vocal cords to relax enough to allow her to speak.

'Hello, Vito,' she murmured huskily. 'It's me— Catherine...'

The bomb went off—in the form of a stunning silence. The kind that ate away at her insides and made nerves twitch all over her. Her mouth was dry, her heart having to force blood through valves that had simply stopped working. She felt light-headed but heavy-limbed, and wanted to start crying suddenly—which was so very pathetic that at least the feeling managed to jolt her into attempting to speak again.

But Vito beat her to it. 'What is wrong with my son?' he lashed out, grating English replacing terse Italian. The sheer violence in his tone was enough to warn Catherine that he had instantly jumped to all the wrong conclusions.

'It's all right,' she said quickly. 'Santo isn't ill.'

There was another short, tense, pulsing moment while Vito took time to absorb that assurance. 'Then why do you break your own court order and ring me here?' he demanded coldly.

Grimacing at his right to ask that question, Catherine still had to bite down on her lip to stop herself from replying with something nasty. The break-up of their marriage had not been pleasant, and the hostility between them still ran strong three years on.

Three years ago Vito had been so incensed when she'd left him, taking Santo with her, that he had made the kind of threatening noises which at the time had made her blood run cold with fear.

She had responded by making Santo a ward of court and serving an order on Vito prohibiting him any contact with her unless it was through a third party. Catherine didn't think Vito would ever forgive her for putting him through the indignity of having to swear before a judge that he would neither contact Catherine personally nor attempt to take Santo out of the country, before he was allowed access to his own son.

They had not exchanged a single word between them since.

It had taken him a whole year to win the legal right to have Santo visit him in Italy. Before that it had been up to him to come to London if he wanted to spend time with his son. And even to this day Santo was collected from and returned to Catherine by his grandmother, so that his parents would not come into contact with each other.

In fact the only area where they remained staunchly amicable was where their son's opinion of the other was concerned. Santo had the right to love them both equally, without feeling the pressure of having one parent's dislike of the other to corrupt his view—a point brought home to them both by a stern grandmother, who had found herself flung into the role of referee between them at a time when their mutual hostility had been running at its highest.

So Catherine had grown used to listening smilingly for hours and hours at a time while Santo extolled all his adored *papà's* many virtues, and she presumed that Vito had grown used to hearing the same in reverse.

But that didn't mean the animosity between them had

mellowed any through the ensuing years—only that they both hid it well for Santo's benefit.

'Actually, I was hoping to speak to Luisa,' she explained as coolly and briefly as she could. 'If you would get her for me, Vito, I would appreciate it.'

'And I repeat,' he responded, tight-lipped and incisive. 'What is so wrong that you dare to ring here?'

In other words, he wasn't going to play the game and allow Luisa to stand buffer between them, Catherine made wry note.

'I would prefer to explain to Luisa,' she insisted stubbornly.

She sensed more than heard his teeth snapping together. 'Then of course you may do so,' he smoothly replied. 'When she arrives to collect my son from you in the morning...'

'No, Vito—wait!' she cried out, her long, slender legs launching her to her feet as panic went rampaging through her when she realised he was actually going to put the phone down on her! And suddenly she was trembling all over as she stood there waiting to find out what he would do, while a taut silence began to buzz like static against her eardrum.

The line was not severed.

As Catherine's stress-muddied brain began to take that fact in, she also realised that Vito was not going to say another word until she said something worth him keeping the line open.

'I'm having problems with Santo,' she disclosed on a reluctant rush.

'What kind of problems?'

'The kind I prefer to discuss with Luisa,' she replied. 'Get her advice on w-what to do be-before she arrives here tomorrow...'

No wonder she was stammering, Catherine acknowledged grimly, because that last bit had been an outright lie. She was hoping to stop Luisa from coming here altogether. But the coward in her didn't dare to tell that to Vito. Past experience warned her that he would just go totally ballistic.

'You will hold the line, please,' his cold voice clipped, 'while I transfer this call to another telephone.'

Just like that, he was going to accede to her wishes and connect her with Luisa? Catherine could hardly believe her luck, and only just managed to disguise her sigh of relief as she murmured a polite, 'Thank you.'

Then the line went dead. Some of the tension began seeping out of her muscles and she sank weakly back down onto the sofa, her insides still playing havoc at the shock contact with their worst enemy. But other than that she congratulated herself. The first words they had spoken to each other in years had not been that dreadful.

They hadn't torn each other to shreds, at least.

Now she had to get her mind into gear and decide what she was going to tell Luisa. The truth seemed the most logical road to take. But the truth had always been such a sensitive issue between them all that she wasn't sure it was wise to use it now.

So, what do you say? she asked herself once again. Blame Santo's distress on something at school? Or on the dual life he is forced to lead where one parent lives in London and the other in Naples?

Then there were the two different lifestyles the little boy had to deal with. The first being where average normality was stamped into everything, from the neat suburban London street they lived in, with its rows of neat middle-class houses, to the neat, normal kind of families that resided in each. While several thousand miles away, in a different country and most certainly in a different world, was the other kind of life. One that was about as far away

from normal and average as life could get for most people,
never mind a confused little boy. For instead of suburban
Naples, Vito lived out in the country. His home was a pal-
ace compared to this house, his standard of living steeped
in the kind of luxury that would fill most ordinary people
with awe.

When Santo visited Naples, his *papà* took time off from
his busy job as head of the internationally renowned
Giordani Investments to give his son his full attention. And
if it wasn't his *papà*, his beloved grandmother was more
than ready to pour the same amount of love and attention
upon him.

Catherine had no other family. And she worked full time
all the time, whether Santo was away or not. He had to
accept that he was collected from school by a child-minder
and taken home with her to wait until Catherine could collect him.

But all of that—or none of that—was what the child
found upsetting. Santo was not really old enough yet to
understand just what it was that was disturbing him so
much. It had taken several skirmishes and a lot of patience
for Catherine to begin to read between the lines of his angry
outbursts.

Then, tonight, the final truth had come out, in the shape
of a name. A name that had sent icy chills sweeping down
her spine when she'd heard it falling from her own child's
lips. And not just the name but the way Santo had said it—
with pain and anguish.

She knew those emotions, had first-hand experience of
what they could do to your belief in yourself, in your sense
of self-worth. She also knew that if what Santo had told
her was the truth then she didn't blame him for refusing to
have anything to do with his Italian family. For hadn't she
responded in the same way once herself?

'Right. Talk,' a grim voice commanded.

Catherine blinked, her mind taking a moment to realise what was going on. 'Where's Luisa?' she demanded, beginning to stiffen up all over again at the sound of Vito's voice.

'I do not recall saying I was going to bring my mother to the phone,' he responded coolly. 'Santo is *my* son, I will remind you. If you are having problems with *my* son, then you will discuss those problems with me.'

'He is *our* son,' Catherine corrected—while busily trying to reassess a situation that had promised to be complicated and touchy enough discussing it with Luisa. The very idea of having to say what she did have to say to Vito, of all people, was probably going to be impossible.

'So at last you acknowledge that.'

The barb hit right on its chosen mark and Catherine's lips snapped together in an effort to stop herself from responding to it.

It was no use. The words slipped out of their own volition. 'Try for sarcasm, Vito,' she drawled deridingly. 'It really helps the situation more than I can say.'

A sound caught her attention. Not a sigh, exactly, more a controlled release of air from his lungs, and then she heard the subtle creak of leather that was so familiar to her that she knew instantly which room he was now in.

His father's old study—now Vito's study, since Lucio Giordani had passed away eighteen months after Santo had been born.

And suddenly she was seeing that room as clearly as she had seen Vito himself only minutes before. Seeing its size and its shape and its old-fashioned elegance. The neutral-coloured walls, the richly polished floor, the carefully selected pieces of fine Renaissance furniture—including the desk Vito was sitting behind.

'Are you still there?'

'Yes,' she replied, having to blink her mind back into focus again.

'Then will you please tell me what problems Santino has before I lose my patience?'

This time she managed to control the urge to retaliate to his frankly provoking tone. 'He's been having problems at school.' She decided that was as good a place to start as any. 'It began weeks ago, just after his last visit with you over there.'

'Which in your eyes makes it my fault, I presume?'

'I didn't say that,' she denied, though she knew she was thinking it. 'I was merely attempting to fill you in with what has been happening.'

'Then I apologise,' he said.

Liar, she thought, heaving in a deep breath in an attempt to iron out any hint of accusation from her tone—though that wasn't easy, given the circumstances. 'He's been disruptive in class,' she made herself go on. 'Angry all the time, and insolent.' She didn't add that Santo had been the same with her because that wasn't important and would only confuse the issue. 'After one such skirmish his teacher threatened to bring his parents in to school to speak to them about his behaviour. He responded by informing the teacher that his father lived in Italy and wouldn't come, because he was rich and too important to bother with a nuisance like him.'

Catherine heard Vito's indrawn gasp in response, and knew he had understood the import of what she was trying to tell him here. 'Why would he say something like that, Vito?' she questioned curtly. 'Unless he has been led to believe it is true? He's too young to have come up with a mouthful like that all on his own, so someone has to have said it to him first for him to repeat it.'

'And you think it was me?' he exclaimed, making Catherine sigh in annoyance.

'I don't know who it was!' she snapped. 'Because he isn't telling!' But I can damn well guess, she tagged on silently. 'Now, to cut a long story short,' she concluded, 'he is refusing to go to Naples with Luisa tomorrow. He tells me that you don't really want him there, so why should he bother with you?'

'So you called here tonight to tell my mother not to come and collect him,' he assumed from all of that. 'Great way to deal with the problem, Catherine,' he gritted. 'After all, Santo is only saying exactly what you have been wishing he would say for years now, so you can get me right out of your life!'

'You are out of my life,' she responded. 'Our divorce becomes final at the end of this month.'

'A divorce *you* instigated,' he pointed out. 'Have you considered whether it is that little event that is causing Santo's problems?' he suggested. 'Or maybe there is more to it than that,' he then added tightly, 'and I need to look no further than the other end of this telephone line to discover the one who has been feeding my son lies about me!'

'Are you suggesting that *I* have been telling him that you think he's a nuisance?' she gasped, so affronted by the implication that she shot back to her feet. 'If so, think again, Vito,' she sliced at him furiously. 'Because it isn't me who is planning to remarry as soon as I'm free of you! And it isn't me who is about to undermine our son's position in my life by sticking him with the archetypal step-*mamma* from hell!'

Oh, she hadn't meant to say that! Catherine cursed her own unruly tongue as once again the silence came thundering down all around her.

Yet, even having said it, her body was pumping with the kind of adrenaline that started wars. She was even breathing heavily, her green eyes bright with a bitter antagonism, her mouth stretched back from even white teeth that desperately wanted to bite!

'Who the hell told you that?' Vito rasped, and Catherine had the insane idea that he too was on his feet, and breathing metaphorical fire all over the telephone.

And this—*this* she reminded herself forcefully, is why Vito and I are best having no contact whatsoever! We fire each other up like two volcanoes.

'Is it true?' she countered.

'That is none of your business,' he sliced.

Her flashing eyes narrowed into two threatening slits. 'Watch me make it my business, Vito,' she warned, very seriously. 'I'll put a block on our divorce if I find that it's true and you are planning to give Marietta any power over Santo.'

'You don't have that much authority over my actions any more,' he derided her threat.

'No?' she challenged. 'Then just watch this space,' she said, and grimly cut the connection.

It took ten minutes for the phone to start ringing. Ten long minutes in which Catherine seethed and paced, and wondered how the heck she had allowed the situation to get so out of control. Half of what she had said she hadn't meant to say at all!

On a heavy sigh she tried to calm down a bit before deciding what she should do next. Ring back and apologise? Start the whole darn thing again from the beginning and hope to God that she could keep a leash on her temper?

The chance of that happening was so remote that she even allowed herself to smile at it. Her marriage to Vito had never been anything but volatile. They were both hot-tempered, both stubborn, both passionately defensive of their own egos.

The first time they met it was at a party. Having gone

there with separate partners, they'd ended up leaving together. It had been a case of sheer necessity, she recalled, remembering the way they had only needed to take one look at each other to virtually combust in the ensuing sexual fall-out.

They had become lovers that same night. Within the month she was pregnant. Within the next they were married. Within three years they were sworn enemies. It had all been very wild, very hot and very traumatic from passionate start to bloody finish. Even the final break had come only days after they'd fallen on each other in a fevered attempt to recapture what they had known they were losing.

The sex had been great—the rest a disaster. They had begun rowing within minutes of separating their bodies. He'd stormed off—as usual—and the next day she'd gone into premature labour with their second child and lost their second son while Vito was seeking solace with his mistress.

She would never, ever forgive him for that. She would never forgive the humiliation of having to beg his mistress to send him home because she needed him. But he'd still arrived too late to be of any use to her. By then she had been rushed into hospital and had already lost the baby. To have Vito come to lean over her and murmur all the right phrases—while smelling of that woman's perfume—had been the final degradation.

She had left Italy with Santo just as soon as she was physically able, and Vito would never forgive her for taking his son away from him.

They both had axes to grind with each other. Both felt betrayed, ill-used and deserted. And if it hadn't been for Vito's mother Luisa stepping in to play arbiter, God alone knew where the bitterness would have taken them.

Thanks to Luisa they'd managed to survive three years of relative peace—so long as there was no personal contact between them. Now that peace had been well and truly shattered, and Catherine wished she knew how to stop full-scale war from breaking out.

But she didn't. Not with the same main antagonist still very much on the scene.

When the telephone began to ring again she went perfectly still, her heart stopping beating altogether as she turned to stare at the darned contraption. Her first instinct was to ignore it. For she didn't feel up to another round with Vito just yet. But a second later she was snatching up the receiver when she grew afraid the persistent ring would wake Santo.

'Catherine?' a very familiar voice questioned anxiously. 'My son has insisted that I call you. What in heaven's name is going on, please?'

Luisa. It was Luisa. Catherine wilted like a dying swan onto the sofa. 'Luisa,' she breathed in clear relief. 'I thought you were going to be Vito.'

'Vito has just stormed out of the house in a fury,' his mother informed her. 'After cursing and shouting and telling me that I had to ring you right away. Is something the matter with Santo, Catherine?' she asked worriedly.

'Yes and no,' Catherine replied. Then, on a deep breath, she explained calmly to Luisa, in the kind of words she should have used to Vito, what Santo's problem was—without complicating the issue this time by bringing Vito's present love-life into it.

'No wonder my son was looking so frightened,' Luisa murmured when Catherine had finished. 'I have not seen that dreadful expression on his face in a long time, and I hoped never to see it again.'

'Frightened?' Catherine prompted, frowning because she couldn't imagine the arrogant Vito being afraid of anything.

'Of losing his son again,' his mother enlightened. 'What is the matter Catherine? Did you think Vito would shrug off Santo's concerns as if they did not matter to him?'

'I—no,' she denied, surprised by the sudden injection of bitterness Vito's *mamma* was revealing.

'My son works very hard at forging a strong relationship with Santo in the short blocks of time allocated to him,' her mother-in-law went on. 'And to hear that this is suddenly being undermined must be very frightening for him.'

In three long years Luisa had never sounded anything but gently neutral, and Catherine found it rather disconcerting to realise that Luisa was, in fact, far from being neutral.

'Are you, like Vito, suggesting that it's me who is doing that undermining, Luisa?' she asked, seeing what she'd always thought of as her only ally moving right away from her.

'No.' The older woman instantly denied that. 'Of course not. I may worry for my son, but that does not mean I am blind to the fact that you both love Santo and would rather cut out your tongues than hurt him through each other.'

'Well, thanks for that,' Catherine replied, but her tone was terse, her manner cooling in direct response to Luisa's.

'I am not your enemy, Catherine.' Luisa knew what she was thinking.

'But if push came to shove—' Catherine smiled slightly '—you know which camp to stand in.'

Luisa didn't answer and Catherine didn't expect her to— which was an answer in itself.

'So,' Luisa said more briskly. 'What do you want to do about Santo? Do you want me to delay my journey to London until you have managed to talk him round a little?'

'Oh, no!' Catherine instantly vetoed that, surprising herself by discovering that somewhere during the two fraught telephone conversations she had completely changed her mind. 'You must come, Luisa! He will be so disappointed if you don't come for him! I just didn't want you to walk in on his new rebelliousness cold, so to speak,' she explained. 'And—and there is a big chance he may refuse to leave with you,' she warned, adding anxiously, 'You do understand that I won't make him go with you if he doesn't want to?'

'I am a mother,' Luisa said. 'Of course I understand. So I will come, as arranged, and we will hope that Santo has had a change of heart after sleeping on his decision.'

Some hope of that, Catherine thought as she replaced the receiver. For Luisa was labouring under the misconception that Santo's problems were caused by a sudden and unexplainable loss of confidence in his *papà*—when in actual fact the little boy's reasoning was all too explainable.

And she went by the name of Marietta, Catherine mocked bitterly. Marietta, the long-standing friend of the family. Marietta the highly trusted member of Giordani Investments' board of directors. Marietta the long-standing mistress—the bitch.

She was tall, she was dark, she was inherently Italian. She had grace, she had style, she had unwavering charm. She had beauty and brains and knew how to use both to her own advantage. And, to top it all off, she was shrewd and sly and careful to whom she revealed her true self.

That she had dared to reveal that true self to Santo had, in Catherine's view, been Marietta's first big mistake in her long campaign to get Vito. For she might have managed to make Catherine run away like a silly whimpering coward, but she would not send Santo the same way.

Not even over my dead body, Catherine vowed as she prepared for bed that night...

CHAPTER TWO

AFTER spending the night tossing and turning, at around five o'clock the next morning Catherine finally gave up trying to sleep, and was just dragging herself out of bed when the distinctive sound of a black cab rumbling to a halt outside in the street caught her attention. A couple of her neighbours often commuted by taxi early in the morning if they were having to catch an early train somewhere, so she didn't think twice about it as she padded off to use the bathroom.

Anyway, her mind was busy with other things, like the day ahead of her, which was promising to be as traumatic as the evening that had preceded it.

On her way past his room, she slid open her son's door to check if he was still sleeping. The sight of his dark head peeping out from a snuggle of brightly printed duvet was reassuring. At least Santo had managed to sleep through his worries.

Closing the door again, she went downstairs with the intention of making herself a large pot of coffee over which she hoped to revive herself before the next round of battles commenced—but a shadow suddenly distorting the early-morning daylight seeping in through the frosted glass panel in her front door made her pause.

Glancing up, she saw the dark bulk of a human body standing in her porch. Her frown deepened. Surely it was too early for the postman? she asked herself, yet still continued to stand there expecting her letterbox to open and a wad of post to come sliding through it. But when instead of bending the dark figure lifted a hand towards her door-bell, Catherine was suddenly leaping into action.

In her urgency to stop whoever it was from ringing the bell and waking up her son she was pulling the door open without really thinking clearly about what she was doing. So it was only after the door opened wide on the motion that she realised she had gone to bed last night without putting the safety chain on.

By then it didn't matter. It was already too late to re-member caution, and all the other safety rules that were a natural part of living these days, when she found herself staring at the very last person she'd expected to see stand-ing on her doorstep.

Her heart took a quivering dive to her stomach, the shock of seeing Vito in the actual flesh for the first time in three long years so debilitating that for the next whole minute she couldn't seem to function on any other level than sight.

A sight that absorbed in one dizzying glance every hard-edged, clean-cut detail, from the cold sting of his eyes to the grim slant of his mouth and even the way he had one side of his jacket shoved casually aside so he could thrust a hand into his trouser pocket—though she wasn't aware of her eyes dipping down that low over him.

He was wearing a black dinner suit and a white shirt that conjured up the picture she had built of him the night be-fore; only the bow tie was missing, and the top button of the shirt yanked impatiently open at his lean brown throat.

Had he come here directly from storming out of his house in Naples? she wondered. And decided he had to have done to get here to London this quickly. But if his haste in getting here was supposed to impress her by how seriously he was taking her concerns about Santo—then it didn't.

She didn't want him here. And, worse, she didn't want to watch those honeyed eyes of his drift over her on a very slow and very comprehensive scan of her person, as if she was still one of his possessions.

And the fact that she became acutely aware of her own sleep-mussed state didn't enamour her, either. He had no right to study the way her tangled mass of copper-gold hair was hanging limp about her shoulders, or the fact that she was standing here in thin white cotton that barely hid what it covered.

Then his gaze moved lower, jet-black lashes sinking over golden eyes that seemed to draw a caressing line across the surface of her skin as they moved over the pair of loose-fitting pyjama shorts which left much of her slender legs on show. And Catherine felt something very old and very basic spring to life inside her.

It was called sexual arousal. The man had always only had to look at her like this to make her make her so aware of herself that she could barely think straight.

'What are you doing here?' she lashed out in sheer re-taliation.

Arrogance personified, she observed, as a black eyebrow arched and those incredible eyes somehow managed to dis-parage her down the length of his roman nose, despite the fact that she stood a deep step higher than him, which placed them almost at a level.

'I would have thought that was obvious,' Vito coolly replied. 'I am here to see my son.'

'It's only five o'clock,' she protested. 'Santo is still asleep.'

'I am well aware of the time, Catherine,' he replied rather heavily, and something passed across his face—a weariness she hadn't noticed was there until that moment.

Which was the point when she began to notice other things about him. He looked older than she would have expected, for instance. The signs of a carefully honed cynicism were scoring grooves into his handsome face where once none had been. And the corners of his firm mouth were turned down slightly, as if he never let himself smile much any more.

Seeing that for some reason made her insides hurt. And the sensation infuriated her because she didn't want to feel anything but total indifference for this man's state of mind.

'How did you get here so quickly, anyway?' she asked with surly shortness.

'I flew myself in overnight,' he replied. 'Then came directly here from the airport.'

Which meant he must have been on the go all night, she concluded. Then another thought sent an icy chill slithering down her spine.

After flying half the night, had he then driven himself here in one of the supercharged death-traps he tended to favour? Glancing over his shoulder, she expected to see some long, low, sleek growling monster of a car crouching by the curbside, but there wasn't one.

Then she remembered hearing a taxi cab pulling up a few minutes earlier and realised with a new kind of shock that Vito must have used it to travel here from the airport.

Now that must have been a novelty for him, she mused, eyeing him curiously. Vito always liked to be in the driver's seat, whether that be behind the controls of his plane or the wheel of a car—or even in his sex-life!

'Which airport did you fly in to?' she asked, the thrifty housekeeper in her wanting to assess the cost of such a long cab journey.

'Does it matter?' He flashed her a look of irritation. 'And do we have to have this conversation here on the doorstep?' he then added tersely, his dark head turning to take in the neat residential street with its rows of neat windows—some of which had curtains twitching curiously because their voices must be carrying on the still morning air.

Vito wasn't a doorstep man, Catherine mused wryly. He was the greatly admired and very respected head of the world-renowned Giordani Investment Bank, cum expert troubleshooter for any ailing business brought under his wing. People valued his opinion and his advice—and welcomed him with open arms when he came to call.

But she was not one of those people, she reminded herself sternly. She owed Vito nothing, and respected him not at all. 'You're not welcome here,' she told him coldly.

'My son may beg to differ,' he returned, responding to her hostile tone with a slight tensing of his jaw.

Much as she would have liked to protest that claim, Catherine knew that she couldn't. 'Then why don't you come back—in a couple of hours', say, when he is sure to be awake?' she suggested, and was about to shut the door in his face when those golden eyes began to flash.

'Shut that door and you will regret it,' he warned very grimly.

To her annoyance, she hesitated, hating herself for being influenced by his tone. And the atmosphere between them thrummed with a mutual antagonism. Neither liked the other; neither attempted to hide it.

'I would have thought it was excruciatingly obvious that you and I need to talk *before* Santo is awake,' he added with rasping derision. 'Why the hell else do you think I have knocked myself out trying to get here this early?'

Once again, he had a point, and Catherine knew she was being petty, but it didn't stop her from standing there like a stone wall protecting her own threshold. Old habits died hard, and refusing to give an inch to Vito in case he took the whole mile from her had become second nature during their long and battle-zoned association.

'*You* called *me*, Catherine,' he then reminded her grimly. 'An unprecedented act in itself. You voiced your concerns to me and I have responded. Now show a little grace,' he suggested, 'and at least acknowledge that my coming here is worthy of some consideration.'

As set-downs went, Catherine supposed that that one was as good as any Vito had ever doled out to her, as she felt herself come withering down from proudly hostile to childishly petty in one fell swoop.

She stepped back without uttering another word and, stiff-faced, eyes lowered, invited her husband of six long years to enter her home for the first time. He did it slowly—stepping over her threshold in a measured way which suggested that he too was aware of the significance of the occasion.

Then suddenly he was there right beside her, sharing the narrow space in her small hallway and filling it with the sheer power of his presence. And Catherine felt the tension build inside her as she stood there and absorbed—literally absorbed—his superior height, his superior breadth, his superior physical strength that had not been so evident while she'd kept him outside, standing nine inches lower and therefore nine inches less the man she should have remembered him to be.

She could smell the unique scent of his skin, feel the vibrations of his body as he paused a mere hair's breadth away from her to send her nerve-ends on a rampage of wild, scattering panic in recognition of how dangerous those vibrations were to them.

Six years ago it had taken one look for them to fall on each other in a fever of sexual craving. Now here they were, several years of bitter enmity on—and yet she could feel the same hunger beginning to wrap itself around her.

Oh, damn, she cursed silently, though whether she was cursing herself for being so weak of the flesh or Vito for being the sexual animal he undoubtedly was, she wasn't quite certain.

'This way,' she mumbled, snaking her way around him so that their bodies did not brush.

She led the way to her sitting room, shrouded still by the curtains drawn across the window. With a jerk she stepped sideways, to allow him to enter, then watched defensively as his eyes moved over his strange surroundings.

Plain blue carpet and curtains, two small linen sofas, a television set, a couple of low tables and a bookcase was all the small room would take comfortably, except for a special corner of the room dedicated to Santo, where his books, games and toys were stacked on and around a low play table.

It was all very neat, very—ordinary. Nothing like the several elegant and spacious reception rooms filled with priceless antiques in Vito's home. Or the huge playroom her son had all to himself, filled with everything a little boy could possibly dream of. A point Catherine was made suddenly acutely aware of when she glimpsed the brief twitch along Vito's jawline as he too made the comparison.

'I'll go and get dressed,' she said, dipping her head to hide her expression as she turned for the door again and—she admitted it—escape, before she was tempted to say something nasty about money not being everything.

But his hand capturing her wrist stopped her. 'I am no snob, Catherine,' he murmured sombrely. 'I know and appreciate how happy and comfortable Santo has been living here with you.'

'Please let go of my wrist,' she said, not interested in receiving his commendation on anything. She was too concerned about the streak of heat that was flowing up her arm from the point where his fingers circled her.

'I am no woman-beater either,' he tagged on very grimly.

'That's very odd,' she countered as he dropped her wrist. 'For I seem to remember that the last time we stood alone in a room you were threatening to do just that to me.'

'Words, Catherine,' he sighed, half turning away from her. 'I was angry, and those words were empty of any real threat to you, as you well know.'

'Do I?' Her smile was wry to say the least. 'We were strangers, Vito. We were strangers then and we are strangers now. I never, ever knew what you were thinking.'

'Except in bed,' he said, swinging back to look at her, the grimness replaced by a deeply mocking cynicism. 'You knew exactly what I was thinking there.'

Catherine tossed her head at him, matching him expression for cynical expression. 'Shame, then, that we couldn't spend twenty-four hours there instead of the odd six,' she said. 'And I really don't want to have this kind of conversation with you,' she added. 'It proves nothing and only clouds the issues of real importance where Santo is concerned.'

'Our relationship—or the lack of it—*is* the important issue for Santo, I would have thought.'

'No.' She denied that. 'The important issue for Santo is the prospect of his father marrying a woman his son is actively afraid of.'

Vito stiffened. 'Define ''afraid'',' he commanded.

Catherine stared at him. 'Afraid as in frightened—how else would you like me to put it?'

'Of Marietta?' His frown was strong with disbelief. 'He must have misunderstood something she said to him,' he murmured thoughtfully. 'You must know his Italian is not as well-formed as his English.'

Oh, right, Catherine thought. It couldn't *possibly* be Marietta's fault. Not in a Giordani's eyes!

'I'm going to get dressed,' she clipped, abandoning the useless argument by moving back into the hallway.

'Do you mind if I make myself a cup of coffee while you do that?'

Without a word, she diverted towards the kitchen—but,

aware that Vito was following her, Catherine sensed him pause to glance up the stairwell, as if he was hoping his son would suddenly appear.

He didn't—and he wouldn't, she predicted, as she continued on into the kitchen. Santo was by nature a creature of habit. His inner alarm clock was set for seven, so seven o'clock was the time he would awaken.

She was over by the sink filling the kettle with water by the time Vito came in the room. The hairs on the back of her neck began to prickle, picking up on his narrowed scrutiny of her, which once again made her acutely aware of the unsuitability of her present clothing.

Not that she was in any way underdressed, she quickly assured herself. The pair of shorts and a shirt-style top she was wearing were adequate enough—it was the lack of anything beneath them that was making her feel so conscious of those oh, too knowing eyes.

'I don't suppose you expect to hear from him until seven,' he murmured suddenly.

Catherine smiled a wry smile to herself as she transferred the kettle to its base and switched it on. So, his attention was firmly fixed on Santo—which put her well and truly in her place!

'You know his routine, then,' she answered lightly. 'And, knowing it, you must also know that if I try to waken him any earlier—'

'He will not be fit to live with,' Vito finished for her. 'Yes, I am aware of that.'

She glanced up at the kitchen clock, heard a sound of rustling cloth behind her and had an itchy feeling that Vito was also checking the time on his wristwatch.

Five thirty, she noted. That meant they had a whole hour and a half to endure each other's exclusive company. Could they stand it? she wondered, counting coffee scoops into the filter jug.

'Your hair is shorter than I remember.'

Her mind went blank, the next scoopful of coffee freezing on its way to the jug. After only just reassuring herself that he wasn't interested in anything about her personally, it came as a shock to discover that her instincts had indeed been working perfectly.

What else had he noticed? The way her shorts tended to cling to the cleft between her buttocks? Or, worse, that as she stood like this, in profile to him, he could see the shadowy outline of her right breast through the thin white cotton?

'I'm three years older,' she replied, though what that was supposed to mean even she didn't know, because she was too engrossed in a whole host of sensations that were beginning to attack her. All of them to do with sex, and sexual awareness, and this damn man, who had *always* been able to do this to her!

'You don't look it.'

And did he have to sound so grim about that?

'You do,' she countered in outright retaliation.

The rollercoaster of her own thoughts sent the coffee into the jug and saw the scoop abandoned onto the worktop with an angry flick of her slender wrist before she turned almost defiantly to face him, with a flat band of a false smile slapped on her face meant to show a clear disregard for his feelings.

But the smiled instantly died, melted away by the megawatt charge of his physical presence. He looked lean and mean, with his shirt hanging open at his brown throat and his jaw darkened by a five o'clock shadow. He had the arrogant nose of a Roman conqueror, the dark honeyed eyes of a charming sneak thief, and the wickedly sensual mouth of a gigolo. His body was built to fight lions in an arena, but men no longer did that to prove their prowess.

'And memories are made of this…' a silk-smooth voice softly taunted.

Her eyes closed and opened very slowly, bringing her fevered brain swirling back from where it had flown off to, to find him standing there taking malicious pleasure in watching her lose herself in memories of him.

It was like being caught with her hand in the sweetie jar. Sweat suddenly bathed her body, heat flushing her fine white skin—not the heat of arousal but the heat of a humiliation that completely demolished her. She didn't know what to do; she didn't know what to say.

'I'll get dressed…' was the wretched thing she actually came out with, and forced her shaking limbs to propel her towards the door and escape—again.

But Vito was not going to let her get off as lightly as that. Oh, no, not this man, with his lethal brand of wit, who also had so many axes to grind on her exposed rear that he was almost gleeful at being given this heaven-sent opportunity.

'Why bother?' he therefore drawled smoothly. 'It is already way too late to cover up what is happening to you, *mia cara.*'

'I am not your darling!' she snapped out in retaliation, knowing she was only rising to his deliberate baiting but unable to stop herself anyway.

'Maybe not,' he conceded. 'But I think you are wondering what it would be like to relive those moments when you were.'

If she didn't suffocate in her own shame then there really was no justice in the world, because it was what she deserved to do, Catherine derided herself bitterly.

'Not with you,' she denied, with an accompanying little shudder. 'Never with you again.'

'Was that a challenge? For if it was I might just take you up on it. You never know,' he mocked. 'It could be an—interesting exercise to see how many times we can ravish each other in the hour and a half we have free before our son comes down. It would certainly keep our minds off all our other problems...'

If the kitchen door handle had been a gun, she would probably have fired it at him. 'And if you need to sink yourself that low just to keep your mind occupied—then call in Marietta!' She used words to slay him with instead. 'She always was much better trained than me at servicing *all* your requirements.'

So what's really new here? she asked herself as a large hand came to land palm flat against the door to hold it shut, making her blink as it landed. 'You may still possess the body of a siren, Catherine,' Vito bit out, 'but you have developed the mouth of a slut! When are you going to listen to me, you blind bitter fool, and believe me when I tell you that Marietta is *not* and has *never* been my mistress!'

She should have left it there; Catherine knew she should. She should have remained perfectly still, pinned her 'mouth of a slut' shut and ignored his wretched lies until he gave up and let her out of here! But she couldn't. Vito had always been able to bring out the worst in her—and she the worst in him. They'd used to fight like sworn enemies and make love as if nothing could break them apart. It was like meeting like. His Latin fire versus her Celtish spirit. His oversized ego versus her fierce pride.

It had been a recipe for utter disaster. But for the first few blissful months of their relationship it had been a glorious blending of both passionate temperaments fused together by that wonderfully enthralling sensation she'd used to describe as—true love.

It hadn't seemed to matter then that the words were never actually spoken, for they had been there in each look, each touch, in the way neither had seemed able to be apart from the other for more than a few hours without making contact—if only with the intimate pitch of their voices via the telephone. Even when she'd fallen pregnant and the warring had begun, she had still believed that love was the engine which had driven them towards marriage.

Meeting Marietta on her wedding day, and learning that this was the woman Vito would have chosen to marry if she had not instead married his best friend Rocco, had placed the first fragile seeds of doubt in her mind about Vito's true feelings for her.

Yet neither by word nor gesture had Vito revealed any hint that there could be truth in the whispers, and she had very quickly managed to dismiss them when his attention towards her remained sound right through her first troubled pregnancy and into her second.

Then Rocco had been killed in a tragic boating accident, followed within weeks by Vito's father dying from a massive stroke. And before she'd realised quite what was happening, Vito and Marietta had hardly ever been seen apart.

'A shared grief', Vito used to call it. Marietta had called it—inevitable. 'What do you think Vito did when you trapped him into marriage—put on a blindfold and forgot it was me he was in love with? While Rocco was alive he may have been willing to accept second best in you. But with Rocco gone…?'

'I'll believe Marietta's not your mistress when hell freezes over.' Catherine came out of her bitter reverie to answer Vito's question. 'Now get away from me,' she commanded, trying to tug open the door.

But Vito's superior strength held it shut. 'When I am good and ready,' he replied. 'For you started this, so we may as well finish it right here and now, before my son arrives.'

'Finish what?' she cried, spinning to stare at him in angry bewilderment. 'I don't even know what it is we're fighting about!'

'This thing you have against Marietta,' he grimly enlightened her, 'is *your* obsession, Catherine. It always has been. So it therefore follows that it must be *you* who has been filling Santo's head full of this nonsense about Marietta and me.'

Catherine stared at him as if she didn't know him. How a man as intelligent and shrewd as Vito was could be so fatally flawed was a real mystery to her.

'You are the blind one, Vito,' she informed him. 'You are a blind, stubborn and conceited fool who could never see through the charm she lays on you that Marietta is as evil as they come!'

'And you are sick,' he responded, his dark face closing into a mask of distaste as he stepped right away from her. 'You have to be sick, Catherine, to think such things about a person who only wanted to befriend you.'

Befriend me—? 'I'm sorry if this offends you, Vito.' She laughed, almost choking on her own fury. 'But I don't make friends of my husband's lovers!'

Honeyed eyes began to flash dire warnings of murder. 'She has never been my lover!' he repeated furiously.

'And you are such a dreadful liar!' she sliced right back.

'I do not lie!'

'I know Marietta has been feeding her poison to Santo just as she once fed it to me,' she doggedly persisted.

'I will not continue to listen to this,' Vito said, reaching out as if to grab her arm so he could shift her away from the door and leave himself.

'Then will you listen to Santo?' she challenged.

The hand dropped away, his chin lifting stiffly. 'It is what I am here for, is it not?'

Why did his accent always thicken when he was under stress? she found herself wondering. Then blinked the silly question away because it had no bearing on what was happening here.

'But will you believe him?' she wanted to know. 'If *he* tells you that what *I* have been telling you is the truth?'

'And what if it is you who has fed him his version of the truth?' he countered.

Catherine sighed in disgust. 'Which I presume means that you have no intention of believing your own son's word—any more than you once believed mine!'

'I repeat,' he said. 'You are the one with the obsession. Not Santo and not me.'

And I am banging my head against a brick wall here, Catherine decided grimly. But what's new about that? she asked herself, with a deriding twist of her mouth that seemed to set his tense frame literally pulsing.

'Then I think you should leave,' she said, moving away from the door and crossing the room to get right away from him. 'Now, before Santo wakes up and finds you here. Because he will not thank you any more than I do for showing such little faith in his word.'

'I did not say that I disbelieve what Santo is thinking, only that I disbelieve his source.'

'Same thing.' Catherine shrugged that line of argument away. 'And all I can say is that I find it very sad that you can put your feelings for Marietta before your feelings for your son—which makes your journey here such a wasted gesture.'

Vito said nothing, his face locked into a tight, grim mask as he went over to the kettle and began pouring boiling water into the coffee jug. From her new place by kitchen sink Catherine watched him with an emptiness that said she saw no hope for happiness for him. The man was bewitched by the devil. He had to be if he was so prepared to risk the love of his son for the love of that woman.

But was he? Catherine then pondered thoughtfully. For he was *here*, wasn't he? Breaking a court order, willing to risk his visitation rights, because it was more important at present for him to be where his troubled son was. Be of help, if he could. Reassure, if he could...?

'Well, as a tit-for-tat kind of thing,' she murmured slowly, 'let's just test your love for Marietta against your love for your son, Vito.'

'It isn't a competition,' he denounced.

'I am making it one,' she declared. 'And I'm going to do it by giving you a straight choice. So listen to me, Vito, for I am deadly serious. Either you renounce all intention of ever marrying Marietta,' she said, 'or you marry her and forfeit all rights of access to Santino.'

Turning with his coffee cup in hand, he murmured levelly, 'Word of warning, *cara*, You will not come between my son and me again, no matter what tricks you try to pull.'

'Yet pull them I will,' she instantly promised. And the tension between them began to edge up to dangerous levels again, because she wasn't bluffing and Vito knew that she wasn't.

Her father had been an eminent lawyer before his premature demise. He'd had friends in the profession, powerful friends, who specialised in marital conflicts and had been more than willing to come to Catherine's aid three years ago when she had needed their expertise. They'd tied Vito up in legal knots before he'd even known what had hit him.

She would let them do it again if she felt she had to protect Santo from the evil that was threatening to take up permanent residence in his father's house. Vito must be as aware as she was that he had already given her the ammunition to fire at him by breaking a court order to come here like this today.

One phone call and she could make good her threat; he knew that.

'So, what is it to be?' She flashed him the challenge. 'Is it Marietta out of your life—or is it going to be Santo?'

He dared to laugh—albeit ruefully. 'You sound very

tough, Catherine. Very sure of yourself,' he remarked. 'But you seem to have overlooked one small but very important thing in all your clever plotting.'

'What?' she prompted, frowning, because as far as she could tell she had all the aces stacked firmly in her hand.

'Our son's clear insecurity and what you mean to do to ease it,' he said, taking a sip of thick black coffee. 'The last time you went to war against me, Santo was too young to know what was going on. But not any longer. Now he is old enough and alert enough to be aware of everything that takes place between the two of us.'

Pausing to watch as the full weight of his words settled heavily on her, he then gently offered a direct counter-challenge. 'Are *you* willing to risk hurting *his* love for me with yet another one of your vindictive campaigns aimed to make me toe the line...?''

CHAPTER THREE

'NO COME-BACK?' Vito softly prompted when she just stood there, staring at him while the full import of what he was pointing out to her slowly drained all the colour out of her face. 'Am I to assume, then, that your lust for revenge on sins imagined done to you does not run to hurting your son also?'

No, she thought on a chilled little shudder that spoke absolute volumes, she wasn't prepared to risk hurting her son's love for his *papà*.

'Well, that makes a refreshing change,' drawled a man who sounded as if he was beginning to enjoy himself. 'It almost—almost—restores my faith in you as the loyal loving mother of my son *cara*—even if it does nothing for my faith in you as the loyal and loving wife.'

Her chin went up, green eyes suddenly awash with derision. 'If we are going to get onto the subject of loyalty, then you're moving onto very shaky ground, Vito,' she warned him darkly.

'Then of course we will not,' he instantly conceded. 'Let us see instead if we can come up with a more—sensible compromise between us, that will adequately meet both our own requirements *and* fulfil our son's needs in one neat move...'

Was there such a thing? Catherine's eyes showed a blankness that said she couldn't think of one. 'So, don't keep me in suspense,' she snapped. 'Tell me this compromise.'

He smiled an odd smile, not quite wry, not quite cynical. 'I am not sure that you are going to like this,' he murmured.

'So long as it will put Marietta out in the cold, I'll be agreeable to anything,' Catherine assured him recklessly.

He didn't answer immediately, but the way his eyes began to gleam in a kind of unholy way made her flesh turn cold on the absolute certainty that she was about to be led somewhere she had no wish to go.

'Look, either cut to the bottom line of what all this taunting is about or get out of here!' she snapped in sheer nervous agitation.

'The bottom line,' he drawled, dropping his eyes down her body, 'is resting approximately midway down your sensational thighs and has the delicious potential of dropping to your lovely bare feet with a bit of gentle encouragement.'

Glancing down to look where his eyes were looking, she almost suffocated in the sudden wave of heat that went sizzling through her when she realised he was referring to her shorts!

'Will you just stop being so bloody provocative?' she choked, not sure if she was angry with him for saying such an outrageous thing or angry with herself for responding to it!

'I wish I could.' He grimaced, taking a languid sip of his coffee. 'But seeing those exquisite legs so enticingly presented has been driving me crazy since I arrived here.'

It was sheer instinct that made Catherine take a step forward with the intention of responding with a slap to his insufferable face!

But his hand deftly stopped her. 'You still have a great body, Catherine,' he told her, his eyes pinning her eyes with a look that made her feel as if she was drowning. 'All long sensual lines and supple curves that stir up some very exciting memories. So exciting in fact,' he murmured, gently stroking his thumb over the delicate flesh covering her wrist where the pulse-point was fluttering wildly, 'that it occurred to me—long before you showed your attraction to me, I should add—that with you back in my bed I would not need to look elsewhere to fill that particular place in my life.'

A stunning silence followed. One that locked the air inside her throat and closed down her brain in complete rejection of what he was actually suggesting here!

'How dare you?' she breathed in harsh denunciation. 'How dare you make such a filthy suggestion?'

'I need a woman in my bed.' He shrugged with no apology. 'And, since my son must be protected from the seedier side of that need, then that woman must therefore be my wife. My proper wife,' he then succinctly extended. 'One who will proudly grace my table, eagerly grace my bed, and love my son as deeply as I do.'

'And you think Marietta fills all of those requirements?' she scoffed in outright contempt for him.

His golden eyes darkened. 'We are not talking about Marietta now,' he clipped. 'We are talking about you, Catherine. You,' he repeated, putting down his cup so he could free his other hand to slide it around her waist. Her flesh tightened in rejection. He countered its response by pulling her that bit closer to the firmness of his body. 'Who, even dressed as you are, would still manage to grace any man's table with your beauty and your inherent sense of style. And as for the sex,' he murmured in that sinfully sensual tone that helped make him such a dynamic lover. 'Since I know your rich and varied appetite as well as I know my own, I see no problem in our resurrecting what used to be very satisfying interludes for both of us.'

Interludes? He called what she would have described as giving herself body and soul to him *satisfying interludes*? She almost choked on her own outrage, feeling belittled and defiled.

But—maybe that had been his intention! 'You're disgusting!' she snapped.

'I am a realist,' he said.

'A realist who is hungry for revenge,' Catherine extended deridingly, well aware of his real motive.

'The Italian in me demands it,' he freely admitted. 'Just think, though,' he added softly, 'how your very British yen for martyrdom could be given free rein. How you could reside in my home with your head held high and pretend that you are only there because of Santo. How you could even share my bed and enjoy every minute of what we do there while pretending to yourself that keeping me happy is the price you have to pay to keep your son happy.'

'And you?' she asked. 'What do you aim to get out of such a wicked scenario?'

'This...' he murmured, and with a tug she was against him, his mouth capturing hers with the kind of kiss that flung her back too far and too swiftly into the realms of darkness, where she kept everything to do with this man so carefully hidden.

Well, they were not hiding now, she noted painfully as the heat from his kiss ignited flaming torches that lit their escape. And suddenly she was incandescent with feeling. Hot feelings, crazed feelings, feelings that went dancing wildly through her on a rampage of sheer sensual greed.

Only Vito could do it. Only he had ever managed to fire her up this way. Her body knew his body, exalted in its hardness pressing against her. His tongue licked the flames; his hands staked their claim on her by skimming skilfully beneath the hem of her top, then more audaciously beneath the elasticated band of her shorts.

She must have whimpered at the shock sensation of his flesh sliding against her flesh, because his mouth left hers and his eyes burned black triumph down at her.

'And I get my pride back,' he gritted. 'A pride you took from me and wiped the floor with the day you forced me into court to beg for the right to love my own son!'

And without warning she was free.

Standing there swaying dizzily, it took several moments for her to realise just what he had done to her. Then the shock descended, the appalled horror of how easy she had made it for him, followed closely by an all-consuming shame.

And all in the name of pride, revenge and of course passion, she listed grimly.

Her chin came up, her green eyes turning as grey as an arctic ocean now as she opened her mouth to tell him what he could do with his rotten proposition, his lousy sex appeal—and himself! when a sound beyond the closed kitchen door suddenly caught their attention.

It had them both turning towards the door, and freezing as they listened to Santo coming down the stairs, bumping something which sounded rather heavy down behind him. And in perfect unison they both then glanced up at the kitchen clock to note that it was only six-thirty, before they looked back at the door again.

The time was significant. It meant that their son was so disturbed by his worries that they'd woken him early.

From the corner of her eye Catherine saw Vito swallow tensely and his hands clench into fists at his sides. His face was suddenly very pale, his eyes dark, and the way his lips parted slightly in an effort to help his frail breathing brought home to her just how worried he was about what his son's reaction was going to be towards him.

She then suggested to herself an alternative. Afraid? Was Vito's expression the one Luisa had described as his frightened look?

Her heart began to ache for him, despite her not wanting it to. Vito loved his son; she had never doubted that. In a thousand other doubts she had never once doubted his love for his son.

Yet still he didn't deserve the way her hand reached instinctively out to touch his arm in a soothing gesture. And beyond the residue of her anger with him over that kiss she felt tungsten steel flex with tension as the kitchen door flew open, swinging back on its hinges against the wall to reveal their son standing there in the opening.

Dressed in jeans and a sweatshirt, a baseball cap placed firmly on his dark head and his travel hold-all, packed to bursting by the look of it, sitting on the floor beside him, while one little fist had a death grip on the bag's thick strap.

If he'd already been aware that his father was here, then the complete lack of expression on his solemn little face would have been understandable. But he hadn't known; Catherine was sure of it. Their home was old and the walls were thick. And no matter how heated their verbal exchanges had grown on occasion, neither of them had raised their voices enough for the sound to filter out of this room.

So her heart stopped aching for the father to begin aching for the son as Santo completely ignored Vito's presence in the room to level his defiant dark brown eyes on his mother.

'I'm running away,' he announced. 'And you're not to follow.'

It could have been comical. Santo certainly looked and sounded comical standing there like that and making such a fantastic announcement.

But Catherine had never felt less like laughing in her life. For he meant it. He truly meant to run away because he believed that nobody loved him.

And if Marietta had done Catherine the favour of walking in here right now she would have scratched her wicked eyes out.

She went to go to him, needed to go to him and simply hug him to her, wrap him in as much love as she could possibly muster.

Only Vito was there before her—and he was wiser. He didn't so much as attempt to touch the little boy as he hunkered down on his haunches in front of him. Instead, he began talking in a deep and soft husky Italian.

Santo responded by allowing himself brief—very brief—eye to eye contact with his *papà*. 'English,' he commanded. 'I don't speak Italian any more.'

To Vito's deserving credit, he switched languages without hesitation, though the significance of his son's rejection must have pierced him like a knife.

'But where will you go?' he was asking gently. 'Have you money for your trip? Would you like me to lend you some?' he offered when the little boy's eyes flickered in sudden confusion because something as unimportant as money hadn't entered into his thoughts while he had been drawing up his plans to run away.

What was in his bag didn't bear thinking about unless Catherine wanted to weep. But she could hazard a fairly accurate guess at several treasured toys, a couple of his favourite tee shirts and his new trainers, since he didn't have them on. And tucked away hidden at the bottom of the bag would be a piece of tatty cotton that the experts would euphemistically call his comforter, though only she was supposed to know about it and he would rather die than let his *papà* find it.

'I don't want your money.' Vito's son proudly refused the offer.

'Breakfast, then,' Catherine suggested, coming to squat down beside Vito, her eyes the compassionate eyes of a mother who understood exactly what a small boy's priorities would be. 'No one should run away without eating a good breakfast first,' she told him. 'Come and sit down at the table,' she urged, holding out an inviting hand to him, 'and I'll get you some juice and a bowl of that new cereal you like.'

He ignored the hand. Instead his fiercely guarded brown eyes began flicking from one adult face to the other, and a

confused frown began to pucker at his brow. Vito uttered
a soft curse beneath his breath as understanding hit him.
Catherine was a second behind him before she realised
what it was that was holding Santo's attention so.

And now the tears really did flood her eyes, because it
wasn't Santo's fault that this had to be the first time in his
young memory that his parents' two faces had appeared in
the same living frame in front of him!

An arm suddenly arrived around her shoulders. Warm
and strong, the attached hand gave her arm a warning
squeeze. As a razor-sharp tactician, famed for thinking on
his feet, Vito had few rivals; she knew that. But the way
he had quickly assessed the situation and decided on ex-
panding on the little boy's absorption in their novel togetherness was impressive even to her.

'We don't want you to leave us, son...' As slick as that
Vito compounded on the 'togetherness'.

Santos's eyes fixed on Catherine. 'Do you want me to
stay?' he asked, so pathetically in need of reassurance that
she had to clench her fists to stop herself from reaching out
for him.

'Of course I do. I love you.' She stated it simply. She
then extended that claim to include Vito. 'We *both* love
you.'

But Santo was having none of it. 'Marietta says you
don't,' he told his father accusingly. 'Marietta said I was a
mistake that just gets in the way.'

'You must have misunderstood her,' Vito said grimly.

The son's eyes flicked into insolence. 'Marietta said that
you hate my mummy because she made you have me,' he
said. 'She said that's why you live in Naples and I live here
in London, out of your way.'

Vito's fingers began to dig into Catherine's shoulder. Did
he honestly believe that *she* would feed her own son this

kind of poison when anyone with eyes could see that Santo was tearing himself up with it all?

'What Marietta says is not important, Santo,' she inserted firmly. 'It's what Papà says and I say that really matters to you. And we *both* love you very much,' she repeated forcefully. 'Would Papà have gone without his sleep to fly himself here through the night just to come and see you if he didn't love you?'

The remark hit a nerve. Catherine saw the tiny flicker of doubt enter her son's eyes as he turned them on his father. 'Why did you come?' he demanded of Vito outright.

'Because you would not come to me,' Vito answered simply. 'And I miss you when you are not there…'

I miss you when you are not there… For Catherine those few words held such a wealth of love in them that she wanted to weep all over again. Not for Santo this time, but for another little person, one who would always be missed even though he could never be here.

Maybe Vito realised what kind of memory his words had evoked, maybe he was merely responding to the tiny quiver she gave as she tried to contain what was suddenly hurting inside her. But his arm grew heavier across her shoulders and gently he drew her closer to his side.

With no idea what was passing through his mother's heart, Santo too was responding to all of that love placed into his father's statement. The small boy let out a sigh that shook mournfully as it left him, but at last some of the stiffness left his body—though he still wasn't ready to drop his guard. Marietta had hurt him much too deeply for her wicked words to be wiped out by a couple of quick reassurances.

'Where's Nonna?' he asked, clearly deciding it was time to change the subject.

His father refused to let him. 'I promised her I would

bring you back to Naples with me, if I could convince you to come,' Vito said.

'I don't like Naples any more,' Santo responded instantly. 'I don't ever—ever—want to go there again.'

'I am very sorry to hear that, Santo,' Vito responded very gently. 'For your sudden dislike of Naples rather spoils the surprise your *mamma* and I had planned for you.'

'What surprise?' the boy quizzed warily.

Surprise? Catherine was repeating to herself, her head twisting to look at Vito with a question in her eyes, wondering just where he was attempting to lead Santo with this.

'I'm not going to live with you in Naples!' Santo suddenly shouted as his busy mind drew its own conclusions. 'I won't live anywhere where Marietta is going to live!' he stated forcefully.

Vito frowned. 'Marietta does not live in my house,' he pointed out.

'But she will when you marry her! I hate Marietta!'

In response, Vito turned to Catherine with a look meant to turn her to stone. He still thought it was she who had been feeding his son all this poison against his precious Marietta!

I'll make you pay for this! those eyes were promising. And as Catherine's emotions began the see-sawing tilt from pain to bitterness, her green eyes fired back a spitting volley of challenges, all of which were telling him to go ahead and try it—then go to hell for all she cared!

He even understood that. 'Then hell it is,' he hissed in a soft undertone that stopped the threat from reaching their son's ears.

Then he was turning back to Santo, all smooth-faced and impressive puzzlement. 'But how can I marry Marietta when I am married to your *mamma*?' he posed, and watched the small boy's scowl alter to an uncertain frown—then delivered with a silken accuracy the dart

aimed to pierce dead centre of his son's vulnerability. 'And
your *mamma* and I want to stay married, Santino. We love
each other just as much as we love you. We are even going
to live in the same house together.'

It was the ultimate *coup de grâce*, delivered with the
perfect timing of a master of the art.

And through the burning red mists that flooded her brain
cells Catherine watched Vito's head turn so he could send
her the kind of smile that turned men into devils. Deny it,
if you dare, that smile challenged.

She couldn't. And he knew she couldn't, because already
their son's face was lighting up as if someone had just
switched his life back on. So she had to squat there, seething but silent, as Vito then pressed a clinging kiss to her
frozen lips as still he continued to build relentlessly on the
little boy's new store of 'togetherness' images.

Then all she could do was watch, rendered surplus to
requirements by his machiavellian intellect, as he turned
his attention back to their little witness and proceeded to
add the finishing touches with an expertise that was positively lethal.

'Will you come too, Santo?' he murmured invitingly.
'Help us to be a proper family?'

A proper family, Catherine repeated silently. The magic
words to any child from a broken home.

'You mean live in the same house—you, me and
mummy?' Already Santo's voice was shaky with enchant-
ment.

Vito nodded. 'And Nonna,' he added. 'Because it has to
be Naples,' he warned solemnly. 'For it is where I work. I
have to live there, you understand?'

Understand? The little boy was more than ready to understand anything so long as Vito kept this dream scenario
flowing. 'Mummy likes Naples,' he said eagerly. 'I know

she does because she likes to listen to all the places we've visited and all the things that we do there.'

'Well, from now on we can do those things together, as a family.' His *papà* smoothly placed yet another perfect image into his son's mental picture book.

At which point Catherine resisted the power of the arm restraining her and got up, deciding that she was most definitely surplus to requirements since the whole situation was out of her control now.

'I'm going to get dressed,' she said. They didn't seem to hear her. And as she stepped around Santo he was already moving towards his darling *papà*. Arms up, eyes shining, he landed in Vito's lap with all the enthusiasm of a well-loved puppy...

'If you still possess a healthy respect for your health, then I advise you to keep your distance,' Catherine warned as Vito's tall, lean figure appeared on the periphery of her vision.

She was in her small but sunny back garden hanging out washing, in the vague hopes that the humdrum chore would help ease some the angst that had built up in her system after having a great morning playing happy families.

Together, they had eaten a delightful breakfast where the plans had flown thick and fast on what to do in Naples during a long hot summer. And she'd smiled and she'd enthused and she'd made suggestions of her own to keep it all absolutely super. Then Santo had taken Vito off to show him his bedroom with all the excitement of a boy who felt as if he was living in seventh heaven.

Now Santo was at his best friend's house, several doors away, where he was excitedly relaying all his wonderful news to a captivated audience, who would no doubt be seeing Santo's change in fortune in the same guise as the child equivalent to winning the lottery.

Which clearly left Vito free to come in search of her, which was, in Catherine's view, him just begging for trouble.

He knew she was angry. He knew she was barely managing to contain the mass of burning emotion which was busily choking up her system at the cavalier way he had decided her life for her.

'Don't you have an electric dryer for those?' he questioned frowningly.

For a man she'd believed had no concept of what a tumble dryer was, the question came as a surprise to her. But as for answering it—she was in no mood to stand here explaining that shoving the clothes into a tumble dryer was no therapy at all for easing what was screaming to escape from her at this moment.

So instead she bent down to pluck one of Santo's tee shirts out of the washing basket, then straightened to peg it to the line, unaware of the way the sunlight played across the top of her neatly tied hair as she moved, picking out the red strands from the gold strands in a fascinating dance of glistening colour.

Nor was she aware of the way the simple straight skirt she was wearing stretched tight across the neat curve of her behind as she bent, or that her tiny white vest top gave tantalising glimpses of her breasts cupped inside her white bra.

But Vito Giordani was certainly aware as he stood there in the shade thrown by the house, leisurely taking it all in.

And a lack of sun didn't detract from his own dark attraction—as Catherine was reluctantly aware. Though you would be hard put to tell when she had actually looked at him long enough to note anything about him.

A sigh whispered from her, and her fingers got busier as a whole new set of feelings began to fizz into life.

'Could you leave that?' Vito asked suddenly. 'We need to talk while we have the chance to do so.'

'I think I've talked myself out today,' Catherine answered satirically.

'You're angry,' he allowed.

'I am?' With a deft flick she sent the rotating line turning, so she could gain access to the next free bit of washing line. 'And here was I thinking I was deliriously ecstatic,' she drawled.

His brows snapped together as her sarcastic tone carried on the crystal-clear morning air. Out there, beyond the low fencing that formed the boundaries between each garden, children's voices could be heard. Any one of them could be Santo, and Vito, it seemed, was very aware of that, because he started walking towards her, closing the gap between them so that their voices wouldn't carry.

'You must see that I really had no alternative but to say what I did,' he said grimly.

'The troubleshooter at work, thinking on his feet and with his mouth.' She nodded, fingers busy with pegs and damp fabric. 'I was very impressed, Vito,' she assured him. 'How could I not be?'

'I would say that you are most unimpressed.' He sighed, stooping to pick up the next piece of washing for her.

Another first, Catherine mused ruefully. Vittorio Giordani helping to hang out washing. For some stupid reason the apparition set her lower abdomen tingling.

'I have a life here, Vito,' she replied, ignoring the sensation. 'I have a job I love doing and commitments I have no wish to renege on.' Carefully, so she didn't have to make contact with his fingers, she took Santo's little school shirt from him.

'With your language and secretarial qualifications you could get a job anywhere.' He dismissed that line of argument. 'Templeton and Lang are not the only legal firm that specialise in European law.'

'You know where I work?' Surprise sent her gaze up to his face. He was smiling wryly—but even that kind of smile was a sexy smile. She looked away again quickly before it got a hold on her.

'Santo has been very vocal about how busy his *mamma's* important job keeps her.'

'You don't approve,' Catherine assumed by his tone.

'Of you working?' Bending again, he selected the next piece of washing. 'I would rather you had been here at home for Santo,' he said, with no apology for his chauvinistic outlook.

'Needs must,' was all she said, not willing to get into that particular argument. They'd had it before, after all, when she'd insisted on continuing to work after they married. Then it had been easy for her, because her multilingual expertise had been well sought after in many fields of modern business. In Naples, for instance, she had managed to pick up a job working for the local Tourist Information Board. Vito had been furious, his manly ego coming out for an airing when he'd wanted to know what the hell people would think of him allowing his pregnant wife to work!

Just another heated row they'd had amongst many rows.

'But the *devil* in this case is definitely not me,' Vito said dryly. 'It is you who refused any financial support when you left me,' he reminded her.

'I can support myself.' Which she always had done, even while she'd been living with Vito in his big house with its flashy cars and its even flashier lifestyle.

She had never been destitute. Her father had seen to that. Having brought her up himself from her birth, he had naturally made adequate provision for the unfortunate chance of his own demise. She owned this little house in middle-class suburbia outright, had no outstanding debts and still had money put away for the rainy days in life. And being reared in a single-parent professional house meant she'd grown up fiercely independent and self-confident. Marrying an arrogant Italian steeped in old-fashioned values had been a test on both qualities from the very start.

But the only time her belief in herself had faltered had been when she was pregnant for a second time and too sick and weakened to fight for anything—and that had included her husband's waning affections.

An old hurt began to ache again, the kind of hurt that suddenly rendered her totally, utterly, helplessly desolate.

'I can't live with you again, Vito,' she said, turning eyes darkened by a deep sadness on him. 'I can't...' she repeated huskily.

The sudden glint of pain in his own eyes told her that he knew exactly what had brought that little outburst on, but where compassion and understanding would have been better, instead anger slashed to life across his lean, dark features.

'Too late,' he clipped. 'The luxury of choice has been denied to you. This is not about what *you* want any more, Catherine,' he stated harshly. 'Or even what I want. It is what our son wants.'

'Our surviving son,' she whispered tragically.

Again the anger pulsed. 'We mourn the dead but we celebrate the living,' he ruthlessly declared. 'I will not allow Santo to pay the price of his brother's tragic ending any longer!'

Or maybe his tactics were the right ones, Catherine conceded as she felt his anger ignite her anger, which sent the pain fleeing. 'You truly believe that's what I've been doing?' she gasped.

His broad shoulders flexed. 'I do not know what motivates you, Catherine,' he growled. 'I never did, and now I have no wish to know. But the future for both of us is now set in stone. Accept it and leave the past where it belongs, because it has outplayed its strength and no longer has any bearing on what we do now.'

With that, he turned away, his black scowl enough to put the sun out.

'Does that include Marietta?' she demanded of his back.

He'd already stopped listening—his attention suddenly fixing on something neither of them had noticed while they'd been so busy arguing. But they certainly noticed now the rows of boundary hedges with varying adult heads peering over the top of them, all of them looking curiously in their direction.

'Oh, damn,' Catherine cursed. At which point, the sound of the telephone ringing inside the house was a diversion she was more than grateful for. Smiling through tingling teeth, she excused herself and went inside, leaving him to be charming to the neighbours, because that was really all he was fit for!

Snatching up the phone from its kitchen wall extension, she almost shot her name down the line.

'Careful, darling, I have delicate eardrums,' a deeply teasing voice protested.

It was like receiving manna from heaven after a fall-out of rats. 'Marcus,' she greeted softly, and leaned back against the kitchen unit with her face softened by its first warm smile of the day. 'What are you doing calling so early in the morning?'

'It's such a beautiful morning, though. So I had this sudden yen to spend it with my favourite person,' he explained, unaware that he had already lost Catherine's attention.

For that was fixed on her kitchen doorway, where Vito was standing utterly frozen, and a hot blast of vengeful pleasure went skating through her when she realised he had overheard her words—and, more importantly, the soft intimacy with which she had spoken them.

'So when I remembered that this was also the day that

your son goes to Italy,' Marcus was saying, 'I thought, Why not drag Catherine out for a leisurely lunch by the river, since she will be free of her usual commitments?'

But 'free' was the very last word that Catherine would use to describe her situation right now. In truth she felt trapped, held prisoner by a pair of gold-shot eyes that were threatening retribution.

CHAPTER FOUR

THE fine hairs all over her body began to prickle as they stood on end in sheer response. 'I'm so sorry, Marcus,' she murmured apologetically, but the way her lungs had ceased to function made every syllable sound soft and breathless and disturbingly sensual. 'But Santo's trip has been—delayed,' she said, for want of a less complicated way of putting it.

'Oh.' He sounded so disappointed.

'Can I call you back?' she requested. 'When I have a clearer idea of when I will be free? Only it isn't—convenient to talk right now...'

'There is someone there,' Marcus realised, the sharp-minded lawyer in him quick to read the subtle intonations in her voice.

'Yes, that's right,' Catherine confirmed with a swift smile.

'Man, woman or child?' he enquired with sardonic humour.

More like frozen beast about to defrost, Catherine thought nervously, but kept that observation to herself. 'Thanks for being so understanding,' she murmured instead. 'I'll—I'll call you,' she promised. 'Just as soon as I can.' And said a hurried farewell before ringing off.

The phone went back on its cradle with the neat precision required of fingers that were trembling badly. 'That was Marcus,' she said, turning a flat-edged smile on Vito meant to hide the flurry of nervous excitement that had taken up residence inside her stomach.

'And?' he prompted, arching an imperious brow at her

when she didn't bother to extend on that. 'I presume this—Marcus has a role to play here?'

A role? A strange way of putting it, Catherine mused. Especially when they both knew exactly the *role* Marcus was supposed to be playing. Still...

'That is none of your business,' she told him, provoking him even though she knew it was a dangerous thing to do. But she was too busy enjoying herself, giving him back what he usually gave to her, to care about the consequences.

And body language is such a rotten tale-teller she thought ruefully when she noticed the way she had folded her arms beneath her breasts in a way that could only be described as defiant.

The back door slammed shut, making her jump. A different kind of body language, she noted warily.

'He's your lover,' Vito bit out condemningly.

'But why look so shocked?' she asked, refusing to deny the charge. 'What's the matter, Vito?' she then taunted goadingly. 'Hadn't it occurred to you before that I might well have a personal life beyond Santo?'

A telling little nerve flicked in his jaw. Catherine enjoyed watching it happen. Did he honestly believe that she'd spent the last three years in social seclusion while he hadn't been around to give her life meaning? The man was too arrogant and conceited for his own good sometimes, she decided. It wouldn't hurt him one bit to discover that he wasn't the be-all and end-all of her existence!

'Or is it your colossal ego that's troubling you?' she said, continuing her thought patterns out loud and with derision. 'Because it prefers to think me incapable of being with another man after having known you? Well, I'm sorry to disappoint your precious ego, but I have a healthy sex drive—as you very well know,' she added before he decided to say it. 'And I can be as discreet as you—if not more so, since it's clear by your face that you knew nothing about Marcus, whereas I've had Marietta flung into my face for what feels like for ever!'

'Leave Marietta out of this,' he warned tightly.

'Not while she remains a threat to my son,' she refused.

'The most immediate threat here, Catherine, is to yourself.' He didn't move a single muscle but she was suddenly aware of danger. 'I want this man out of your life as of now!'

'When Marietta is out of your life,' she threw back promptly. 'And not before.'

'When are you going to accept that I cannot dismiss Marietta from my life!' he said angrily. 'Her husband was my best friend! She holds shares in my company! She works alongside me almost as my equal! She is my mother's only godchild!' Grimly, precisely, he counted off all the old excuses that gave Marietta power over them.

So Catherine added to it. 'She sleeps in your bed,' she mimicked him tauntingly. 'She slips poison into your son's food.'

'You are the poisonous one,' he sighed.

'And you, Vito, are the fool.'

He took a step towards her. Catherine's chin came up, green eyes clashing fearlessly with his. And the atmosphere couldn't get any more fraught if someone had wired the room up with high-voltage cable. He looked as if he would like to shake her—and Catherine was angry enough to wish he would just try!

What he actually did try to do was put the brakes on what was bubbling dangerously between them. 'Let's get this discussion back where it should be,' he gritted. 'Which is on the question of your love-life, not mine!'

'My love-life is flourishing very nicely, thank you,' she answered flippantly.

It was the wrong thing to say. Catherine should have seen

the signs—and maybe she had done. Afterwards she couldn't quite say she hadn't deliberately provoked him into action.

Whatever. She suddenly found herself being grabbed by hands that were hell-bent on punishment. 'You hypocrite,' he gritted. 'You have the damned cheek to stand in judgement over my morals when your own are no better!'

'Why should it bother you so much what I do in my private life?' Catherine threw back furiously.

'Because you belong to me!' he barked.

She couldn't believe she was hearing this! 'Which makes you the hypocrite, Vito,' she told him. 'You want me—yet you don't want me,' she mocked him bitterly. 'You like to play around—but can't deal with the idea that I might play around!'

With a push, she put enough space between them to slide sideways and right away from him. But inside she was shaking. Shaking with anger or shaking with something far more basic. She wasn't really sure.

'Until last night—' Was it only last night? She paused to consider. 'We hadn't even exchanged a single word with each other for the past three years! Then you suddenly walk in through my front door this morning and start behaving as if you've never been away from it!' The way the air hissed from her lungs was self-explanatory. 'Well, I've got news for you,' she informed him grimly. 'I have a life all right. A good one and a happy one. Which means I resent the hell out of you coming here and messing with it!'

'Do you think that I am looking forward to having you running riot through *my* life a second time?' he responded. 'But you *are* my wife! Mine!' he repeated. 'And—'

'What a joke!' Catherine interrupted scornfully. 'You only married me because you had to! Now you are taking me back because you have to! Well, hear this,' she announced. 'You may have walked me into a steel trap by saying what you did to Santo. But that doesn't mean I am willing to stay meekly inside it! Anything you can do I can do,' she warned him. 'So if Marietta stays then Marcus stays!'

'In your bed,' he gritted, still fixed, it seemed, on getting her to admit the full truth about her relationship with Marcus.

'In my bed,' she confirmed, thinking, What the hell— why not let him believe that? 'In my arms and in my body,' she tagged on outrageously. 'And so long as my son doesn't know about it, who actually cares, Vito?' she challenged. 'You?' she suggested as she watched his face darken with contempt for her. 'Well, in case you haven't realised it yet, I don't care what you think. The same way that you didn't care about me when you went from my arms to Marietta's arms the day I lost our baby!'

Seven o'clock, and Vito still hadn't come back.

Catherine stood by her bedroom window staring down at the street below and wondered anxiously whether she had finally managed to finish it for them.

She shouldn't have said it, she acknowledged uncomfortably. True though it might have been, those kind of bitter words were best kept hidden within the dark recesses of one's own mind. For it served no useful purpose to drag them all out, and if anything only added more pain where there was already enough pain to be felt.

She knew that he had felt the loss of their second child just as deeply as she had done. And had suffered guilt in knowing that she had known exactly where he had been and with whom he had been when she'd needed him. But in the thrumming silence which had followed her outburst, while she'd stood there sizzling in her own corrosive bitterness, she'd had to watch that tall, dark, proudly arrogant man diminish before her very eyes.

His skin had slowly leached of its colour, his mouth began to shake, and with a sharp jerk of his head he wrenched his eyes from her—but not before she'd seen the look of hell written in them.

'Oh, God, Vito.' On a wave of instant remorse she'd taken a step towards him. 'I'm so...'

'Sorry,' she had been going to say. But he didn't give her the chance to, because he'd just spun on his heel and walked out of the house.

And if the kitchen floor had opened up and swallowed her whole at that moment, she would have welcomed the punishment. For no man deserved to be demolished quite so thoroughly as she had demolished Vito.

Par for the course, she thought wearily now, as she stood there in the window. For when had she and Vito *not* been hell-bent on demolishing each other? They seemed to have been at loggerheads from day one of their marriage— mostly over Marietta. And the final straw had been her miscarriage.

In the ensuing dreadful hours after being rushed into hospital she had almost lost her own life. She'd certainly lost the will to live for several long black months afterwards. She felt she had failed—failed her baby, failed in her marriage and failed as a woman. And the only thing that had kept her going through those months was Santino, and a driven need to wage war on Vito for coming to her hospital bed straight from Marietta's arms.

But that was three years ago, and she had truly believed that she had put all of that anger and bitterness behind her. Now she knew differently, and didn't like herself much for it. Especially when she knew that downstairs in the sitting room, already fed and bathed and in his pyjamas, was their son, kneeling on the windowsill doing exactly the same as his mother was doing. Staring out of the window anxiously waiting for his father's return even though she'd assured him that his *papà* had merely rushed off to keep an appointment in the City and would be back as soon as he was able.

The throaty roar of a powerful engine reached her ears just before she saw the sports car turn the corner and start heading down the street towards them.

And Catherine's hand shot up to cover her mouth as tears of relief, of aching gratitude, set her tense mouth quivering.

From the excited whoop she heard from her son, Santo had heard the sound and recognised it instantly.

Low, long, black and intimidating, Vito's car hadn't even come to a halt when she heard the front door open then saw her son racing down the path towards him. As he climbed out on the roadside, Vito's face broke into a slashing grin as he watched his son scramble up and over the gate without bothering to open it.

He must have gone back to his London home as he had changed his clothes, she noticed. The creased suit and shirt swapped for crease-free and stylishly casual black linen trousers and a dark red shirt that moulded the muscular structure of his torso. And his face was clean shaven, the roguish look wiped away so only the smooth, dark, sleek Italian man of means was visible.

Coming around the long bonnet of the car, Vito only had time to open his arms as his son leapt into them. Leaning back against the passenger door of the car, he then proceeded to listen as Santo rattled on to him in a jumble of words that probably didn't make much sense he was so excited. But that didn't matter.

What Santo was really saying was all too clear enough. I've got my *papà* back. I'm happy!

Glancing up, Vito saw her standing there watching them, and his eyes froze in that instant. Take this away from me if you dare, he seemed to be challenging.

But Catherine didn't dare—she didn't even *want* to dare.

Turning away from the window, she left them to it and went to sink weakly down on her bed while she tried to decide where they went from here.

To Naples, of course, a dryly mocking voice inside her head informed her. Where you will toe the line that Vito will draw for you.

And why will you do that? she asked herself starkly.

Because when you brutally demolished him today, what you actually did was demolish your will to fight him.

Getting wearily to her feet, she grimly braced herself, ready to go down and face Vito. She found them in the sitting room and paused on the threshold to witness the easy intimacy with which Santo sat on Vito's lap with his latest reading book open. Between them they were reading it in English then translating into Italian in a way that told Catherine that they did this a lot back in Naples.

And still she didn't know what her place was going to be in this new order of things. But when Vito glanced up at her and she saw the residue of pallor that told her he still had not recovered from all of that ugliness earlier, she knew one thing for an absolute certainty as shame went riddling through her.

Vito might be feeling the weight of his own guilt but he would never forgive her for making him remember it.

'I'm sorry,' she murmured, because it had to be said now or never, even if their son was there to hear it. 'I didn't mean to—'

'Santo and I are going to spend the day out tomorrow,' Vito coolly cut in. 'To give you chance to close up your life here. We fly back to Naples the day after...'

'Damn...' Catherine muttered as she lost the end to the roll of sticky tape—again. 'Damn, damn, blasted damn...'

With an elbow trying to keep the cardboard box lid shut,

she used a fingernail to pick carefully at the tape while her teeth literally tingled with frustration.

She'd had a lousy day and this stupid sticky tape was just about finishing it. First of all she'd had a row with Santo just before he'd gone off with his father and she'd walked into his bedroom to find it in complete upheaval.

'Santino—get up here and clean this mess up!' she'd yelled at him down the stairwell.

He'd come, but reluctantly. 'Can't you do it, this once?' he'd asked her sulkily. 'Papà is ready to go now!'

'No, I cannot,' she refused. 'And Papà can wait.'

'I never have to do this in Naples,' her son muttered complainingly as he slouched passed her.

In the mood she was in, mentioning Naples was the equivalent of waving a red flag at a bull.

'Well, in this house we clean up after ourselves, and *before* we get treats out!' Catherine fired back. 'And guess what, sweetie?' she added for good measure. 'From now on Mummy is going to be in Naples to make sure you don't get away with such disgraceful behaviour!'

'Maybe you should stay here, then,' the little terror responded.

'Santino!'

Catherine hadn't realised that Vito called his son Santino, as she did, when the boy was in trouble. And it had a funny little effect on her to hear him doing it this morning.

'Apologise to your mother and do as she tells you!'

The apology was instant. And Catherine sighed, and seethed, and resented the hell out of Vito for getting from her son what she had been about to get from him herself.

But then that was just another little thing about herself she'd learned that she didn't like. She was jealous of Santo's close relationship with his father. It had shown its ugly green head when Santo had insisted Vito take him to bed last night, leaving her feeling pathetically rejected.

And the pendulum had swung back the other way, just like that, putting her right on the attack again. So when Vito had come down half an hour later and coolly informed her that their son was expecting him to stay the night—she exploded.

'You've got your own house only two miles up the road. Use it!' she'd exclaimed. 'I don't want you staying here.'

'I didn't say that *I* wanted to stay,' he'd drawled. 'Only that our son expects it.'

'Well, I expect you to leave,' she'd countered. 'Now, if possible. I've got things to do and you—'

'Or people to see?' he'd silkily suggested. 'Like your lover, for instance?'

So, they were back to that already, she'd noted angrily, realising that neither seemed to have learned much from their row that morning. 'I do not bring my lovers into this house,' she'd informed him haughtily. 'Behaviour like that might be acceptable in Italy but it certainly isn't here!'

As a poke at Marietta without actually saying her name, it had certainly hit its mark. His hard face had shut down completely. 'Then where do you meet him? In a motel under assumed names?'

'Better that than allocating him the room next to my room,' she'd said.

The remark had sent his eyes black. 'Marietta never occupied a room within ten of ours, Catherine,' he'd censured harshly.

But at least he had voiced whom it was they were talking about. 'Well, rest assured she won't be occupying *any* room when I move back in,' she'd informed him. 'And if I see her with so much as a toothbrush in her hand, I'll chuck her through the nearest window.'

To her annoyance he'd laughed. 'Now that I would like to see,' he'd murmured. 'After all, Marietta stands a good two inches taller than you and there is a little bit more of her—in every way.'

'Well, you should know,' she'd drawled, in a tone that had wiped that grin right off his face!

He'd left soon after that, stiffly promising to return before Santo woke up the next morning. He'd left soon after her argument with Santo this morning too, she recalled now, with a grimace. One glance at her face as she'd walked down the stairs must have told him she was gunning for yet another round with him.

Next she'd had to beg an immediate release from her contract, which Robert Lang had not taken kindly. Then she'd had to say her goodbyes to people she had been working with for over two years, and that had been pretty wretched. Then—surprise, surprise—something nice had happened! One of the new recruits at the company had come to search her out because he'd heard she was leaving London and wanted to know if he could lease her house from her.

Why not? she'd thought. It was better than leaving it unlived in, and she liked the idea of him and his small family looking after the place for her.

But she hadn't bargained on the extra work it would entail to leave the house fit for strangers. Instead of just doing the usual preparations, then shutting the front door on everything as she left it, she'd had to go hunting round for anything and everything of a personal nature and box it up ready to go into storage, arrange for that darned storage, and also arrange for a company of professional cleaners to come in and get the place ready for her new tenants.

Now she was tired and fed-up and harassed, and all she wanted to do was sit down and have a good weep because everything she'd grown to rely on for security in her life had been effectively dismantled today!

But she couldn't weep because Vito and her son were

due back at any minute, and she would rather die than let Vito catch her weeping!

But none of that—or even all of that put together—compared with the awful lunch she had endured with Marcus Templeton.

Okay, she reasoned, so their relationship was not quite on the footing that she had led Vito to believe. But it had been getting there—slowly. And she liked Marcus—she really did! He was the first man she had allowed to get close to her after the disastrous time she'd had with Vito.

He was good and kind and treated her as an intellectual equal rather than a potential lover. And she liked what they'd had together. It was so much calmer and more mature than the relationship she'd had with Vito.

No fire. No passion to fog up reality.

Marcus was tall, he was dark—though not the romantically uncompromising dark that was Vito's main weapon of destruction. And he was very good-looking—in a purely British kind of way.

She'd wanted to want him. She'd wanted to stop comparing every other man she met with Vito and actually take a chance on Marcus being the one to help her remove Vito's brand of hot possession from her soul for ever. But had she been in love with Marcus? She asked herself. And the answer came back in the form of a dark shadow. For, no, she had not fallen in love with him nor even been close to falling, she realised now.

But what really hurt, what really shocked and shamed and appalled her, was that she hadn't realised just how seriously Marcus had fallen in love with her—until she'd broken her news to him today.

With a heavy sigh she sat back against the wall behind her, her packing forgotten for the moment while she let herself dwell on the biggest crime of blindness she had ever been guilty of.

She had stunned Marcus with her announcement that she was going back to Naples and to her husband. She had knocked the stuffing right out of him. So much so, in fact, that he hadn't moved, hadn't breathed, hadn't done anything for the space of thirty long wretched seconds but stare blankly into space.

The threatened tears arrived. Catherine felt them trickle down her dusty cheeks but didn't bother to stop them.

Because Marcus loved her—and she'd always wanted to be loved like that—for herself and not just the heat of her passion!

Oh, he'd pulled himself together eventually, she recalled with bittersweet misery. Then he'd said all the nice, kind gentlemanly things aimed to make her feel better when really it should have been the other way around and her consoling him.

But how do you console someone you know you've hurt more than you would ever want to be hurt yourself?

'Mummy?' The concerned sound of her son's voice reached deep inside to where she'd sunk in, and brought her shuddering back to a sense of where she was. She opened her eyes to find him squatting beside her with a gentle hand resting on her shoulder and his brown eyes looking terribly anxious. 'What's the matter?' he asked worriedly.

'Oh,' she choked, hurriedly pulling herself together. 'Nothing,' she said huskily. 'Just some dust in my eye. How...?' She rubbed at the offending evidence. 'How did you get in?' she asked.

'The front door was open,' another deeper and very protracted voice grimly informed her.

Vito. Her heart sank. And now she felt thoroughly stupid.

'You left it on the latch.' Her small son took up the censure. 'And we couldn't find you anywhere so we thought something might have happened to you.'

Couldn't find her? Why, where was she? she asked herself with a blank stare at her immediate surroundings.

She was in her bedroom, she realised. Sitting on the floor between the chest of drawers and the wardrobe while the space around her was piled with hastily filled cardboard boxes.

Boxes in which to pack her life away, she thought tragically. And without any warning the floodgates swung wide open. It was terrible—the lowest moment of her whole rotten day, in fact.

So the tears flowed in abundance and she couldn't stop them, and beside her Santo began crying too. He tried to hug her and she tried to comfort him by hugging him back and mumbling silly words about his mother being silly, and somewhere in the background she could hear things being shifted and someone cursing, but didn't even remember who that someone was until her son was plucked away from her and put somewhere so a pair of strong arms could reach down and gather her up.

She simply curled up against a big, firm male body and continued weeping into its shoulder. Oh, she knew it was Vito, but to admit that to herself meant fighting him again, and she didn't want to fight right now. She wanted to cry and be weak and pathetic and vulnerable. She wanted to be held and clucked over and made to feel safe.

He sat down on the bed with her cradled against him and beside them Santo came to put his arms back around her; he was still sobbing.

'Santino, *caro*,' Vito was murmuring with husky firmness. 'Please stop that crying. Your *mamma* is merely sad at having to leave here, that is all. Females do this; you must learn to expect it.'

The voice of experience, Catherine mocked within her own little nightmare. Yet she'd never cried on him like this—ever. So where had he acquired that experience?

'I hate you,' she whispered thickly.

'No, you don't. Your *mamma* did not mean that, Santo,' Vito coolly informed his son. 'She merely hates having to leave this house, that is all.'

In other words, Remember who is listening.

'We'll have to stay here, then,' his young son wailed, his arms tightening protectively around Catherine.

'We will not.' His father vetoed that suggestion. 'Your *mamma* loves Naples too; she is just determined to forget that for now.' The man had no heart, Catherine decided miserably. 'Now be of use,' he instructed his son sternly, 'and go and get your mother a glass of water from the kitchen.'

The sheer importance of the task diverted Santo enough to stop his tears and send him scrambling quickly from the bed.

'Now, try to control yourself before he comes back.' Vito turned his grimness onto Catherine next. 'You are frightening him with all of this.'

She didn't need telling twice to realise that Vito was only being truthful and she had frightened Santo by breaking down. So she made a concerted effort to stem the tears, then pulled herself free of his arms and crawled off his lap and beneath the duvet without uttering a single word.

What could she say, after all? she pondered bleakly. I'm crying because I hurt the man I wanted to replace you with? Vito would really love to know that!

By the time Santo came back, carefully carrying the glass of water in front of him, her tears had been reduced to the occasional sniffle. Smiling him a watery smile, she accepted his offering and added a nasal-sounding thank you that didn't alter his solemn stare.'

I don't like to see you upset, Mummy,' he confessed.

'I'm sorry, darling,' she apologised gently, and pressed a reassuring kiss to his cheek. 'I promise I won't do it again.'

And to think, she slayed herself guiltily, only this morning she had been shouting at him, and here he was being so excruciatingly nice to her! It was enough to make her want to start crying all over again.

Maybe Vito saw it coming, because as quick as a flash he was ushering Santo out of the room with murmured phrases about Catherine needing to rest now.

Oddly enough she did rest. Lying there, huddled beneath the duvet, she started out by thinking about Marcus and Santo and herself and ended up falling asleep, to dream about Vito coming back into the bedroom, she didn't how much later, and silently but gently undressing her before slipping the duvet back over her boneless figure. She could remember dreaming that she had a one-sided conversation with him, but before she could remember what that conversation was about sleep claimed her yet again.

The next time she awoke she knew it was the middle of the night simply by the hushed silence beyond the closed curtains. She lay there for a while, feeling relaxed and comfortable—until something moved in the bed beside her that had her shimmying over on a gasp of alarm.

She found Vito asleep in the bed beside her. Lying flat on his back, with an arm thrown in relaxed abandon on the pillow behind his head, he looked as if he had been there for hours!

But that wasn't all—not by a long shot. Because from what she could see of his bronze muscled torso, he had also climbed into her bed naked!

CHAPTER FIVE

'Vito!' she cried in whispering protest, and issued an angry push to his warm satin shoulder.

'Hmm?' he mumbled, black-lashed eyelids flickering upwards to reveal slumberous eyes that were not quite in focus.

'What do you think you are doing here?' Catherine demanded.

'Sleeping,' he murmured, and lowered his eyelids again. 'I suggest that you do the same thing.'

'But I don't want you in my bed!'

'Tough,' he replied. 'Because I am staying. You could not be left alone here in the state you were in, and Santo needed the reassurance of my presence. So be wise, *cara*,' he advised. 'Accept a situation you brought upon yourself. Shut up and go to sleep before I awaken properly and begin thinking of other things we can do to use up what is left of the night.'

'Well, of all the—' She couldn't believe she was hearing this. 'What makes you think that all of that gives you the right to climb into bed with me?'

'Arrogance,' he replied, so blandly that Catherine almost choked on the sudden urge to laugh!

Only this was no laughing matter. 'Just get out of here,' she hissed, giving his rock-solid shoulder yet another prompting push.

'If I open my eyes, Catherine, you will intensely regret it,' he warned very grimly.

She was no fool; she recognised that tone. On an angry

73

flurry of naked flesh, she flung herself onto her back, to lie seething in silence.

Naked. Her heart stopped beating as a new kind of shock went rampaging through her.

So it had not been a dream and Vito *had* undressed her! The man's self-confessed arrogance knew no bounds! she decided as she sent one of her hands on a quick foray of her own body to discover just how naked she was.

She was very—very naked.

'Did you know you have developed a habit of talking in your sleep?' he said suddenly.

Catherine froze beside him. She heard a very muddled and very disjointed echo of words being spoken by her that should have taken place in the privacy of her head.

Regretful words about Marcus.

'Shut up,' she gasped, terrified of what was coming. 'He must be quite something, this man you weep for.' He ignored her advice in the dulcet tones of one readying for battle. 'To reach the frozen wastelands where your heart lies hidden. Maybe I should take the trouble to meet him, see what he's got that I never had.'

'Why bother?' she slashed back. 'When you would never find the same qualities inside yourself if you searched for ever.'

'Is he good in bed?'

Her next gasp almost strangled her. 'Go to hell,' she replied, turning her back towards him.

As an act of dismissal it had entirely the opposite effect, because Vito's arm had scooped around her and rolled her back before she even knew what was happening.

And suddenly he was leaning right over her, all glinting eyes and primitive male aggression. 'I asked you a question,' he prompted darkly.

Her mouth ran dry, the tip of her tongue slinking out to moisten parted lips that were remaining stubbornly silent because she was damned if she was going to tell the truth—that she had never even been tempted to go to bed with Marcus—just to soothe Vito's ruffled ego! Luxurious dark eyelashes curled down over shimmering eyes as he lowered his gaze to observe the nervous action—and completely froze it as an old, old sensation went snaking through her.

He was going to kiss her. 'No, Vito,' she breathed, but even she heard the weakness in that pathetic little protest.

It was already too late. His mouth claimed hers with the kind of deeply sensual kiss that could only be issued by this wretched man. It was like drowning in the most exquisite substance ever created, she likened dazedly as she began to sink on a long, spiralling dive through silken liquid kept exactly at body heat so it was impossible to tell what part of the kiss was hers and what part was his.

The man, his closeness, even the antipathy that was pulsing between them, was so sexual that she found herself thinking fancifully of lions again. Her skin came alive, each tiny pore beginning to vibrate with an awareness that held her trapped by its power and its intensity.

Whether it was she who began to touch him first or whether Vito was the one to begin their gentle caresses, she didn't know—didn't really care. Because the heat of his flesh felt so exquisitely wonderful to her starved fingertips, and where he touched she burned, and where he didn't she ached.

She tried to drag some air into lungs that had ceased working, felt the tips of her breasts briefly touch his hair-roughened breastplate, felt her nipples sting as they responded to the contact and moaned luxuriously against his mouth.

With a sensual flick of his tongue, Vito caught that little moan, took possession of it as if it belonged to him. And as his hands worked their old magic on her flesh with the sensual expertise of a master, he watched in grim triumph as, bit by bit, she surrendered herself to him.

'Does he make you feel like this, *cara*?' he grated with electric timing across the erect tip of one pouting nipple. 'Can he send you this far, this fast?' he demanded as his fingers, so excruciatingly knowing, slid a delicate caress over her sex.

She shuddered, moaned again, flexed and unflexed muscles that were moving to their own rhythm. 'Vito,' she breathed, as if her very life depended on her saying that name.

'Yes,' he hissed. 'Vito,' he repeated in rough-toned satisfaction. 'Who touches you—here—and you go up in flames for me.'

She went wild then. Three years of abstinence was no defence against what he could do for her. She moved for him, breathed for him, writhed and begged for him.

His laugh of black triumph accompanied the first deep penetrating thrust of his body. But Catherine was too busy exalting in the power of his passion to care that he seemed to be taunting her surrender. And as Vito gritted his teeth and began to ride her his eyes remained fixed on her shuttered eyelids, because he knew her so well and did not want to miss that moment when those eyelids flicked upwards just before she shot into violent orgasm.

Then let him see if she was shocked to find *his* dark face bearing down on her instead of her damned lover's face! 'Me,' he muttered tautly as he grappled with his own soaring need to surrender. 'Vito,' he gritted.

Why? Because despite what he was telling himself the very last thing he needed right now was Catherine shattering his ego by expecting it to be another man making her feel this good!

So he repeated his name. 'Vito, *cara*.' And kept on repeating it with each powerful thrust of his powerful frame,

'Vittorio—Adriano—Lucio—Giordani,' in the most seductive accent ever created.

Her answering whimper caught him in mid-thrust. Her eyes flicked open. She looked straight at him. *'Pidoccio,'* she said, then shot into a flailing orgasm.

They lay there afterwards, sweat-soaked, panting, utterly spent. He on his back, with his arm covering his face, she on her side, curled right away from him. 'Louse,' she whispered again—in English this time.

She was right and he was. So he didn't deny it. 'You are *my* wife,' Vito stated flatly. 'Our separation is now officially over. So take my advice and be careful, *cara*, who you dream about in future.'

That was all. Nothing else needed to be added to that. Catherine had unwittingly struck at the very centre of his pride when she'd mumbled mixed-up words about Marcus in her sleep. The experience just now had not been performed for mere sexual gratification's sake, but in sheer revenge.

Naples was shimmering beneath a haze of heat that made Catherine glad they were taking the coast road towards Mergellina then on to Capo Posillipo, where most of the upper echelons of Neapolitan society had their residences.

Vito was driving them in an open-top red Mercedes Cabriolet that must be a recent buy judging by the newness of the cream leather. And driving alfresco like this beat air-conditioned luxury any day, to Catherine's way of thinking. She could feel the breeze in her hair and the sun on her skin, and if it hadn't been for the man beside her she would have been enjoying this. The views were every bit as spectacular as she'd remembered them to be. And Santo was safely strapped into the rear seat, happily singing away to himself in whichever language took his fancy.

The three of them must look the perfect family, she mused. But they weren't.

In fact she and Vito had hardly swapped three words with each other since they got up this morning. He'd risen first, rolling out of the bed and striding off to the bathroom very early—but then he always had been an early riser. Catherine had stayed huddled where she was, listening until she'd heard Santo go down the stairs before she made any attempt to stir herself.

She'd needed her son as a buffer. Catherine freely acknowledged that. At least with Santo there she could try to behave with some normality. But Vito had been as withdrawn and reticent as she had been, as if his behaviour last night had pleased him as little as it had done Catherine.

'...sunglasses in the glove compartment.'

Catching only the tail end of Vito's blunt-edged comment brought her face automatically swinging around from the view to find him looking directly at her. Blinking uncomfortably, she turned quickly away again.

It was all right for him, she thought as she leant forward to open the door to the glove box, his eyes were already hidden behind silver-framed dark lenses, but he hadn't been able to look at her before he'd put the darn things on!

Once through Mergellina the car began the serpentine climb on the Via Posillipo. As Catherine turned her attention to enjoying the spectacular view now unfolding beneath them, a flash of gold caught her eye.

It was Vito's wedding ring, gleaming in the sunlight where his fingers were hooked loosely around the steering wheel. Glancing down at her lap, she saw her own slender white fingers suddenly looked distinctly bare. In what had been meant to be a dramatically expressive gesture she had left her rings behind when she left Vito all those years ago.

But now she shifted uncomfortably, a sudden wistfulness

sending her thumbpad on a stroke of the empty space where her rings should be.

'Do you want them back?'

Catherine jumped, severely jolted by the fact that he wasn't only looking at her now, but was doing it enough to miss nothing!

'It seems—practical,' she said, using the same flat tone as he. 'To avoid any—speculation. For Santo's sake.'

For Santo's sake. She grimaced at the weakness of her excuse, and even though she didn't check she knew that Vito was grimacing too. Because they both knew that if she put her rings back on she would be doing it for her own sake.

Pride being another sin they were all victim to in different ways. And her pride wanted her to wear the traditional seal of office that stated clearly her position in Vito's life. That way she could hold her head up and outface her critics—of which she expected to meet many—and feel no need to explain her arrival back to those people who probably believed their marriage had been dissolved long ago.

The car moved on up the hillside, and the higher it went the bigger the residential properties became and the more extensive and secluded became the land surrounding them. As they reached a pair of lattice iron gates that automatically swung open as they approached them, Catherine's attention turned outwards again, her interest picking up as she viewed the familiar tree-lined approach to her old home and found herself watching breathlessly for the house itself to come into view.

The gardens were a delight of wide terraces, set out in typically Italian formality, with neat pathways and hedgerows and elegant stone steps leading down to the next terrace and so on. There were several tiny courtyard areas fashioned around tinkling fountains framed by neatly clipped box hedgerows of jasmine and bougainvillea that were a blaze of colour right now.

As they rounded a bend in the driveway the house suddenly came into view. The Villa Giordani had been standing here for centuries, being improved on and added to until it had become the most desired property in the area.

Bright white walls as thick as four feet in places stood guarding an inner sanctum. Good taste and an eye for beauty had always been present in the Giordani genes. There was no upper floor terrace exactly, but each suite of rooms had its own balcony set flat against the outer wall and marked by a thick stone arch and balustrade supported on turned stone supports. The balconies went deep—deep into the house itself—in an effort to offer shade to their occupants, who might want to sit there and enjoy the view over the Bay of Naples, which was nothing short of breathtaking from this high on the hill.

In keeping with the upper floor, the ground floor kept to the same arched theme, only the low stone balustrades had been extended out to the edge of the wide terrace which circumvented the whole house.

Nothing had ever been skimped on in the creating of the Giordani residence. Even the four deep steps leading up to the terrace had been designed to add to the overall grandeur of the place.

The driveway continued on to curve round towards the back of the house, where Catherine knew the garages lay along with a stable block, two tennis courts and a swimming pool tucked away in a natural bowl in the landscape. But Vito brought the car to a halt at the front steps and shut down the engine.

Santo was already scrambling at the back of Catherine's seat in an effort to get out. 'Hurry up, Mummy!' he commanded impatiently. 'I want to go and surprise Nonna before she knows we're here!'

Climbing out of the car, Catherine unlocked the back of her seat to set her impatient son free, then stood watching as he raced off towards the house, bursting in through the front doors with a, 'Nonna, where are you?' at the top of his voice. 'It's me, Santo! I'm home!'

I'm home... Catherine felt her mouth twist in bitter rueful acknowledgement at just how much 'at home' her son had looked and sounded as his dark-eyed, dark-haired little body had shot him through those doors without a thought given to knocking first. And the words had burst from him in free-flowing Italian, as if it was the only language he knew how to speak.

As if he belonged here.

On the other side of the car, Vito stood watching also. And as her top lip gave a quiver in response to an unacceptable hurt she was suddenly feeling, he murmured, 'Here...' and Catherine turned only just in time to catch what it was he was tossing to her. 'A sweet to follow the bitter pill,' he drawled sardonically.

Frowning slightly, puzzled by both the cryptic remark and what he had tossed to her, she looked down to find that she was holding the keys to the Mercedes in her hand.

Her frown deepened, and for a confused moment she actually wondered if he was ordering her to go and garage the car! Then enlightenment struck. The sardonic words began to make sense.

He had not been watching their son; he had been watching her. And the sweetener remark had been a sarcastic reference to her reaction to the confidence with which Santo knew his place here!

But, worse than that, the keys had not been tossed to her to use to garage anything.

Vito was making her a gift of this beautiful Mercedes!

Her eyes shot up to clash with his, shaded lenses trying to probe through shaded lenses in an effort to try and discover before she responded if this was some kind of joke! Out here beneath his native skies he looked more the arrogant Italian than he had ever done. The darkness of his hair, the richness of his skin and the proud angle at which he held his head all sent the kind of tingling messages running through her that she did not like to feel.

Sexual messages. Without her being able to do a single thing to control it, the soft, springy cluster of curls nestling at the crown of her thighs began to tingle and stir beneath the covering of her thin jade summer dress. And her nipples gave a couple of sharp pricking stings in response.

It was awful, like being bewitched. She even found it shamefully sexy to note the way he had rolled up the sleeves on his pale blue shirt—as if it came as supremely natural for him to have them settle at just the right place to draw attention to the hair-peppered strength in his forearms.

'I can't accept this!' she burst out shrilly—and secretly wondered if it was the car or the man's sexual pull that she was refusing to accept. 'It's too much, Vito,' she tagged on hurriedly. 'And I have a car tucked away here somewhere,' she remembered, glancing around her as if she expected her little Fiat runabout to suddenly appear of its own volition.

'It lost the will to live over a year ago,' he informed her with yet more dry sarcasm. 'When no one else bothered to use it.'

And when she still hovered there in the sunlight, so conditioned to accepting nothing from Vito that she couldn't bring herself to accept this gift now, she heard him release a small sigh. 'Just bite the bullet and say thank you graciously,' he grimly suggested.

'As gracious as you were in offering the car to me?' she couldn't resist flashing back.

His grimace acknowledged her thrust as a hit. And he

opened his mouth to say something, but whatever it was stalled by the sudden appearance of his mother on the terrace.

In her sixties now, Luisa was still a truly beautiful woman. Only slightly smaller than Catherine, and naturally slender, she was a walking advert for eternal youth. Her skin was as smooth as any twenty-year-old's, and her hair kept its blackness with only the occasional help from her talented hairdresser.

But it was the inner Luisa that drew people to her like bees to the sweetest honeypot ever found. There wasn't a selfish bone in her body. She was good, she was kind, she was instinctively loving. And if she had one teeny-teeny fault, then it was an almost painful refusal to see bad in anyone.

And that included her daughter-in-law, most definitely her son, and of course her goddaughter—Marietta.

'Darling, I cannot tell you how wonderful it is to see you standing here!' Luisa murmured sincerely as she walked down the steps and right into Catherine's open embrace. 'And you look so lovely!' she declared as she drew away again. 'Vittorio, the Giordani eye for true beauty did not escape you,' his mother informed him. 'This woman will still be a source of pride to you when you are both old and grey.'

Off with the old, on with the new, Catherine wryly chanted to herself. In true Luisa form she was discarding the last three intensely hostile years as if they'd never happened.

'Come,' Luisa said, linking her arm through Catherine's and turning them both towards the house. 'Santo is already raiding the kitchen for snacks, and I have a light tea prepared in the summer room. The special carrier bringing your luggage will not be here for another couple of hours, so we have time to sit and have a long chat before you need worry about overseeing your unpacking...'

Behind her, Catherine was aware of Vito's shaded gaze following them as arm in arm they mounted the steps. And there was an unexpected urge in her to turn round and invite him to come and join them. But somehow she couldn't bring herself to do it. That kind of gesture had no place in what they had with each other.

Yet...

With her fingers curling around the bunch of keys she still held in her palm, she paused on the top step that formed the beginning of the wide terrace.

'Wait,' she murmured to Luisa. And on impulse turned and strode back down the steps to where Vito was still standing where they had left him.

An excuse? she asked herself as she drew to a stop in front of him. Had she needed an excuse to justify coming back to him? Yes, it was an excuse, she answered her own question. And, yes, she needed one to approach Vito in any way shape or form.

'Thank you for the car,' she murmured politely.

He was gazing down at her through those dratted glasses, though in a way she was glad they were there so she didn't have to read his expression.

She saw his mouth twitch. 'My pleasure,' he drawled with super-silken sardonicism.

It put her set teeth on edge. 'I really do appreciate the thought,' she added through them.

'My heart is gladdened by your sincerity,' he replied with taunting whimsy.

Her eyes began to flash behind the glasses. Maybe he caught a glimpse of it, because his hand suddenly shot up and in the next moment both pairs of sunglasses had been whipped away and tossed casually onto the back seat of the car.

Stripped bare of her hiding place, Catherine didn't know what to do other than release a stifled gasp. Then, on another move that left her utterly floundering, he dipped his head and caught her parted mouth with his own.

His kiss was deep and very intimate, and his body heat was stifling. The way his fingertips were sliding feather-light caresses up and down her arms was just another distraction she would have preferred to do without.

But her lips softened beneath his, and she swayed even closer to the source of heat, and the shaky sigh that escaped from her was really a shiver of pleasure at what his fingers were doing to her.

'Now I feel thanked,' he murmured as he drew away again. 'And my mother is enchanted. That is two birds killed with one small stone, Catherine. You may commend yourself.'

'You sarcastic rat,' she hissed at him, stepping away from him with a sudden flush to her cheeks that had nothing whatsoever to do with pleasure.

'I know,' he agreed, still smiling that sardonic smile as he leant back against the car and folded his arms across his pale-blue-covered chest. 'But it was either sarcasm or ravish you,' he said, and when she blinked, he grimaced. 'You turn me on, hard and fast, Catherine. I thought you were aware of that. Watching you walk up the steps to my house was, in fact, the biggest turn-on I've experienced in a long—long time.'

'You're over-sexed,' she snapped, turning away from him.

'And under-used,' he tagged on dryly.

Catherine walked off back to his waiting mother with her chin up and her expression a comical mix of angst and sweetness. The angst was for Vito, the sweetness a sad attempt to show Luisa that everything was fine! But she dropped the Mercedes car keys on the nearest flat surface

she passed as she entered the elegant Giordani hallway—
and gained a whole lot of satisfaction from knowing that
Vito had arrived at the front door in time to see her doing
it.

He knew why she had done it. He knew she was discarding both him and his sex appeal—and the darn gift—
with that one small gesture. But, in usual arrogant Vito
form, he ignored it all, politely declined to join them for
refreshment and went off instead to find his son—which
was all that really mattered to him anyway.

Afternoon tea was surprisingly pleasant, mainly because
both Luisa and Catherine were careful not to broach any
tricky subjects. Afterwards Santo came looking for his
mother, so he could take her up to show her his bedroom.
They spent a while in there together, looking at and discussing all the surprisingly well-used things he had in there.
There was a nice informality about the place that touched
her a little, because it was really only a bigger version of
Santos's bedroom at home.

Home. Once again the word brought her up short. Home
is here now, she told herself sternly. Home is here…

After that Santo was taken by his grandmother to visit
friends he had in the area, and after watching them stroll
away hand in hand down one of the pathways towards the
lowest part of their huge garden, where Catherine remembered there was a small gate which led out onto the road,
she decided to fill in her time by making a tour of the
house, to reacquaint herself with all of its hidden treasures.

Nothing had changed much, she noted as she strolled
from elegantly appointed room to room. But then, why
mess with perfection once you'd achieved it? Most of the
rooms were furnished with the kind of things which had
been collected through several centuries, by Giordanis adding to rather than discarding anything, so the finished result

was a tasteful blending of periods that gave an impressive picture of the family's successful history.

Vito was proud of his heritage. And it meant a lot to him to have a son to follow after him. Coming here for the first time, Catherine had admitted to feeling rather in awe of the kind of rarefied world she was being drawn in to. But by then it had already been too late to have second thoughts about whether she wanted to marry a man who in name alone was a legend in his own country. Already heart and soul in love with Vito, *and* pregnant with the next Giordani heir, she'd had her freedom of choice taken away from her.

And there had been so many people very eager to remind her of just how lucky she was to be marrying Vito. He was special, and being treated as special had also made him arrogant, she thought dryly, as she stood gazing around the huge ballroom which still looked exactly as it had done in the early eighteenth century when it had been constructed. To her knowledge it was still used for formal occasions.

Her own wedding ball had taken place here, she recalled. It had been a wonderful extravagant night, when the house had been filled with light and music and laughter, and the gardens hung with romantic lanterns so their guests could take the air if they felt like it. A reminiscent smile touched her lips as she watched herself being danced around the vast polished floor in the arms of her new husband in her flowing gown of gold which had been specially designed for her.

'Have I told you today how beautiful you are?' Vito's softly seductive voice echoed back to her through a trail of memories. 'You outshine every woman here tonight.'

'You're only saying that because it flatters your own ego,' she'd mocked him.

She could still hear the sound of his burst of appreciative laughter ringing around this room even as she drew the doors shut on the ballroom. And she was smiling wryly to herself as she turned to make her way to the elegant central stairway. For Vito had laughed like that because the man *was* conceited enough to know that having a beautiful wife flattered his ego for choosing her, not her ego for *being* her.

That was the way it was with a Giordani, she mused whimsically as she strode along the upper mezzanine and in through one of the many doors that lined the elegant two-winged landing. To them, other people were the satellites which revolved around *their* rich and compellingly seductive world. It was supposed to be a privilege to be invited to enter it.

Enter where? she then thought suddenly, and brought her wayward attention to an abrupt standstill along with her feet, when she realised just where it was she was standing.

A bedroom. *Their* bedroom. The one she'd used to share with Vito before she ran away.

Her heart began to thud, her throat closing over as she took on board just what she had done while her mind had been elsewhere.

She had walked herself right into the one room in the house she had been meaning to steer well clear of.

Her first instinct was to get out of there again as quickly as she could! Her second instinct had her pausing instead, though, giving in to an irresistible urge to check out the one place where she and Vito had always managed to be in harmony.

The bedroom. The bed, still standing there like a huge snow sleigh, made of the richest mahogany and polished to within an inch of its life. The width of three singles, it still had the same hand-embroidered pure white counterpane covering its fine white linen, still had its mound of fluffy white pillows they'd used to toss to the floor before retiring each night.

Then she recalled why they'd used to toss those pillows

away so carelessly, and felt the tight sting of that memory attack the very centre of her sexuality.

Was that all to begin again? she asked herself tensely. All the rowing and fighting, followed by the kind of sexual combat that used to leave them both a little shell-shocked afterwards?

It has already started again, she reminded herself. And on that grim acknowledgement let her eyes drift around the rest of the room to discover that not a single thing had been changed since she'd last stepped into it.

Yet, *she* had changed. She wasn't the same person she had been three years ago. In fact, at this precise moment she felt rather like a lost penny that had found itself being tossed back, only to land in the wrong place entirely.

She didn't want to be here, didn't think she *should* be here, even though she knew without a single doubt that this was the room Vito would be expecting her to share with him again.

Not that she'd asked the question, and would not be doing when she knew it would only give Vito the chance to taunt her with the fact that she had been brought back here to provide him with sex.

Sex, lies and pretence—the status quo re-established for Santo's sake—and to slake Vito's thirst for revenge. She was about to turn back to the door when—without any warning at all—the bathroom door suddenly flew open and Vito appeared in its aperture. He must have come directly from the shower, because all he had on was a white towel slung around his lean hips and he was rubbing briskly at his wet hair with another towel.

His arrival froze her to the carpet. And seeing her standing there had the same effect on him. So for the next few pulsing seconds neither seemed able to move another muscle as shocked surprise held them utterly transfixed.

CHAPTER SIX

WAS he seeing her like a lost penny that really shouldn't be where it was standing? she wondered as she watched those lush dark sensual lashes slowly lower over eyes that were determinedly giving nothing away.

The silence between them stretched into tension, and within it Catherine tried to stop her gaze from drifting over him. But it was no use. She had been drawn to this man's physical attraction from the first moment she ever set eyes on him. And nothing had changed, she realised sadly as, dry-mouthed, she watched crystal droplets of water drip from his hair onto his wide tanned shoulders then begin trailing into the crisp dark hair covering his chest.

He was male beauty personified, his face, his body, the long lean muscular strength in his deeply tanned legs.

'Have your things arrived yet?' Deep and dark, and unusually sedate for him in this kind of situation, Vito's voice held no hint of anything but casual enquiry.

Yet her skin flinched as if he'd reached out and touched it with the end of an electric live wire. 'I...n-not that I know of,' she replied, eyelashes fluttering as she dragged her gaze away from him. 'I've been—showing myself around,' she then added on a failed attempt at sounding casual.

'No surprises?' he asked, drawing her eyes back to him as he began to rub at his wet hair with the towel again.

She watched his biceps flex and his pectorals begin to tremble at the vigorous activity. 'Only Santo's room,' she murmured, and wished she knew how to cure herself of wanting this man. 'It's nice,' she tagged on diffidently.

'Glad you think so.' There should have been a hint of sarcasm when he said that, but there wasn't. In fact he was playing this all very casual—as if the last three years had never happened and they shared this kind of conversation in this room all the time.

But then, wasn't she trying to treat it the same way herself?

The towel was lowered and cast aside. Catherine bit her inner lip and tried desperately to come up with some excuse to leave that wouldn't make her appear a total coward.

In the end it was Vito who solved the dilemma for her. 'Sorry,' he apologised suddenly, and took a step sideways. 'Did you come here to...?'

He was asking if she needed to use the bathroom. 'N-No,' she murmured. Then, 'Yes!' she amended that, seeing the bathroom, with the lock it had on its door, as the ideal place to escape to.

But it was only as she pushed her tense body into movement that she realised she was going to have to pass very close by him to gain that escape. And Vito didn't move another muscle as he watched her come towards him. So her tension grew with each step that she took, and by the time she reached him her heart was thumping, and her breathing was so fragile that it was all she could do to murmur a frail, 'Thank you,' as she went to pass by him.

'Are you going to take a shower?'

Her senses were lost to a medley of tingles, all of which were set on high red alert. 'Y-Yes,' she heard herself answer, seeing yes as good as no at this precise moment, when she had absolutely no idea what she was intending to do in there! She didn't even need to use the bathroom!

'Then allow me...' his smooth voice offered.

At which point she found herself freezing yet again as his hands came to rest upon her shoulders. Then his fingers began trailing downwards over her pale skin until they reached the scooped edge of her jade linen dress where the long zip lay.

Gritting her teeth, Catherine prayed for deliverance. He was standing so close she could actually feel his lightly scented dampness eddying in the air surrounding her. It was incredibly alluring, the kind of scent that conjured up evocative pictures of warm, naked bodies tangled in loving.

She shivered delicately when, with a deftness that had always been his, he sent the zip of her dress skimming downwards. By the time the fabric parted her shivers had become tremors, and she had to close her eyes and grit her teeth harder while she waited for the ordeal to be over.

But Vito didn't stop there. Next his fingers were unclipping the catches on her bra and her breasts were suddenly free to swing unsupported. And in all of their long and intimate association she had never felt so wary and unsure of his intentions.

Even the way he ran the back of one long finger down the rigid length of her spine was telling her one thing while his voice, as cool as a mountain spring, was telling her another when he suggested levelly, 'Make it a long shower, Catherine, you are as tense as a bowstring.'

Make it a long shower, she repeated to herself. Make it a long, *cold* shower, she helplessly extended.

'But of course,' he then added, and suddenly his voice was as silken as his wretched voice ever could be, 'there are other, much more pleasurable ways to cure your tension.'

And before she could react his mouth landed against the side of her neck and, like a vampire swooping on its chosen prey, he bit sensually into the pulsing nerve there that lay alongside her jugular. At the same time his hands slid inside her dress and took possession of her recently freed breasts.

Sensation went streaking through her. After the day-long build-up of sexual tension, it was like being sprung free from the unbearable restraints that had been binding her, though she did at least try to put up some kind of protest.

'Vito, no,' she groaned. 'I need a shower—'

'I like you just the way you are,' he huskily counter-manded. 'Smelling of you, and tasting of you.'

He was already urging her dress to slither down her body, and in seconds she was standing there in just her panties. As those long, knowing fingers moulded her breasts so his thumbpads could begin drawing circles around their tips to encourage them to peak for him, his mouth continued to suck sensually on her neck.

It was all so exquisite, the caress of his hands, the wet-ness of his mouth, the way he was pressing her back against him. When he stroked one hand down the flat wall of her stomach and beneath the fabric of her briefs she simply gave up trying to fight it. On a shaky little sigh that her-alded her complete surrender her eyes drifted shut, and, tilting her head back against his shoulder, she allowed him to arouse her in a way only a deeply familiar lover would arouse a woman.

But not enough—not enough. Her hands reached behind him to rip away the towel so she could press him against her, and her head turned against his shoulder, searching out his mouth so she could join her own with it. 'Kiss me properly,' she commanded, no shrinking violet when it came to her body's pleasures.

On an answering growl he swung her around, lifted her up his body until she was off her feet—then kissed her hard and hot and deeply. The wall not far away was a godsend as he pressed her back against it and let her feet find solid ground again. Catherine parted her thighs and pressed him even closer, then tightened herself around him.

He was very aroused, and with the towel gone it left him free to use other, far more invigorating methods to keep her riding high on the crested wave of pleasure. Dragging her mouth free from his, she tilted her head back and simply let herself concentrate on the stroke of his body.

'You're wearing too much,' he murmured sensually.

'I'll never wear panties again,' she agreed with him.

Vito laughed, but it was a hard, tense, very male laugh, and it set fires alight inside her that did nothing for her self-control as he caught her mouth again and began kissing her greedily.

'I need the bed,' she groaned, when things began to get too much for her and her legs threatened to completely give away.

'I'm way ahead of you, *cara*,' he murmured raspingly.

Opening her eyes, Catherine found herself looking directly into two hot, hard golden points of passion that were doing nothing to hide the intensity of what he too was experiencing.

And they were moving. Catherine hadn't even noticed until that moment that he was actually carrying her. They arrived at the bed. With a complete lack of ceremony he dropped her to her feet, then bent to get rid of her last piece of clothing.

As he buried his mouth into this newly exposed part of her body, she stretched out an arm behind her and began tossing away pillows, raking back bedcovers. It was all very urgent, very hectic, very fevered. No time for lazy foreplay, no hint of romance. She wanted him now, and it was patently obvious that he was the same.

As she lowered herself onto the bed, then began sliding backwards so she could lie down flat, she remembered the door. 'Lock us in first,' she whispered.

'To hell with the door,' he refused, following her onto the bed as if they were joined at the hip. 'I'm not stopping this if the whole house walks in to watch.'

With that he entered her, sure and swift, and as she cried out in sheer surprise he laughed again, the same very male laugh, caught her face between his hands then made her look at him.

'Hi.' He grinned, as her lashes flickered upwards. 'Remember me? I am your fantastic lover.'

He wasn't even moving. He was playing with her, toying with her. He had fired her up until she didn't know her own name any more. Now he was trying to lighten the whole thing!

With a flash from vengeful green eyes, she tightened the muscles around her abdomen. The motion made him suck in his breath. 'Want to play, Vito?' she taunted, and raked her fingernails along his lean flanks where some of this man's most vulnerable erogenous zones were situated.

The breath left his lungs on a driven hiss. Catherine put out her tongue and licked the sound right off his warm, moist, pulsing lips. He began cursing in Italian, and there was no hint of humour left in him when he began moving on her with a fierceness that sent her reeling away into a pool of hot sensation.

When she shattered her arms flew out, wide, like a swimmer floating on its back. Vito slid his hand beneath her head to her nape, then lifted her towards him. It was a need he'd always had, to capture her desperate little gasps as she went into orgasm, and Catherine didn't deny him them now as she breathed those helpless little sounds into his mouth and felt his body quicken as he too came nearer to his peak.

After that she remembered nothing. Not his own intense climax, not the swirling aftermath, not even the way he slid away from her, then lay fighting for recovery.

Outside it was still daylight. Inside the air-conditioning was keeping the room temperature at a constant liveable level. But Catherine was bathed in sweat from tingling toes to hairline. And beside her she could see the same film of sweat glistening on Vito's skin.

She watched him for a little while, enjoying the way he

was just lying there, heavy-limbed and utterly spent. Yet, even spent, Vito was physically imposing. A man with the normal potency of ten.

Potent…

Catherine stiffened—then went perfectly still, the sweat slowly chilling her flesh as she lay there, held by a sudden thought so terrible that her mind literally froze rather than dare let her face it. Beside her, sensing the change in her, Vito turned his dark head, then began frowning as he watched her steadily draining pallor.

But before he had a chance to say anything she sat up with a jerk, then began sliding frantically for the edge of the wide bed. Her long legs hit the ground at a run, her hair flying out behind her as she streaked like a sprinter for the bathroom.

Whatever she was looking for wasn't there, because she appeared again almost immediately. To say she was in shock was an understatement. White-faced, and shaking so badly that her teeth chattered, she looked at Vito, who was only just pulling himself into a sitting position.

'My things,' she shot out in a taut staccato. 'Where are my things?'

Still frowning in complete bewilderment as to what was going on, he shrugged. 'They have not arrived yet, remember?'

'Not arrived,' she repeated, then her eyes went blank, and Vito shot off that bed like a bullet from a gun because he thought she was actually going to pass out where she stood!

'For goodness' sake, *cara*,' he rasped. 'What is wrong with you?'

'M-my bag, then,' she whispered shakily, and when all he did was come striding towards her without bothering to answer she hit the hysteria button. 'My *handbag*, Vito!' she actually screamed at him. 'Where is it? My handbag—*my handbag*!'

It brought him to a stop in sheer astonishment. 'Catherine—what the hell is this?' he demanded, beginning to sound shaken himself.

She didn't answer, instead she suddenly burst into action again. Darting down to snatch up her dress, she began to pull it on. She was trembling so badly she could barely manage the simple task, but when he attempted to help her she slapped him away.

'I can't believe I let you do this!' she launched at him shrilly. 'I can't believe I let myself!'

'Do what, for God's sake?' he shouted back angrily. 'Make love?' He decided that was the only answer. 'Well, that's rich coming from the woman who just ravished me!'

If anything, her face went even whiter, though it didn't seem possible. And, on a pained whimper that did nothing for his temper, she turned and ran for the bedroom door with her fingers still grappling with the zip on her dress and the rest of her still completely naked.

'Catherine!' Vito barked at her in a command meant to stop her leaving the room.

But Catherine was already out of it and running down the stairs. Outside in the late-afternoon sunshine she found her handbag, still lying where she had left it on the floor of the red Mercedes.

By the time Vito had pulled some clothes on and followed her Catherine was just sitting there on the bottom step in front of the house, with the bag and its spilled contents lying beside her.

And there was such an air of fragility about her that he made his approach with extreme caution, walking down the steps to come and squat down in front of her. 'Are you going to tell me what that was all about now?' he requested carefully.

She shook her head and there were tears in her eyes. He sighed, his mouth tightening as he began flicking his gaze across the contents of her bag as if the answer would show itself there.

But it didn't. All he saw was the usual clutter of personal things women tended to carry around with them. Lipstick, wallet, the passport she'd needed to get her into the country. A packet of paper tissues, a couple of spare clips she used to hold back her hair sometimes, and a hair comb. He looked back at Catherine, looked at the way she was staring out at nothing, and automatically looked down, expecting to find the cause of all of this—trauma clutched in her hands. But her hands were empty, their palms pressed together and trapped between her clenched knees.

It was then that he spied it, lying on the ground between her bare feet, and slowly, warily, he reached out and picked it up.

It took him about five seconds after that to realise what was wrong with her. Then the cursing started. Hard words, hoarse words, words that had him lurching to his feet and swinging around to slam his clenched fist into the shiny bodywork of the Mercedes.

After that, he too went perfectly still, frozen by the same sense of numbing horror that was holding Catherine. And the ensuing silence throbbed and punched and kicked at the both of them.

Until a sound in the distance grabbed Vito's attention. His dark head went up, swinging round on his shoulders so he could scan the furthest corner of the garden, where a gate out onto the road served as a short cut to their nearest neighbours.

Then suddenly he was bursting into action again, spinning back to Catherine and stooping down to gather her into his arms before turning to dump her into the passenger seat of the Mercedes.

'What—?' she choked, coming out of her stunned stupor on a gasp of surprise.

'Stay put,' he gritted, then turned back to the house and disappeared inside it, only to come back seconds later with a bunch of keys in his hands. On his way past her bag he bent to gather in its contents; it landed on the back seat beside two pairs of sunglasses as he climbed behind the wheel.

The engine fired first time, and with the efficiency of a born driver he turned the car around and took off at speed down the driveway.

'Santo and my mother are on their way back.' He grimly explained his odd behaviour. 'I did not think you would want them to see you looking like this.'

Like this... Catherine repeated to herself, looking down at herself with the kind of blank eyes that said she couldn't see, as he could see, the changes that had come over her in a few short, devastating minutes.

Stopping at the end of the drive, Vito Giordani looked at this woman who had known more than her fair share of pain, heartache and grief in her life, and felt the air leave his lungs on a constricted hiss.

'How many have you missed?' he questioned flatly.

Catherine lifted those wretched dull grey eyes to him and a nerve began ticking along his jawline as he set the car going again, taking them not down the hillside but up it, out into open country.

'You can count as well as I can,' she answered dully.

Vito grimaced. 'I am afraid my eyes glazed over when I noticed that yesterday's was still there.'

Yesterday's, the day before—and the day before, Catherine counted out bleakly. A contraceptive pill for each day since Vito had come back into her life, in fact.

'I hate you,' she whispered. 'You've been messing up

my life since I was twenty-three years old, and here you are, six years on, still messing it up.'

About to remind her that it wasn't him who'd forgotten to take the damn pills, Vito bit the words back again. 'Getting embroiled in a fight about whose fault it is is not going to solve the problem,' he threw at her instead.

'Nothing can solve it,' Catherine countered hopelessly. 'The damage has already been done.'

Mouth set in a straight line, Vito said not another word as he drove them higher and higher, until eventually he pulled the car off the road and onto a piece of scrub land that overlooked the kind of views people paid fortunes to see.

They didn't see the beauty in it, though. There could have been pitch-blackness out there in front of them for all they knew. And they were surrounded by perfect silence. Not a bird, not a house, not another car, not even a breeze to rustle the dry undergrowth. In fact they could have been the only two people left in the world, which suited exactly how they were both feeling.

Two people alone with the kind of problem that shut out the rest of the world.

'I'm sorry,' Vito murmured.

Maybe he felt he needed to say it, but Catherine shrugged. 'Not your fault,' she absolved him. 'It's me who's been unforgivably stupid.'

'Maybe we will get lucky and nothing will come of it,' he suggested, in an attempt to place a glimmer of light into their darkness.

'Don't count on it,' Catherine replied heavily. 'Twice before we've taken risks, and twice I got pregnant. Why should this time be any different?'

Why indeed? was the echo that came back from the next drumming silence.

'There has to be something we can do!' he muttered

harshly. And on a sudden flash of inspiration said, 'We will drive to the doctor's. Get that—morning-after pill—or whatever it is they call it...'

Catherine flinched as if he had plunged a knife in her. 'Do you know what they call those pills, Vito?' she whispered painfully. 'Little abortions,' she informed him starkly. 'Because that's what they do. They abort the egg whether it is fertilised or not.'

'But you also know what they told you,' he reminded her. 'Another pregnancy like the last one could be dangerous.'

Her tear-washed eyes shimmered in the sunlight. 'So I abort one life to safeguard my own life?'

The anguish she saw in his eyes was for her; Catherine knew that. But she couldn't deal with it. And on the dire need to escape from both him and the whole wretched scenario, she opened the car door and climbed out.

Leaving Vito sitting there staring ahead of him, she walked, barefooted, across the dusty ground to a lonely cypress tree and leaned against its dry old trunk.

First she had almost lost Santo, due to mid-term complications. She had managed to hold onto him until he was big enough to cope outside his mother's womb, and the doctors had assured her that the same condition rarely struck twice in the same woman. But they had been wrong. And the next time it had happened she'd almost lost her own life along with her baby.

'No more babies,' they had announced. 'Your body won't take the physical trauma.'

No more babies...

A movement beside her made her aware that Vito had come to lean a shoulder on the other side of the tree. For a man who had only had enough time to drag on the first clothes that came to hand he looked remarkably stylish in his light chinos and a plain white tee shirt. But then, that was Vito, she mused hollowly. A man so inherently special that no one in the world would believe that anything in his life would ever go wrong for him.

His marriage had. From its unfortunate beginning to its tragic ending.

Catherine didn't count this latest encounter. Because in truth she no longer felt married to Vito; if anything, she felt more as she had done when she first met him: alive, excited, electrifyingly stimulated. Which was why they'd ended up in bed making love like there was no tomorrow. It was a taste of the old days—irresistible.

And now the piper demands his payment, she concluded dully.

'Santo needs his mother, Catherine,' Vito stated levelly—nothing more. He didn't need to elaborate. Catherine knew exactly what he was telling her here.

They were back to celebrating the living, she supposed. Santo needs his mother alive and well and very much kicking. Tears burned her eyes again. She blinked them away. 'I'll take the pill,' she said.

He didn't say anything. Instead he just continued to lean there, staring out at his homeland as if he was watching Naples sink beneath a sea of lava and was as helpless to stop that from happening as he was to stop Catherine from having to make that decision.

Without another word, she walked back to the car and climbed into it. Vito followed her, got in, fired the engine and drove them away, down the hillside this time, and into Naples proper, where he took grim pleasure in fighting with the unremitting flood of traffic before eventually turning into an arched alleyway which led through to a private courtyard belonging to his offices.

Climbing out of the car, he came around to Catherine's side, opened her door and helped her to alight. She didn't put up any protest, not even when he silently turned her around and did up the rest of her zip before leading the way into the building. His concierge took one look at his face and with only a brief nod of his head backed warily away, but his glance swept curiously over Catherine's dusty bare feet and tangled mane of bright hair as the lift doors shut them away.

It was getting late by now. The working day was over so the place was empty of people. Leading the way to his own office suite, Vito pointed to a door. 'Take a shower,' he instructed, and walked off to his desk to pick up the telephone.

As she stepped into the bathroom she heard him talking to his mother, making some excuse about them going shopping on impulse and forgetting to tell anyone before leaving.

It was as good an excuse as any, she supposed, so long as no one had thought to check their bedroom, where the evidence of what they had been doing before they went out was painfully clear to see.

The next call Vito made was out of her hearing. It was curt, it was tight, and it didn't improve his temper as he began his third call, instructing a fashion boutique a short block from here, that knew him through his mother, to deliver the full range of whatever they had in stock to fit a British size ten, including shoes and underwear.

Catherine still hadn't emerged from the bathroom by the time the concierge came in, laden down with the boutique's delivery. In any other mood Vito might have been interested in what he had got for his money, but since most of the items were simply a bluff to fool his mother, he merely told the man to place the purchases on the low leather sofa beneath the window, then dismissed him.

But before he went the concierge handed him a different kind of purchase entirely. It was small, it was light, and it bore the name of a well-respected medical practice in Naples.

Vito was still staring grimly down at it when Catherine emerged from the bathroom, wrapped in his own short white towelling robe that was way too big for her. She looked wet, she looked clean—and utterly miserable.

'I couldn't find a hairdryer,' she said, indicating her head, where her hair hung straight and at least five shades darker against the whiteness of her face.

'I'll find it in a minute,' he replied, walking towards her.

She wasn't looking at him, but then she hadn't done so since they'd made love earlier—not with eyes that could see him anyway.

'Here,' he said gruffly, and handed her the small package.

She knew what it was the moment she looked at it, even though her eyes couldn't focus on the writing. 'Two now, two more in twelve hours,' he instructed.

A cold chill went sweeping through her, turning her fingers to ice as she reached out and took the packet from him.

'I need a drink,' she said.

He nodded briskly and moved away. 'Tea, coffee, iced water?' he enquired, opening the doors to a huge drinks cabinet equipped with everything from kettle to cocktail shaker.

'Water,' she chose, then slid her hands into the cavernous pockets of the robe before lifting herself to take a forced interest in her surroundings.

This place hadn't changed much since she'd last been here either, she saw. Same classic trappings of a well-to-do businessman, same hi-tech equipment, only a lot more of it.

He turned with the glass of water. 'Catherine—'

'Shut up,' she said flatly, and, ignoring the grim tension

in his stance, she made herself walk over to the sofa where the concierge had placed Vito's purchases. 'For me?' she asked.

'Take your pick,' he replied. 'There should be a selection of everything you will require.'

'The man thinks of everything,' she dryly mocked as her fingers flicked open boxes and checked out bags with about as much interest as a hungry dog being offered a plastic bone to eat. 'Troubleshooter extraordinaire.'

He didn't answer, but then, why should he bother? It was only the truth after all. For who else did she know who could achieve so much in the time it took her to have a shower?

'I'll take these,' she said, choosing at random a teal blue silk dinner dress and some matching underwear. Going back towards the bathroom, she paused in the doorway. 'The hairdryer?' she prompted him.

He walked over to her, then stopped to silently hand her the requested glass of water that she seemed to have had already forgotten about, before he slid past her into the bathroom and unearthed a hairdryer from the back of a vanity unit.

Grimly plugging it in, he left it ready for her on the marble top, then turned to leave her to it. In her hand was the glass of water. The water was to help her swallow the medication he had given to her. He walked past her, then stopped, tensely swung back. 'Catherine—'

She shut the door in his face.

Fifteen minutes later she came out again, hair dried into some semblance of a style, her clothes looking unexpectedly fantastic, considering the way they had been chosen. The dress was short, slim, and edged with a layer of fine black lace. Standing staring out of the window, Vito turned when he heard her, then went still, his sombre eyes hooding over as they slid down her.

'Shoes,' was all he said, though, pointing to a pair of

teal-blue strappy sandals standing neatly by the sofa. Everything else had gone—where to Catherine didn't know, nor care.

She found out when they arrived back at the car and saw the back seat was full of packages. The car's roof had been raised, and as they climbed inside she felt the difference as a humid heat quickly enveloped her. Vito started the car and switched on the air-conditioning system, then they drove off, back home to their twisted version of normality.

It was growing quite dark by the time they arrived at the house. Lights were burning on the driveway, offering a warm welcome that didn't touch Catherine.

As they walked into the house Santo appeared, already dressed for bed in his pyjamas. With a delighted whoop he came running towards them. Whether it was deliberate, Catherine wasn't certain, but Vito took a small step backwards then slid stealthily behind her, as if he was trying to reduce Santo's options so he would run into his mother's arms and not his father's.

If it was deliberate then it was a very selfless gesture, one that showed a deep sensitivity to her needs right now. And an understanding that her emotions had taken a big enough battering today without having her son giving it a further knock by choosing to hug his father before hugging her.

So she received her warm bundle of love and hugged him to her as if her life depended on holding this precious child of theirs. And with his arms around her neck and his legs around her waist Santo chatted away about what he had been doing, with absolutely no idea that his mother was frantically fighting a battle with tears again.

It was only when she eventually set her son down again, so he could go to his father, and she saw the way Vito held Santo to him in much the same way that she had done, that she allowed herself to acknowledge that he too was suffering.

It was too much—much too much for her to cope with right now, when she could barely cope with her own inner agony. So she walked away, wishing she could just go and crawl into bed, pull the covers over her head and stay there for ever.

But she couldn't do that, because Luisa was waiting for them and expected bright smiles and conversation. Catherine played the game to the best of her ability, and even managed to smile at Luisa teasing Vito about the new wardrobe of clothes he had just bought Catherine because her own luggage hadn't arrived.

'But it came while you were out!' her mother-in-law laughingly informed them. 'How terribly impatient and extravagant of you, darling!' Her eyes twinkled teasingly at her son, and why were they twinkling? Because Luisa was seeing the gesture as a demonstration of how wonderfully romantic things must be between her son and his wife—when really things couldn't be more wretched. 'And what a lovely treat for you, Catherine...!'

Dinner that night was just another ordeal she had to force herself to get through. She had to eat when she didn't want to, smile when she didn't want to, had to make pleasant innocuous conversation when she didn't want to. And through it all she had to watch Vito watch her from beneath heavily veiled eyes, as if he was expecting her at any moment to jump up and start screaming the place down.

She didn't really blame him, for she knew that beneath her relaxed exterior she was so uptight it was actually beginning to hurt. She had been avoiding him like the plague since they got back. If he walked into a room then she walked out of it; if he went to speak to her she pretended she didn't hear. Now, across the dinner table, if she found herself being forced into making eye contact with him she did it from behind a frosted veil, which thankfully kept him out of focus.

But that didn't mean that she wasn't aware of *his* tension, or of the greyish pallor sitting just beneath the surface of his golden skin that had been there ever since he had handed her that packet in his office.

'...Marietta...'

Suddenly feeling as though a thousand sharp needles were embedding themselves into her flesh, Catherine blinked her mind back into focus on the conversation at the table.

'She was sorry she couldn't be here to welcome you home today,' Luisa was saying innocently. 'But Vito saw fit to send her off to New York on some wild-goose chase she insists did not really warrant her attention.' A censorious glance at her son gained no response whatsoever. 'Still, since Vito's priority had to be here with you and Santo, one of them had to go, I suppose,' Luisa allowed, with a little shrug meant, Catherine presumed, to dismiss her son's silence. 'She will be back by the weekend, though, so maybe we could all get together then for a celebratory dinner—which would be nice, don't you think, Catherine? The two of you were such good friends once upon a time. I'm sure you must be looking forward to reviving the friendship.'

'Excuse me.' She stood up with an abruptness that surprised everyone. 'Forgive me, Luisa, but I'm afraid I can't sit here any longer—'

'Aren't you well, Catherine?' It was a logical conclusion to make, bearing in mind that her dinner plate was sitting untouched, right in front of her. And at last Luisa seemed to notice Catherine's strained pallor, while, with the kind of good manners that had been bred into him, Vito rose gracefully to his feet also. But he was still watching her like a hawk, and Catherine wanted to scratch his blasted eyes out because he knew his mother had just advantageously stopped her from saying something she would have regretted later about Luisa's precious Marietta!

'Just tired, that's all.' She smiled a weak smile that was

really an acknowledgement of her own sense of relief at Luisa's interruption. For hadn't it always been easier to leave Luisa with her rose-tinted glasses in place than be the one to rip them from her? 'It has been a long day in one way or another.'

'Of course, dear,' Luisa murmured understandingly. 'And you are not used to our late dining habits—which probably accounts for your lack of appetite tonight...'

'Yes.' Catherine kept on smiling the wretched smile and bent to brush a kiss across Luisa's cheek before mumbling some incoherent remark about seeing Vito later as she stumbled wearily from the table.

By the time she had prepared for bed and carried out her most dearest wish by crawling beneath the sheets and pulling them right over her, she had hardly any energy left to do much more than switch her brain off.

So she was completely lost to a blessed oblivion when a pair of arms firmly gathering her in brought her swimming back to consciousness.

'No.' Her response was instant rejection.

'Be still,' Vito's deep voice flatly countered, and, drawing her into the warm curve of his body, he firmly clamped her there. 'You may wish to pretend that I do not exist right now, but I do, and I am here—'

'While your lover is several thousand miles away,' she tagged on waspishly.

'Marietta is your obsession, not mine,' he replied. 'But since you have decided to bring her into this bed with us, may I remind you that you are here to replace her? So stop fighting me, Catherine.' Once again his arms tightened to subdue her wriggling struggles. 'You may like to believe that you are the only miserable one in this bed, but you are not. And I need to hold you as much as you need to be held like this.'

He wasn't talking about Marietta now, she realised. He was talking about something far more emotive. Impulsively she opened her mouth to say something about that—then changed her mind, for her emotions were in such a dreadful mess that remaining silent seemed wiser at this moment than saying anything that could well start another quarrel.

So she subsided, reluctantly, into the warmth of his embrace, felt his muscles relax when he recognised her surrender. And as she began taking on board other things, like his nakedness against her thin cotton pyjamas, she bitterly wished that the man wasn't so physically alluring.

Wished to God that she wasn't so useless as a woman. She wished her heart didn't hurt so much and her brain was more able to make a clear-cut decision between what was right and what was wrong.

And she wished so very sincerely that the world would stop turning, so that she could get off it and never come back to it again!

'Cry if you want to,' his rusty voice encouraged.

'No,' she refused, but her body was already trembling with the effort it was costing her not to.

'It was the right thing to do, Catherine. The only thing to do.' Vito's mouth pressed a kiss to the back of her head. 'But that does not mean you must not mourn the decision.'

But it did—it did! And Vito was never going to understand what that decision was costing her because she was not going to tell him—or tell anyone for that matter.

'I just want to go to sleep and forget all about it,' she whispered thickly.

'Then do so,' he allowed. 'But I will be here if you change your mind, *cara*. Right here beside you.'

Was this his way of making up for the time when he hadn't been there for her? If it was then Catherine was not going to taunt him with it. Because she might be absorbed by her own torment right now, but she could feel the way his hands were tensely gripping her hands, that Vito was no less tormented.

CHAPTER SEVEN

His arms stayed wrapped around her throughout the long night. Each time Catherine swam up from the dark well of sleep towards reality she felt him there, and drew enough comfort from that to help sink her back into oblivion once again.

The next morning he woke her up very early and gently reminded her to take her second set of pills. Without a word she dragged herself out of the bed and disappeared into the bathroom. But it was only as she stood there in the middle of the bathroom floor, feeling a bit like a spare part that had no useful function, that the sudden realisation that something was different had her glancing down at her left hand—then going perfectly still when she saw her rings winking up at her.

The first one—an exquisite square-cut diamond set to stand on its own—she'd received a week after she'd told Vito she was pregnant with Santo. The second was the plain gold band given to her on her wedding day that matched the one Vito wore on his finger. And the third—a diamond-encrusted eternity ring—arrived the day after she'd announced the coming of their second baby.

When had he done this? she wondered frowningly, remembering that there hadn't seemed to be a single moment during the night when she hadn't been aware of him right there beside her. Yet he must have left her at some point and gone downstairs to his safe in the study, where she presumed he had placed her rings when she'd left them behind her, then come back upstairs to slide the rings on her finger—carefully, so as not to waken her.

But *why* had he done it? That was the much more disturbing question. And why last night, of all nights, when she couldn't have felt less deserving of these rings if she'd tried?

What kind of message was he trying to convey to her? There had to be some significance in him replacing these rings on her finger last night when things could not have been more pitiable between them.

A statement of intent? 'I am here for you, Catherine,' he had told her. And the appearance of her rings seemed to be telling her that he wanted her to know he was seriously committing himself to this ailing marriage of theirs, when really what had happened yesterday could not have been a better reminder as to why he was better off without her!

Guilt riddled through her. The guilt of a woman who knew she wasn't being entirely truthful with him.

But then, she asked herself, when had she ever felt that she could be? She had always only ever felt like a means to an end for Vito. First as a very compatible lover, then as the mother of his future child, and now as a necessary means of making his son happy. You couldn't build trust and honesty on foundations as shaky as theirs were.

Rings or no rings, none of that had changed since yesterday. She still felt as alone now as she had done on the day she'd lost their baby three years ago.

'Forgive me, Catherine,' he had pleaded at that time. 'If there was anything I could do to make the last twenty-four hours go away then I would do it. You have to believe me.'

But no one, not even Vito, was able to turn back time. It had already been too late for them by then. Just as it was also too late to change the consequences of the last twenty-four hours now.

And right now as she stood here, staring at these rings which seemed to be making such an important statement, she wished he hadn't done it when it only complicated a situation that was complicated enough already. Because he didn't know.

He didn't know...

A point which made her manner awkward when she returned to the bedroom a few minutes later. 'Thank you,' she mumbled, making a gesture with the hand bearing the rings.

He smiled a brief, tight smile. 'I missed them last night,' he explained. 'Then could not go to sleep without putting them back where they belonged.'

That word 'belonged' made her aching heart flinch. And for the life of her she couldn't think of a single thing to say in reply. So a tension built between them, a different kind of tension that lacked the old hostility that usually helped to keep them going.

Vito eventually filled it. 'So—what would you like to do today?' he asked briskly. 'I usually take Santo on a short horse-ride on his first day here, to brush up on his riding skills.'

'Fine.' It was her turn to flash a brief, brisk smile. 'I'll come too, if I may.'

But her light reply sent his eyes dark. 'That was the idea, Catherine,' he said soberly. 'That we do things together as a family.'

'I thought I just agreed to that,' she countered blankly.

'It was the way that you said it,' Vito grimly replied. 'As if you were afraid you may be an intrusion.'

This time Catherine's smile was wry to say the least. 'Let's face it, Vito. I wouldn't be here at all if Santino hadn't backed you into a corner.'

His eyes began to flash. And, snap—just like that the antagonism was back. 'Well, you are here,' he grated. 'And this is your home. We are your family and the sooner you come to terms with that, the sooner you will stop being an intrusion!'

With that, Catherine watched him slam himself into the bathroom, leaving her to wonder what the hell had motivated it.

Going back over the conversation, the only thing she could come up with that could have ignited his temper was her silence after he had explained about her rings.

Had he been expecting a whole lot more than a blank stare? A declaration of mutual intent, maybe? But why he should expect or even want that baffled her. He had never looked for those kind of declarations before when—marginally—they'd had something more substantial to work with than they had now.

And anyway, she concluded as she went to find something suitable to wear to go riding in, she felt more comfortable with antagonism than she did with the terrible lost and vulnerable feeling that she'd woken up with this morning. So let him stew, she decided. Let him bash his ego against the brick wall of her defences if that was what he wanted to do. Because there was no way that even Vittorio Giordani could really believe he had a right to expect more from her than he was willing to give out himself!

Yet something fundamental had altered inside him, Catherine had to admit as her first week in Naples drew to a close. For after that one show of his Italian temperament Vito had never uttered another harsh word to her, and seemed to be very careful not to give her the opportunity to flash hers at him.

He had allotted this week to spend with Santo, and work had been set to one side so he could play the loving family game their son had been promised. So they'd filled in their days by riding and swimming, and with trips out around Naples. And their nights had been spent in each other's arms, without even the slightest question of sex rearing its emotive head between them.

And slowly—slowly—Catherine had begun to relax her

guard a little, begun to cautiously enjoy herself. And without the sex to complicate matters, they had actually managed to achieve a kind of harmony that was almost as seductive as the sex used to be.

But it couldn't last. Did she honestly believe that it could? Catherine asked herself as she lay, supposedly relaxing with a book at the poolside, left entirely to her own devices for the first time since she had arrived back here. Luisa had announced her intention to take Santo and a group of his friends off to the beach for the day, and Vito had informed her that he planned to spend the day in his study, putting in some work for his neglected company.

Nothing particularly life-changing in those events, you would think, she mused to herself. But, for reasons she refused to let herself delve into, the book she was reading wouldn't hold her attention. After having pounded out a dozen or so laps of the pool, she had hoped she would just collapse on the sunbed in exhaustion, but she hadn't.

She felt tense and edgy, and kept glancing at the sky, as if she expected to find thunderclouds gathering on the horizon, which would explain this strange tension she was experiencing. But no hint of grey spoiled the perfect blue. In the end she gave up trying to be relaxed when she so obviously wasn't, and went back indoors to shower the suncream from her skin and get dressed with the vague intention of driving herself into Naples in an effort to kill some time.

She had rubbed herself dry, and was just in the process of smoothing body lotion into one of her long slender thighs when the bathroom door swung open. Standing there completely naked and with one foot lifted onto the bathroom stool to make her task easier, she glanced up, saw Vito filling the doorway—and knew in that instant that the storm she had been expecting all day had finally arrived.

It was a storm called desire. Pure and simple, hot and

hungry, tense and tight. It raged in the burning intensity of his eyes and pulsed in the tautness of his stance.

He was wearing a casual wine-red shirt and a pair of lightweight black linen trousers, but as his gaze glittered over her she saw his hand lift up and begin unfastening shirt buttons—and the frisson of response which went shimmering through her was electric.

She had to move. It was a point of necessity that she drop her raised foot to the floor so she could squeeze her pulsing thighs together. The shirt fell apart to reveal a wide bronzed breastplate covered in short, crisp devil-black hair.

'I w-was about to go out,' she heard herself stammer, really as a vehicle to break the raging tension now filling the space between them. 'Drive in-into Naples.'

'Later,' he murmured as the shirt landed on the bathroom floor. Then he half bent so he could slide off his shoes and socks before moving his attention to his trousers.

This was one hell of a strip show. Catherine clutched the bottle of lotion in one hand and felt her flesh begin to tingle. As the trousers parted to reveal that dark patch of body hair she knew thickened beneath the covering of his briefs panic erupted, though it was a very sexual kind of panic and had nothing to do with any dismay at what he was clearly intending.

Yet something made her put up a protest. Maybe it was the knowledge that the trousers were about to go, as she saw his fingers grip at the waistband in readiness to rake them down his legs.

'I... Vito, you—I—we c-can't,' she mumbled incoherently.

'Why not?' he countered.

'Y-your mother—Santo...'

But he shook his dark head. 'I've waited a full week for you to tell me it is okay for us to do this,' he said rawly.

'I am not waiting any longer, Catherine. I *cannot* wait any longer—'

Was that what had been holding him back for all of this time? Because he had assumed she would be rendered unavailable by the pill-induced menstrual cycle?

Chagrined heat blushed her skin from toes to hairline. Seeing it happen brought his strip show to a taut standstill. 'Is it okay?' he then demanded, and his consternation was so great that Catherine almost let out a giggle.

Except that this was no moment for humour. The man in front of her was suffering too badly to appreciate it—as his next gruff statement clearly illuminated. 'For goodness' sake, answer me, Catherine,' he commanded. 'The tension is starting to kill me, very slowly and very painfully.'

'It's okay,' she whispered.

Honey-gold eyes grew suddenly darker, their heat piercing her in all the right places. The trousers went the same way as the shirt, taking his underwear with them to leave only the man in his full and sexual glory to come walking towards her.

The tip of her tongue came out to moisten her lips as he took the bottle of lotion from her nerveless fingers then set it aside. And, without taking his eyes from her eyes, he bent his dark head to capture the tongue-tip between his own lips and draw it into his mouth in an act so inherently erotic that she whimpered in protest when he withdrew again almost immediately.

But his eyes continued to make love to her eyes as one of his hands slid around her waist while the other hand reached up to release her hair from the knot she had it twisted in for her shower. As her hair tumbled down over his fingers to brush sensually against her naked shoulders, he slowly drew her against him.

The contact was utterly scintillating, a fine brushing of warm flesh against flesh that set every nerve-end she possessed singing. Then he kissed her again, slowly and deeply, while stroking her with featherlight fingertips until she was breathless and trembling.

It was all too much for her to just stand there passive while he did this to her. With a sigh that was about as tactile as a sigh could be, she wound her arms around his shoulders, caught his head in her palms and began kissing him hungrily.

It was all the encouragement he needed to pick her up in his arms and carry her to the bed. The pillows went the way they usually did, to the floor, sent there by his urgent hands while Catherine dragged back the covers.

They came together in a tangle of limbs on the smooth, cool linen. It was all very deep, very unconstrained—very erotic, very definitely them at their most sensuously intense. Nothing was taboo, no means to give pleasure ignored— no words uttered. And their silence in itself was deeply seductive. Only the sounds of their breathing and their bodies moving in unison towards the kind of finale that stripped the soul.

Afterwards they lay just touching and kissing, communicating by all other means than talking, because words were dangerous, and neither of them wanted to spoil the special magic they had managed to create, that enclosed them in this wonderful bubble of tactile contentment. Of course they made love again several times during that long, quiet, lazy afternoon, then eventually slept in a possessive love-knot while the sun died slowly out of the room. This was fulfilment at its most sweetest.

Catherine came awake to find herself lying on the bed with a sheet draped strategically across her. Vito had gone from his sleeping place beside her, but her initial sense of loss was quickly replaced with a gasp of shock when she glanced at the bedside clock and actually saw what time it was!

Seven o'clock—Luisa and Santo would have been home for ages! What must they be thinking of her? What had Vito given as an excuse for her being so lazy? How could he just leave her to sleep like this?

'You rat, Vito,' she muttered to herself as she scrambled off the bed, then hurried to find some clothes to drag on.

The thin blue summer dress she had been intending to put on after her shower earlier still lay draped over a chair where she had left it. Scrambling into her underwear, then the dress, she was acutely aware of a series of deep inner aches that offered a good reason why she had slept so heavily. She had never been so thoroughly ravished!

She even felt herself begin to blush as she slid her bare feet into a pair of casual sandals, remembering just what they had done to each other. Or *for* each other, she then corrected, and on an agitated mix of pleasure and embarrassment she began finger-combing her tumbled hair as she made for the door.

The moment that she stepped out onto the landing she knew something was wrong, when the first thing that she heard was Santo's voice raised in anger.

What could be the matter? she wondered frowningly as she followed the sound of her son's angry voice down the stairs and into the main drawing room.

The sight that hit her eyes as she arrived in the doorway sent her still in dismay. Both Luisa and Vito were staring at a surly-faced Santo, who was standing there belligerently facing up to—none other than Marietta.

Of course it had to be Marietta causing all of this mayhem, Catherine grimly acknowledged as she watched the other woman bend at her slender waist to smile sweetly at Santo and say gently. 'But, darling, *you* told *me* that *you* would like your *papà* to marry me.'

'No, I didn't.' Santo angrily denied it. 'Why would I say that when I don't even like you?'

'Santino!' his father cautioned sternly. 'Apologise—now!'

If Catherine thought Santo had been difficult enough during the week before Vito arrived, when she'd endured some spectacular tantrums from him, she was now seeing he had not even got started.

For his face was hot, his eyes aflame, and his stance was more than ready for combat. Turning his glare on his father, he spat, 'No!' with enough force to make Vito stiffen. 'She's lying, and I won't let her!'

'Oh, please...' It was Luisa who tried to play peace-maker, by hurrying forward in an attempt to put herself between Santo and Vito. 'This is just a silly misunderstanding that has got out of hand,' she said anxiously. 'Please don't be alarmed by it, Vito.'

'Alarmed?' Vito bit out. 'Will you explain to me, then, why I walk in this room to the alarming sounds of my son being rude to a guest in this house?'

'A language thing, obviously,' his mother suggested. 'Marietta said something to Santo the last time he was here that he clearly misunderstood, and he said something to Marietta that she misunderstood. Such a silly thing to get fired up about.'

'I didn't misunderstand,' Santo insisted.

'Santino!' Vito turned his attention back to his son. Everyone had been talking in Italian until that point, but Vito's next sentence was delivered in clear, crisp English. 'You will apologise to Marietta now! Do you understand that?'

The little boy was close to tears; Catherine could see that, even though he was determined to face the whole thing out with an intransigence that was promising to be his downfall.

'Oh, don't make him do that, Vito.' It was Marietta who came to Santo's rescue. Marietta sounding beautifully placating. 'He meant no offence. He's just a little angry because I corrected his Italian.'

'No, you didn't!' the little boy protested. 'You said I was a nuisance and that when *papà* married you he wouldn't want me any more! And I hate you, Papà!' he turned to shout at his father. 'And I won't say sorry! I won't—I won't—I won't!'

Shocked surprise at his son's vehemence hardened Vito's face. 'Then you—'

'Santo,' Catherine said quietly, over whatever Vito had been about to say to him, and brought all four pairs of eyes swinging around in her direction.

And if Catherine had never been made to feel like the poor relation in this house before, she was certainly feeling that way now, as she stood there in her scrap of cheap cotton and took in with one brief, cold glance Marietta, looking smooth and sleek and faultlessly exquisite in her shiny black dress and shiny black shoes and with her shiny black hair stroking over one shoulder.

'Oh, Catherine!' It was poor, anxious Luisa that burst into speech. 'What must you be thinking?'

'I am thinking that this—altercation seems to be very lopsided,' she answered, without taking her eyes from her belligerent son. Silently she held out a hand to him, and with that simple gesture brought him running to her.

Vito was glaring at her for overriding his authority. Luisa was wringing her hands because her peaceful little haven had been shattered and she never could cope with that. And Marietta watched sympathetically as Catherine knelt down so her face was at her son's level.

'Santo, were you rude to Marietta?' She quietly requested his opinion.

He dropped his eyes. 'Yes,' he mumbled truculently.

'And do you think that deserves an apology?'

The dark head shook, then came back up, and Catherine

could see that the tears were real now in big brown eyes. 'I never said what she said I did, Mummy,' he whispered pleadingly. 'I just wouldn't,' he added simply. 'I *like* Papà being married to you.'

Catherine nodded. As far as she was concerned Santo had stated it as honestly as he knew how and the conflict was now over, because she was not going to make her son apologise to a woman she knew from personal experience could twist any situation round to suit her own purposes.

'Then you go off to your room,' she told Santo. 'And I'll come and see you there in a few minutes.'

'Catherine—' Vito wanted to protest, seeing his influence being thoroughly undermined here, but Catherine continued to ignore him as she came upright and sent her son off without offering anyone the chance to do anything about it.

When she turned to face all of those that were left, she found three completely different expressions being aimed right back at her. Vito—angry. Luisa—upset. And Marietta—smiling like a cat who'd pinched the last of the cream.

And why not? Catherine allowed. Within minutes of arriving here she had managed to stir up trouble between every single one of them.

'Good grief, Catherine, what a temper your son has!' Marietta broke the silence with a mocking little laugh. 'Sadly, I seem to have a knack of inadvertently sparking it off! I shall attempt to stay out of his way while I am staying here,' she determined ruefully.

Staying here? Catherine turned to look at Vito, who was looking as puzzled as she was by the comment.

'Marietta arrived home from the States this morning to find her apartment under water,' Luisa jumped in hurriedly. 'A burst water pipe while she was away has ruined everything, so of course I invited her to stay here while the repair work is being done.'

Of course, Catherine parodied, feeling an old-remembered weariness begin to settle over her like a thick black cloud.

'I have just placed my things in the rooms next to Vito's rooms,' Marietta inserted sweetly. 'If you want to know where to find me.'

'No.'

The harsh negative did not come from Catherine's lips, though it very well could have done, since she was thinking the exact same thing as Vito obviously was by the way he had stiffened his stance. Was he remembering a conversation they'd had recently, where the question of which rooms Marietta used when she stayed here had been the one of too many points of conflict between the two of them?

The woman had a special knack of making other people out to be liars.

'Whoever put you there has made a mistake,' he said tersely. 'If you need to stay here, Marietta, then stay in my mother's wing of the house. Catherine and I desire our privacy.'

'Of course,' Marietta instantly conceded. 'I will move rooms immediately. And I apologise that Luisa and I did not take into consideration the—newness of your reconciliation when we chose my rooms.'

And the poison barbs fly thick and fast, Catherine observed as Luisa began to look anxious again, which made her wonder if her mother-in-law had had any say at all in which room Marietta had chosen to use.

On top of that, Vito was getting really touchy now, she noted, as his frown deepened into a real scowl. First his son had annoyed him, then his wife by interfering, and now his mother, by placing Marietta where he didn't want her to be.

In fact the only person he did not seem cross with was dear Marietta. Clever girl, Catherine silently commended her as Marietta deftly flipped the conversation over to business things and proceeded to dominate his attention to the exclusion of everyone else.

Catherine left them to it to go in search of her son, whom she found sitting slouched over a large box of building blocks from where he was picking one up at random then throwing it sullenly back into the pile.

Chivvying him up with a determined brightness aimed to overlay the ugliness of the scene downstairs, she helped him with his bath then curled up on the bed beside him to read a couple of his favourite stories to him. Then, when she saw his eyes begin to droop, she kissed him gently goodnight and got up to leave.

'I don't like Marietta,' he mumbled suddenly. 'She's always spoiling things.'

Out of the mouths of babes, Catherine thought dryly.

'Do you like her?' he shot at her.

Well, do I lie or tell the truth? she wondered ruefully. And on a deep breath admitted, 'No. But Nonna does. So for Nonna's sake we have to be nice to her, okay?'

'Okay,' he agreed, but very reluctantly. 'But will you tell Papà for me that I'm sorry I shouted at him? I don't think he likes me now.'

'You can tell me yourself,' a voice said from the doorway.

They both glanced around to find Vito leaning there, looking as if he had been standing like that for ever—which probably meant he had overheard everything.

A quick glance at his face as she walked towards him told Catherine he didn't look pleased. But then, who did around here? she wondered grimly.

'We need to talk,' he murmured as she reached him.

'You just bet we do,' she replied. And once again the mutual antagonism was rife between them. Whatever they had managed to achieve in bed today had now been almost wiped away by one very clever lady.

They met in their bedroom when it was time to change for dinner. Catherine was already there, waiting for him when he came through the door with all guns blazing.

'Right,' he fired at her. 'What the hell did you think you were doing undermining my authority over Santo like that?'

'And what the hell did you think *you* were doing forcing him to take no other stand in front of everyone?' she shot right back.

'The boy was rude,' Vito gritted unapologetically.

'Our *son* was upset!' Catherine snapped. 'Have you any idea how it must have felt to him to have his own words twisted around like that?'

'Maybe he was the one who did the twisting, Catherine,' Vito grimly pointed out. 'Marietta was only trying to make pleasant conversation with him and...'

Catherine stopped listening. She'd heard more than enough as it was. On an angry twist of her heel she turned and walked out onto the balcony, leaving Vito talking to fresh air.

Out here the air was warm, after the air-conditioned coolness of the bedroom, and tiptoe quiet—soothing in its own way. Leaning her forearms on the stone balustrade, she tried breathing in some deep gulps of that warm air in an effort to dispel the angry frustration that was simmering inside her.

Because the hurt she felt, the disappointment and frustration at Vito's dogged championship of Marietta, only made her wonder why Vito had gone chasing all the way to London when it was so very clear to her that Santo came in a poor second-best to dear Marietta.

Pulling the glass French door shut behind him, Vito came to lean beside her. He knew as well as she did that the earlier row was not over.

'You can be so aggravating sometimes,' he censured. 'Did no one ever tell you that it is rude to walk out when someone is speaking to you?'

'Which makes me rude and Santo rude all in one day,' she said tartly. 'My, but we must be hell to live with.'

His sigh was almost a laugh, his sense of humour touched by her sarcasm, which actually managed to cool some of the angry heat out of her. And for the next few moments neither said anything as they gazed out at the view.

It was fully dark outside, but a three-quarter moon was casting silver shadows on the silk-dark water, and Naples was sparkling like fairy dust on a blanket of black velvet.

A beautiful sight. A sensually soothing sight.

'Did you tell Santo off just now?' she asked eventually.

'No, of course not,' he denied. 'I apologised to him for losing my temper. I'm not a fool, Catherine,' he added gruffly. 'I know I behaved no better down there than Santo did.'

Well, that was something, she supposed. 'So you're both friends again?'

'Yes,' he said, but he wasn't comfortable with it all. 'Marietta's right,' he muttered frowningly. 'He does seem to have developed a temper—'

'Marietta can keep her opinion about my son to herself!' Catherine returned tightly. 'And while she's at it she can go and stay at a damned hotel!'

'Hell, don't start on that one, for goodness' sake,' Vito pleaded wearily. 'You know I can't stop her from staying here!'

'Well, either she goes or we go,' Catherine informed

him. 'And while we are on the subject of Marietta,' she added tightly, 'you lied to me about her.'

'I did?' he sighed wearily. 'When was that, exactly?'

'When you led me to believe that you would be marrying her after we divorced. But the question of marriage between you two was never an option, was it?'

'Ah.' Vito grimaced. 'Would you care to tell me how you came to that conclusion?'

'Marietta herself told me,' she replied. 'When she was forced into twisting Santo's words around to cover up her own lies.'

'Or corrected a misunderstanding between two people who naturally speak two different languages?' he smoothly suggested.

A shrug of her shoulders dismissed the difference. 'Whichever, it still means that our son upset himself badly over nothing, and you brought me back here under a threat that was a lie.'

'I did not lie,' he denied. 'In fact I told you quite plainly why I wanted you back here with me.'

'You mean the revenge for your hurt pride thing?' she said, turning to look at him.

He was already looking at her, and their eyes clashed with a heat that set her insides burning. 'Did what we shared today feel like revenge to you?' he countered very softly.

No, it hadn't. Catherine silently admitted it. But the only other alternative she could come up with for his motives was just too unreliable to contemplate.

So she changed the subject. 'But you did promise me that if I came back here, then Marietta would be kept out of our lives.'

'I never made that promise.' He denied that also. 'If you remember, Catherine, I told you that I *couldn't* make that kind of promise.'

She released a small sigh, anger coming to life on the wings of frustration. 'In the name of decency, Vito. A man does not keep his mistress under the same roof as his wife!'

'I'm not telling you again that she isn't my mistress,' he snapped.

'Ex-mistress, then. Whatever.' She shrugged. 'She should not be here and you know she should not be here!'

'I know that you are crazy, obsessed and just downright delusional,' he told her.

Catherine's chin came around, eyes flashing green in the darkness. 'Okay, so I'm crazy.' She freely admitted it. 'You have married yourself to an absolute lunatic with obsessive tendencies and paranoid delusions. Now deal with the lunatic's delusions before she does something about them herself!' she advised.

Despite himself, Vito laughed. 'Now I do know you are crazy, for admitting all of that,' he murmured ruefully.

'Comes with the hair and the green eyes,' she explained. 'I believe I can cast spells too, and ride on a broomstick. Which also means I can tell a fellow witch when I meet one.'

'Meaning?' He was still smiling, fooled by her light tone into thinking the other subject was over.

But the smile died when she said. 'Marietta. Wicked Witch of the North, complete with black hair, black eyes, black heart—and a yen for other people's husbands.'

'She has been a close friend of this family for as far back as I care to remember,' Vito reminded her. 'I will not, on that point alone, think of alienating Marietta simply because you cannot like her.'

And that, Catherine acknowledged, is telling me.

'What about doing it because your son cannot like her?' she therefore suggested.

'He dislikes what you dislike.'

'Ah, so it's my fault,' she mused dryly. 'I should have expected it.'

But what really annoyed her was that he didn't deny it. 'I refuse to pander to unfounded prejudice,' he stated firmly instead.

Staring out across the bay, Catherine's eyes changed from flashing green to winter-grey, as if they were absorbing the bleakness in the moonlight. So he wanted sound proof of Marietta's prejudice towards them? she pondered. Well, she had that proof, circumstantial though it was.

The point was, did she tell him? For the last time she had brought up the subject she had demolished him so utterly that she'd vowed never to do that to him again.

Then she remembered their son, and the kind of depths Marietta's obsession with Vito had forced her to sink to— and with a sigh that told of a heaviness which went too deep for words, she made her decision. 'On the day I started to lose our baby,' she began, 'I rang around everywhere looking for you. I eventually tracked you down at Marietta's apartment.'

'I know that.' He was already stiffening. 'I have never denied to you where I was.'

Only *his* excuse for being there had been to get drunk and find oblivion from his nagging wife. Marietta's version had been very different.

'Why, then, if Marietta *woke* you immediately, did it take you six hours after that call to arrive at my hospital bed?' she asked. 'The traffic bad, was it?' she taunted softly as his face began to drain. 'Or maybe you ran out of petrol? That is another male euphemism for being busy in bed with someone else, I believe. Or maybe—just maybe,' she then added grimly, 'Marietta didn't bother to pass on my message until she felt like it, hmm? What does that tell you about your precious Marietta?' she demanded—only to instantly withdraw the question.

'No, don't tell me,' she said. 'Because in truth I don't really care what it tells you, when really there is no excuse you can offer as to why you went from me to her that day, or why you weren't there for me when I needed you to be. But from now on when I tell you that that woman is poison where I am concerned, you believe me,' she insisted. 'And you keep her away from both me and my son or we leave here. And if that is prejudice, then that's fine by me. But it is also a rock-solid promise.'

After that, the silence droned like the heavy pulse of a hammer drill while they both stood there watching Naples twinkle. How much of that Vito had already known and how much he had been stubbornly hiding from himself was impossible to tell. But Catherine knew one thing for sure, and that was if he still persisted in standing in Marietta's corner after what she'd just said, then it really was over for them.

Okay,' he said finally, deeply—flatly. 'I will see what I can do about the situation. There are a couple of new ventures on the planning table at the moment,' he murmured—thinking on his feet again, Catherine made note. 'One in New York, one in Paris. Marietta would be the ideal person to oversee either one of them. But it will take time for me to set it up,' he warned. 'She is going to need time to clear any outstanding projects from her desk before she can go anywhere. And my mother's birthday is coming up,' he then reminded her. 'It will be her sixty-fifth and she is planning a big party here to celebrate. She will expect Marietta to be here for it, Catherine, you must see that.'

Did she? she asked herself. No, actually, she didn't. But she could accept that Vito had a right to protect his mother from hurt just as Catherine had a right to protect herself and her son.

'Two weeks,' he repeated huskily. 'And I promise you that she will be gone from this house and gone from Naples...'

Two weeks, Catherine pondered. Can I live through two whole weeks of Marietta?

Do you really have a choice here? she then asked herself bleakly. For she could spout out threats about leaving until she was blue in the face, but she knew—probably as well as Vito knew—that she was trapped here no matter what the circumstances, so long as this was where Santo wanted to be.

'All right, you have your two weeks,' she agreed. 'But in the interim you keep her well away from both me and Santo,' she warned him. And with that she straightened away from the balcony, then turned to make her way back inside.

'I did not sleep with Marietta the day you lost our baby.' His deep voice followed her.

'"Sleep" being the operative word there, I suppose,' she derided.

The harsh hiss of air leaving his lungs had him spinning angrily round to glare at her. 'Did I ever call out Marietta's name in my sleep while you were lying beside me?' he rasped out bitterly.

About to open the French doors, Catherine went perfectly still, understanding exactly where he was going with this. 'No,' she admitted.

She heard him shift his tense stance a little, as if maybe relief had riddled through him.

'Unlike you and your Marcus. At least you were saved that bloody indignity.'

'I never slept with Marcus,' Catherine countered stiffly.

On the next balcony Marietta sat forward, the new name being inserted into the conversation sparking her back to life when only a moment before she had been almost defeated.

'Funny, that,' Vito drawled. 'But I don't believe you. So now what is left of trust?'

'We never really had any to begin with,' Catherine denounced. 'You married me because you had to. I accepted that because I felt I had to. You don't build trust on foundations like those.'

It seemed he didn't have an answer to that one, because the silence behind her deepened again. So, opening the French door, she stepped back into the bedroom. Vito didn't follow her. In fact he remained outside, leaning against the balcony for ages afterwards, thinking—she knew not what. But when he did eventually reappear, one brief glimpse of his closed, very grim expression was enough to tell her that his thoughts had not been pleasant ones.

And what bit of closeness they had managed to find in their bed that afternoon had now been well and truly obliterated.

CHAPTER EIGHT

So DINNER that evening was a strained affair. Luisa clearly had not yet recovered from the angry scene with her grandson in her drawing room earlier. And the way she kept on looking anxiously from Vito to Catherine said she too was acutely aware that the fine peace they had all been enjoying since Catherine had come back here to live had been completely shattered.

Did she ever bother to ask herself why that was? Catherine wondered, and decided not, because to do so would mean Luisa seeing the faults in her wonderful family.

Even Marietta was unusually quiet for her. She spent most of the wretched meal seemingly lost in her own deep train of thought.

Jet-lag, she called it when Luisa anxiously asked her if anything was the matter. But she did briefly raise herself to attempt polite conversation with Catherine. 'I believe you have been working for Templeton and Lang while living in London,' she remarked.

Go to hell, Catherine wanted to snap. But she smiled a civilised smile and answered cordially enough. 'Yes. I originally trained as a legal secretary, so it was nice to get back to it.'

'And your gift for languages must have been very useful to a firm which specialises in European law.' Marietta nodded in understanding. 'Have we ever used them, Vito?' she asked.

Busy glowering into his wine glass, Vito seemed to

133

stiffen infinitesimally, though why he did Catherine had no idea. 'Not that I recall,' he answered briefly.

'That is very odd.' Marietta frowned. 'For I am sure I know them. Marcus Lang is one of the senior partners, is he not?' she enquired of Catherine.

'No. *Robert* Lang and *Marcus* Templeton,' she corrected, feeling Vito's tension like a sting in her throat as she said Marcus's name.

'Ah. My mistake,' Marietta replied. 'Still…you are going to miss the stimulation, no doubt,' she murmured sympathetically. 'I know I would not like to go back to doing nothing again.'

'I have some work to do.' Vito rose so abruptly that everyone was taken aback. 'Marietta, I could do with going over a few things with you before you retire, if you are not too tired.'

'Of course,' Marietta agreed, but she was already talking to Vito's back, because he was striding from the dining room.

She followed very soon after him, which left Catherine to smooth out poor Luisa's ruffled feathers before she too could escape to the relative sanctuary of the bedroom. And by the time she had undressed and crawled into bed, she was ready—more than ready—to switch today off by dropping herself into the oblivion of sleep.

So having Vito arrive only minutes later was the last thing she needed.

Presuming he was coming to bed, she lay curled on her side with her eyes closed and pretended to be asleep. So when his finger gently touched her cheek only seconds later, her eyes flicked open in surprise to find him squatting down by the bed beside her.

'Something has come up,' he told her quietly. 'I need to go into Naples to my office for a while.'

'Alone?' The question shot from her lips without her

expecting it, never mind Vito. And instantly she wanted to kick herself as she watched his expression harden.

'Yes, alone,' he gritted. 'And if you don't watch out, Catherine, your mistrust is going to eat you alive!'

With that, he levered himself upright, turned and walked out of the room.

She didn't blame him. And he was right about her lack of trust eating her alive. Because it was already doing it.

'Oh damn,' she breathed, rolling onto her back to stare at the ceiling. 'What am I *doing* to myself?'

You know what you're doing, she immediately answered her own question. You are tearing yourself apart over the same man you have been tearing yourself apart over for the last six years.

Hearing the sound of a car engine firing into life, she got up and walked out onto the balcony to watch Vito leave. She arrived at the balcony rail just in time to see his red tail-lights gliding down the driveway.

'I love you,' she whispered after him. 'Even though I don't want to.'

And miserably she watched those tail-lights snake their way down the hillside until they became nothing but red dots among a million other red dots. She was about to go back inside when the sound of yet another car engine firing caught her attention. Turning back to the rail, she watched a black BMW come around from the back of the house where the garages were situated.

It was Marietta.

Even though it was too dark to see from up here who was driving, she just knew it was Marietta, and that she had to be following Vito to wherever they had arranged to meet.

So much for my paranoid delusions, she thought, and oddly didn't feel angry, or hurt, or even bitter any more.

But then she had a feeling that she had no more hurt left to feel about what Vito and Marietta did together.

She didn't sleep much that night. And was still awake when one car came back up the driveway at around four-thirty. The other she didn't hear, because she had eventually fallen into a heavy pre-dawn slumber.

Sounds in the bedroom eventually awoke her, and, opening her eyes, she found Vito quietly readying himself for the day. But a swift glance at his side of the bed told her it had not been slept in. On that observation alone, she shut her eyes again and pretended that she didn't know he was there.

An hour later she came downstairs in an outfit she'd had for years. The classic cut of the calf-length pin-straight cream skirt was timeless, the crocheted silk sleeveless top a soft coffee shade that went well with her warm autumn colouring.

Walking into the sunny breakfast room, she found Vito and Marietta there sharing a working breakfast. There was a scatter of paperwork lying on the table between them, and Marietta was busily scribbling notes across one of them while Vito sat scanning the contents of another.

All very businesslike, Catherine dryly observed, very high-executive, with Marietta wearing her habitual black and Vito in tungsten-steel-grey. And, considering he was supposed to have been up working all night, he looked disgustingly well on it, she mocked as she watched his dark head come up at the sound of her step and his eyes narrow as they took in her own coolly composed demeanour today.

He knew the look. He knew the outfit. He even knew the neat way she had loosely tied back her hair with a large tortoiseshell clip at her nape that gave the red-gold threads chic without being too formal.

'Going somewhere?' he questioned, not pleased, by the sound of it.

Catherine smiled a bland smile. 'To re-establish links with some old contacts,' she replied, and walked towards one of the vacant chairs at the table as Marietta's dark head lifted and her eyes drifted over her.

'Buon giorno,' she greeted. 'So you mean to go back to work,' she observed, like Vito, recognising the outfit.

'Better than ''doing nothing again'', don't you think?' she answered sweetly as she sat herself down, then reached for the coffee pot.

'Did I draw blood when I said that?' the dark beauty said. 'I'm sorry, Catherine, it was not intentional.'

Of course it was, Catherine silently countered, while Marietta turned her attention back to the business presently in hand across the breakfast table and began discussing figures with Vito.

He, on the other hand, wasn't listening. His whole attention was arrowed on his wife, who was now calmly pouring herself a cup of coffee as if this was just any ordinary day. But there was nothing ordinary about it. He knew it—she knew it. Catherine was angry and she was in rebellion.

'Santino is with his grandmother,' he said, over the top of what Marietta was saying. 'They are spending the day at the beach again.'

'I know. I waved them off.' Catherine smiled serenely and reached for a slice of toast from the rack, then the bowl of thick, home-made orange marmalade.

'Vito, if you—'

'Shut up, Marietta,' he interrupted.

Her lovely eyes widened. 'Am I interrupting something?' she drawled.

'Not at all,' Catherine assured her, spreading marmalade on her toast.

'Yes!' Vito countered. 'Please leave us.'

Marietta's expression revealed no answering irritation as,

on her feet in an instant, she obediently gathered up her papers and left them alone.

Biting neatly into her slice of toast, Catherine watched her go. But Vito pushed back his chair and got to his feet. A few strides had him rounding the table, then he was lowering himself into the chair next to Catherine's.

'I don't want you to go out to work,' he said curtly.

'I wasn't aware that I was giving you a choice,' she replied.

His lean face snapped into irritation at her very dry tone. 'Rushing out there and taking the first job that is offered to you just because you are angry with me is childish,' he clipped.

'But I'm not angry with you,' she denied, taking another bite at her toast.

'Then for what reason are you doing this?' he demanded. 'You have not once mentioned going to work since you came back here!'

'Myself,' she explained. 'I am doing it for myself.'

It was a decision she had come to at some very low point during the night. That there was very little she could do to change the status quo, so she might as well just get on with it.

Which was the reason why she was dressed for the city this morning. Getting on with it meant getting a life. A life outside the suffocating confines of this house, anyway.

'What about Santino?' Vito tried another tack.

Catherine smile a rueful smile. 'Santino has more people eager to amuse him here in this house than a whole school of normal children have.'

'He prefers to have his *mamma* at home with him. *I* prefer to have his *mamma* at home with him. What is the use of my providing all of this,' he said, with a wave of a hand meant to encompass their luxury surroundings, 'if you will not let yourself appreciate its advantages?'

'That is a terribly arrogant thing to say,' Catherine replied.

'I don't feel arrogant,' he confessed. 'I feel damned annoyed that you did not discuss this with me before making your decision. It is so typical of you, Catherine,' he censured, unaware that her face had quite suddenly gone very pale. 'You are so stubbornly independent that you just go ahead and do whatever it is you want to do and to hell with what anyone else may think!'

'I'm sorry you think that,' she murmured, but her tone said she was not going to change her mind.

Vito released a driven sigh. 'Listen to me...' he urged, curling his fingers tensely around her fingers. 'I don't want to wage war with you every time that we speak. I want you to be happy here. I want *us* to be happy here!'

'With you as the family provider and me as the trophy you keep dusted in the corner?' she mocked. 'No, thank you, Vito. I'm not made of the right kind of stuff to play that particular role.'

'That woman should learn to curb her stupid tongue!' he muttered.

A criticism of Marietta? Catherine almost gasped at the shock of it—albeit sarcastically. 'Don't you have some work to do?' she prompted him.

As if on cue, the door suddenly opened. 'Have you two finished?' a cool voice questioned. 'Only we have a lot to get through, Vito, if we are to catch that noon flight to Paris today.'

The air in the sunny breakfast room suddenly began to crackle. Catherine glared at Vito. 'You're going to Paris today—with her?' she demanded.

He looked fit to wreak bloody murder. 'I—'

'Oh—didn't you know, Catherine?' Marietta inserted. 'I assumed Vito would have told you.'

'I was about to,' he gritted—at Catherine, not Marietta.

'No need now, though,' Catherine pointed out, raking her fingers from beneath his as she shot stiffly to her feet. 'Since your ever-efficient compatriot has done the job for you.'

'Catherine—' Vito's voice was harsh on a mixture of fury and frustration.

'Excuse me,' she spoke icily over him, 'I have some calls to make.' And she walked towards the door. 'Enjoying yourself?' she asked sweetly of Marietta as she passed by her.

The other girl's eyes widened in mock bewilderment. 'I don't know what you mean,' she lied.

Catherine just laughed—a hard, scoffing sound that jarred on the eardrums—and left the two of them to it, with Marietta's voice trailing after her. 'Vito, I am so sorry. I just thought…'

Vito followed her. Catherine would have been more surprised if he hadn't. He found her standing in their bedroom grimly pulling on the jacket to match her cream skirt.

'Don't you have a plane to catch?' she questioned sarcastically.

His angry face hardened. 'Don't do this, Catherine,' he warned. 'Don't rile me today when I've worked right through the night and am low on sleep and on patience.'

'And where were you *working* last night?' she challenged.

'You know where. The office,' he said heavily. 'I told you.'

'Alone?'

'Yes—alone!' he snapped.

'What time did you come home?'

'Around five—why the inquisition?' he asked dazedly.

'Marietta left here straight after you last night and arrived back half an hour before you say you got back,' she informed him. 'Is that the standard time-lapse for secret trysts these days? Only it's best to know the form when I start some trysts of my own.'

'You think I was with Marietta.' He began to catch on at last. *'Madre di Dio,'* he sighed. 'When are you going to try trusting me?'

Not in this lifetime, Catherine thought bitterly. 'How long will you be away?'

'About a week—' He went to say more, but Catherine beat him to it.

'Staying where?'

'The company apartment—where else?' he sighed out heavily. 'Catherine, it was you who told me to keep her out of the way,' he tagged on impatiently. 'And that is exactly what I am trying to do!'

'Enjoy yourself, then.'

Wrong thing to say, she realised as he suddenly leapt at her. She was trapped in his arms before she could gasp. And his mouth, when it found hers, was intent on taking no prisoners.

Yet—what did she do? She surrendered was what she did. Without a fight and without dignity she let her head tilt backwards, parted her lips—and let him do whatever it was that he wanted to do.

The slave for her master, she likened, not even bothering to be disgusted with herself as her fingers turned into claws that took a grip on his head and she let the power of his hungry, angry passion completely overwhelm her.

And his hands were everywhere, yanking off her little jacket, raking up her top, and the flimsy lace bra she was wearing beneath it, was no barrier at all against those magic fingers. She started whimpering with pleasure. He laughed into her mouth, then reached up to grab hold of one her hands and dragged it down to press it hard against his rising sex.

'Now this is what I call enjoying myself,' he muttered,

as he transferred his mouth to one of the breasts he had prepared for himself.

As he sucked, and sensation went rampaging through her, the telephone by the bed began to ring. His dark head came up. It would be Marietta, telling him to get a move on.

'Answer that and you're dead,' Catherine told him, and to state her point her fingers closed more tightly around him.

On a growl of sheer sensual torment he caught her mouth again, sent her mind spinning, drove her straight back out to where they'd both briefly emerged from, while the ring of the telephone acted like a spur to every single sense they possessed as she slowly eased her grip to begin sliding her palm along the full throbbing length of him with the intention of finding the tab to his trouser zip—

He stepped away from her so quickly she barely registered what was happening. And as her confused eyes focused on the wicked grin slashing his arrogant features she realised why he had stepped away as abruptly as he had.

Or he would not have escaped without injury. Vito was well aware that his wife could be a little hell-cat when she wanted to be, and the grin he was offering her was one of triumph, because he knew he had just stage-managed his own very lucky escape.

'Hold that thought,' he commanded. And with one flashing, gleaming dip at the way she was standing there—looking utterly ravaged without the ravaging—he had the damn audacity to wink! 'I will be back to collect the rest at the end of the week.'

He was gone before she could answer. And as she stood there blinking bemusedly at the back of the door, unable to believe she had let him do this to her, the telephone kept on ringing with a ruthless persistence that was Marietta.

Yet what did she find herself doing? She found herself standing there loving the sound of that ringing telephone, knowing that Marietta must be seething in frustration while she stubbornly hung on there, waiting for one of them to answer. And also knowing, by the length of time it took the ringing to stop, that Vito had needed to take time to compose himself before going to find Marietta.

It ended up being a strange week all told. A long week that made her feel a bit like a bride marking time before her big day—though she was truly annoyed with herself for feeling like that.

The man leaves one decidedly provocative taunt hanging in the air and you respond to it like this, she scolded herself crossly. But it didn't stop her from feeling pumped up with a waiting expectancy which had her almost floating hazily through the ensuing days until Vito's return.

The man was her weakness, his body a temple at which she worshipped whether she liked it or not. Control was a no-word where he was concerned. It always had been. Weak of the mind, weak of the flesh and weak of the spirit was what she was.

So she tried very hard to combat all of that by throwing herself into a whirl of activity that didn't seem to achieve anything. She had lunch each day with old acquaintances, put out feelers about a job, then found herself in no rush to take one—though she didn't understand it, since she had thought a job was her number one priority if she was going to make her life bearable here.

Another thing she learned was that Luisa was no part-time grandmother. She adored Santo. In fact she loved nothing better than to have her grandson with her all day and every day. She *did* things with him, took him places with her, was always interested in everything he had to say. And Santo blossomed under her loving attention. Not that he hadn't been happy with just Catherine back in London, because he had been—very happy. It was just that watching from the sidelines how Luisa treated Santo made Catherine realise why Vito was the man he was. Luisa seemed to instinctively instill confidence and self-belief into Santo, and she would have done the same for her own son.

A son who rang home every evening religiously. Spoke to his mother, spoke to his son—and spoke to Catherine.

Neither of them mentioned Marietta during those telephone calls. Catherine wouldn't in case the wretched woman was there in the room with him and would therefore know that her existence worried Catherine. And Vito didn't mention her because, Catherine presumed, Marietta *was* right there with him and he didn't want *Catherine* to know.

Oh, the evils involved in feeling no trust, she mused grimly one afternoon while she was standing beneath the shower attempting to cool herself, because Naples had been hit by the kind of heatwave that even the air-conditioning system was struggling to cope with.

But it wasn't just the heatwave that had forced her into taking her second shower of the day. The real culprit for that was Vito. He had left her hungry, and hungry she had stayed. So much so that even standing here like this, with a cold jet of water pouring all over her, she couldn't stop her body from responding to the knowledge that he was coming home today. Her breasts were tingling, their sensitive tips tightly peaked, and a permanent throb had taken up residence deep down in her abdomen. And if she kept her eyes closed she could even imagine him stripping off his clothes to come and join her here.

So when a naked, very male body slid in behind her she thought for a moment that she was fantasising his presence.

'Vito!' she gasped, almost slipping on the wet tiles in shocked consternation. His arms wound around her, to hold her steady. 'You frightened the life out of me!' she protested.

'My apologies,' he murmured. 'But hearing you in here was an irresistible temptation.'

'I thought you weren't due back until this evening,' she said, trying desperately to steady her racing heartbeat.

'I caught an earlier flight.' He was already bending his dark head so that he could press his open mouth to the side of her throat. 'Mmm, you taste delicious.'

And you feel delicious, Catherine silently countered.

'The water is a bit cold, though,' he complained, reaching over her shoulder to alter the temperature gauge slightly. 'What are you trying to do—freeze yourself?'

'It's so hot,' she murmured in idiot-like explanation. But the blush that suffused her skin told its own wretched story.

He knew it too. 'Ah,' he drawled. 'Missed me, hmm?'

'I have hardly given you a second thought,' she lied.

'Well, I missed you,' he murmured as he turned her round to face him. 'And please do note that *I* am not too proud to admit it.'

'Only because you want something,' she mocked.

But he just laughed softly, then proceeded to show her exactly what he wanted. And as she wound her long legs around his body, while Vito loved her into ecstasy, she let herself smile. Because a man couldn't be this hungry if he had spent the whole week doing this with someone else, could he?

Because even though it was her mouth that was gasping out its little sounds of pleasure, she wasn't so mindless with sensation that she wasn't aware that Vito was trembling, that despite the rhythmic power of his thrusts he was struggling to hang onto control here.

'Kiss me,' she groaned, as if in agony. 'I need you to kiss me!'

On a growl, he did so, felt her begin to quicken as his

mouth fused with her mouth and sent her spinning into orgasm, and almost instantly joined her, their mutual gasps mingling with the sound of the shower spray.

Afterwards he carried her out of the shower before letting her stand on her own shaky legs again. She leaned weakly against him while he set about drying her, her mouth laying lazy kisses across his hair-roughened chest while her arms rested limply against his lean hipline.

They didn't speak. It didn't seem necessary—or maybe they were both too aware that words tended to ruin everything. So when he made her stand up properly, so he could dry her front, Catherine stood staring wistfully up at his beautiful face and wished she could dare love him again.

Wished it with all she had in her to wish.

'Keep looking at me like that...' his smile was rueful '...and you will be spending the rest of the day in the bedroom.'

'Santo is spending the day with his friend Paolo,' she murmured.

A sleek eyebrow arched. 'Is that your way of telling me that you don't mind spending the day in the bedroom with me?' he asked.

'Got any better ideas?' she softly queried.

It was Luisa who asked about Marietta over dinner that night.

'She remained in Paris,' Vito replied. 'But she will be back in time for your birthday party next week.'

No Marietta for another whole week. Catherine's mood suddenly felt positively buoyant. And remained like that throughout the next few days as their life returned to the same routine it had developed before Vito had taken Marietta to Paris. He spent his mornings in his study and his afternoons with his wife and son while his mother became deeply involved in the preparations for her party at the weekend.

In fact, life could almost be described as happy. They swam in the pool and took drives into the mountains in an attempt to escape the oppressive heat. And Vito took Santo and a small group of his friends out for the day so that Catherine could help Luisa. Then a job cropped up that Catherine quite fancied, because it involved working freelance from home, translating manuscripts for a publishing company.

'I must be getting lazy,' she confessed to Vito that evening as they lay stretched out on the bed together.

'It could not be, I suppose, that you are merely contented?' he suggested.

Is that why I've been working so hard through the last few years? she asked herself. Because I was so discontented with my life?

It could be, she had to admit, because she certainly hadn't felt this relaxed with herself in a very long time.

'Well, I am going to have to commandeer the library to use as my workplace,' she warned him. 'It's either there or your study, and I don't think you would like it if I moved in there with you.'

'We would neither of us get much work done,' he agreed. Then, 'Mmm,' he groaned. 'You are very good at this.'

He was lying stretched out on his stomach and Catherine was running her nails down the muscle-cushioned tautness of gold satin skin covering his long back while he enjoyed the sensation with all the self-indulgence of a true hedonist.

'I know,' she replied with a bland conceit. 'I've had loads of practice, you see.'

She'd meant with him, because once upon a time they'd used to lie for ages just doing this. But from the way his muscles tensed Catherine knew he had misunderstood her.

'How much practice?' he demanded.

Sighing, she sat up and away from him.

He moved too, rolling onto his back to glare up at her. 'How many lovers have there been, Catherine?' He insisted on an answer.

'You know there was no one before you,' she reminded him. 'So why start asking questions like that now, all of these years later?'

'I meant *since* we married.'

Turning her head, she looked down at this man who was lying beside her in all his naked arrogance, with the power of his virility on blatant display, and wished she knew what made his mind tick as well as she knew his body.

'How many for you?' she counter-challenged.

'None,' he answered unhesitatingly.

'Same here,' she replied, and knew they both thought the other was lying. 'Does it matter?' she asked.

'No.' He grimaced, and she knew that was a lie also.

Her hand reached out to lightly stroke him. Releasing a small sigh, he closed his eyes. 'Okay,' he said. 'I can take a hint. You can ravish me.'

Coming on top of him, Catherine eased him inside her then sighed herself. 'Talking never did us any favours, Vito,' she murmured sombrely. 'Let's make a pact not to do it more than is absolutely necessary.'

Then, before he could answer, she closed her own eyes and began to move over him. And she rode him with a muscular co-ordination that soon sent any arguments he might have been about to voice fleeing in favour of more pleasurable pursuits.

CHAPTER NINE

THE house was on show tonight, lit by strategically placed halogens that turned its white walls a seductive gold, and its many garden features were subtly lit from within the shrubbery that lined its many pathways. Inside, everything had been cleaned or swept or dusted or polished, and in the large formal dining room attached to the ballroom a buffet banquet fit for kings had been laid.

Which left only the house occupants to dress themselves up in the kind of clothes that would complement the house. Catherine had achieved this by deciding to wear a striking long red silk gown with a strapless and boned basque-style bodice that was as bold as it was stunning with her colouring. She had dressed her hair into an elegant twist held in place by a diamond clasp that allowed a few stray tendrils to curl around her nape and around the diamond earrings she had dangling from her earlobes. And on her feet she wore very high, very strappy, shiny red shoes that forced her to move in a way that set men's pulses racing.

It certainly set Vito's pulses racing as he watched her come gliding down the stairs towards him. He had just returned from delivering Santo into the care of Paolo's *mamma*, where he was to enjoy his first sleep-over.

Which did not mean he had missed out on the fun. Luisa had been all for thoroughly enjoying her whole day, so when Santo decided that she should have a special birthday tea party with him and his friends, his *nonna* had been more than willing to play along. So it had been a balloons and red jelly party, with a novelty cake and the kind of games children believed a prerequisite for birthdays.

149

It had been fun. Probably would turn out to have been more fun than the grown up party that was about to follow, Catherine mused wryly as she watched Vito watch her come towards him. And the dark gleam in his eyes was telling her everything she wanted to know. Pride and appreciation were the words that came to mind, underpinned by the ever-present sexual vibrations that were such an integral part of what they had always shared.

'You look as if you have just stepped out of one of my father's Pre-Raphaelites,' he murmured deeply as she reached him, then frowned. 'But something is missing…'

'Jewellery,' Catherine agreed, touching her bare throat. 'You have most of it locked away in your safe, if you remember.'

'Then lead the way to my study,' he commanded, 'and we will rectify the situation immediately.'

Walking off in the direction of his study, she could feel the heat of his eyes as he followed behind her, and her ruby-painted mouth gave a rueful twitch because she was aware that he was now able to see how her gown dipped at the back in an audaciously deep V to her slender waistline.

'Very provocative,' he drawled.

Casting him a flirtatious glance over her shoulder, she replied, 'I *like* being provocative.'

His answering laugh was low and husky as they entered his study. And he was still smiling when he turned back to her after extracting something from the safe. Expecting him to come towards her with her old jewellery box in his hands, she was surprised, therefore, when he held only a flat black velvet case. 'Don't I get to choose?' she asked.

'No,' he replied. 'And that dress is most definitely an outright provocation,' he added, again eyeing censoriously the amount of naked back she had on show. 'Make sure I vet every man you dance with tonight.'

Catherine mocked him with a look as he came to stand behind her. 'You're being very imperious,' she complained. 'Choosing my dance partners and choosing my jewellery. What if I don't like your choice—like what you have in that box, for instance?'

'Tell me, then, what you think,' he said, and with that deftness that was his, something cool and heavy landed against her chest.

She transferred her eyes from him to herself, and an instant gasp of surprise whispered from her as she stared at the most exquisite diamond-encrusted heart resting just above the valley between the creamy slopes of her breasts.

'Oh, but this is beautiful,' she breathed, lifting slender fingers to gently touch the heart.

'Don't sound so surprised,' he drawled as he concentrated on fastening the intricate clasp which would lock the necklace safely in place. 'I may be imperious, but my taste is usually faultless.'

'It's a locket,' she realised, ignoring his conceit. 'If I look inside will I find your arrogant face looking out at me?'

'No,' he laughed. 'It is for you to decide who you carry around in there.'

You, Catherine thought. It would only ever be his image he would find nestling in any heart she possessed.

'Well, thank you.' She smiled up at him, keeping the tone as light as it had been between them despite the sudden wistfulness she was feeling inside. 'Now I feel properly decked out to grace the arm of the imperious Italian with the faultless taste.'

She knew the moment she saw his eyes cloud over that her response had disappointed him. 'You've always been fit to grace the arm of any man, Catherine,' he informed her deeply. 'I just happen to be the lucky one who claims the right to have you there.'

It was too much, too intense. They just didn't share these kind of deep and meaningful discussions. Never had done, never would do. It was the way of their relationship.

Shallow, she wanted to call it, but shallow didn't really say it either. Because there had never been anything shallow in the way she and Vito responded to each other.

What they really did was muddle on, never knowing what the other felt inside, because it was safer not knowing than finding out and being mortally wounded. So instead they used their love for their son as the common denominator to justify their being together—and the sex, of course, which had never been a problem where they were concerned.

And maybe her own clouding expression reminded him of all of that, because in the next moment Vito was smiling again, and the mockery was back when he ran a long finger down her spine and allowed it to settle low in the hollow of her back where the deep V in her dress finished.

'I have this terrible archaic urge to send you back to your room to change,' he admitted.

Turning to face him, Catherine baited him with a look. 'Just remember who gets to remove it himself later,' she softly suggested.

Luisa appeared then, saving Catherine from a rather delicious bit of punishing ravishment for that piece of seduction. 'Oh, Catherine, what a lovely necklace!' she exclaimed when she saw it.

'I am reliably informed by the man who gave it to me that his taste is faultless,' Catherine replied mock solemnly.

'Vittorio, your conceit will one day be your downfall,' his mother scolded.

'And there was I about to say that I get my faultless good taste from you,' Vito sighed—then, quite seriously, 'You look beautiful, *mi amore*. How can a man be so lucky to have a *mamma* like you?'

MICHELLE REID   153

'Now he is trying to use his charm on me to get him out of trouble,' Luisa confided to a smiling Catherine. 'It was always the same, even when he was as small as Santino.'

But she did look beautiful. A beautiful person dressed in shimmering gold satin who, two hours later, was wearing the soft flush of pleasure from the wealth of compliments that had flooded her way about her looking not a day over forty.

'She's enjoying this,' Catherine murmured to Vito as she caught sight of no less than three gentlemen gallantly vying for his mother's hand for the next dance.

'More than you are, I think,' he replied quietly.

But then, she'd had to outface a lot of curiosity from people she'd used to know three years ago. Not that any of them had been allowed to quench their curiosity about the present state of her marriage, because Vito had remained steadfastly at her side throughout the whole evening, as if to act as a shield to that kind of intrusion.

And with a hand lightly resting on the curve of her hip, so his thumb could make the occasional caressing stroke across the skin left exposed at the base of her spine, if she moved he moved with her; if she was invited to dance he politely refused for her. It was all very possessive, and deliciously seductive.

So the evening wore on, the champagne flowed freely, and the hired eight-piece orchestra played while some people danced and others went to help themselves to the buffet. And the only thing that seemed to be missing was— Marietta.

'Where is she?' she asked Vito.

'Delayed, so I believe,' he answered briefly.

'But your mother will be disappointed if she isn't here to toast her birthday.'

'Oh, don't worry,' he said dryly. 'I would say that you

can virtually count on her being here at some point or other.'

Catherine frowned, not liking the abrasion she had caught in his tone when he'd said that. In fact, when she thought about it, Vito's tone had been distinctly abrasive whenever Marietta's name had come up since their trip to Paris.

Had they had a row? she wondered. Then felt something disturbingly like hope curl her stomach. Had Vito actually come to accept that if he wanted his marriage to succeed this time then it had to be without Marietta in its shadows, and had he already called the parting of the ways he had promised?

Hope was a seed that could bloom all too quickly when its host was so eager to feed it. And Catherine was more than ready to do that tonight, with her man behaving so very possessively and with his diamond heart lying against the warm skin just above her breasts.

Good or bad timing on his part that he sent that intrusive thumbpad of his skating across the triangle of flesh exposed by the V of her gown? Whatever, she quivered, and she quivered violently enough to make Vito utter a soft curse beneath his breath.

'Let's dance,' he determined huskily.

It was an excuse to hold her closer. Catherine knew that as she let him guide her out onto the dance floor. His palm flattened against the silk-smooth skin of her back as his other hand closed around her fingers, and as she rested her free hand against his lapel he set them moving to one of those soulful melodies that had a nasty habit of touching the heartstrings. The usual vibrations that erupted between the two of them the moment their bodies were in touch with each other began to pulse all around them.

It was dangerously seductive, wholly mesmerising. They didn't attempt to talk, and the silence itself added fuel to their growing awareness of each other. When his lips touched her brow it was like being bathed in static. When his thigh brushed her thighs it set the soft curls of hair around her sex stinging in reaction.

And, in response to it all, she felt Vito's inner self quicken, felt his heart pick up pace beneath her resting hand and that familiar tension enter his body. Unable to resist the urge, she lifted her chin to look at him at the same moment that his lush, long curling lashes gave a flicker as he lowered his gaze and looked at her.

Their eyes suddenly locked. And for a short, stunning moment it was as if everything going on around them faded into the ether. It was seduction at its most torturously exquisite. He held her captive with eyes that were saturating her in the liquid gold heat they were pouring into her.

It was total absorption. Utterly enthralling. Because right there in the middle of a hundred other people she was sure she could feel love come beating down upon her from the one place she had never expected to find it.

'Vito…' she heard herself whisper, though she didn't know why.

'Catherine,' he said tensely. 'We have to—'

'Luisa. Happy birthday, darling!' a beautifully rich female voice called out in its warmest Italian and—snap—the link between them was broken.

Marietta had arrived. Dear Marietta. Even the music came to an abrupt standstill.

But then, if anyone could make a perfectly timed entrance, it was Marietta, Catherine mused cynically as she turned within Vito's slackened grasp to view her worst enemy.

At which point everything alive inside her froze to a complete cessation.

For there, framed by the open glass doors of the glittering ballroom, stood Marietta, dressed in a silver sequinned creation that was as bold as it was beautiful and did tremendous things for her wonderful figure.

But it wasn't what Marietta was wearing that was paralysing Catherine. That achievement was down to the man who was standing at Marietta's elbow. Tall, dark, extremely attractive in a very British kind of way, he was looking distinctly uncomfortable with his own presence here...

'Marcus,' she breathed, too shocked to even think of holding the name back.

So the tensing she felt taking place behind her sent her heart plummeting in a sinking dive to her stomach as she watched Marcus give a tense tug at his shirt collar before offering the hand and a stiff smile to Luisa, who was being formally introduced to him.

Marietta was smiling serenely while Luisa attempted to put Marcus at his ease, as you would expect from Luisa. But Marcus was beyond being put at his ease. It was so obvious he did not want to be here that Catherine could not understand why he was!

Confusion began to replace the numbing sense of surprised horror. 'But what is he doing here?' she murmured, bewildered.

'You mean you cannot guess?' Vito taunted grimly.

'It has nothing to do with me, if that's what you're thinking!' she protested.

'No? I would say that his being here has everything to do with you,' he coolly informed her.

As if to confirm that, Marcus's restless eyes suddenly alighted on her standing there, with Vito tall and grim behind her. And colour rushed into the other man's face. It was awful. Like watching, helplessly from the sidelines, someone slowly drown without being able to do a single thing to help him.

Then she caught the flash from a pair of malevolent eyes, and suddenly realised that this was all Marietta's doing.

Marietta had somehow managed to find out about Catherine's more personal association with Marcus and she had brought him here with the single intention of using that information to cause trouble.

But who could have told her? Her mind quickly tried to assess the situation. Certainly not Marcus himself. Besides his clear discomfort with his present position, he was not the kind of man who told kiss and tell stories.

And what was even more worrying was how Marietta was no longer attempting to hide her malevolence. It was out of the closet and on show for anyone to see—including Vito, if he wanted to.

Determined to find out just what was going on, Catherine went to break free from Vito. But his steely grip held her.

'No,' he refused. 'This is Marietta's game. We will let her play it.'

And he wasn't shocked. He wasn't even angry! 'You knew he was coming,' she realised shakily.

'It is very rare that anyone enters my home without my prior knowledge,' Vito replied smoothly.

Beneath his resting hands her stomach gave a quiver of dismay as a brand-new suspicion began to form like a monster, and she spun around angrily. 'This is all your doing,' she accused him. 'You told Marietta about Marcus and me. You helped her to arrange this!'

He didn't answer, and his expression was so coldly implacable that for Catherine it was an answer in itself.

Contempt turned her green eyes grey. 'I despise you,' she breathed, and turned back to look at the trio by the doorway just in time to see Marcus excuse himself to Luisa so he could come striding purposefully towards them.

He looked angry, he looked tense, and his eyes were filled with a mute plea for understanding even before he spoke. 'Catherine...' he said as he reached them. 'My sincere apologies, but I had no idea whose party this was until I was introduced to your mother-in-law just now.'

'It is called being set up,' Vito dryly inserted.

As Marcus glanced warily at him, Catherine took her moment to break free from his grasp and stepped towards Marcus. 'Dance with me,' she said, and before he could protest she had pulled him into the middle of the dance floor and placed herself firmly in his arms.

'I don't think your husband is pleased that we are doing this,' Marcus said uneasily.

Well, I'm not pleased with him, Catherine countered silently. 'Just smile, for goodness' sake,' she told him. 'And tell me what you are doing here.'

On a low groan that was packed full of contempt for his own gullibility, he explained about Marietta turning up at his offices that week, asking specifically for him. 'Having never heard of a Signora Savino before, I had no idea at all about her connection to the Giordani family.'

'She is my mother-in-law's goddaughter,' Catherine informed him.

'So I've just discovered.' Marcus nodded. 'She seems a nice lady, your mother-in-law,'

'She is,' Catherine confirmed. Shame about the rest of her family.

'But the goddaughter doesn't seem quite so nice.'

Catherine's eyes turned arctic grey. 'How did she get you here?' She prompted him to continue.

'With that magical word *business*,' he replied. 'And can we go somewhere less public, do you think?' he pleaded. 'Only I am beginning to feel distinctly *de trop* here...'

'Sure,' Catherine agreed, and stopped dancing to lead the way out through the open French doors which led into the lantern-lit garden, without even bothering to check out what Vito was doing. She wasn't interested. In fact, she didn't care at this moment if she never set eyes on the manipulative, vengeful swine ever again!

The air out here was warm and silken on the flesh. Catherine breathed in a couple of deep breaths of it, then said, 'Let's walk,' and began strolling down one of the pathways with Marcus pacing grimly beside her. 'Go on with your story,' she instructed.

'She lured me to Naples on the information that a well-known investment bank was looking for a new legal firm that specialises in European law,' he explained. 'When I asked her the name of the company she said she wasn't at liberty to give it until she had the go-ahead to make an official approach, but invited me over here this weekend—to meet some people—was the way she baited it. She sounded very plausible,' he added in his own defence. 'Extremely knowledgeable about what kind of legal expertise is required in the investment field.'

'She is,' Catherine confirmed. 'She owns stock in Giordani's, has a place on the board, holds some of their most lucrative portfolios.'

'Then she wasn't lying.' He frowned thoughtfully.

'About Girodani's wanting to change lawyers? I don't know, is the honest answer,' she replied. 'All I do know is that Marietta was one of the main causes for my marriage break-up three years ago. And since I came back here I have been expecting her to try the same thing again.'

'She's in love with your husband,' Marcus assumed from that.

Catherine didn't deny it, though she would probably use the word 'obsessed' instead of love. 'They work very closely together,' she murmured. 'Marietta is a natural charmer and Vito is—'

'Renowned for his troubleshooting qualities.' Marcus nodded. 'He turned Stamford Amalgamates round from bankruptcy in weeks only last year.'

'I didn't know that!' Catherine admitted, impressed without wanting to be, since most people knew that Stamford Amalgamates was about as big as a giant conglomerate could get.

'The fact that they were in trouble was kept secret to save the stock price,' Marcus explained. 'It was only after your husband had been in and waved his magic wand that those in the know discovered just how close things had been to collapse. He impresses me,' he added. 'Even though I don't want him to.'

'I know the feeling,' Catherine said grimly.

'Which means he's a dangerous man to cross.'

'I know that too.' She nodded.

'So why is Marietta attempting to cross him?'

'Because she is one of the only people Vito lets get away with it.' Catherine's smile was bitter.

'And the reason he does that?'

'Now there is the big question,' she mocked. 'I can give you a dozen maybes, Marcus. But no absolute certainties.'

'Okay,' he said. ' So give me the maybes.'

He was frowning thoughtfully—thinking on his feet just like Vito, Catherine likened wryly.

Which was probably why she liked him so much, she then realised, and didn't like the feel of that, since it also probably meant that she had always been looking for Vito-type qualities in every man she had come into contact with over the last three years.

'Because she is his mother's beloved goddaughter?' she suggested. 'Or because she was married to his best friend? Or maybe it could have something to do with the fact they are lovers?'

'Lovers in the past tense or the present?' Marcus asked sharply.

Catherine shrugged a slender shoulder. 'Both,' she replied.

'Rubbish,' Marcus denounced. 'That man has too much *nous* to play around with another woman when he's got you to come home to.'

Turning towards him, Catherine let her eyes soften. 'That was sweet of you,' she murmured softly.

But Marcus gave an impatient shake of his head. 'I wasn't being sweet, I was being truthful. I know men, Catherine. I am one myself, after all, so I should do. And I am telling you as a man that your husband is married to the only woman he wants to share his body with.'

Catherine stopped walking to turn sombre eyes on him. 'Then you tell me why you think you were brought here tonight?' she prompted gently.

He frowned, not understanding the question. 'It was Signora Savino who brought me here, in her quest to stir up trouble between you and your husband,' he replied.

'But who gave her the idea to use you as a weapon?' she posed. 'Who, in other words, told Marietta that you and I were more intimately involved than mere employer and employee?' she asked. 'Was it you who told her?'

'No!' he denied.

'And it wasn't me,' she said. 'Which leaves only one other person who knew about us.'

'Your husband?' Marcus stared at her in complete disbelief. 'You think your husband confided in that bitch about you and me?'

'Vito knew you were coming here tonight.' Catherine shrugged. 'He told me himself.'

'Then none of this makes any sense.' Marcus was frowning again. 'Because I can't see what either of them aimed to gain by bringing me face to face with you again. It served no useful purpose except to give us both a couple of embarrassing moments.'

He was right, and it hadn't. And they fell into a puzzled silence as their feet set them moving again—only to come to an immediate stop when the angry sounds of a familiar voice suddenly ripped through the air.

'You think you are so very clever, Marietta,' Vito rasped out. 'But what the hell do you think you have gained by bringing him here with you tonight?'

'Vengeance,' Marietta replied, and Catherine turned in time to see the metallic flash of Marietta's dress as it caught the light from one of the many hidden halogens. They were standing facing up to each other on the path that ran parallel with the one Catherine and Marcus were walking along. A neat boxed hedge surrounding a bed of pink roses was separating them. But that didn't mean Catherine couldn't see the malice in Marietta's face when she tagged on contemptuously, 'You have been flaunting Catherine at me since the day you married her—why the hell should I not flaunt her lover at you?'

'They were never lovers,' Vito denied as, beside Catherine, Marcus released a protesting gasp.

'They were lovers,' Marietta insisted. 'The same as *we* were once lovers! And when she tells you otherwise you know she is lying, Vito,' she added slyly. 'In the same way that she knows you lie every time you deny ever making love to me!'

'No,' Catherine murmured, closing her eyes as she waited tensely for Vito to deny the charge—now—when she could then let herself believe him at last!

But he didn't. 'That was a long time ago,' he bit out dismissively. 'Before I ever met Catherine—and therefore has no place in our lives today.'

Catherine felt Marcus's arm come around her shoulders when she must have swayed dizzily.

'It does to me!' Marietta insisted. 'Because you loved me then, Vito! You were supposed to have married me! Everyone expected it. *I* expected it! But what did you do?' she said bitterly. 'You settled for a short affair with me, then dropped me. And I had to settle for second best and marry Rocco—'

'Rocco was not second best, Marietta,' Vito denied. 'And he loved you—genuinely loved you! Which from the sound of it was more than you deserved from him!'

'Is that why you did it?' she asked curiously. 'Because Rocco loved me, did you step gallantly to one side and let him have me?'

'No. I stepped gallantly to one side because *I* didn't want you.' Vito stated it brutally.

'Shame you didn't let Rocco know that,' Marietta threw back. 'For he died believing he had come between the two of us.'

'Oh, my God.' Catherine breathed out painfully, remembering that bright shining star that had always been Rocco, scintillating the world while inside he must have been feeling wretched.

As wretched as she was feeling right now, she likened bleakly.

'When you brought Catherine here and made her your wife he actually apologised to me,' Marietta told Vito.

'Not on my behalf,' Vito rejected. 'Rocco knew exactly how I felt about Catherine.'

'Are you suggesting that you married her for love?' Marietta mocked. 'Don't take me for a fool, Vito,' she scoffed. 'Like everyone else around here, we all know you married her because you had to if you wanted to uphold family tradition and make Santo legitimate. If I had known that getting pregnant was what it would have taken to get you to marry me I would have used the tactic myself! But such a sneaky manipulation didn't occur to me—unlike her,' she added witheringly. 'With her cool English ways and clever independent streak that kept you dancing on your toes in sheer fear that she was going to do something stupid enough to risk your precious son and heir!'

'I think you've said enough,' Vito gritted.

'No, I haven't,' Marietta denied. 'In fact I haven't even got started,' she pronounced. 'You had the arrogance to think that all you needed to do was banish me to Paris and all your marital problems would be over. Well, they will never be over while I still have a brain in my head to thwart you with!'

'So you intend to do—what?' Vito challenged. 'Lurk in some more dark corners listening in on private conversations in the hopes that you can discover some more dirt to throw?'

'Ah,' Marietta drawled. 'So you knew I was there.'

'On the balcony next to ours? Yes,' Vito confirmed, unwittingly answering one question that had been burning a hole in Catherine's brain. 'When you later began quizzing Catherine about Marcus Templeton, I then found it a simple step to put two and two together and realise that you were planning to do something as—crass as this. But what I still don't understand is what you aim to gain by it?'

'That is quite simple. I mean to bring about the absolute ruin of your precious marriage,' Marietta coolly informed him.

'By bringing Marcus Templeton here?' It was Vito's turn to scoff. 'Do you really think that my feelings for Catherine are so fickle that I would throw her out because you brought me face to face with her supposed ex-lover?'

'No. But by having him here Catherine will have someone to fall upon when I tell her that I am pregnant with your baby.'

'That's a filthy lie!' Vito raked out harshly as Catherine swayed in the curve of Marcus's arm.

'But Catherine doesn't know that,' Marietta pointed out. 'She believes we have been lovers since before she lost your second baby. For a woman like Catherine, who cannot have more children, believing that I am pregnant with your child will finish her, believe me,' she advised. 'And I am going to enjoy watching her walk away from you with her darling Marcus after I break the news to her.'

'But why should you want to hurt her like that?' Vito demanded hoarsely.

'I couldn't care less about Catherine's feelings,' Marietta stated carelessly. 'But I do care about hurting you, Vito,' she told him. 'Just as you made me hurt when you passed me on to Rocco like a piece of used baggage!'

'You were lucky to have him!' Vito rasped out painfully. 'He was a good man! A caring man!'

'But not a Giordani.'

'My God,' Vito breathed, sounding truly shaken. 'Catherine was right. You are poison to whatever you come into contact with.'

'And, being so, I really do think, Marietta, that it is time for you to leave now.' Another voice arrived through the darkness.

Four people started in surprise, then watched with varying expressions as Luisa moved out from the shadows of yet another pathway. And the moment that she could see her face clearly Catherine felt her heart sink in sorrow. She looked so dreadfully—painfully wounded.

Yet what did Luisa do? She looked towards Catherine and murmured anxiously, 'Catherine, are you all right, darling? I would have given anything for you not to have witnessed this.'

It was almost worth having her cover exposed just to see the look of stark, staring dismay that was Marietta's face when she spun round to face her. But if it hadn't been for Marcus's arm grimly supporting her, she knew she wouldn't still be standing on her own feet, right now.

'Catherine—you heard...' Vito murmured, and sounded so relieved that it was almost painful.

'Well, well,' Marietta drawled. 'None of us are above lurking in dark corners to eavesdrop, it seems.'

But they were the satirical words of a woman who knew she was staring right into the face of her own ruin...

CHAPTER TEN

CATHERINE stood on the balcony watching the red tail-lights from the final few stragglers snake stealthily down the hillside.

The party was well and truly over at last, though it had gone on for another few nerve-stretching hours after Marietta had left here.

Marcus had taken on the responsibility of her removal, and the way he had guided her away without uttering a single word in anger to her Catherine had, in a strange way, found vaguely comforting. Because she was not the kind of person that liked to watch someone being kicked when they were already down, and Marietta had certainly been right down by the time that she had left.

It had been Luisa's icy contempt that had finally demolished her. Luisa who could usually be relied upon to find some good somewhere in any situation. But for once she had chosen not to, and watching a relationship that was as old as Marietta herself wither and die, as it had done out there in the garden, had been terrible.

Luisa had wept a little, which had helped to fill in an awkward moment between Catherine and Vito while they attempted to comfort her. And then there had been a house full of guests to sparkle for, plus questions to field about Marietta's whereabouts and...

She released a small sigh that sounded too weary for words, because she knew that this wretched night was still far from over.

'Quite an evening, hmm?' a deep voice murmured lightly behind her.

Too light, Catherine noted. Light enough for the true tension to come seeping through it. Vito knew as well as she did that, no matter what had been cleared up during that ugly scene in his garden, the two of them had not even got started yet.

'How is your mother?' she asked, without bothering to turn and look at him.

'She is still upset, naturally,' he replied. 'But you know what she is like,' he added heavily. 'She never could cope well with discord.'

'She loved Marietta.' Catherine stated it quietly. 'Discovering that someone you love is not the person you thought they were can be shattering.'

There was a moment of stillness behind her, then, 'Was that a veiled prod at me?' Vito asked.

Was it? Catherine asked herself. And shrugged her creamy shoulders because, yes, it had been a prod at him. 'You lied to me,' she said. 'About your previous relationship with Marietta.'

His answering sigh was heavy. 'Yes,' he finally admitted. And as that little truth came right out into the open he walked forwards, to come and lean against the rail beside her. 'But it happened a long time ago, and—arrogant as I am,' he acknowledged wryly, 'I did not think you had any right questioning me about my life before you came into it.'

'It gave Marietta power,' Catherine explained. 'With you persistently denying you'd ever been her lover, it left her free to drop nasty hints all over the place. When you insisted you were doing one thing she insisted you were doing another. And she...' Turning to look at him, she felt her soft mouth give a telling little quiver. 'She—knew things about you that only a lover would know.'

Wincing at the implication, he reached out to touch a

gentle fingertip to that telling little quiver. 'I'm sorry,' he said huskily.

It didn't seem enough somehow. And Catherine turned away from him to stare bleakly out across a now dark and very silent garden while beside her Vito did the same thing, their minds in tune to the heaviness Marietta had left behind her.

'She was out here that night, sitting on the next balcony listening to us bash out the same old arguments that we always used to share,' Vito said eventually. 'She must have lapped it all up. My continued lying, our lack of trust in each other, the mention of Marcus that must have seemed like a heaven-sent gift to her to use as yet another weapon.'

Standing in more or less the same place they had been standing that night, Catherine felt her skin begin to crawl at the mere prospect of anyone—worst of all Marietta—sitting there on the next balcony, eavesdropping on what should have been a very private conversation.

'How did you know she was there?' Catherine murmured.

'After you had gone back inside I remained out here, if you remember,' Vito explained. 'I was thinking—trying to come to terms with the very unpalatable fact that if your version of what happened the day you lost the baby was true, then a lot of other things you had said to me could also be true,' he admitted grimacingly. 'At which point I heard a movement on the next balcony—a chair scraping over the tiles, then a sigh I recognised, followed by the waft of a very distinctive perfume. Then I heard her murmur *"Grazie Caterina,"* and the way she said it made my blood run cold.'

He even shuddered. So did Catherine. Then, on a sigh that hissed almost painfully from him, he hit the stone balustrade with a clenched fist. 'How can you *know* someone as well as you think you know them—yet not really know them at all?' he thrust out tragically.

'She loved you.' To Catherine it seemed to explain everything.

But not for Vito. 'That is not love, it is sick obsession,' he denounced. And his golden eyes flashed and his grim mouth hardened. 'I decided she was out of my house by the morning and I didn't care what it took to achieve it,' he went on. 'So I went in to the office, worked all night clearing *her* desk, not my desk, and the rest you know— except that I used that week in Paris with her to let her know that her place in this family was over.'

'What did she say to that?' Catherine asked curiously.

'She reminded me that my mother may not like to hear me say that,' he dryly responded. 'So I countered that piece of blatant blackmail—by sacking her from the bank.'

Catherine stared at him in stunned disbelief. 'Can you do that?' she gasped.

His answering smile wasn't pleasant. 'She may own a good-size block of stock in the bank, but not enough to sway the seat of power there. And, although this is going to confirm your opinion about my conceit, I am the main force that drives Giordani's. If I say she is out, then the board will support me.'

'But what about her client list—won't you lose a lot of very lucrative business?'

'Given the option between going elsewhere with their investment portfolios or transferring them to me, her client list, to the last one, transferred to me,' Vito smoothly informed her.

'No wonder she was out for revenge tonight,' Catherine breathed, feeling rather stunned by the depths of his ruthlessness. 'You frighten me sometimes,' she told him shakily.

Catching hold of her shoulders, he turned her to face

him. 'And you frighten me,' he returned very gently. 'Why else do you think we fight so much?'

Because I love you and I still daren't tell you, Catherine silently answered the question. 'We married for all the wrong reasons,' she said instead. 'You resented my presence in your life and I resented being there.'

'That is not entirely true, Catherine,' he argued. 'At the time I truly believed we were marrying because we could not bear to be apart from one another. '

'The sex has always been good.' She nodded.

His fingers tightened. 'Don't be flippant,' he scolded. 'You know we have always had much more than that.'

Did she? Catherine smiled a wry smile that made his eyes flash with anger.

'Is it too much to ask of you to give an inch?' he rasped out. 'Just a single small inch and I promise you I will repay you with a whole mile!'

'Meaning what?' she demanded, stiffening defensively in his grasp.

A nerve began to tick along his jaw. 'Meaning I married you because I was, and still am, head over heels in love with you,' he raked out. 'Will that help you to respond in kind?'

'Don't,' she protested, trying to turn away from him, knowing it wasn't true. 'You don't have to say things like that to make me stay here. Marietta didn't do that kind of damage.'

'It is the truth!' he insisted. 'And it should have been said a long time ago—I know that,' he admitted tightly. 'But now it has been said you could at least do me the honour of believing me!'

Staring up into those swirling dark gold burning eyes of his, Catherine wished—*wished* she dared let herself do just that. But...

Lifting her shoulders in a helplessly vulnerable gesture,

she murmured dully, 'A man in love doesn't go from the arms of a woman he loves straight into the arms of another.'

He went white in instant understanding, and she felt like crying for bringing it all up again. But it had to be said. It had to be dealt with.

His heavy sigh as he dropped his hands away from her seemed to be acknowledging that.

'I did *not* sleep with Marietta on the night you lost our baby,' he denied. 'Though after tonight's little revelations I can understand why you may choose not to believe that.' Glancing at her, Vito searched her face for a hint of softening, only to grimace when he didn't find it. 'You used to drive me crazy,' he confessed. 'From day one of our marriage you made sure I knew that you were not so content with your lot as my wife. You were stubborn, fiercely protective of your independence and so bloody steadfast in your refusal to let me feel needed by you—except in our bed, of course.'

'I needed you,' she whispered.

He didn't seem to hear her. 'As hot as Vesuveus in it and as cold as Everest out of it.' He sighed. 'I began to feel like a damned gigolo, useful to you for only one purpose...'

And I felt like your sex slave. Catherine silently made the bleak comparison.

'But at least I *could* reach you there,' he went on heavily. 'So I didn't take it kindly when you fell pregnant once again and were so sick with it that the doctors were insisting on no exertion—and suddenly I found myself robbed of my only excuse to be close to you when making love was banned also.'

'We made love!' she protested.

His eyes flashed darkly over her. 'Not the grit your teeth, feel the burn, all-out physical love we had always indulged in.'

'Life can't always be perfect, Vito!' she cried, shifting uncomfortably at his oh, so accurate description of their love-life.

'The sex between us was perfect,' he responded. 'We blended like two halves coming together in the fiery furnace. And I missed it when I wasn't allowed to merge like that any more, and I found the—other stuff,' he described it with a contemptuous flick of his hand, 'bloody frustrating, if you want to know.'

Listening to him so accurately describe how she had been feeling herself, Catherine stared at his grim face and wondered how two people could be so wonderfully in tune with each other—and yet not know it!

'So I grew more frustrated and resentful of what you did to me week by wretched week,' he went on. 'Until it all exploded in one huge row, followed by the most glorious coming together.'

'Then you stormed off.' She nodded, bringing this whole thing painfully back to where it had started. 'To Marietta, in search of consolation.'

'I stormed off feeling sick with my lack of self-control,' he brusquely corrected. 'But I did not start out at Marietta's apartment. I started out at the office—where she found me too drunk to do much more than let her take me home with her while I attempted to sober up before coming back to make my peace with you. Only it didn't work out like that,' he sighed. 'Because I fell into a drunken stupor on her sofa, muttering your name and pleading for your forgiveness. And the next thing I know I wake up, too many hours later to even count, to find myself in hell, where everything I held dear in my life was being wrenched away from me. By the time I stopped spinning round like a mad dog trying to catch its own tail, months later, I realised that I deserved what I had got from you—which only made me resent you all the more.'

'I felt the same,' Catherine confessed.

'But never, since the day I set eyes on you, have I so much as *wanted* to sleep with another woman—and that includes Marietta!' he vowed. 'In fact,' he then added reluctantly, 'the three years without you were the most miserable of my life, if you want to know the truth.'

Catherine smiled in wry understanding, and felt herself beginning to let herself believe him. Maybe he saw it, because he reached out to gently touch her cheek. 'But I never knew just how miserable until the night I picked up the phone and heard your voice...' he told her softly. 'It was as if someone threw a switch inside me to light me up.' He smiled.

'You were as cold as ice with me!' she charged.

'Not beneath the surface,' he denied. 'Beneath the ice I felt very hot and very angry—it was marvellous! Even fighting with you was wonderful,' he confessed as the hand moved to her throat, while the other slid stealthily around her waist to draw her up against him.

She didn't fight—didn't want to fight. She was too busy loving what he was saying here, with his eyes so dark and intense and so beautifully sincere.

'I was not in your home for five short minutes before I knew without a doubt that I was going to get you back in my life, no matter what it took to do it.' He stated it huskily. 'Because I want you here. I want you to *know* I want you here. I want to wake up every morning to see your face on the pillow beside me and I want to go to sleep every night with you cradled in my arms.'

Bending his head, he brushed his mouth against her own. 'In short, I want us to be a warm, close, loving family,' he said as he drew away again. 'Just me, you, Santo and Mamma, in a small tight unit of four with no lies to cloud our horizon and no— What?' he said, cutting off to frown at her as Catherine's softened expression took on such a radical change that he couldn't miss it. 'What did I just say? Why are you looking like that?'

She was already trying to get away from him. 'I...'

'Don't you dare claim that you don't want these things also!' he exploded angrily, completely misreading the reason for the sudden way she had just shut him out again. 'Because I know that you do! I *know* you love me, Catherine!' he insisted forcefully. 'As much as I love you!'

Oh, God help me! she prayed as his angry declaration shuddered through her. 'Please, Vito!' she begged. 'Don't be angry. But—'

'But nothing!' he growled, and took ruthless possession of her mouth in a blatant act meant to stop her from speaking.

It was hard and it was urgent, and she loved him for it. But in all her life Catherine had never felt so wickedly wretched—because he was trembling—all of him! His mouth where it crushed her mouth, his arms where they bound her tightly to him. She could even feel his heart trembling where her hand lay trapped against the wall of his chest.

And if she had never believed a single word he had said to her before this moment, then she suddenly knew that she had to believe that any man who could be as affected as this must truly love her!

'Y-You don't understand,' she groaned as she wrenched her mouth free of him. 'I need to—'

'I have no *wish* to understand,' was his arrogant reply. But it was hoarsely said, and the look on his face was the one Luisa would call his frightened expression. 'You are mine! You *know* you are!' And on that he picked her up and began striding inside with the grim-faced, hard-eyed, burning intention of ravishing her—Catherine knew that.

'You just said that you wanted no more lies between us!' She tried to plead with him for reason. 'Well, at least give me a chance to be as honest with you as you have just been with me!'

'No.' The refusal was blunt and uncompromising as he fell with her onto the bed.

'I do love you!' she cried—and effectively brought him to a stop just as his mouth was about to take hers prisoner.

'Say that again,' he commanded.

'I love you,' she responded obediently. 'But I have a terrible confession to make, Vito!' she hurried on anxiously. 'And I need you to listen before you—'

'If you are going to admit that you and Marcus Templeton were lovers,' he cut in, 'then believe me, Catherine, when I tell you that I do not want to hear it!'

'Marcus and I were never lovers,' she shakily assured him.

His eyes drew shut, long dark lashes curling over dark golden iris in an effort to hide his deep sense of relief. And Catherine's teeth pressed deep indentations into her lower lip as she waited while some of the fierce tension began to ease out of him.

She watched those eyelids rise up again slowly to show her the eyes of a man who was not quite as driven by fear any more, though still dark and dynamic, with the kind of inherent passions that curled around the soul.

'Okay,' he invited grimly. 'Make your damned confession and get it over with.'

'I *do* love you,' she repeated urgently. 'I always have! Wh-which—which is why I just couldn't do it!'

'Do what?' he frowned.

She lost courage, and with it the words to speak. So instead she kissed him gently, softly, tenderly. But her heart was beating like a hammer drill and, lying on top of her as he was, Vito had to be aware of it.

His head came up. 'For goodness' sake,' he breathed. 'It cannot be this bad, surely?'

The fear was filtering back into his eyes. She bit her bottom lip again. Then the tears began to flood her own eyes as she forced herself to say what had to be said.

'I didn't take the morning-after pills,' she confessed in a frightened little rush of words that had him staring down at her uncomprehendingly. 'I couldn't, you see, wh-when it came right down to it. I mean—how could I destroy the chance of a new life we may make between us? It was just too—'

'No,' he cut in as understanding finally began to dawn on him. 'You would not be so stupid.'

'I'm sorry,' she breathed. With trembling fingers Catherine reached up to gently cover the sudden white-ringed tension circling his mouth. 'But I couldn't do it. I just—couldn't do it...'

Rolling away from her, Vito jack-knifed to his feet, then just stood staring down at her as if he didn't know who she was. It was awful—much, much worse than she had expected it to be.

'What is it with you?' he demanded hoarsely. 'Do you harbour some kind of death-wish or something?'

Catherine sat up to hug her knees and murmured shakily, 'It was too late.'

He let out a laugh—only it wasn't a laugh but more a burst of something else entirely. 'No, it damn well wasn't!' he exploded. 'You had seventy-two hours to take the bloody things after we made love that day!'

'I meant it was too late for me!' she yelled back in pained rebuttal. 'What if we'd conceived, Vito?' She begged for understanding. 'It would have been like killing Santino!'

'That's just so much rot, Catherine, and you know it,' he denounced. 'You have been taking the contraceptive pill for years! What difference could a couple of extra hours be to what you do every single day?'

'Not then.' She shrugged. 'But the night before, when we...'

She didn't finish, but then she didn't need to. Vito was well ahead of her. 'That is no excuse,' he denounced, 'for putting your own life on the line!'

'We don't know if I have done yet,' she pointed out. 'But at least I can be sure that I didn't deliberately kill another baby.'

His face turned pure white. 'You didn't kill the last one!' he shouted furiously.

Catherine flinched at his anger. 'I don't want to talk about it,' she said, and buried her face in her knees.

'Well, you are going to talk about it!' he rasped, and a pair of hands gently took hold of her head to pull it upwards again. 'You are going to talk about the fact that once again you have made a decision that should have been mine to share with you!'

'You wanted me to take the pills!' she cried. 'That isn't sharing a decision; that's me bowing down to what you decide!'

'Well, that has to be better than this!' he said in a voice that shook, then removed his hands and turned right away from her.

'I'm sorry,' she whispered again, but he didn't acknowledge it. Instead he strode into the bathroom, slamming the door shut behind him.

And Catherine lowered her head again, allowing him the right to be so angry—which was why she had let him go on believing she had taken the damned—stupid—rotten pills!

And actually—she had meant to take them. It had only been when it had come to the point of actually putting them in her mouth that she'd discovered she just couldn't do it.

Not to herself, not to the child that might already have been forming its tenuous grasp for life deep inside her. So she'd binned the pills right there in Vito's bathroom then continued the lie with a determined blank disregard of the consequences.

Maybe Vito was right and she did harbour a secret death wish, she mused hollowly. But she knew deep down inside that this had nothing to do with death but to do with a chance of life. The maternal instinct to protect that life was as strong in a woman as the natural need to keep drawing in breath.

She hadn't been able to fight it, and somehow she had to make Vito understand that, she decided as she dragged herself off the bed and walked on shaking limbs towards the bathroom.

It had to mean something that he hadn't bothered to lock the door, she told herself bracingly as she twisted the handle and stepped bravely inside.

The room was steamy. Vito was already in the shower and his clothes lay in an angrily discarded heap over in one corner. Not really sure that she was doing the right thing here, Catherine walked over to the shower cubicle and pulled open the door.

He was standing with his back to the shower spray. Hands on narrow hips, wide shoulders braced, dark head thrown back to receive the full blast of the hot water right on his grim face.

A truly dynamic sensual animal, she mused, then smiled wryly at letting herself think of such things at a dire moment such as this.

'Vito,' she prompted quietly. 'We need to talk about this...'

His dark head tilted forward, then turned towards her. And his utterly cold dark golden eyes ran slowly over her while the water sluiced down his bronze back.

'You will ruin that dress in this steam,' was all he said, then turned his face back up to the shower.

Catherine gritted her teeth as her old enemy anger began to raise its dangerous head. And without thinking twice about it she stepped into the shower with him, silk dress and all, and firmly pulled the door shut.

She'd surprised him, she noted with some satisfaction as his dark head shot forwards again to stare at her in disbelief. 'What the hell do you think you are doing?' he protested.

'You are going to have to listen some time.' She shrugged determinedly. 'So it might as well be now.'

Forever the man to think fast on his feet, Vito responded by taking a small step sideways. Doing so gave the water spray unrestricted passage towards her, and, with a grim intention that galled, he leaned his shoulders into the corner of the shower, folded his arms across his impressive chest, then watched uncaringly as the water turned her red silk dress almost transparent before his ruthless eyes.

Diamonds glittered at her throat, at her ears, and on her finger. Her chin was up, her eyes flashing green fire at him at his black-hearted retaliation. But she didn't so much as gasp as the hot water hit her.

'Okay,' he said coolly. 'Talk.'

'I am a woman,' she announced, earning herself the mocking arch of an arrogant brow in response. Gritting her teeth, she ignored it. 'Being a woman, the urge to nurture and protect new life is so deeply entrenched in my very psyche that I would probably find it easier to shoot myself than harm that new life.'

'This is not the Dark Ages,' he grimly derided. 'In case you have forgotten, your sex stopped being slaves to your hormones a long time ago.'

'I'm not talking about hormones,' Catherine refuted. 'I am talking about instinct—the same kind of instinct that gives your sex the desire to impregnate mine!'

'Once again, *my* sex stopped being slaves to our sperm banks with the advent of condoms.' He also derided that.

'It is called free sex—enjoyed by millions for its pleasure, not its original function.'

'Since when have you ever thought of using a condom?' Catherine scoffed at that. 'I don't remember you considering protection, even when you knew it was dangerous for me to risk getting pregnant!'

His jaw clenched on a direct hit, and Catherine noted it with a nod in acknowledgement. 'You left the protecting up to me, Vito,' she reminded him. 'Which therefore gives me the right to call the shots when that protection is breached!'

'Not at the risk of your own life,' he denied.

'You said it,' she agreed. 'It *is* my life. I made a decision that might risk everything—but might also be risking absolutely nothing, depending on how my pregnancy goes. That's a fifty-fifty chance either way,' she told him. 'Fifty-fifty odds are just too even for me to justify stealing from any child the right to survive them!'

'For goodness' sake,' he rasped. 'Your own mother died in childbirth, Catherine! What does that tell you about the risk you are taking!'

Tears burst into her eyes, making them glint like the diamonds she was wearing. 'I didn't say I wasn't frightened,' she whispered shakily.

On the kind of curse that turned the air blue Vito snapped off the gushing water, then reached out to drag her against him.

'You stupid woman,' he condemned, but it was a darkly possessive and very needy condemnation. 'How could you do this to us now, when we are actually beginning to *know* each other?'

'I need you to be strong for me—not angry,' Catherine sobbed against his shoulder.

'I will be strong,' he promised gruffly. 'But not yet,

while I still cannot make up my mind whether I want to kill you for doing this to us!'

Despite the tears, Catherine lifted her face to smile wryly at him. 'That was a contradiction in terms if ever I heard one.'

He gave a muttered growl of frustration and bent to kiss her. Then, 'Turn around,' he commanded gruffly, and without waiting for her to comply he twisted her round himself, then began dealing with the sodden length of zip down one of her sides which helped hold the dress in place. With an efficiency that had always been his, he stripped her bare, and, leaving her clothes in a wet puddle on the shower floor, he led her out of the cubicle, found a towel and began drying her with all the grimness of a man still at war with himself.

Or with her, Catherine corrected as she gazed at the top of his dark head while he briskly dried her legs for her.

'It might never happen,' she huskily pointed out.

'With our past record?' His mouth took on a scornful grimace as he rose to his full height. 'You are pregnant, Catherine,' he announced as he wrapped the towel around her and neatly tucked the ends in between her breasts. 'You know it and I know it. We don't need to await the evidence to be that sure.'

'I'm sorry,' she murmured yet again, with a glum sense of utter inadequacy.

'But not regretful,' he said, clearly not very impressed by the apology.

Catherine gave a mute shake of her head. He reached for another towel, which he tucked around his own lean waist, then grabbed hold of her hand to lead her back into the bedroom.

The bed awaited. He trailed her directly to it, bent to toss back the covers—then paused. 'Your hair is wet,' he observed belatedly.

'Just the loose ends,' she dismissed, not in the least bit interested in her wet hair because she was too busy waiting for whatever it was he had damped down inside him to come bursting through the restraints of his control.

'I love you,' she said, and inadvertently helped it to explode when he turned on her, grabbed her by the shoulders and gave her an angry shake.

'You don't deserve me, Catherine,' he informed her darkly. 'You give me nothing but arguments, heartache and grief and yet I love you. You mistrust me, leave me, and make me go through the horror of fighting to see my own son, and still I continue to love you!'

'I didn't know that then,' she reminded him.

'Well, you damn well do now!' he grimly responded. 'So now what do I have?' he asked her. 'I have you back where you belong, is what I have. I have you back in my home, in my bed and in my life, and what do you do? You tell me I have to go through the worry and stress and fear of losing you all over again because you hold your own life in lower regard than I do.'

'It isn't that simple—'

'It is from where I stand,' he informed her. 'In fact it is elementary from where I stand! Because this time you are going to do as you are told. Do you understand me?'

His hands gave her another small shake. 'Yes,' she answered meekly.

'No more working for money we do not need. No more fights to establish your precious independence. You will rest when I tell you to, and eat when I tell you to, and sleep when I tell you to!'

'You're being very masterful,' she said.

'You think this is masterful?' he questioned darkly. 'Wait until you have lived for nine months with me as your jailer and you will be very intimate with just how masterful I am going to be!'

'Sounds exciting,' she said, her green eyes glinting up at him with the kind of suggestion that had him tensing.

'Well, that is just something else you are going to have to learn to do without,' he informed her deridingly. 'Because sex is out for the next nine months, if you recall.'

'Are you joking?' she flashed. 'I'm not giving up sex until I have to!'

'You will do as you are told,' he informed her coldly.

That's what you think, Catherine thought, with the light of battle burning in her eyes. On an act of rebellion she whipped both towels away, then, with a push to his arrogant chest, sent him toppling backwards onto the mattress.

'I want you now, while you are still wet from your shower and I am dripping in diamonds!' she informed him as she followed him down so she was stretched out down his full length. Then she kissed him so sensuously that he didn't stand a cat in hell's chance of arguing the point with her.

'You are right; you are a witch,' he muttered when she eventually released him.

'A happy witch, though,' she said. 'I love you. You love me. It makes me feel so wickedly aroused,' she confessed as she trailed the heart-shaped diamond locket across his kiss-warmed mouth. 'So, do you want to fight some more or make love?' she asked. 'Bearing in mind, of course, that you have just ordained that we are not allowed to fight any more...'

Eight months later, Catherine was relaxing on one of the sun loungers reading a book while Santo played around in the pool. It was April, and the weather had only just turned warm enough to indulge in this kind of lazy pastime. But she put her book aside when Vito suddenly appeared around the corner of the house and came to join her.

'You're home early,' she remarked, accepting his warm kiss as he bent over her.

'I have some news for you,' he explained. 'But first— how are my two precious females?'

Catherine smiled serenely as his hand reached out to lay a gentle stroke across her swollen stomach. Learning the sex of their baby had been a decision they had made together very early on in her pregnancy, when neither knew what the future was going to offer them. Catherine had wanted to know as much about her baby as she could know—just in case. And Vito had not demurred. So Abrianna Luisa had become a very real little person to all of them, and that included her brother and her grandmother. But in the end they needn't have worried, for she had sailed through this pregnancy without so much as a hiccup to spoil its calm, smooth development.

'We are fine,' she assured him. 'But—what is this?' She frowned as he dropped a very official-looking document with red seals and signatures on her lap.

'You can read Italian,' he reminded her lazily, then walked off to collect a red and white football that was lying beside the pool and toss it playfully at his son.

It was several minutes before he came back to her. By then Catherine had finished reading and was waiting for him. 'She sold out to you at last,' she said.

'Mmm,' was all he said, but his brief smile held a wealth of grim satisfaction. 'Once our daughter has arrived as safely as the doctors have assured us she will, I will have the stock transferred to her.'

'Not Santino?' Catherine queried.

Vito shook his dark head. 'He already has a similar block of my own stock placed in his name. So…' He bent down to touch a gentle hand to Catherine's stomach. 'Marietta's block will belong to my Abrianna Luisa,' he ordained. 'And we can now put Marietta out of our lives.'

With a sigh, Catherine gazed out in front of her and thought about Marietta, living in New York now and working for another investment bank of great repute. She was happier there, so they'd heard via the Neapolitan grapevine. Like any addict denied her fix, she had eventually learned to overcome her obsessive desire to be a Giordani. And, as Vito had just more or less said, her willingness to sell him her shares in the company was final proof of that. 'It's time Santo came out of the water before he catches a chill,' she murmured. And just like that Marietta was set aside.

Vito nodded. 'Santino!' he called. 'Come and help me heave Mamma off this lounger. It is time for her rest!'

'Rest,' Catherine mocked as she watched her son power his wiry little frame to the edge of the swimming pool. 'What else do I ever get to do but rest?'

'Ah,' Vito smiled. 'But this one will be different. For I shall be there to share it with you.'

And his eyes were gleaming, because he was talking about spending an hour or so loving her—not the sexual kind of loving, but the other kind, that nourished the soul...

A PASSIONATE MARRIAGE

MICHELLE REID

CHAPTER ONE

LEANDROS PETRONADES sat lazing on a sunbed on the deck of his yacht and looked out on the bay of San Estéban. Satisfaction toyed with his senses. The new Spanish resort had developed into something special and having enjoyed a very much hands-on experience during its development, he felt that sense of satisfaction was well deserved. Plus the fact that he had multiplied his original investment, he was business-orientated enough to add.

He had done a lot of that during the four years since he took over from his late father, he mused idly. Multiplying original investments had become an expectation for him.

Which was probably why he'd found this project just that bit different. It had always been more than just another investment. He had been in on it from the beginning when it had been only an idea in an old friend's head. Between them, he and Felipe Vazquez had carefully nurtured that idea until it had grown into the fashionable new resort he was seeing today.

The problem for him now was, where did he go from here? The resort was finished. The luxury villas dotted about the hillside had their new owners, the five-star hotel, golf and leisure complex was functioning like a dream. And San Estéban itself was positively bustling, its harbour basin filled with luxury sail crafts owned by the rich and famous looking for new places to hide out while they played. By next week even this yacht, which had been his home while he had been based here, would have slipped her moorings. She would sail to the Caribbean to await the

5

arrival of his brother Nikos, who planned to fly out with his new bride in three weeks.

It was time for him to move on, though he did not know what it was he wanted to move on to. Did he go back to Athens and lose himself in the old cut and thrust of the corporate jungle? His wide shoulders shifted against the sun bed's padded white cushion as an old restlessness began to stir deep within his bones.

'No, it is not possible to go over the top with this.' A soft female voice filtered through the open doors behind him. 'It is to be a celebration of San Estéban's rebirth, and a thanks and farewell to all who worked so hard to make the project happen. Let it be one of fireworks and merriment. We will call it—the Baptism of San Estéban, and it will become its annual day of carnival.'

A smile eased itself across his mouth as Leandros listened, and his shoulders relaxed as the restlessness drained away. The Baptism of San Estéban, he mused. He liked it.

He liked Diantha. He liked having her around because she was so calm and quiet and so terribly efficient. When he asked her to do something for him she did it without bothering him with the irritating details. She was good for him. She tuned in so perfectly to the way of his thinking.

He was almost sure that he was going to marry her.

He did not love her—he did not believe in love any more. But Diantha was beautiful, intelligent, exceedingly pleasant company, and she promised to be a good lover—though he had not got around to trying her out. She was also Greek, independently wealthy and was not too demanding of his time.

A busy man like him had to take these things into consideration when choosing a wife, he pondered complacently. For he must be allowed the freedom to do what was necessary to keep himself and the Petronades Group of companies streets ahead of their nearest rivals. Coming from a similar background to his own, Diantha Christophoros understood and accepted this. She would not nag and complain and make him feel guilty for working long hours, nor would she expect him to be at her beck and call every minute of the day.

She was, in other words, the perfect choice of wife for a man like him.

There was only one small obstacle. He already had a wife. Before he could begin to approach Diantha with murmurings of romance and marriage he must, in all honour, cut legal ties to his current spouse. Though the fact that they had not so much as laid eyes on each other in three years meant he did not envisage a quick divorce from Isobel being a problem.

Isobel...

'Damn,' he cursed softly as the restlessness returned with enough itchy tension to launch him to his feet. He should not have allowed himself to think her name. It never failed to make him uptight. As time had gone by, he had thought less and less of her and become a better person for it. But sometimes her name could still catch him out and sink its barbed teeth into him.

Going over to the refrigerated drinks trolley, he selected a can of beer, snapped the tab and went to rest his lean hips against the yacht rail, his dark eyes frowning at the view that had only made him smile minutes before.

That witch, the hellion, he thought grimly. She had left her mark on him and it still had not faded three years on.

He took a gulp of his beer. Behind him he could still hear Diantha's level tones as she planned San Estéban's celebration day with her usual efficiency. If he turned his head he would see her standing in his main stateroom, looking as if she belonged there with her dark hair and eyes and olive-toned skin, her elegant clothes chosen to enhance her beauty, not place it on blatant display like...

He took another pull of the beer can. Up above his head the hot Spanish sun was burning into his naked shoulders. It felt good enough to have him flexing deep-bedded muscles wrapped in rich brown skin.

Recalling Isobel, he felt a different kind of bite tug at his senses. This one hit him low down in his gut where the sex thing lurked. He grimaced, wondering if or when he would ever want another woman the way he'd wanted Isobel? And hoped he never had to suffer those primitive urges again.

They had gone into marriage like two randy teenagers, loving each other with a passion that had them tearing each other to pieces by the time they'd separated. He had been too young—she had been too young. They'd made love like animals and fought in the same ferocious way until— inevitably probably—it had all turned so nasty and bitter and bad that it had been easier to lock it all away and forget he had a wife than to risk allowing it all to break out again.

But, like his sojourn in San Estéban, it was over now— time to move on with his life. He was thirty-one years old and ready to settle down with a *proper* wife, maybe even a family...

'Why the frown?'

Diantha had come up beside him without him noticing. Turning his head, he looked down into warm brown eyes, saw the soft smile on her lips...and thought of a different smile. This mouth didn't smile, it pouted—provokingly. And those intense green eyes were never warm but just damned defiant.

'I am attempting to come to terms with the fact that it is time for me to leave here,' he answered her question.

'And you do not want to leave,' Diantha murmured understandingly.

Leandros sighed. 'I have come to love this place,' he confessed, looking outwards towards San Estéban again.

There followed a few moments of silence between them, the kind that allowed his mind to drift without intrusion across the empty years during which he had hidden away here, learning to be whole again. San Estéban had been his sanctuary in a time of misery and disillusionment. Isobel had—

It took the gentle touch of Diantha's fingers to his warm bicep to remind him that she was here. They rarely touched. It was not yet that kind of relationship. She was his sister Chloe's closest friend and he was honour-bound to treat her as such while she was here. But his senses stirred in response to those cool fingers—only to settle down again the moment they were removed.

'You know what I think, Leandros,' she said gently. 'I think you have been here for too long. Living the life of a lotus-eater has made you lazy—which makes it a good time for you to return to Athens and move on with your life, don't you think?'

'Ah, words of wisdom,' he smiled. It was truly uncanny how Diantha could tap in to his thinking. 'Don't worry,' he said. 'After the San Estéban celebration I have every intention of returning to Athens and…move on, as you call it,' he promised.

'Good,' she commended. 'Your mama will be pleased to hear it.'

And with that simple blessing she moved away again, walking gracefully back into the stateroom in her neat blue dress that suited her figure and with her glossy black hair coiled with classical Greek conservatism to the slender curve of her nape.

But she did so with no idea that she had left behind her a man wearing another frown because he was seeing long, straight, in-your-face red hair flowing down a narrow spine in a blazing defiance to everything Greek. Isobel would have rather died than wear that neat blue dress, he mused grimly. She preferred short skirts that showed her amazing legs off and skinny little tops that tantalised the eyes with the thrust of her beautiful, button-tipped breasts.

Isobel would rather have cut out her tongue than show concern for his mother's feelings, he mentally added as he turned away again and took another grim pull of his beer. Isobel and his family had not got on. They had rubbed each other up the wrong way from the very beginning, and both factions hadn't attempted to hide that from him.

Diantha, on the other hand, adored his mother and his mother adored her. Being such a close friend to his sister, Chloe, she had always hovered on the periphery of his life, though he had only truly taken notice of her since she had arrived here a week ago to step into the breach to help organise next week's celebration because Chloe, who should have been here helping him, had become deeply embroiled in Nikos's wedding preparations.

It had been good of Diantha in the circumstances. He appreciated the time she had placed at his disposal, particularly since she had only just returned to Athens, having spent the last four years with her family living in Washington, D.C. She was well bred and well liked—her advantages were adding up, he noted. And, other than for a brief romance with his brother Nikos to blot her copybook, she was most definitely much more suitable than that witch of a redhead with sharp barbs for teeth.

With that final thought on the subject he took a final pull of his beer can, saw a man across the quay taking photographs of the yacht and frowned at him. He had a distinct dislike of photographers, not only because they intruded on his privacy but also because it was what his dear wife did for a living. When they had first met she had been aiming a damned camera at him—or was it the red Ferrari he had been leaning against? No, it had been him. She had got him to pose then flirted like mad with him while the camera clicked. By the end of the same day they'd gone to bed, and after that—

He did not want to think about what had happened after that. He did not want to think of Isobel at all. She no longer belonged in his thoughts, and it was about time that he made that official.

The man with the camera turned away. So did Leandros, decisively. He suddenly felt a lot better about leaving here and went inside to…move on with his life.

Isobel's own thinking was moving very much along the same lines as she sat reading the letter that had just arrived from her estranged husband's lawyer giving her notice of Leandros's intention to begin divorce proceedings.

She was sitting alone at a small kitchen table. Her mother hadn't yet risen from her bed. She was glad about that because the letter had come as a shock, even though she agreed with its content. It was time, if not well overdue that one of them should take the bull by the horns and call an official end to a marriage that should have never been.

But the printed words on the page blurred for a moment at the realisation that this was it, the final chapter of a four-year mistake. If she agreed to Leandros's terms, then she knew she would be accepting that those years had been nothing but wasted in her life.

Did he feel the same? Was that why he had taken so long to get to this? It was hard to acknowledge that you could be so fallible, that you had once been stupid enough to let your heart rule your head.

Or was there more to it than a decision to put an end to their miserable marriage? Had he found someone with whom he felt he could spend the rest of his life?

The idea shouldn't hurt but it did. She had loved Leandros so badly at the beginning that she suspected she'd gone a little mad. They'd been young—too young—but oh, it had been so wildly passionate.

Then—no, don't think about the passion, she told herself firmly, and made herself read the letter again.

It was asking her if she would consider travelling to Athens to meet with her husband—in the presence of their respective lawyers, of course—so they could thrash out a settlement in an effort to make the divorce quick and trouble-free. A few days of her time should be enough, Takis Konstantindou was predicting. All expenses would be paid by Leandros for both herself and her lawyer as a goodwill gesture, because Mr Petronades couldn't travel to England at this time.

She paused to wonder why Leandros couldn't travel. For the man she remembered virtually lived out of a suitcase, so it was odd to think of him under some kind of restraint.

It was odd to think about him at all, she extended, and the letter lost its holding power as she sat back in the chair. They'd first met by accident right here in England at an annual car exhibition. She'd been there in her official capacity as photographer for a trendy new magazine—a bright and confident twenty-two-year-old who believed the whole world was at her feet. While he was dashing and twenty-seven years old, with the looks and the build of a genuine dark Apollo.

They'd flirted over the glossy bonnet of some prohibitively expensive sports car. With his looks and his charm and his immaculate clothing, she'd assumed he was one of the car's sales representatives, since they all looked and dressed like a million dollars. It had never occurred to her that far from selling the car they were flirting across he owned several of them. Realisation about just who Leandros was had come a lot later—much too late to do anything about it.

By then he'd already bowled her over with his dark good looks and easy charm and the way he looked at her that left her in no doubt as to what was going on behind his handsome façade. They'd made a date to share dinner and ended up falling into bed at the first opportunity they were handed. His finding out that he was her first lover had only made the passion burn all the more. He'd adored playing the role of tutor. He'd taught her to understand the pleasures of her own body and made sure that she understood what pleasured his. When it came time for him to go back to Greece he'd refused to go without her. They'd married in a hasty civil ceremony then rushed to the airport to catch their flight.

It was as he'd led her onto a private jet with the Petronades logo shining in gold on its side that she started to ask questions. He'd thought it absolutely hilarious that she didn't know she'd married the modern equivalent of Croesus, and had carried her off to the tiny private cabin, where he'd made love to her all the way to Athens. She had never been so happy in her entire life.

But that was it—the sum total of the happy side of their marriage was encapsulated in a single hop from England to Greece. By the time they'd arrived at his family home the whole, whirling wonder of their love was already turning stale. 'You can't wear that to meet my mother;' his first criticism of her could still ring antagonistic bells in her head.

'Why, what's wrong with it?'

'The skirt is too short; she will have a fit. And can you not tie your hair up or something, show a little respect for the people you are about to meet?'

She had not tied her hair up, nor had she changed her clothes. But she had soon learned the hard way that stubborn defiance was one thing when it was aimed at a man who virtually salivated with desire for you even as he criticised. But it was not the same as being boxed and tagged a cheap little floozy at first horrified glance.

Things had gone from bad to worse after that. And— yes, she reiterated as her gaze dipped back to the letter, it *was* time that one of them took the initiative and drew the final curtain across something that should never have been.

In fact, Isobel had only one problem with the details Takis Konstantindou had mapped out in the letter. She could not see how she could spend several days in Athens because she could not leave her mother on her own for that long.

'What time does her flight come in?'

Leandros was sitting at his desk in his plush Athens office. In the two weeks he had been back here he had changed into a different person. Gone was the laid-back man of San Estéban and in his place sat a sharp-edged, hard-headed Greek tycoon.

Was he happy with that? No, he was not happy to become this person again, but needs must when the devil drives, so they said. In this case the devil was the amount of importance other people placed on his time and knowledge. His desk was virtually groaning beneath the weight of paperwork that apparently needed his attention as a matter of urgency. He moved from important meeting to meeting with hardly a breath in between. His social life had gone from a lazy meal eaten in a restaurant on the San Estéban boulevard, to a constant round of social engagements that literally set his teeth on edge. If he lifted his eyes someone jumped to speak to him. If he closed those same eyes someone else would ensure that he opened them again. The wheels of power ground on and on for twenty-four hours of every day and the whole merry-go-round was made all the more intense because his younger brother Nikos was off limits while he prepared for his wedding day.

On his father's death Leandros had become the head of the Petronades family, therefore it was his duty to play host in his father's stead. His mother was becoming more neurotic the closer it came to Nikos's big day, and was likely to panic if she did not have an open line to her eldest son's ear. If he complained she told him not to spoil this for her then reminded him that he had denied her the opportunity to stand proud and watch him make his own disastrous union. And because thoughts of marriage were already on his mind, he was hard put not to snap at her that maybe Nikos could take a leaf out of his own book and run away to marry secretly. At least the day would belong only to him and Carlotta. If there was anything about his own marriage he could still look back on with total pleasure, it was that moment when Isobel had smiled up at him as he placed the ring upon her finger and whispered, 'I love you so much.' He had not needed five hundred witnesses to help prove that vow to be true.

His heart gave him a punishing twinge of regret for what he had once had and lost.

'This evening.' Takis Konstantindou pulled him back from where he had been in danger of visiting. 'But she insisted on making her own arrangements,' Takis informed him. 'She will be staying at the Apollo near Piraeus.'

Leandros frowned. 'But that is a mediocre place with a low star rating. Why should she want to stay there when she could have had a suite at the Athenaeum?'

Takis just shrugged his lack of an answer. 'All I know is that she refused our invitation to make arrangements for her and reserved three rooms, not two, at the Apollo, one of which must have wheelchair access.'

Wheelchair access? Leandros sat forward, his attention suddenly riveted. 'Why?' he demanded. 'What's wrong with her? Has she been hurt...is she ill?'

'I don't know if the special room *is* for her,' Takis answered. 'All I know is that she has reserved such a room.'

'Then find out!' he snapped. Suddenly the thought of his beautiful Isobel trapped in a wheelchair made him feel physically ill!

He must even have gone pale because Takis was looking at him oddly. 'It could change everything, do you not see that?' His tycoon persona jumped to his rescue. 'The whole structure on which we have based our proposals for a settlement may need to be revised to take into account a physical disability.'

'I think you have adequately covered for any such eventuality, Leandros.' The lawyer smiled cynically.

'*Adequate* is not good enough.' He was suddenly furious. 'Adequate is not what I was aiming towards! I am no skinflint! I have no wish to play games with this! Isobel is my wife.' Hearing that 'is' leaving his lips forced him to stop and take a breath. 'I will leave my marriage with no sense of triumph at its failure, Takis,' he informed the other man. 'But I will hopefully leave it with the knowledge that I treated her fairly in the end.'

Takis was looking surprised at his outburst. 'I'm sorry, Leandros, I never meant to—'

'I know what you meant,' he interrupted curtly. 'And I

know what you think.' Which was why that derisory comment about Isobel being *adequately* compensated had made him see red. He knew what his family thought about Isobel. He knew that they probably discussed her between themselves in that same derogatory way. He had even let them—if only by pretending it wasn't happening. But they were wrong if they believed his failed marriage was down to Isobel, because it wasn't. Not all of it anyway.

Takis was wrong about him if he believed that he was filing for divorce because he no longer cared about Isobel. He might not want her back to run riot through his life again, but... 'Whatever anyone else thinks about my marriage to Isobel, she deserves and *will* get my full honour and respect at all times. Do you understand that?'

'Of course.' For a man who was twice his own age and also his godfather, Takis Konstantindou suddenly looked very much the wary employer as he gave a nod of his silvered head. 'It never crossed my—'

'Find out what you can before we meet with her,' Leandros interrupted, glanced at his watch and was relieved to see he was due at a meeting elsewhere so could end this conversation.

He stood up. Takis took his cue without further comment and went off to do his bidding. Leandros waited until the door closed behind him, then threw himself back down into his chair. He knew he was behaving irrationally. He understood why Takis no longer understood just where it was he was coming from. Only two weeks ago Leandros had called up his godfather and informed him he wanted to file for divorce. It had been a brief and unemotional conversation to which Takis had responded in the same brisk, lawyer-like way.

But a few weeks ago, in his head, Isobel had been a witch and a hellion with barbs for teeth. Now, on the back of one small comment she was the young and vulnerable creature he had dragged by the scruff of her beautiful neck out of sensual heaven into the hell of Athenian society.

On a thick oath he stood up again, paced around his desk. What was going on here? he asked himself. What was the matter with him? Did he have to come over all macho and feel suddenly protective because there was a chance that the Isobel he would meet tomorrow was going to be a shadow of the one he once knew?

A wheelchair.

Another oath escaped him. The phone on his desk began to ring. It was Diantha, gently reminding him that his mother would prefer him not to be late for dinner tonight. The tension eased out of his shoulders, her soft, slightly amused tone showing sympathy with his present plight where his mother was concerned. By the time the conversation ended he was feeling better—much more like his gritty, calm self.

Yes, he confirmed. Diantha was good for him. She refocused his mind on those things that should matter, like the meeting he should be attending right now.

'You're asking for trouble dressed like that,' Silvia Cunningham announced in her usual blunt manner.

Isobel took a step back to view herself in the mirror. 'Why, what's wrong with it?' All she saw was a perfectly acceptable brown tailored suit with a skirt that lightly hugged her hips and thighs to finish at a respectable length just below her slender knees. The plain-cut zip-up jacket stopped at her waist and beneath it she wore a staunchly conventional button-through cream blouse. Her hair was neat, caught up in a twist and held in place by a tortoise-shell comb. She was wearing an unremarkable flesh-coloured lipstick, a light dusting of eye-shadow and some black mascara, but that was all.

In fact she could not look more conservative if she tried to be, she informed that hint of a defiant glint she could see burning in her green eyes.

'What's wrong with that suit is that it's an outright prov-ocation,' her mother said. 'The wretched man never could keep his hands off you at the worst of times. What do you think he's going to want to do when you turn up wearing a suit with a definite slink about it?'

'I can't help my figure!' Isobel flashed back defensively. 'It's the one you gave to me, along with the hair and the eyes.'

'And the temper,' Silvia nodded. 'And the wilful desire to let him see what it is he's passing up.'

'Passing up?' Those green eyes flashed. 'Do I have to remind you that I was the one who left him three years ago?'

'And he was the one who did not bother to come and drag you back again.'

Rub it in, why don't you? Isobel thought. 'I haven't got time for this,' she said and began searching for her hand-bag. 'I have a meeting to go to.'

'You shouldn't be going to this meeting at all!'

'Please don't start again.' Isobel sighed. They had al-ready been through this a hundred times.

'I agree that it is time to end your marriage, Isobel,' her mother persisted none the less, 'and I am even prepared to admit that the letter from Leandros's lawyer brought the best news I'd heard in two long years!'

Looking at the way her mother was struggling to stand with the aid of her walking frame, Isobel understood where she was coming from when she said that.

'But I still think you should have conducted this busi-

ness through a third party,' she continued, 'and, looking
at the way you've dressed yourself up, I am now absolutely
positive that coming face to face with him is a mistake!'

'Sit down—please,' Isobel begged. 'Your arms are shaking. You know what they said about overdoing it.'

'I will sit when you stop being so pig-stubborn about
this!'

A grin suddenly flashed across Isobel's face. 'Pot calling
the kettle black,' she said.

Her mother's mouth twitched. If Isobel ever wanted to
know where she got her stubbornness from then she only
had to look at Silvia Cunningham. The hair, the eyes, even
her strength of will came from this very determined
woman. Though all of those features in her mother had
taken a severe battering over the last two years since a
dreadful car accident. Silvia was recovering slowly, but the
damage to her spine had been devastating. Fortunately—
and her mother was one for counting her blessings—her
mind was still as bright as a polished button and unwav-
eringly determined to get her full mobility back.

But Sylvia had a tendency to overdo it. Only a few
weeks ago she had taken a bad fall. She hadn't broken
anything but she'd bruised herself and severely shaken her
confidence. It had also shaken Isobel's confidence about
leaving her alone throughout the day while she was at
work. Then Leandros's letter had arrived to make life even
more complicated. It had been easier to just bring Silvia
with her than to leave her behind then worry sick for every
minute she was away from her.

On a tut of impatience Isobel went to catch up the nearest chair and settled it behind her mother's legs. Silvia
lowered herself into it without protest, which said a lot
about how difficult she'd been finding it to stand. But that
was her mother, Isobel thought as she bent to kiss her

smooth cheek. She was a fighter. The fact that she was still of this world and able to hold her own in an argument was proof of it.

'Look,' Isobel said, coming down to her mother's level and moving the walking frame out of the way so that she could claim her hands. 'All right, I confess that I've dressed like this for a reason. But it has nothing to do with trying to make Leandros regret this divorce.' It went much deeper than that, and her darkened eyes showed it. 'He did nothing but criticise my taste in clothes. When he did, I was just too stubborn to make even one small concession to his opinion of what his wife should look like, wear or behave.'

'Quite right too.' Her beautiful, loyal mother nodded. 'Pretentious oaf.'

'Well, I mean to show him that when I have the freedom to choose what the heck I want to wear, then I can be as conventional as anyone.'

A pair of shrewd old eyes looked into their younger matching pair, and saw cracks a mile wide in those excuses just waiting for her daughter to fall right in.

A knock sounded at the door. It would be Lester Miles, Isobel's lawyer. With a hurried smile, Isobel got up to leave. But her mother refused to let go of her hand.

'Don't let him hurt you again,' she murmured urgently.

Isobel's sudden flash of annoyance took Silvia by surprise. 'Whatever else Leandros did to me, he *never* set out to hurt me, Mother.' *Mother* said it all. For Silvia was *Mum* or *sweetheart*, but only ever *Mother* when she was out of line. 'We were in love, but were wrong for each other. Learning to accept that was painful for us both.'

Silvia held her tongue in check and accepted a second kiss on her cheek while Isobel wondered what the heck she was doing defending a man whose treatment of her had been so indefensible!

What was the matter with her? Was it nerves? Was she more stressed about this meeting than she was prepared to admit? Hurt her? What else could Leandros do that could hurt her more than he'd already done three years ago?

Another knock at the door and she was turning towards it, her mind in a sudden hectic whirl. She tried to fight it, tried to stay calm. 'What are you going to do while I'm out?' she asked as she walked towards the door.

'Clive has hired a car. We are going to do some sight-seeing.'

Clive. Isobel's mouth tightened. There was another point of conflict she had not yet addressed. Clive Sanders was their neighbour and very good friend. He was also what Isobel supposed she could call the new man in her life. Or that was what he could be if Isobel gave Clive the green light.

Clive had somehow managed to invite himself along on this trip—aided and abetted by her mother, she was sure. The first she'd known about it was when she'd been in the hotel foyer last night and happened to see him arrive. Clive had just smiled at her burst of annoyance, touched a soothing hand to her angry cheek and said innocently, 'I am here for your mother. You're supposed to be pleased by the surprise, you ungrateful thing.'

But she had been far from pleased or grateful. Too many people seemed to believe they had a right to interfere in her life. Clive insisted the trip to Athens fitted in with his plans for a much-needed break. Her mother insisted it made her feel more secure to have a man like Clive around. Isobel thought there was a conspiracy between the two of them, which involved Clive keeping an eye on her in case she went totally off the rails when she met up with Leandros again.

But she knew differently. For all that she'd just defended Leandros, she knew there was not a single chance that seeing him was going to send her toppling back into the madness of their old love affair. She didn't hate him, but she despised him for the way he had treated her. He'd killed her confidence and her spirit and, finally, her love.

'Don't let him tire you out,' was her clipped comment to Silvia about Clive's presence here.

'He's a fully trained physiotherapist,' Silvia pointed out. 'Give him the benefit of some sense.' Which was her mother's way of making it known that she knew Isobel disapproved of him being here. 'And Isobel,' Silvia added as she was about to pull the door open, 'a brown leather suit is not conventional by any stretch of the imagination, so stop kidding yourself that you're out to do anything but make that man sit up and take note.'

Isobel left the room without bothering to answer, startling Lester Miles with the abruptness with which she appeared. His eyes widened then slid down over the leather suit before carefully hooding in a way that told her he thought her attire inappropriate too.

Maybe it was. Her chin went up. Suddenly she was fizzing like a simmering pot ready to explode because her mother was right—she was out to blow Leandros right out of his shoes.

'Shall we go?' she said.

Lester Miles just nodded and fell into step beside her. He was young and he was eager and she had picked him out at random from the Yellow Pages. Yes, she was dressed for battle, because she didn't think she needed a lawyer to fire her shots for her—though she was happy for him to come along and play the stooge.

For today was redemption day. Today she intended to take back all of those things that Leandros had wrenched from her and walk away a whole person again. She didn't want his money or to discuss *settlements*. She had nothing he could want from her, unless he planned to fight over a gold wedding ring and a few diamond trinkets that had made his mother stare in dismay when she'd found out that her son had given them to Isobel.

Family heirlooms, she recalled. 'A bit wasted on you, don't you think?' his sister Chloe had said. But then, dear Mama and Chloe had not been in the bedroom when the precious heirlooms had been her only attire. They'd not seen the way their precious boy had decked out his wife in every sparkle he could lay his hands on—before he enjoyed the pleasure they gave.

Those same heirlooms still lay languishing in a safety deposit box right here in Athens. Leandros was welcome to them as far as she was concerned. It was going to be interesting to discover just what he was willing to place on the table for their safe return—before she told him she wanted nothing from him, then gave him back his damned diamonds and left with her pride!

The journey across Athens in a taxi took an age in traffic that hardly seemed to move. Lester Miles kept on quizzing her as to what was required of him, but she answered in tight little sentences that gave him no clue at all.

'You are in such a powerful position, Mrs Petronades,' he pointed out. 'With no pre-nuptial agreement you are entitled to half of everything your husband owns.'

Isobel blinked. She hadn't given a single thought to a pre-nuptial agreement or the lack of one, come to that. Was this why Leandros wanted to see her personally? Was he out to charm her into seeing this settlement thing from his point of view? The stakes had quite suddenly risen. A few family heirlooms didn't seem to matter any more when you put them in the giant Petronades pot of gold.

'Negotiations will stand or fall on which of you wants this divorce more,' Lester Miles continued. 'As it was your husband who instigated proceedings, I think we can safely say that power is in your hands.'

'You've done your homework,' she murmured.

'Of course,' he said. 'It is what you hired me to do.'

'Does that mean you might know *why* my husband has suddenly decided he wants this divorce?' she enquired curiously.

'I have not been able to establish anything with outright proof,' the lawyer warned her, then looked so uncomfortable Isobel felt that fizz in her stomach start up again. 'But I do believe there is another woman involved. She goes by the name of Miss Diantha Christophoros. She is from one of the most respected families in Greece, my sources tell me...'

His sources couldn't be more right, Isobel agreed as she shifted restlessly in recognition of the Greek beauty's name. A union between the Petronades and Christophoros families would be the same as founding a dynasty. Mama Petronades must be so very pleased.

'She spent some time with your husband on his yacht recently,' her very efficient lawyer continued informatively. 'Also, your brother-in-law—Nicolas Petronades— will be marrying Carlotta Santorini next week. Rumour has it that once his brother is married your husband would like to follow suit. It could be an heir thing,' he suggested. 'Powerful families like the Petronades prefer to keep the line of succession clear cut.'

An heir thing, Isobel repeated. Felt tears sting the backs of her eyes and the fizz happening inside her turn to an angry ache.

To hell with you, Leandros, she thought bitterly.

CHAPTER TWO

To HELL with you, Isobel repeated fifteen minutes later, when finally they came face to face in the elegant surroundings of Leondros's company boardroom with all its imposing wood panelling and fancy portraits of past masters.

Here stood the latest in a long line of masters, she observed coldly. Leandros Petronades, lean, dark and as arrogant as ever. A man built to break hearts, as she should know.

He stood six feet two inches tall and wore a grey suit, white shirt and a grey silk tie that drew a line down the length of a torso made up of tensile muscle wrapped in silk-like bronze skin. He hadn't changed, not so much as an inch of him; not the aura of leashed power beneath the designer clothing, or the sleek, handsome structure of his face. His hair was still that let-me-touch midnight-black colour, his eyes dark like the richest molasses ever produced, and his mouth smooth, slim, very masculine—the mouth of a born sensualist.

She wanted to reach out and slap his face. She wanted to leap on him and beat at his adulterous chest with her fists. The anger, the pain, the black, blinding pulse of emotional fury was literally throbbing along her veins. It was as if the last three years hadn't happened. It could have been yesterday that she had walked out of his life. Diantha Christophoros of all women, she was thinking. Diantha, the broken-hearted one who had had to be taken out of

26

Athens by her family when Leandros arrived there with his shocking new wife.

Did he think she didn't know about her? Did he really believe his awful sister would have passed up the opportunity to let her know what he had thrown away in the name of hot sex? Did he think Chloe would have kept silent about the trips he made to Washington D.C. to visit his broken-hearted ex?

I hate you, her eyes informed him while the anger sang in her blood. She didn't speak, she didn't want to. And as they stared at each other along half the length of his impressive boardroom table the silence screamed like a banshee in everyone's ears. His uncle Takis was there but she refused to look at him. Lester Miles stood somewhere behind her, watchful and silent as the grave. Leandros didn't make a single move to come and greet her, his dark eyes drifting over her as if they were looking at a snake.

Well, that just about says it all, she thought coldly. His family has finally managed to indoctrinate him into their speciality of recognising dross.

Having just watched his wife of four years walk into his boardroom—and scanned her sensational legs—Leandros was held paralysed by the force of anger which roared up inside him like a lion about to leap.

So much for killing himself by imagining her a mere shadow of her former self, he was thinking bitterly. So much for feeling that overwhelming sense of relief when he'd found out it was not Isobel who was confined to a wheelchair but her mother—then feeling the guilt of being relieved about something so painfully tragic, whoever the victim! Silvia Cunningham had been a beautiful woman, full of life and energy. To think of that fine spirit that she had passed on to her daughter now quashed into a wheelchair had touched him deeply.

He was in danger of laughing out loud at his latest plan to make sure that Isobel's mother was provided for within the settlement. Indeed that plan was not about to change because of what he now knew.

Only his plans for this beautiful, adulterous creature standing here in front of him, with her glossed-back hair, spitting green eyes and tight little mouth with its small upper lip and protruding bottom lip that made him want to leap on it and bite.

Where only hours ago he had been content to be unbelievably kind and gentle. He now wanted to tear her limb from limb.

Four years—for four long years this woman had lived inside him like a low, throbbing ache. He'd felt guilt, he'd felt sadness, he'd wanted to accord her the respect he'd believed she deserved from him by making no one aware of his plans to remarry until he had eased himself out of this marriage in the least hurtful way that he could.

But that was until he discovered that his wife was suffering from no such feelings of sensitivity on his behalf, for she had brought her lover with her to Athens! Could she not manage for two days without the oversized brute? Did he satisfy her, did he know her as intimately as he did? Could he make her tremble from her toes to her fingertips and cry out and grab for him as she reached her peak?

Cold fury sparked from his eyes as he looked her over. Bitterness raked its claws across his face. She was wearing leather. Why leather? What was it she was aiming to prove here, that she was brazen enough to wear such a fabric— bought with his money, no doubt—but worn to please another man?

'You're late,' he incised, flicking hard eyes up to a face that was even more treacherously perfect than he remembered it. The gentle hairline, the dark-framed eyes, the straight little nose and that provoking little mouth. A mouth that knew how to kiss a man senseless, how to latch on to his skin and drive him out of his mind. He'd seen the oversized blond brute with the affable smile, standing in the hotel foyer wearing cotton sweats and touching her as if he had every right.

He should not have gone there. He should not have been so anxious to find out the truth about the wheelchair, then he would not have had to witness that man touching his wife in full view of anyone who wanted to watch.

His wife! Touching *his* wife's exquisite, smooth white skin, making that skin flush when it only used to flush like that for him! She had not been wearing leather then, but tight jeans and a little white top that showed the fullness of her beautiful breasts!

Her wonderful hair had been flowing down her back, not pinned up as if she was some little prude. A lying prude, he extended.

'This meeting was due to begin fifteen minutes ago. Now we will have to keep it brief,' he finished his cutting comment.

Then watched as her witch's green eyes narrowed at his clipped, tight tone. 'The traffic was bad—'

'The traffic in Athens is always bad,' he inserted dismissively. 'You have not been away from this city for so long that you could have forgotten that. Please take a seat.'

He took a seat. He pulled out a chair at random and threw himself into it with a force that verged on insolence. Takis was frowning at him but he ignored this lawyer's expression. The other lawyer was trying not to show anything, though Leondros could see he was thoroughly engrossed.

Perhaps fascinated was a better word, he decided as he

studied his wife's lawyer through glassed-over eyes. The man was nothing but a young hawk, still wet behind the ears, he noted with contempt. What was Isobel thinking about, putting a guy like this up against himself and Takis? She knew of his godfather's brutal reputation, she knew of his own! The only thing that Lester Miles seemed to have going for him was the cut of his suit and his boyish good looks.

Maybe that was it, he then thought with a tightening of just about every nerve. Maybe the body-builder was not her only man. Maybe this guy held a different place in her busy private life.

Irritation with himself made him take out his silver pen and begin tapping it against the polished boardroom table while he waited for this meeting to begin. Takis was shaking hands with Lester Miles and trying to appear as if Isobel's husband always behaved like this. Isobel, on the other hand, was walking on those long legs down the length of the boardroom table on the opposing side to his. The leather suit stretched against her slender thighs as she moved and the jacket moulded to the thrust of her breasts. Was she wearing anything beneath it? Did she have the jacket zipped up to her throat simply to taunt him with that question?

Her chin was set, her flesh so white and smooth it didn't look real—but then it never had. She chose to take the seat right opposite him. As she pulled the chair out his gaze moved to the smooth length of her slender neck, then up to the perfect shell-like shape of her ear, and his teeth came together with a snap. One cat-like lick of that ear and all of that cool composure would melt like wax to her dainty feet, he mused lusciously. He knew her, he knew her likes and dislikes, he knew every single erogenous zone, had been the one to take her on that journey of glorious discovery. He knew how to make her beg, cling, cry out his name in a paroxysm of ecstasy. Give him two minutes alone with her and he could wipe away that icy exterior; give him another minute and he could have her naked and begging for him. Or maybe he should be the one to strip his clothes off, he mused grimly. Maybe he should take her on the ride of their lives up against the panelled wall, with her skirt hitched up just high enough for his flesh to enjoy the erotic slide against leather while other parts of him enjoyed a different kind of slide, inside the hot, moist core of her ever-eager body.

It was almost a shame that he wasn't into sexual enhancers, though it suddenly occurred to him that the body-builder looked the type. A new and blistering flash of his recently constructed fantasy now being enacted by the lover sent his eyes black with rage.

She sat down, bent to place her handbag on the floor by her chair, then sat up straight again—and looked him right in the eye. Hostility slammed into his face. His pulse quickened as the glinting green look lanced straight through him and war was declared. Though he wasn't sure which of them had done the declaring.

She had certainly arrived here ready for a battle, though why that was the case he had no idea. It was not as if *he* had done anything other than suggest this divorce. Since it was very clear that she had not spent the last three years pining for him, her hostility was, in his opinion, without cause.

Whereas his own hostility... His narrowed eyes shot warning sparks across the table. She lifted her chin to him and sent the sparks right back. His fingers began to tingle with an urge to do something—they began tapping the pen all the harder against the polished table-top.

What is it you think you are going to get out of this,

you faithless little hellion? he questioned silently as his lips parted to reveal the tight, warning glint of clenched white teeth. You had better be well prepared for this fight, because I am.

She placed her hands down on the table, long white fingers tipped with pink painted fingernails stroked the polished wood surface like a caress. His loins tightened, his chest began to burn. She saw it happen and her upper lip offered a derogatory curl.

Takis took the chair beside him. Lester Miles sat down beside Isobel. She turned to her lawyer and sent him a smile that would have made an iceberg melt. But Lester Miles was no iceberg. As he watched this little byplay, Leandros saw the young fool's cheekbones streak with colour as he sent an answering smile in return.

It's OK, I am here, that smile said to her. Leandros felt the lion inside him roar again. She turned to fix her gaze back on him. I am going to kill you, he told her silently. I am going to reach out and drag you across this table and spoil your little piece of foreplay with the kind of real play that shatters the mind.

'Shall we begin?' Takis opened a blue folder. Lester Miles had a black leather one, smooth, trendy and upwardly mobile. Isobel slid her hands to her lap.

Leandros continued to tap his pen against the desk.

'In the midst of all of this tension, may I begin by assuring you, Isobel, that we have every desire to keep this civil and fair?'

Leandros watched her shift her gaze from his face to Takis. He felt the loss deep in his gut. 'Hello, Uncle Takis,' she said.

It was a riveting moment. Takis froze, so did Lester Miles, glancing up sharply from his trendy black leather dossier to sniff the new tension suddenly eddying in the air. The deeply respected international lawyer of repute, Takis Konstantindou, actually blushed.

He came back to his feet. 'My sincere apologies, Isobel,' he murmured uncomfortably. 'How could I have been so crass as to forget my manners?'

'That's OK,' she replied and, as Takis was about to stretch across the table to offer her his hand, she returned her eyes back to Leandros, leaving Takis suffering the indignity of lowering his hand and returning to his seat.

So she could still twist a room upon its head without effort, Leandros noted. You bitch, he told her silently.

The mocking movement of a slender eyebrow said— Maybe I am, but at least I won't be your bitch for much longer.

The air began to crackle. 'As I was about to say...' clearing his throat, Takis tried again '...with due regard to the sensitivities of both parties, at my client's instruction I have drawn up a draft copy of proposals to help ease us through this awkward part.' Taking out a sheet of paper, he slid it across the table towards Isobel. She didn't even glance at it, but left Lester Miles to pick it up and begin to read. 'As I think you will agree, we have tried to be more than fair in our proposals. The financial settlement is most generous in the circumstances.'

'What circumstances?' her lawyer questioned.

Takis looked up. 'Our clients have not lived together for three years,' he explained.

Three years, one month and twenty-four days, Isobel amended silently, and wished Leandros would stop tapping that pen. He was looking at her as if she was his worst enemy. The tight mouth, the glinting teeth, the ice picks flicking out from stone-cold black eyes, all told her he could not get rid of her quick enough.

It hurt, though she knew it shouldn't. It hurt to see the

way he had been running those eyes over her as if he could not believe he'd ever desired someone like her. So much for dressing for the occasion, she mused bleakly. So much for wanting to blow him out of his handmade shoes.

Lester Miles nodded. 'Thank you,' he said and returned his attention to the list in front of him, and Takis returned to reading out loud the list of so-called provisions. Isobel wanted to be sick. Did they think that material goods were all she was here for? Did Leandros truly believe she was so mercenary?

'When,' she tossed at him, 'did I ever give you the impression that I was a greedy little gold-digger?'

Black lashes that were just too long for a man lifted away from his eyes. 'You are here, are you not?' he countered smoothly. 'What other purpose could you have in mind?'

Isobel stiffened as if he'd shot her. He was implying that she was either here for the money or to try to win him back.

'Both parties have stated that the breakdown in their marriage was due to—irreconcilable differences,' Takis put in swiftly. 'I see nothing to be gained from attempting to apportion blame now. Agreed?'

'Agreed,' Lester Miles said.

But Isobel didn't agree. She stared at the man she had married and thought about the twenty-three hours in any given day when he'd preferred to forget he had a wife. Then, during the twenty-fourth, he'd found it infuriating when she'd chosen to refuse to let him use it to assuage his flesh!

He'd met her, lusted after her, then married her in haste to keep her in his bed. The sex had been amazing, passionate and hot, but when he had discovered there was more to marriage than just sex, he had repented at his leisure *during* the year it had taken her to commit the ultimate sin in the eyes of everyone—by getting pregnant.

Leandros must be the only Greek man who could be horrified at this evidence of his prowess. How the hell did it happen? he'd raged. Don't you think we have enough problems without adding a baby to them? Two and a half months later she'd miscarried and he could not have been more relieved. She was too young. He wasn't ready. It was for the best.

She hated him. It was all coming back to her how much she did. She even felt tears threatening. Leandros saw them and the pen suddenly stopped its irritating tap.

'Your client left my client of her own volition,' Takis was continuing to explain to Lester Miles while the two of them became locked in an old agony. 'And there has been no attempt at contact since.'

Yes, you bastard, Isobel silently told Leandros. You couldn't even bother to come and find out if I was miserable. Not so much as a letter or a brief phone call to check that I was alive!

'By either party?' Lester Miles questioned.

The pen began to tap again, Leandros's lips pressing together in a hardening line. He didn't care, Isobel realised painfully. He did not want to remember those dark hours and days and weeks when she'd been inconsolable and he had been too busy with other things to deal with an over-emotional wife.

'Mr Petronades pays a respectable allowance into Mrs Petronades' account each month but I do not recall Mrs Petronades acknowledging it,' Takis said.

'I don't want your money,' Isobel sliced across the table at Leandros. 'I haven't touched a single penny of it.'

'Not my problem,' he returned with an indifferent shrug.

'Now we come to the house in Hampshire, England,'

Takis determinedly pushed on. 'In the interests of goodwill this will be signed over to Mrs Petronades as part of the—'

'I don't want your house, either,' she told Leandros.

'But—Mrs Petronades. I don't—'

'You will take the house,' Leandros stated without a single inflexion.

'As a conscience soother for yourself?'

His eyes narrowed. 'My conscience is clear,' he stated.

She sat back in her chair with a deriding scoff. He dropped the pen then snaked forward in his chair, his black eyes still fixed on her face. 'But why don't you tell me about your conscience?' he invited.

'Leandros, I don't think this is getting us—'

'Keep your house,' Isobel repeated. 'And keep whatever else you've put on that list.'

'You want nothing from me?'

'Nothing—' Isobel took the greatest pleasure in confirming.

'Nothing that is on this list!' Lester Miles quickly jumped in as a fresh load of tension erupted around them. Leandros was looking dangerous, and Isobel was urging him on. Takis was running a fingertip around the edge of his shirt collar because he knew what could happen when these two people began taking bites out of each other.

'Mrs Petronades did not sign a pre-nuptial agreement,' Lester Miles continued hurriedly. 'Which means that she is entitled to half of everything her husband owns. I see nothing like that amount listed here. I think we should…'

Leandros flashed Lester Miles a killing glance. If the young fool did not keep his mouth shut he would help him. 'I was not speaking to you,' he said and returned his gaze to Isobel. 'What is it is that you do want?' he prompted.

Like antagonists in a new cold war they faced each other

across the boardroom table. Anger fizzed in Isobel's brain, and bitterness—a blinding, stinging, biting hostility—had her trembling inside. He had taken her youth and optimism and crushed them. He had taken her love and shredded it before her eyes. He had taken her right to feel worthy as the mother of his child and laughed at it. Finally, he had taken what was left of her pride and been glad to see the back of her.

She'd believed there was nothing else he could do to hurt her. She'd actually come here to Athens ready to let go of the past and leave again hopefully feeling whole. But no. If just one name had the ability to crush her that bit more, then it would be that of Diantha Christophoros.

For that name alone, if she only could reach him she would scratch his eyes out; if she could wrestle him to the ground she would trample all over him in her spike heels.

But she had to make do with lancing him with words. 'I don't want your houses, and I don't want your money,' she informed him. 'I don't want your name or you, come to that. I don't even want your wedding ring…' Wrenching it off her finger, she slid it across the table towards him, then bent and with a snatch caught up her bag. 'And I certainly don't want your precious family heirlooms,' she added, holding her three witnesses silent as she took a sealed envelope out of the bag and launched it to land beside the ring. 'In there you will find the key to my safety deposit box, plus a letter authorising you to empty it for yourself,' she informed Leandros. 'Give them to your next wife,' she suggested. 'They might not be wasted on her.'

Leandros did not look anywhere but at her face while she spat her replies at him. 'So I repeat,' he persisted, 'what is it that you do want?'

'A divorce!' she lanced back through tear-burned eyes. 'See how much you are worth to me, Leandros? All I want is a nice quick divorce from you so that I can put you right out of my life!'

'Insult me one more time, and you might not like the consequences,' he warned very thinly.

'What could you do to me that you haven't already done?' she laughed.

Black eyes turned into twin lasers. 'Show you up for the tramp you are by bringing your muscle-building lover into this?'

For a moment Isobel did not know what he was talking about. Then she issued a stifled gasp. 'You've been having me watched!' she accused.

'Guilty as charged,' he admitted and sat back indolently, picked up the pen again and began weaving it between long brown fingers. 'Adultery is an ugly word,' he drawled icily. 'I could drag you, your pride and your lover through the courts if you wish to turn this into something nasty.'

Nasty. It had *always* been nasty since the day she'd married him. 'Do it, then,' she invited. 'I still won't accept a single Euro from you.'

With that she stood up and, to both lawyers' deepening bewilderment, snatched up her bag and turned to leave.

'Isobel, please—' It was Takis who tried to appeal to her.

'Mrs Petronades, please think about this—?' Lester Miles backed him up.

'Get out of here, the pair of you,' Leandros cut across the two other men. 'Take one more step towards that door, Isobel, and you know I will drag you back and pin you down if necessary.'

Her footsteps slowed to a reluctant standstill. She was trembling so badly now she actually felt sick. In the few seconds of silence that followed she actually wondered if the two lawyers were about to caution him.

But no, they weren't that brave. He was bigger than them in every way a man could be. Height, size—bloody ego. They both slunk past her with their heads down, like two rats deserting a sinking ship.

The door closed behind them. They were alone now. She spun on her slender heels, her eyes like glass. 'You are such a bully,' she said in disgust.

'Bully.' He pulled a face. 'And you, my sweet, are such an angelic soul.'

The *my sweet* stiffened her backbone. He had only ever used the endearment to mock or taunt. He was still flicking that wretched pen around in his fingers. His posture relaxed like a big cat taking its ease. But she wasn't fooled. His mouth was thin, his eyes glinting behind those carefully lowered eyelashes, his jaw rigid, teeth set. He was so angry he was literally pulsing with it beneath all of that idleness.

'Tell me about Clive Sanders.'

There was the reason for it.

She laughed, it was that surreal. He dared to demand an explanation from her after three years of nothing? Walking back to the table, she leaned against it, placed the flat of her palms on its top then looked him hard in the face. 'Sex,' she lied. 'I'm good at it, if you recall. Clive thinks so too. He...'

The table was no obstacle. He was around it before she could say another word. The cat-like analogy had not been conjured up out of nowhere; when he pounced he did it silently. In seconds she was lying flat on her back with him on top of her, and in no seconds at all she was experiencing a different kind of sensation.

This one involved his touch and his weight and his lean, dark features looming so close that her tongue actually moistened with an urge to taste. It was awful. Memories of never holding back whenever he was this close. Memories of passion and desire and need neither had bothered to hold in check.

'Say that again, from this position,' he gritted.

'Get off me.' In desperation she began pushing hard against his shoulders, but the only things that moved were her clenched fists slipping against the smooth cloth of his jacket. She could feel the heat of his body, its power and its promise.

'Say it!' he rasped.

Her eyes flashed like green lightning bolts filled with contempt for everything he stood for. His anger, his arrogance, his ability to make her feel like this. 'I don't have to *do* anything for you any more, *ever*,' she lashed at him.

He released a hard laugh that poured scorn onto her face. 'Sorry to disappoint you, angel, but you still do plenty for me,' and he gave a thrust of his hips so she would know and understand.

Shock brought the air from her lungs on a shaken whisper. 'You're disgusting,' she gasped.

But no more than she was, when the cradle of her own hips moved in response and that oh, so damning animal instinct to mate dragged a groan from her lungs.

He laughed again, huskily, then reached up to tug the comb from her hair. 'There,' he growled as red fire uncoiled across his fingers, 'now you look more like the little wanton I married. All we need to do now is see how wanton,' and his fingers moved down to deal with the jacket zip. The leather slid apart to reveal her neat cream blouse with its pearly buttons up to her throat. Whatever the blouse was supposed to say to him, she did not expect the flaming clash of her eyes with his, as if she'd committed some terrible sin.

'Why the sexy leather?' he demanded. 'Why the prim

hairstyle and a blouse my mother would refuse to wear? What are you trying to prove, Isobel?' he lanced down at her. 'That there are different kinds of sexual provocation? Or is this the way you've learned to dress for your new lover? Does he like to peel you, layer by exquisite layer, is that it?'

'Yes,' she hissed into his hard face. 'The more layers I have on the more I excite him! Whereas you lacked the finesse to notice me at all unless I was already naked in bed and thoroughly convenient for a quick lay!'

The *quick lay* struck right at his ego. Both saw the blistering flashback of his last urgent groping before she'd left him for good. Sparks flew, heat, pain then an anguish that coiled a sound inside his throat.

'You bitch.' The sound arrived in a hoarse whisper.

He'd gone pale and tears were suddenly threatening her again. On a thick whimper she tried to dislodge him with the pushing thrust of her body, making leather squeak against polish wood and the heels of her shoes come close to scoring deep marks in the wood.

'Let me go!' she choked out helplessly. He caught the sound with his mouth and his tongue, and a full onslaught followed of someone who needed to assuage what she had just flung up into his face. Within seconds she had lost the will to fight this man who knew exactly how to kiss her senseless and make her cling with the hungry need for more.

One of his hands was in her hair while the other was sliding between their bodies, making her spine arch sensually as the backs of his knuckles skidded over her breasts. The blouse sprang free, he was that deft with buttons, long fingers slid beneath a final covering of flimsy brown lace and claimed her nipple. She groaned in dismay but was already threading her fingers into his hair as she did so, making sure that he didn't break away.

It was all so primitively, physically *basic*! The harried sound of their laboured breathing, the squeak of leather on polished wood. The heat of his lips and the lick of his tongue and the slow, deep, sinuous thrust of his hips against the eager thrust of her own, that even with the thickness of her skirt was pulling her deeper into a morass of desire. If he reached down and touched the naked flesh at her thighs she would be his for the taking; the tingling already happening there was so tight she could barely stop herself from begging for it.

Suddenly she was free. It happened so quickly that she wasn't expecting it. Dizzy, disorientated, she lay there gasping and blinking as he arrived lightly on his feet by the table and between two chairs. She'd forgotten the anger with which he'd started this. But now she remembered, felt tears of humiliation fill her eyes and didn't even bother to fight him when he took hold of her by the waist, lifted her up and swung her to her trembling feet.

He saw the tears, and a sigh rasped from him. 'I hate you,' she whispered shakily. 'You always were an animal.'

'You should not have brought your lover to Athens!' he ground out. 'You insulted me by doing so!'

She responded by instinct. A hand went up, caught him a hard, stinging slap to the side of his face, then she was grabbing up her bag and turning to walk away. Unsteady legs carried her forward, as her trembling fingers hurriedly tried to zip up her jacket—while her hair flowed down her spine like a red-hot flag that proclaimed what they had been doing.

He didn't stop her, which she took as a further insult. When she arrived in the next room the two lawyers stared at her tear-darkened eyes and dishevelled appearance in open dismay.

'Whatever he wants,' she instructed Lester Miles. 'Have him draw up the papers and I'll sign them.'

With that she just kept on walking.

Leandros had never been so angry with himself in a long time. He'd just treated her like a whore and for what reason?

He didn't have one. Not now that sanity had returned, anyway.

Three years.

He couldn't believe his own crassness! Three years apart and he had reacted to the sight of her with her lover as if he'd caught them red-handed in his own bed! She was young and normal and perfectly healthy. She was beautiful and desirable and she had a sex-drive like anyone else! If she had utilised her right to sleep with another man, then what did that have to do with him now?

It had a great deal to do with him, he grimly countered that question. On a dark and primitively sexual level she still belonged to him. Not once in the last three years had he thought about her taking other lovers. How stupid did that make him? Supremely, so he discovered, because from the moment she'd stepped into this room he'd tossed half a century out of the window to become the jealously possessive Greek male.

Then he remembered the expression in her eyes that had brought with it the memory of the last time they had been together. Something thick lurched in his gut and he reeled violently away from what it was trying to make him feel.

Guilty as charged. An animal lacking the finesse of which he was once so very proud. The boardroom door opened as he was splashing a shot of whisky into a glass.

It was Takis. 'She slapped your face,' the lawyer commented, noticing the finger marks standing out on his cheek. 'I suspect that you deserved it.'

Oh, yes, he'd deserved it, Leandros thought grimly and picked up the glass of whisky then stood staring at it. 'What did she say?' he asked grimly.

'Give him anything he wants,' Takis replied. 'I am to draw up the papers and she will sign them. So take my advice, Leandros, and do it now before she changes her mind. That woman is dangerous. Whatever you did to her here has made her dangerous.'

'She admitted it—to my face—that she's sleeping with that bastard,' he said as if it should explain away everything.

To another Greek male maybe it did in some small part. 'Did you tell her that you want this divorce because you already have her replacement picked out and waiting in the wings to become your wife?'

Shock spun him on his heel to stare at Takis. 'Who told you that?' he demanded furiously.

Takis suddenly looked wary. 'I believe it is common knowledge.'

Common knowledge, Leandros repeated silently. Common knowledge put about by whom? His hopeful mother? His matchmaking sister? Or Diantha herself?

Then, no, not Diantha, he told himself firmly. She is not the kind of woman to spread gossip about. 'Gossip is just that—gossip,' he muttered, more to himself than to Takis. 'Isobel will not be here long enough to hear it.'

Did that matter to him? he then had to ask himself, and sighed when he realised that yes, it mattered to him. What was wrong with him? Another sigh hissed from him. Why was he feeling like this about a woman he hadn't wanted in years?

He detected a pause, one of those telling ones that

grabbed your attention. He glanced at Takis; saw his expression. 'What?' he prompted sharply.

'She knows,' he told him. 'Her lawyer mentioned the Christophoros name before he went after Isobel.'

Leandros felt his mind go blank for a split-second. She cannot know, he tried to convince himself.

'The guy knew quite a lot as a matter of fact,' Takis went on and there was surprise and reluctant respect in the tough lawyer's voice. 'He knew that Diantha spent time alone with you on your yacht in Spain, for instance. He also mentioned conservative attitudes in Greece to extramarital affairs, then suggested we review the kind of scandal it would cause if two big names such as Petronades and Christophoros were linked in this way in a court battle. He's a clever young man,' Takis concluded. 'He needs watching. I might even use him myself one day.'

Leandros was barely listening. His mind had gone off somewhere else. It was seeing Isobel's face when she'd walked in here, seeing the anger, the hate, the desire to tear him to shreds where he stood.

'Dear God,' he breathed. Where had his head been? Why had he not read the signs? When she hurt she came out fighting. Make her feel vulnerable and expendable and she unsheathed her claws. Let her know she wasn't good enough and she spat fire and brimstone over you then ran for cover as quickly as she could. Let her think she was being replaced with one of Athens' noblest, and you could not hurt her more deeply if you tried.

'The lack of a pre-nuptial is beginning to worry me.' Takis was still talking to a lost audience. 'She could take you to the cleaners if she decided she wanted to roll your name in the mud.'

Turning, Leandros looked at the table where the imprint of her body had dulled the polished wood surface. His stomach turned over—not with distaste for what he had done there but for other far more basic reasons. He could still feel the imprint of her down his front, could still taste her in his mouth.

Not far away, resting where it had landed when she tossed them at him, lay her wedding ring and the envelope containing access to the so-called family heirlooms.

What family heirlooms? he thought frowningly. It was not something his family possessed.

Until today she had still worn her wedding ring, even after three years of no contact with him, he mused on while absently twisting his own wedding ring between finger and thumb. Did a woman do that when she took herself a lover? Did she flout convention so openly?

Ah, the lover, he backtracked slightly. The muscle-building blond with the lover's light touch. His senses began to sizzle, his anger returned. Getting rid of the whisky glass, he walked up to the table and picked up the envelope and the ring.

'We need to start moving on this, Leandros,' Takis was prompting him.

'Later,' he said absently.

'Later is not good enough,' the lawyer protested. 'I am telling you as your lawyer that if you want a quick, clean divorce then you have to move now.'

But I don't want a divorce, was the reply that lit up like a halogen light bulb in his head. I want my wife back. *My wife!*

CHAPTER THREE

OUT in the street Isobel hailed a passing taxi, gave the driver the name of her hotel then sank back in her seat with a shaking sigh. Maybe she should have waited for Lester Miles to join her but at this precise moment she didn't want anyone witnessing the state she was in.

'You OK, *thespinis*?' the taxi driver questioned.

Glancing up, she saw the driver studying her through his rear-view mirror, his brown eyes clouded by concern.

Did she look that bad?

Yes, she looked that bad, she accepted. Inside she was a mass of shakes and tremors. Beneath her zipped-up jacket her blouse was still gaping open and there wasn't an inch of flesh that wasn't still wearing the hot imprint of a man's knowing touch. Her hair was hanging around her pale face and her mouth was hot, swollen and quivering from the kind of assault that should have set her screaming for help but instead she just—

'Yes—thank you,' she replied and lowered her eyes so he wouldn't see just how big a lie that was.

She felt like a whore. Her eyes filmed over. How could he do that to her? What had she ever done to him to make him believe he had the right to treat her that way?

You riled him into doing it is what happened, a deriding little voice in her head threw in. You went in there wanting to rip his unfaithful heart out and ended up with him ripping out yours!

She stared at the fingers of one hand as they rubbed anxiously at the empty place on another finger where her

47

wedding ring had used to be, and tried to decide if she hurt more because of the way he had just treated her, or because she was still flailing around in the rotten discovery that she was still in love with the over-sexed brute!

It had hit her the moment Lester Miles had mentioned a future wife and Diantha Christophoros in the same, soul-destroying breath. Couldn't he have come up with someone fresh instead of picking out his old love to replace her with?

He'd also been having her watched, she suddenly remembered. Had he been that desperate to find a solid reason to bring their marriage crashing down that he'd had to go to such extremes?

I hate him, she thought on a blistering wave of agony. And she did. The two opposing emotions of love and hatred were swilling around inside her in one gigantic, dizzying mix. The man was bad for her. He had always been bad for her. Three years on, she thought wretchedly, and her stupid heart had not learned anything!

The taxi pulled into the kerb outside her hotel. Fumbling in her purse, Isobel unearthed some money to pay the driver then climbed out into the heat of a midday sun. Within seconds she felt as if she was melting, which only made a further mockery of her sanity in coming here to Athens at all *and* wearing leather of all things in this city famous for the oppressive weight of its summer heat.

Her mother had been right; she'd been asking for trouble—and had certainly found it! Returning to her hotel room, she stripped off the wretched suit and walked into the bathroom to shower his touch from her skin.

Never again, she vowed as she scrubbed with a grim disregard for her skin's fragile layers. By the time she had finished drying herself she was tingling all over for a different reason and her mood had altered from feeling destroyed to mulish. If she'd ever needed to be reminded why she left Leandros in the first place then that little scene in his boardroom had done it.

She didn't need a man like him. Let him pour his money into his settlement, she invited, as she dressed in a pair of loose-fitting green cotton trousers and a matching T-shirt. Let him have his divorce so he can marry Diantha Christophoros and produce black-eyed, black-haired little thoroughbreds for his dynasty—

Was that it? Her head shot up, the brush she was using on her hair freezing as she struck at the heart of it. Had Leandros changed his mind about children and decided it was time he made an effort to produce the next Petronades heir?

What was it Lester Miles had said? She tried to remember as she brushed her hair into one long, thick, silken lock. Nikos was getting married. The lawyer called it an heir thing. Nikos might be three years younger than his brother but if Leandros wanted to keep the line of succession clear in his favour, then he needed to get in first with a son.

The tears came back. I would have given him a son. I would have given him a hundred babies if he'd only wanted them. But he didn't, not with me for a mother. He wanted a black-haired Greek beauty with a name exalted enough to match his own.

I'm going to be sick, she thought and had to stand there for a few minutes, fighting the urge as a three-year-old scar ripped open in her chest.

She had to get out of here. The need came with a sudden urgency that left her no room to think. Securing her hair into a simple pony-tail, she snatched up her camera case and slung the strap over her shoulder, slid a pair of sunglasses onto the top of her head then headed for the outer door.

It was only when she stepped out into the hotel corridor that she remembered her mother, and felt guilty because she didn't want to see her right now while she was in this emotional mess. But in all fairness she could not just walk out of here without checking Silvia was back. With a deep breath for courage, she knocked on the door next to her own room. There was no answer. Silvia must still be out with Clive. Relief flicked through her. In the next minute she was riding the lift to the foyer, so eager to escape now that she could barely contain the urge long enough to leave a message for her mother at Reception to let her know what she was doing.

As luck would have it, she was about to step outside when Lester Miles strode in.

'How quickly did they draw up the papers?' she questioned tartly.

'They didn't.' The lawyer frowned. 'Mr Petronades left just after you did.'

To dance attendance on his future bride? Isobel wondered, and felt another burst of bitterness rend a hole in her chest.

'So what happens now?' she asked.

'I am to wait further instruction,' Lester Miles informed her.

'Really?' she drawled. At whose command—Leandros's or Takis Konstantindou's? 'Well, since I am the one you are supposed to take instruction from, Mr Miles, take the afternoon off,' she invited. 'Enjoy a bit of sightseeing and forget about them.'

It was what she intended to do anyway.

'But, Mrs Petronades,' he protested, 'we are due to fly

home tomorrow evening. We really should discuss what it is you want from—'

'I don't want anything,' she interrupted. 'But if this thing can be finished by me accepting everything, then I will.' End of subject, her tight voice intimated. 'They will be back tomorrow with their proposed settlements,' she predicted. 'I'll sign and we will catch our flight home.'

Never to return again, she vowed as she left the poor lawyer standing there looking both puzzled and frustrated. He'd been looking forward to a good fight. He'd had a taste of it and liked it; she'd recognised that in the Petronades boardroom today.

As she stepped outside, the full heat of the sun beat down upon her head. She paused for a moment to get her bearings before deciding to revisit some of her old haunts that did not remind her of Leandros. There were plenty of them, she mused cynically, as she flopped her sunglasses down over her eyes then walked off down the street. While Leandros had played the busy tycoon during her year here in Athens, she had learned to amuse herself by getting to know the city from her own perspective rather than the one her privileged Greek in-laws preferred.

Leandros had just managed to park his car when he saw Isobel step into the street. About to climb out of the vehicle, he paused to watch as she stood for a moment frowning fiercely at everything before she reached up to pull her sunglasses over her eyes, then walked off.

Where was she going? he mused grimly. Why wasn't she sitting in her room sobbing her heart out—as he'd expected her to be?

A stupid notion, he then decided when he took in what she was wearing. It was what he had used to call her battle-dress. When the hair went up in a pony-tail and her camera swung from her shoulder, and those kinds of clothes came out of the closet, his aggravating wife was making a determined bid for escape. How many times had he watched the back of that fine, slender figure disappear into the distance without so much as a word to say where she was going or why she was going there?

His jaw clenched because he knew *why* she had used to disappear like this. It had usually occurred after a row, after she'd asked him for something and he'd snapped at her because he'd been too busy to listen properly, and thought the request petty in the extreme. Guilty conscience raked its sharp claws across his heart. He'd been hell to live with, he recognised that now. He'd done nothing but pick and gripe and shut her up with more satisfying methods. And had never seen how lonely she'd been as she had walked away.

Climbing out of his sleek red Ferrari, he paused long enough to remove his jacket and tie then lock them in the boot. Then he intended to go after her.

But Leandros remembered the lover, and stopped as a whole new set of emotions gripped. Was he still in the hotel? Had she just come from him? Was he receiving the same walk-away treatment because he hadn't listened to what she had been trying to say? Had they rowed about the disaster this morning's meeting had turned into? Had she told the lover that she'd almost made love with her husband on the boardroom table before she walked away? Had *they* made love just now, in there, in that shabby hotel that suited clandestine relationships?

His mind knew how to torment him, he noted, as he slammed the car boot shut.

Where was his mother-in-law while all of this was going on? Was she lying on her sickbed with no idea that her daughter was romping with the body-builder in the next room? Maybe he should go and talk to Silvia. Maybe he should tackle the lover while Isobel was out of the way.

But his mother-in-law was a dish best eaten cold, he recalled with a rueful half-grin at the memory of her blunt tongue. And he wasn't cold right now, he was hot with jealousy and a desire to beat someone to a pulp.

Isobel disappeared around a corner; the decision about whom he was going to tackle first was made there and then. To hell with everyone else, he thought. This was between him and his wife.

It was good to walk. It was good to feel the tension leave her body the deeper she became lost in the tourist crowds. Isobel caught the metro into Piraeus, drank a can of Coke as she walked along the harbour, pausing now and again to snap photos of the local fishermen and their brightly painted boats. She even found her old sense of fun returning when they tossed pithy comments at her, which she returned with a warm grasp of Greek that made them grin in shocked surprise. Most people hated the busy port of Piraeus but she'd always loved it for its rich and varied tapestry of life.

An hour later she had walked to Zea Marina where the private yachts were berthed and ended up getting out of the heat of the sun in Mikrolimano beneath the awning of one of her favourite restaurants that edged the pretty crescent-shaped waterfront. She couldn't eat. It seemed that her stomach was still plagued by a knot of tension even if the rest of her felt much more at peace. But she was content to sit there sipping the rich black Greek coffee while taking in the spectacular views across the Saronic Gulf to the scatter of tiny islands glinting in the sun.

Eventually Vassilou, the restaurant owner, came out to greet her with a warm cry of delight and a welcoming kiss to both cheeks. It was that time of the day when Athens

was at its quietest because most people with any sense
were taking a siesta. The restaurant had very few custom-
ers and Vassilou came to sit beside her with his coffee
while he tested her Greek.

It seemed crazy now, that she'd learned the language
down here with the real people of Athens and not up there
in the rarefied air on Lykavittos Hill, or Kolonáki, where
the wealthy Athenians lived in their luxury villas. No one
up there had thought it worth coaching her in the Greek
language. They spoke perfect English so where was the
need?

The need was sitting right here beside her with his thick
thatch of silver hair and craggy brown face and his gentle,
caring eyes. Not many minutes later they were joined by
a retired sea captain, who began telling her some of his
old sea yarns. Soon the chairs at her small table had dou-
bled along with the circle of men. The restaurant owner's
son brought coffee for them all and sat down himself.

Isobel was relaxed; she was content to sit and be enter-
tained by these warm-hearted people. Despite her nightmare marriage to Leandros, she'd loved Athens—*this*
Athens—and she'd missed it when she returned to London.

Suddenly she sensed someone come to stand behind her
chair. Assuming it was another local, drawn to the little
coffee-drinking group, she didn't think to glance round.
She simply continued to sit there on a rickety chair with
her coffee-cup cradled between her fingers and her smile
one of wicked amusement while she listened—until a hand
settled on her shoulder.

His touch caused a jolt of instant recognition. Her body
froze and she lost her smile. The old sea captain's voice
trailed into silence, and as each set of eyes rose to look at
Leandros she had to watch the warmth die.

Not into frozen shock, she noted, but into looks of respect, the kind men gave to another when they recognised a superior man come down into their midst.

They also understood the gentle claim of possession when they saw it. These shrewd men of Greece understood the light, *'Kalimera,'* when it was spoken with the smoothness of silk. 'I understand now why my wife goes missing,' Leandros drawled lazily. 'She has other suitors with whom she prefers to spend the siesta hours.'

The words were spoken in Greek with the aim to compliment, and Isobel was not surprised when the grins reappeared. Men were always first and foremost men, after all. She sat forward to put down her coffee-cup, though ostensibly the movement was supposed to dislodge his hand. It didn't happen; the long brown fingers merely shifted to curve her nape then he bent and she felt the warmth of his breath brush her jawbone just before the brush of his kiss on her cheek followed suit.

He must know that her expression did not welcome him, but he was trusting her not to reject him here in view of all of these interested eyes. And, oddly, she didn't. Which troubled and confused her as she watched the sudden genial shift of bodies and listened to the light banter that involved excuses as the others left the lovers to themselves while they made a mass chair-scraping exodus to another table.

It took only seconds for her to know she'd been deserted. The reason for that desertion chose one of the vacated chairs and sat down. He didn't look at her immediately but frowned slightly as he gazed into the distance his mouth pressed into a sombre line and the length of his eyelashes hiding his thoughts. He had lost his jacket and tie, she noticed, and the top two buttons to his shirt had been tugged free. He looked different here in the humid weight of natural sunlight, less the hard-headed business tycoon and more the handsome golden-skinned man she had first fallen in love with.

Her heart gave an anxious little flutter. She converted the sensation into a sigh. 'How did you know where to find me?' she asked then added sardonically, 'Still having me watched, Leandros? How quaint.'

The sarcasm made his dark head turn. Their eyes connected, the flutter dropped to her abdomen and she sank back in her chair in an effort to stop herself from being caught in the swirling depths of what those dark eyes could do to her if she let them.

'You speak and understand my language,' he said quietly.

It was not what she had been expecting him to say. But she hid her surprise behind a slight smile. 'What's the matter?' she mocked. 'Did you think your little wife too stupid to learn a bit of Greek?'

'I have never thought you stupid.'

Her answering shrug dismissed his denial. 'Inept and uninterested, then,' which added up to the same thing.

He didn't answer. He was studying her so intently that in the end she shifted tensely and found herself answering the dark question she could see burning in his eyes. 'I have always had a natural aptitude for languages,' she explained. 'And this...' her hand gave a gesture to encompass Piraeus in general '...was my classroom three years ago, where I learned Greek from the kind of people you've just scared off in your polite but esoteric way.'

'Esoteric,' he repeated. 'You little hypocrite,' he denounced. 'I have yet to meet a more esoteric person than you, Isobel, and that is the truth. You lived right here in Athens as my wife for a year. You slept in my bed and ate at my table and circulated on a daily basis amongst my family and friends. Yet not once can I recall you ever

mentioning your trips down here to your *classroom* or revealing to any one of those people who should have been
important to you that you could understand them when
they spoke in Greek.'

'Oh, but I heard so many interesting titbits I would never
have otherwise, if they'd known I understood,' she
drawled lightly.

'Like what?'

Light altered to hard cynicism. 'Like how much they
disliked me and how deeply they wished poor Leandros
would come to his senses and see the little hussy off.'

'You didn't want them to like you,' he denounced that
also. And his eyes threw back the cynical glint. 'You made
no attempt to integrate with anyone who mattered to me.
You just got on with your own secret life, picking and
choosing those people you condescended to like and holding in contempt those that you did not. If that isn't bloody
esoteric then I misunderstand the word.'

'No, you just have a very selective memory,' she replied. 'Because I don't recall a moment when any of those
people you mention cared enough to show an interest in
anything I said or did.'

'Most of them were afraid of you.'

She laughed, that was so ridiculous. His expression
hardened. The anger of this morning's confrontation had
gone, she noticed, but what had taken its place was worse
somehow. It was a mood with no name, she mused, that
hovered somewhere between contempt and dismay. 'You
slayed them with your fierce British independence,' he
continued grimly. 'You sliced them up with your quick,
sharp tongue. You mocked their conservative beliefs and
attitudes and refused to make any concessions for the differences between your cultures and theirs. And you did it
all from a lofty stance of stubborn superiority that only

collapsed when you were in my bed and wrapped in my arms.'

Isobel just sat there and stared as each accusation was lanced at her. Did he really see her as he'd just described her? Did he truly believe everything he'd just said?

'No wonder our marriage barely lasted a year,' she murmured in shaken response to it all. 'You thought no better of me than they did!'

'I loved you,' he stated harshly.

'In that bed you just mentioned,' she agreed in an acid-tipped barb. 'Out of it? It's no darn wonder I came looking for my own world down here where I belonged!'

'I was about to add that unfortunately love is not always blind.' He got in his own sharp dig. 'I watched you cling to your desire to shock everyone. I watched you take on all-comers with the fierce flash of your eyes. But do you know what made all of that rather sad, Isobel? You were no more comfortable with your defiant stance than anyone else was.'

He was right; she'd hated every minute of it. Inside she had been miserable and frightened and terribly insecure. But if he thought that by telling her he knew all of this gave him some high moral stance over her then he was mistaken. Because all it did was prove how little he'd cared when he'd known and had done nothing to help make things easier for her!

Love? He didn't know the meaning of the word. She had loved. She had worshipped, adored and grown weaker with each small slight he'd paid to her, with his *I'm too busy for this* and *Can you not even attempt to take the hand of friendship offered to you?* What hand of friendship? Why had he always had something more important to do than to take some small notice of her? Hadn't he seen how unhappy she was? Had he even cared? Not that she could recall, unless the rows had taken place in their bed at night. Then he'd cared because it had messed with that other important thing in his life—his over-active desire for sex! If she'd sulked, he'd thrown deriding names at her. If she'd said no, he'd taught her how quickly no could be turned into a trembling, gasping yes!

'Talk, instead of sitting there just thinking it!' he rasped at her suddenly.

She looked at him, saw the glint of impatience, detected the pulsing desire to crawl inside her head. Well, too late, she thought bitterly. He should have tried crawling in there three years ago!

'What do you want, Leandros?' she demanded coldly. 'I presume you must have a specific reason for tracking me down—other than to slay my character, of course.'

'I was not trying to slay anything. I was attempting to...' He stopped, his mouth snapping shut over what he had been about to say. 'I wanted to apologise for this morning,' he said eventually.

'Apology accepted.' But as far as Isobel was concerned, that was it. He could go now and good riddance.

He surprised her with a short laugh, shook his dark head then relaxed into his chair. 'Bitch,' he murmured drily.

It was not meant to insult, and oddly she didn't try and turn the remark into one.

Maybe this was a good time for Vassilou to bring them both fresh cups of coffee. He smiled, murmured a few polite pass-the-time-of-day phrases to which Leandros replied. Then, as he was about to leave, he turned back to send Isobel a teasing look. 'You never mentioned your handsome husband to me. Shame on you, *pethi mou*,' he scolded. 'Now see what you have done to my son? His hopes are dashed!'

With that he walked away, leaving her alone to deal with Leandros's new expression. 'Never?' he quizzed.

'For what purpose?' She shrugged. 'Our relationship had no place here.'

'You mean I had no place here—other than to keep eager young waiters at bay, of course,' he added silkily.

Without thinking what she was about to do, Isobel lifted her left hand up with the intention of flashing her wedding ring, which to her made the statement he was looking for without the need of words.

Only the ring wasn't there. Tension sprang up, her ribcage suddenly felt too tight. No ring, no marriage soon, she thought and tugged the hand back onto her lap as an unwanted lump of tears tried to clog up her throat. Leandros looked on with his eyes faintly narrowed and his expression perfectly blank.

'Vassilou was making a joke.' Impatiently she tried to cover up the error.

'I know it was a joke,' he answered quietly.

'Then why have you narrowed your eyes like that?' she flashed back.

'Because the young waiter in question has been unable to take his eyes from you since you sat down at this table.'

'You've been watching for that long, have you? What did you do, hide behind a pillar and take snapshots every time he smiled at me?'

'He smiled a lot.'

She sat forward, suddenly too tense to sit still. She was beginning to fizz inside again, beginning to want to throw things at this super-controlled, super-slick swine! 'Why don't you just go now that you've made your apology?' she snapped, and picked up her coffee-cup.

Those luxurious lashes of his lowered to the cup; he knew what was going through her head. She'd done it before and thrown things at him when he'd driven her to it. Punishment usually followed in the shape of a bed.

But not this time, because she was not going to give him any more excuses to jump on her, she vowed, and took a sip at her coffee. It was hot and she'd forgotten to put the sachet of sugar in that she found necessary when drinking the thick, dark brew the Greeks so liked.

'Where is the lover?'

'What…?' Her head came up, green eyes ablaze because she was at war.

With herself. With him. She didn't know any more what was going on inside. She wished he would go. She didn't want to look at him. She did not want to soak in the way his head and shoulders were in a shaft of sunlight that seeped in through a gap in the striped awning above. She didn't want to see strength in those smooth golden features, or the leashed power in those wide shoulders.

He was gorgeous. A big, dark Latin-hot lover, with a tightly packed body lurking beneath his white shirt that could turn her senses to quivering dust. She could see a hint of black hair curling over the gap where he'd undone the top few buttons of the shirt. She knew how those crisp, curling hairs covered a major part of his lean torso. His rich brown skin was gleaming in the golden sunlight, and the sheen of sweat at his throat beneath the tough jut of his chin was making the juices flow across her tongue.

He was a man whom you wanted taste. To touch all over. A man whom you wanted to touch you. His hands were elegant, strong, long-fingered and aware of what they could do for you. Even now as they rested at ease between the spread of his thighs they were making a statement about his masculinity that sent desire coursing through her blood. His mouth could kiss, his eyes could seduce, his arms could support you while you flailed in the wash of rolling ecstasy the rest of him could give to you.

In other words he was a dark, sensual lover and she suspected one did not need personal experience of that to know it. A few weeks spent on his yacht in Spain and Diantha Christophoros must know it by osmosis. He was not the kind of man to hold back from something he wanted—as *she* knew from experience.

'The blond hunk with the lazy smile,' he prompted. 'Where is he?'

She blinked again and lowered her eyes. Oh, the temptation, she mused, as she stared at her coffee. Oh, the desire to say what was hovering right on the end of her tongue. 'His name is Clive and he's a physiotherapist.' She managed to control the urge to draw verbal pictures of Clive left sleeping off an hour's wild sex.

But her heart was still hammering out the temptation. She heard Leandros utter a soft, mocking little laugh. 'That cost you,' he taunted softly. 'But you had the sense to weigh up the odds of my response.'

'How is Diantha?' she could not resist that one.

Touché, his grimacing nod reflected. 'I have changed my mind about the divorce,' he hit back without warning.

'Well, I haven't!' she responded.

'I was not aware that I gave you a choice.'

'I don't think you have much control over my choice, Leandros,' she drawled witheringly. 'Why have you changed your mind?'

'Simple.' He shrugged, and with a bold lack of conscience lifted his hands enough for her to see what he was talking about. Pure shock sent a whole tidal wave of sensations washing through her.

'You should be ashamed of yourself!' she gasped in stunned reaction as heat poured into her cheeks.

He grimaced as if he agreed. 'I cannot seem to help it. I have been like this since you walked into my boardroom today. So, no divorce,' he explained. 'And definitely no other lovers until I get this problem sorted out.'

The problem being her and his desire for her, Isobel realised with a choke and incredulous disbelief that this was even happening.

'You are so excitingly beautiful,' he murmured as if that justified everything.

'But a bitch,' she reminded him.

'I like the bitch. I always did. It is part of your attraction I find such an irresistible challenge. Like the warning-red hair and the defy-me green eyes and the sulky little mouth that threatens to bite when I step out of line.'

His eyes were dark on her, his tone serious, the fact that he had already stepped out of line all part of what was beginning to burn between them. 'Everything about you I find an outright irresistible challenge,' he continued in a smooth, calm tone that could have been describing the weather, not what turned him on. 'When you walked into my boardroom this morning wearing leather, of all things, and it is thirty degrees out here, it was a challenge. When you sat there spitting hatred at me I don't know how I remained in my chair as long as I did before I leapt. I surprised myself,' he confessed. 'Now you sit here in military-style trousers and a T-shirt with your hair stuck in that pony-tail and you challenge me to crack the tough-nut you are pretending to be.'

'It's no pretence. I am tough,' she declared.

'So am I. And you can leap on me and try scratching my eyes out if you want to, but what *I* want will be the end result.'

'You still haven't told me what you want!' Isobel sliced

back at him. 'I haven't the slightest idea where you think you are going with this!'

'I want you, right at this moment,' he answered without hesitation. 'I thought I had made that absolutely clear. I want to close my mouth around one of those tight button breasts I can see pushing against your tough-lady top and simply enjoy myself,' he informed her outrageously. 'Though I would not protest if you dropped to your knees, unzipped my trousers and enjoyed yourself by taking me into your mouth—only I don't think the setting is quite right for either fantasy.'

'I think you're right, and I've had enough of this.' She got to her feet. 'Go to hell with your fantasies, Leandros.' She turned to leave.

As he'd done once before today, he moved with a silent swiftness that gave her no room to react. His hand curled around her wrist and with the simplest tug he brought her toppling down onto his lap. Her stifled cry of surprise slithered through the humid air and had a table of interested witnesses turning their way.

To them it must look as if she'd dived on Leandros rather than been pulled there, she realised, even as his eyes told her what was coming next.

'Don't you dare,' she tried to say but it was already too late. His mouth crushed the refusal, then began offering an alternative to both his fantasies with the help of his tongue.

It lasted short seconds, yet still she was too lost to understand what was happening when he broke the kiss, then quite brutally sat her back on her own chair again. Dizzy and dazed, flushed and shaken, she watched as he climbed to his feet. For a horrible moment she thought it was him who was going to walk away now and leave her to the humiliating glances.

Was that why he'd come here, tracked her down like

this and said what he had just said, just to pay her back for the way she had walked out on him this morning?

His hand dipped into his trouser pocket then came out again. Something landed on the table with a metallic ping. Money. She began to feel as if she had walked into hell without realising it. Had he thrown money down on the table to pay for the pleasure of treating her like this?

Stinging eyes dropped to stare and took long seconds to comprehend what it was they were staring at. Leandros sat down again. She couldn't breathe or think. Lifting her eyes, she just stared at him, her mouth still pulsing from the pressure of his kiss and her heart beating thickly in her throat.

Yes, Leandros thought with a grim lack of humour as he watched her flounder somewhere between this stunning moment and the kiss. You might be in shock, and you might be unable to believe I've just done what I did in broad daylight and in public view of anyone wanting to watch. But just keep watching this space, my beautiful wife, because I haven't even begun to shock you.

I should have done it years ago. I should have taken you by the scruff of your beautiful, stubborn, *tough*, slender neck and dragged you back into my life.

He was angry. Why was he angry? he asked himself. And knew the answer even before he asked the question. Every time he touched her she fell apart at the very seams with her need for him. Each time their eyes clashed he could see the hurt burning in hers because she was still so in love with him.

Which all added up to three empty, wasted years. Because if he'd faced her with their problems three years ago they would not be sitting here like two damned fools fighting old battles with new words. They would be in a bed somewhere enjoying each other in the traditional

Greek way. There could even have been another child to replace the one they'd lost, sleeping safely in a room close by.

And she would certainly not have let another man touch her! How could she do that anyway? he extended furiously.

'Put it back on,' he instructed, even though he knew she was incapable of doing anything right now.

'I don't—'

'Not your choice.' He was back to choices. 'While you are married to me you will wear my ring.'

'We are about to end our marriage,' she protested. 'What use is a wedding ring in a divorce?'

But even as she made that bitter statement he could see his kiss still clinging to the swollen fullness of her lips. The tip of her tongue could not resist making a sensual swipe across them in an effort to cool their pulsing heat. He mimicked the action with his own tongue, saw her breath shorten and her throat move convulsively. The old vibrations came to dance between them. The air became filled with the heady promise of sex. They had been here before, felt this before. Only then they had been eager to follow where those senses led them.

Now...?

'It means nothing any more,' she said and broke eye contact.

Was she referring to the ring or the sexual pull? he mused, and decided to deal with the former because the latter, he knew, was going to take care of itself in the not too distant future.

Leaning forward, he brought his forearms to rest on the top of the small wooden table, forcing a wary glance from her because she wasn't sure what was coming next. Once he had her gaze, he drew it down with the slow lowering of his lashes and let her watch as he worked his own ring free from his finger then placed it next to hers.

She was so very still he knew she understood what he was doing. The pulse in his throat began to pound. The two rings lay side by side in the sunlight, one large, one small, both an exact match to the other, with their gloss smooth outer surface and the inner circle marked by an inscription that said *My heart is here*.

How could he have forgotten that when he'd stood upon the deck of his yacht in San Estéban complacently making plans to finish their marriage? How could she have forgotten it when she tossed her ring back at him with such contempt earlier today? They had done this together. They had chosen these rings with their arms around each other, and hadn't cared how soft and stupidly romantic they must have appeared as they'd made the decision to have those words inscribed in those inner circles so they would always rest next to their skins!

'Now tell me it means nothing.' He laid down the rasping challenge as he watched her face grow pale. 'If you can bear to walk away and leave your ring on this table, then I will do the same. If you cannot bear to do that, put it back on your finger and we will talk about where we can go from here.'

Her tongue made a foray of her lips again. His teeth came together with a snap to stop him from moving close enough so his own tongue could follow in its wake. She was his, and the sooner she came to accept that the sooner they could work out their problems.

'The divorce—'

'The ring,' he prompted firmly.

She swallowed tensely. The mood began to sizzle with the threat of his challenge and her defiant need to get up and walk away.

But she could not do it. In the end and with a lightning flash of fury, she reached out, snatched her ring up and pushed it back onto her finger.

It went on easily because it belonged there. The next lightning bolt came his way. 'Now what? Do we go back to your office and talk divorce settlements again?'

Her waspish tone didn't hide anything. She was shaking all over and almost on the point of tears. She wanted him. She could not let him go. His ring was back where it belonged and he'd never felt so good about anything in a long time. Picking up his own ring, he slid it back where *it* belonged then sat back with a sigh.

'No,' he answered her question. 'We go somewhere more private where we can talk.'

Her look poured scorn all over that lying suggestion. She knew what he was intending. She was no fool. 'Try again, Leandros,' she murmured bitterly.

'Dinner, then. Tonight,' he came back. 'We will drive out of the city to that place you like in the mountains. Eat good food, drink champagne and reminisce over the good points in our marriage.'

His mockery flicked her temper to life, and he was pleased to see it happen because it was just the mood he was pushing for. Put Isobel in a rage and you had yourself an easy target, because as one guard fell the others quickly followed. So he relaxed back and waited for the sarcastic, What good points? to come slashing back at him. But what he actually got threw him completely.

'Sorry, my darling,' she drawled. 'But I already have a date tonight.'

Just like that it was his own temper deserted him. The lion inside him roared. He retaliated with swift and cruelly cutting incision. 'And there I was about to break my date with Diantha for you. But—no matter, you may bring your lover; we will make it a foursome. Maybe we will go home with different partners. Who knows?' He added a casual shrug. 'Maybe I will ache like this for Diantha and all my problems will be solved.'

He knew the moment he had shut his mouth that he had made some terrible tactical mistake. She'd gone so white he thought she might be going to faint away on him and her eyes stood out like two deep green pits of pain. She was standing up, not in anger, but on legs that did not wish to support her.

'I was referring to my mother,' she breathed, and this time she did walk away.

CHAPTER FOUR

YOU little liar, Isobel accused as she made good her escape. You meant what he thought you meant. What you didn't expect was the counter-thrust that punched another hole in your stupid heart!

But he wasn't coming after her, which probably meant they were back to square one, she thought heavily. Why am I here? Why am I letting him get to me like this? A three-year long separation should have dulled these wretched emotions out of existence!

The hotel was only a short walk away but by the time she arrived there she had the beginnings of a headache, so the last thing she needed was to walk into the hotel foyer and straight into a bored and weary reception party. Her mother, Clive and Lester Miles were all sitting on the few comfortable chairs the dingy foyer possessed. On a low table in front of them lay the remains of an indifferent-looking afternoon tea.

'Where have you been?' her mother demanded the moment she saw her. 'I've been worrying myself sick about you.'

'But I left you a message at Reception,' she said frowningly as she walked towards them.

'I got your message, Isobel,' her mother said impatiently. ' "*I've gone out for while,*" does not really cover a three-hour disappearance, does it? Having dragged me all the way to Athens, I did think you would have spared a little time to be with me.'

'But I thought...' she began, then changed her mind.

Her mother was right and attempting to shift responsibility on to the fact that Clive was supposed to be taking her out for the day wasn't good enough. Especially when it only took a glance at Clive to know he was wishing he hadn't invited himself along on this trip.

'I'm sorry,' she murmured, and bent to press a contrite kiss on her mother's cheek. It felt warm and she looked flushed. It occurred to her that they all looked flushed. Clive was sweating and Lester Miles had lost his suit jacket and tie and was fanning himself with an ancient-looking magazine.

It was then that she realised the air-conditioning wasn't working, and that it was as warm inside as it was out.

'It's broken,' Clive offered, noticing the way she'd glanced up at the air-conditioning vents set in the walls.

Broken, Isobel echoed wearily. No wonder her mother was cross. She had promised her faithfully that the hotel would be cool when she'd bullied her into coming here with her. With a deep breath she braced herself. 'Look,' she said. 'Why don't we go upstairs and all take a nice shower, then we can find somewhere to—?'

'We can't go upstairs, either.' It was Lester Miles that spoke this time. 'The lift has broken down as well.'

'As well?' she gasped. 'You have to be joking.'

'Nope.' It was Clive again. 'We are in the middle of a power cut, in case you haven't noticed. No lights, no air-conditioning and no lift,' he pointed out. 'Apparently it happens all the time.'

'So you tell me, Isobel,' Silvia said crossly, 'how a wheelchair-bound, feeble woman climbs four flights of stairs to get her much-needed cool shower?'

I don't know, she thought, and wondered what they would do if she plonked herself down on the floor and had a good weep? Nothing had gone according to plan from the moment she'd left here this morning. She wished she hadn't come to Athens. She wished she was still at home in rainy England, plodding away at her mundane photo-imaging job! She certainly wished she hadn't had to set eyes on Leandros again. He cut her up, he always had done. She lost her calm and steady sense of proportion whenever she was around him.

'You two men don't have to stay down here if you pre-fer to go and cool off in your rooms,' she murmured a trifle unsteadily. 'I'll see if Mum and I can find—'

'Trust me, Isobel,' Clive put in deridingly, 'we are sit-ting in the coolest place right now.'

'This place is a dump,' her mother added.

'I'm sorry,' her daughter apologised once again, real-izing she *was* going to cry. She placed a hand to her aching head and tried to think. 'Just give me a few minutes—all of you—and I'll see if I can find us another hotel to—'

'Is there a problem here?' another, deeper voice in-serted.

If it was possible, Isobel's spirits sank even lower as she turned with fatalistic slowness to face her nemesis. Leandros didn't look hot, she noticed. He didn't look any-thing but cool and smooth, suave and handsome and...

'What are you doing here?' It was her mother who asked the abrasive question.

'And good day to you, too, Silvia.' Leandros smiled, but his eyes remained fixed on Isobel's pale face. 'What's wrong?' he asked her gently.

Gentle did it. Her mouth began to wobble. The tears bulged in her eyes. 'I...' She tried to think but found that she couldn't. 'I...' She tried to speak again and couldn't even do that. It wasn't fair. *He* wasn't fair. He'd spun her round in circles until she didn't know what she was doing any more.

Leandros's hand came out in front of him. She saw he was holding her camera case out by its strap. She must have left it at Vassilou's restaurant. Maybe she'd left her courage there too. She reached out to take the camera back, missed the strap and found herself clutching at a solid male wrist instead. He didn't even hesitate, but just used her grip to propel her towards him and the next moment her face was pressed into his shoulder and she stayed there, not even caring who watched her sink so easily into the enemy.

One of his hands was gently cupping her nape; the other just as gently curved her waist. The camera was knocking against the back of her leg and her fingers were clutching at a piece of his shirt. He felt strong and reassuringly familiar and, though she did not want to feel it, there was not another place that she would rather be right now.

Someone was talking, someone was tutting. Someone else was also sobbing quietly and she knew it was her. He didn't speak. He just stood there and held her and listened.

Then she heard her mother snap, 'This it is all your fault, Leandros.'

'Quite,' he agreed, the single word vibrating in his deep chest and against Isobel's hot forehead. 'Mr Miles,' he spoke to her lawyer, 'would you do me a great favour and go over to that excuse for a hotel receptionist and tell him that Leandros Petronades wishes to speak to him?'

This blatant bit of name-dropping brought Isobel's face out of his chest. 'What are you going to do?' she asked.

'What you once told me I am good at,' he replied. 'Which is solving other people's problems.'

It was an old gripe, and it stiffened her spine to be reminded of it. 'I can do that for myself.'

'Stay where you are.' The hand at her waist slid up her back to keep her still. 'This is turning out to be one of the best days of my life, and you are not going to spoil it by turning back into the tough-lady I know so well.'

Her worst day, his best day. That just about said it all for Isobel.

As you would have expected, when Leandros threw his weight around, the hotel manager came out of his hide-away at great speed to begin apologising profusely in Greek. Leandros answered him in equally profuse but incisive Greek. The conversation was so swift and tight that Isobel couldn't follow it all. By the time the little man had hurried away again, Leandros was letting her ease away from him, and she then had to brace herself to face their audience.

Which made it the third time in one day she'd had to do it. Well, they said that bad things always come in threes, so maybe her luck was about to change, she thought hopefully as she glanced from hot face to hot face.

Her mother was staring at her as if she couldn't quite believe that her daughter had just wept all over her estranged husband. Lester Miles had put his jacket back on and was looking invigorated because he had been given something to do. Clive had come to his feet and was weighing up the competition. If he had any sense, it was all he would do, Isobel thought, then took in a deep breath and decided it was time to introduce him to Leandros.

'Clive, this is my husband Lean—'

'Silvia, *thoes*! You do not look well.' Cutting her off with a brusque exclamation, Leandros didn't even glance at Clive as he went to lean over her mother. 'This has been too much for you,' he murmured concernedly and took possession of one of her hands. 'You must accept my sincere apologies on behalf of Athens. You will give me five minutes only and I will make your life more comfortable, *ee pethera,* I promise you. If the manager is doing as I instructed then a car is on its way here as I speak. It will carry you with air-conditioned swiftness away from this miserable place.'

As Isobel watched, her stubborn, tough, I-hate-this-man mother melted before her very eyes. 'This hotel was all we could afford,' she told him miserably. 'Isobel wouldn't listen to sense. She wouldn't let you pay. And she wouldn't let me stay in my own home where at least I could make myself a cup of tea if I pleased.'

'Away to where?' Isobel cut in on this very enlightning conversation.

'To our home, of course,' Leandros replied. 'Isobel is a very stubborn woman, is she not?' he conspired with her mother. 'Which she gets from you, of course,' he added with a grin.

'I don't cut my nose off to spite my face,' Silvia pointed out.

'What do you mean, to your home?' Isobel gasped in outrage.

'*Our* home,' he corrected. 'I am relieved to hear that, *ee meetera*. It is such a beautiful nose. Perhaps between us we could persuade Isobel to leave her nose where it is?'

'You always were an inveterate charmer, Leandros,' Silvia huffed, but her cheeks were now flushed with pleasure rather than heat.

'Leandros. We are not going to stay at your house,' Isobel protested. 'The power cut will be over in a minute or so, then everything here will be back to normal!'

'And if it happens again when your mother is in her room?' he challenged. 'Is it worth risking her being trapped up there?'

'Just what I'd been about to say before you arrived.' Her wretched mother nodded.

Isobel threw herself into one of the chairs and gave up

the fight. 'What about Clive and Mr Miles?' she tossed into the melting pot of calamities that were befalling her today. 'They will have to come too.'

There was a sudden and stunningly electric silence. Then Leandros rasped, 'Your lover can sleep where the hell he likes, so long as it is not in my house.'

Her mother stared at him. Clive looked as if he had turned to stone. Lester Miles just watched it all avidly, like a man watching some gripping drama unfold.

Isobel's heart stopped dead. Oh, dear God, she groaned silently and covered her eyes and wished the world would swallow her up. Too late, she remembered that she'd left Leandros with the impression that she and Clive were lovers.

She couldn't take any more. She stood up. 'I'm going to my room,' she breathed shakily, and headed for the stairwell on legs that shook.

By the time she'd climbed up four flights and felt her way down a dingy inner corridor to her room, she was out of breath and so fed up that she headed straight for the telephone and got Reception to connect her with the airport. If she could get them home tonight then they were going, she decided grimly. Even if that meant travelling in the cargo hold!

No such luck. When a day like this began it didn't give up on turning one's life into a living hell. No seats were available on any flight out of Athens. She was stuck. Her mother was stuck.

'I'm sorry,' a voice said behind her. 'My coming here seems to have made a lot of problems for you.'

'Why did you come, Clive?' She swung round on him. 'I don't understand what you aimed to gain!'

He was standing propping up the doorway. 'I thought I might be of some use.' His shrug was rueful. 'Your mother agreed. It didn't occur to me that your husband would view my presence here with such suspicion.'

He didn't just suspect—he *knew* because she had told him! Oh, heck, she thought and sighed heavily. 'He's been having me watched,' she explained. 'When he heard that you were here he automatically assumed the worst.'

'It's nothing to do with him any more what I am to you,' Clive responded curtly. 'You came here to agree a divorce, not ask his permission to take a lover.'

Isobel released a thick laugh. 'Leandros is a very powerful, very arrogant, and very territorial man. The moment he heard about you, the divorce thing was dropped. Now I'm stuck with a man who has decided to work on his marriage rather than give me up to someone else.'

'That's primitive!'

'That's Leandros,' she replied, then sighed and sat down on the end of the bed.

'You don't have to go with him.'

No? I wish, she thought. 'He's already sweet-talked my mother with promises of air-conditioning and I can't even begin to list the rest of the luxury she is now looking forward to.'

'She doesn't even like the man.'

'Don't you believe that front she puts up,' she said heavily. 'My mother used to think he was the best thing that ever happened to me.' Until it all went wrong; then she'd wished him in hell.

Clive slouched further into the room. He was built like a cannon. All iron with a sunbed-bronzed sheen. The women adored him and flocked after him in droves. He worked at a fitness club. He spent hours patiently helping broken people to mend. He was *nice*!

'You came to Athens hoping I would need putting back

together again after meeting Leandros, didn't you?' she suddenly realized.

The painful part of it was that he didn't deny it. 'A man can hope.'

And a woman could dream. Her dream was downstairs right now, taking over her life. 'I'm sorry,' she murmured huskily.

He came to sit beside her on the bed. 'What are you going to do?' he asked.

Cry my eyes out? 'Give it a chance.' She shrugged.

On a sigh, Clive put a big arm around her and gave her a sympathetic hug. It was a nice arm, strong and secure and safe. But it was the wrong arm and the wrong man, though she wished it wasn't.

'Well, this is nice,' a very sardonic voice drawled.

Isobel felt her heart sink to her toes. Clive gave her shoulder a final squeeze then stood up. As he walked towards Leandros she could feel the hostility bouncing between the two of them. It conjured up images of dangerous cats again, only these were two big male predators considering testing each other's weight. They didn't speak. It was all part of the test to keep silent. Clive didn't stop walking and Leandros didn't move so their shoulders brushed in one of those see-you-later confrontations you expected from a pair of strutting thugs.

The moment Clive had gone, the bedroom door closed with a violent thud. Isobel got up and went over to the small chest of drawers and pulled open the top drawer for some reason she couldn't recall.

'My car has arrived,' Leandros informed her levelly. 'Lester Miles and my driver are taking your mother on ahead.'

'You should have gone with them.' It was not meant nicely.

'And leave you alone with the body-builder? You must think I am mad.'

'Clive is a friend, not my lover.' There, she'd told him. Now he could relax and return to the issue of divorce.

'Too late for that, *agape mou*,' he said deridingly. 'Though *ex*-lover, he most definitely is.'

'He is not my lover!' she swung on him furiously.

His black eyes flared. He moved like lightning, making her heart pound as he pushed his angry face up to her. 'Don't lie to me!' he barked at her. 'I am not a fool! I can count as well as you can!'

'Count?' She frowned. 'What are you talking about?'

His breath left his lips through clenched white teeth. If he touched her she had a feeling he would end up strangling her, he was in such a rage. But he didn't touch. He brought up his hand and placed four long fingers in front of her face. 'Four people. Three rooms,' he breathed severely. 'You tell me how that adds up! You tell me where the extra person sleeps!'

'Why, you…' The words got lost in a strangled gasp as it sank in what he was getting at. 'Clive did not share this room with me!' she denied shrilly. 'He didn't come as one of my party. He came under his own steam. Booked in under his own name—and his room is not even on this floor!'

He didn't believe her, she could see it as the savagery locked into his face. Without another word she slapped his hand away then stalked across to the wardrobe, threw open the doors then stood back. 'My room. My clothes!' she said furiously. 'My single bed!'

Her hand flicked out, sending his angry gaze lashing across the utilitarian plainness of a three-foot divan set in the shoebox this hotel called a single room.

'You know what you are, Leandros? You're the original

chauvinist pig! You dare to come up here showing me your contempt for what you believe I've been doing with my sordid little life—while you shack up with Diantha Christophoros on your super-expensive bloody yacht!'

He spun to stare at her. 'What I said before about Di—'

'Talk about double standards,' she sliced over him. 'I really ought to go and confront her now, just to even things up a bit. Shall I do that, Leandros?' She threw out the challenge. 'Shall I strut the strut? Get all territorial and threaten to smack her in the face if she so much as looks at my man? Maybe I should.' She sucked in a fiery breath, breasts heaving, eyes flashing on the crest of a furious wave. 'Maybe I should just do that and let the whole upper echelons of this damn city know that Isobel, your scary slut, is back!'

She was gasping for breath by the time she had finished. He wasn't breathing at all and his face had gone pale. But the eyes were alive with a dangerous glitter. 'Slut,' he hissed out. 'You're no scary slut but just an angry woman on the defensive!'

'Defending what?' she asked blankly.

'Your blond Adonis.'

At which point she knew she was in trouble. He didn't believe her about Clive, and was coming towards her with the slow tread of a man about to stake his claim on what he believed belonged to him.

'Don't you dare,' she quavered, beginning to tremble as his arm came up. His hand purposefully outstretched and angled to take hold of her by the waist. If she backed up she would be inside the wardrobe; if she stayed where she was she was as good as dead meat for this predatory male.

'Andros—no,' she murmured shakily and tried a squirming shift of her body in an attempt to evade what was going to come.

His hand slid further around her waist and banded her to him. 'Say that again,' he gritted.

'Say what?' Too distracted by his closeness, she just looked blank.

'*Andros,*' he murmured in that low, deep, huskily sensual way that robbed her of her ability to breathe. Had she said his name like that? She couldn't remember. She hoped she hadn't because it gave too much away.

His other hand came up to coil around the thick silk lock of her pony-tail and began tugging with gentle relentlessness so he could gain access to the long column of her neck. She knew what was coming, her breath caught in her throat. If she let him put his tongue to that spot beneath her earlobe she was going to explode in a shower of electric delight.

'Say it,' he repeated, his eyes dark like molasses, his face locked in the taut mask of a man on the edge. His lips had parted, and were coming closer to her angled neck.

She released a stifled choke. '*Andros,*' she whispered.

His mouth diverted. It was so quick, so rewarding that she didn't stand a single chance. He claimed her mouth with devastating promise. He devoured it while she fought for breath. Her breasts heaved against his hard chest, her hips ground against the glorious power of his. Nothing went to waste, the kiss, touch, taste, scents, and even the sounds they made were collected in and used to enhance the whole experience.

It had always been like this. One second nothing, the next they were embroiled in a heady, sensuous feast. His fingers were in her hair. The next moment it was flowing over his hand and she quivered with pleasure because it always felt so very sexy when he set it free like this. Her T-shirt was easy; it disappeared without a trace. His shirt came next, revealing a torso that made her groan as she scraped her fingernails into the curling black mass of hair.

They kissed like maniacs; she nipped his lip, he bit back. Their tongues danced, their eyes locked together. She slid down his zip and covered him with the flat of her hand. He groaned something. He was hot and hard and out of control but then so was she. With one of his swift silent moves he picked her up and put her down on the divan bed then bent to rake the rest of her clothes down her legs.

'I'm going to eat you alive,' he said as he stripped himself naked. And he meant it. He began by bending his dark head and fastening on to one of her breasts. She squirmed with pleasure, her fingers clutching at his shoulders so she could pull him down next to her on the bed. He was magnificent, he was beautiful, his skin felt like oiled leather and she stroked and scored and kneaded it until he couldn't take any more and came to claim her mouth.

Every single inch of him was pumped up and hard with arousal. Every single inch of her was lost in a world of fine, hungry tremors that demanded to be quelled. They kissed, they touched, they rolled as a single sensual unit. When he reached between her legs, she cried out so keenly that he uttered a black oath and had to smother the sound with his mouth. The room shimmered in the golden light of the low afternoon sun. The heat was tremendous, their bodies bathed in sweat. His first plunge into her body brought forth another keening cry. He muffled this one with his hand. She turned her teeth on him, latching on to the side of his palm until he groaned in agonised pleasure, then pulled the hand away and finally buried his mouth in her neck.

Starbursts swirled in the steamy atmosphere. Her legs wrapped around his waist. With each thrust of his body she released another thickened cry and he groaned deep in his throat. It was a blistering, blinding coupling, incandescent and uncompromisingly indulgent in every sense. He brought her to the edge, then framed her face with his hands. His heart was pounding. His eyes were black, his beautiful mouth tight, his total commitment to what was about to happen holding his features drawn and tense.

The first flutters of orgasm took her breath away. He groaned, 'Oh, my God,' as her muscles rippled along the length of his shaft. His eyes closed, her eyes closed, and each flutter lengthened with each driving thrust until the whole experience became one long, tempestuous shower of sensation. It had always been like this for them; there wasn't a place where they could separate the sensuous storm at work inside each other.

Tenderness followed. It had to. They couldn't share something so deeply intimate and special then get up and walk away. Leandros rolled onto his back and took Isobel with him, curving her into his side with a possessive arm while he took deep breaths. Her cheek lay in the damp hollow of his shoulder; her arm lay heavy across his chest. She could feel the aftershocks at work inside him and turned her mouth to anoint him with a slow, moist kiss. It was one of those exquisite moments in time when nothing else mattered but what they were feeling for each other and through each other.

Then the lights flicked on. The small refrigerator in the corner began to whir. Muffled cheers sounded through the thin walls and reality returned with the electricity.

Leandros jerked into a sitting position then jackknifed off the bed. 'Tell me again that this bed is not big enough for two people,' he rasped and strode off to her tiny bathroom, slamming the door behind him in his wake.

He must be mad, he told himself as he turned on the poor excuse for a shower and attempted to wash the sweat from his flesh with tepid water that dribbled rather than sprayed.

Did he really want all of this back again? Did he want to feel so out of control all the time that he could barely think? She touched him and his skin was enlivened, she spat fury at him and it excited him out of all that was sane. She hated his family, she hated his lifestyle, she had learned his language but had not bothered to tell him so she could listen in like a sneaky spy on every conversation happening around her. She was already threatening to cause trouble and he would be a fool not to take her seriously.

He knew her. She was a witch and a hellion. Had he not reminded himself of these things only two weeks ago in Spain? Sluicing water down the flatness of his stomach, his hand brushed over the spot where she had laid her final kiss. Sensation quivered through him; hot and sweet, it caused a fresh eruption of flagrant passion to flow through his blood. Her barbs were not always sharp, he recognised grimly as he switched off the shower.

Grabbing one of the stiff hotel towels, he began to rub himself dry with it. It smelled of Isobel—her perfume was suddenly back on his skin and floating round his senses like a magic potion meant to keep him permanently bewitched. Did this dump of a hotel not even change the towels daily? Glancing around the tiny bathroom, he saw the signs of female occupation but no sign of a man's stamp anywhere.

No hint of a man's scent lay on the towels. Was she telling the truth? Ah, he would be a bigger fool to believe it, he told himself harshly. If the muscle-bound hulk did not know what it was like to fall apart in that woman's arms then he was no man, in his estimation.

Did he really want all of this back in his life?

It had been a day of madness, that was all; pure madness. He had seen and remembered and wanted and now had. It should be enough to let the rest of Isobel return to her other life so he could return to his.

But it wasn't, and he knew it the moment he stepped out of the bathroom with one of the towels wrapped round his hips. She was standing by the window in a blue towelling bathrobe, which looked familiar to him. Could it be the same one of his from his house in Athens that she used to pinch all the time because she liked to feel him close to her skin? Her hair lay down the back of it, her hands were lost in its cavernous pockets. He wanted to go over there and wind his arms around her but anger and frustration and outright damn *need* held him back from doing it.

Did he want to let her go again? Not in this lifetime. 'You can use the bathroom now,' he said as calmly as he could do and turned away from her.

'I will when you've gone,' she replied.

He was about to recover his scattered clothes when she said that but his movements froze on a sudden warning sting. 'In case you have forgotten,' he finished, bending to pick up his trousers, 'you are coming with me.'

'No, I'm not.'

His legs suddenly felt like lead beneath him. 'Of course you are,' he insisted. 'You cannot stay in this place, and your mother is…'

She turned to look at him then. His ribcage tightened in response. She looked so pale and fragile—ethereal, as if she could float away if the window were open.

'I would appreciate it if you could put my mother up for tonight,' she requested politely. 'You are right about this hotel; it isn't the place for her and I don't want to upset her further by moving her on again. But I'll stay here and collect her tomorrow in time for us to catch our flight home.'

'You come with me,' he insisted yet again and did not want to think about tomorrow.

But she shook her head. 'I think we've made enough mistakes for one day.'

'This is not a mistake.' Had he really just said that? While he had been locked away in the bathroom he had agreed with her. Now, when he could look at her again, he did not want it to be a mistake! 'We've just made love—'

'No,' she denied that, and what made it all the more frightening was that she did it so calmly. 'You've made your point.' A slight tilt of her head acknowledged his success at it. 'Two can lie in that narrow bed—I stand corrected. Now I would like you to leave.'

Leave, he repeated inwardly. She was dismissing him. 'So that the Adonis can get back in?'

Spark, he urged her silently. Say something like—Of course, he's waiting outside the door! Then I can retaliate swiftly. I can toss you back down on that blasted bed!

But she didn't say anything. She just turned and walked into the bathroom and left him standing there like a fool!

CHAPTER FIVE

LEANDROS turned to stare at the small hotel bedroom, with its scuffed grey marble flooring and the furniture that must have been there since the First World War. He stared at the bed with its coffee-coloured sheets covered with an orange spread made of cheap nylon, and thought of his own luxurious seven-foot bed set upon smooth white tiling and draped in cool mint-green silk over the finest white cotton sheets.

No effort was required to place Isobel's image on the mint-green coverlet, or to sit her cross-legged on the cool white floor while she sorted through a new set of photographs. Wherever he placed her in his bedroom, she created a glorious contrast to everything. He had missed that contrast in more ways than he had dared let himself know.

But he now had to ask himself if it was because he had missed her that he had gone to Spain and rarely returned to Athens for two years. Was it her ghost that had driven him out of his home and even now forced him to take a deep breath before he could walk back into it?

The sound of the shower being shut off had him moving out of his bleak stasis. By the time the bathroom door opened he knew what was going to happen next and that Isobel was going to have to accept it.

'What do you think you are doing?' Isobel came to a halt in surprised protest.

He was dressed and in the process of packing her suitcase. Beside the case, draped like a challenge on the bed, lay fresh underwear and the only dress she had brought with her to Greece.

'I believe that must be obvious,' he answered coolly.

'But I said…'

His glance flicked towards her. The way it slithered down her front made her heart give a shuddering thump. 'I recognise the robe,' he announced.

Without thought, her fingers went up to clutch the edges of her robe together across her throat. 'I…'

'You what?' he prompted, his dark eyebrows rising to challenge the guilty flush trying to mount her cheeks. 'You took it with you by mistake when you left me, then forgot to send it back to me? Or you stole it because you needed to take a part of me with you and have been hugging me next to your beautiful skin each time you have worn it since?'

'It's comfortable, that's all,' she snapped, shifting impatiently. 'If you want it back—'

'Yes, please.'

Without hesitation he walked towards her as if he was going to drag the stupid robe from her back! His dark eyes mocked the jerky step she took. They also saw the darkening swirl taking place in her eyes. He knew what that swirl meant. He knew everything about her.

Too much! she acknowledged helplessly as her senses began to clamour and he reached towards her with a hand. Prising her unwilling fingers free of the robe's collar, he then bent his dark head, buried his face in the soft towelling and inhaled.

'Wh-what are you doing?' she jerked out on a strangled breath.

'I am checking to see if you douse the robe with my aftershave,' he explained as he lifted his head. 'But no,' he sighed. 'It smells of you.' He took a step closer. 'And the promise of what awaits beneath.'

'I wish you would just stop this and leave,' she murmured crossly.

'Liar,' he drawled. 'What you want is for me to take the robe from you. You would love me to rip the thing from your body then throw you back on the bed and spend the next few minutes reminding you *why* I am still here!'

She was beginning to tremble. 'This is intimidation.'

'No,' he denied. 'It is a case of pandering to your preference for melodrama.' His fingers moved, releasing the towelling so he could brush a lazy fingertip across her pouting bottom lip. There was contempt in the small action but still her lip pulsed as the finger moved; it heated and quivered. 'You want me to *make* you surrender,' he said huskily. 'You would love me to use due force to make you come home with me so that you do not have to give up your precious stubbornness.'

Was he right? Yes, he was right, she conceded bleakly. Beneath the robe her body was already alive with anticipation, her breasts were tight, her abdomen making those soft, deep, pulsing movements that said fresh arousal was on its way.

With a toss of her head, she displaced his finger. 'It isn't home to me,' she denounced, utilising that stubbornness he spoke about. Then spoiled it all when her tongue slipped out to moisten the point where his finger had lingered.

Dark lashes lowered over even darker eyes as he watched the revealing little gesture. The power of his sexuality had never been a question for any woman who could witness that look. He was a dark golden figure with a dark, honeyed, sensual promise attached to everything he did.

'But it will be,' he assured, dragging her attention back

to the argument. 'Just as soon as you take off that robe and put on the clothes I have laid out for you, then we will drive *home*, together, as husbands and wives do—and find the nearest bed to finish what we have started here.'

With that, he turned and walked back to the suitcase, leaving her standing there having to deal with a sense of quivering frustration, which converted itself into a spitting cat. 'Will Diantha be joining us for a cosy little three-some?' she asked tartly. 'Or is this the point where I call up Clive and invite him along just in case we need the extra…?'

Her tongue cleaved itself to the roof of her mouth when he looked at her. Like the swinging gauge on a barometer, his mood had turned from tauntingly sexual to a cold contempt.

'There is no Diantha. There is no Adonis,' he clipped out with thin incision. 'This will be the last time either name will be mentioned in the context of our marriage again. Our marriage has just been re-consummated in this bed,' he added tightly. 'Here in Greece men still hold some authority over their women. Don't force me to impress upon you what that means, Isobel.'

He would, too, she realised as she stood staring at him while her mind absorbed his coldly angry expression. His willingness to be ruthless if she forced him into it was scoring lines of grim certainty into the lean cast of his face. Maybe she paled; she was certainly taken aback by his manner. They'd had many fights in their short-lived, highly volatile marriage, but she could not remember another time when he had used an outright threat.

Frissons sparked from one set of eyes to the other. Her fingers jerked up to clutch the robe again, closing the soft towelling across the pulse working in her throat. He watched it happen while he waited for a response from her. She saw a hard man, a tough man—much tougher than he had been three years ago. It was as if those years had taught him how to hone his strengths and use them to his own advantage. Four years ago he had been coming to terms with the knowledge that he no longer had a father to check every decision he made before it was put into action. Aristotle had been dead for only six months when Leandros and Isobel married. Leandros had been living with the stress of having to walk in a highly revered man's shoes. Advisors had hung around him like circling vultures, vying for a position of power in the new order of things that would eventually emerge from the melting pot of chaos into which his father's sudden death had thrown the Petronades empire. Leandros had lived in a permanent preoccupied state in which small things irritated the hell out of him because the big things totally obsessed his mind.

She had been a small thing. She had been a nagging irritant that he did not need during this dangerous cross-over period of his life. Oh, he had loved her to begin with. During that two-week sojourn in London, when most of the vultures had been left behind in Athens, he had been able to cast off his cloak of responsibility and become a carefree young man again for a while. So they met, fell in love, almost drowned in their happiness. Then they had come here to Athens, and he'd donned his heavy cloak again and become a stranger to her.

She hadn't understood then. She had been too young—only twenty-two herself. She had been too demanding, selfish and possessive and resentful of everything he placed higher on his list of priorities than her. Understanding had come slowly during the years they'd been separated, though the resentments had remained and hurts he'd inflicted upon her had refused to heal.

But she was now realising that Leandros had changed also. The circling vultures were no longer in evidence. The stress-packed frown of constant decision-making no longer creased his brow. He had grown into his father's shoes— had maybe even outgrown them to become a man who answered to no one, and was even prepared to be ruthless to get his own way.

'Why?' she breathed shakily. 'Why have you changed your mind about me?'

He did not even attempt to misunderstand the question. He knew they were back to divorce. 'I still want you,' he said. 'I thought that was obvious. All you need to do now is accept that you still want me and we can move on without all of this tedious arguing.'

'And if we make each other miserable again?'

He turned abruptly as if the question annoyed him. 'We will deal with that if or when it happens. Now, can we finish up here? Your mother's possessions still need to be packed and I would like to get away from here before the next power cut hits.'

He wasn't joking, she realised only half a second later, when there was a click, the lights went out and the fridge shuddered to a protesting halt. Problem solved, she mused bleakly. Stubborn desire to keep fighting him appeased.

Without another word she collected her clothes and returned to the bathroom, where it was pitch-black because there was no natural source of light in there. By the time she had fumbled into her clothes and knocked different joints against hard ceramic, she was more than ready to leave this hotel. Coming out of the bathroom, she found Leandros waiting for her by the open outer door.

'We are getting out of here while there is still enough light left to get down the stairs,' he said impatiently.

'But the bags—'

'The hotel will finish it and send your things on,' he announced with an arrogance that had always been there.

Before she knew it she was feeling her way down the dim corridor with her hand trapped securely in his.

'The city is being hit by lightning strikes due to a pay dispute,' he explained as they made it to the stairwell. 'The strikers are working on the principle that, because it is high season here in Athens, if they hit the tourist areas the government will sit up and take more notice, so the main residential areas are being left alone.'

'For how long, do you think?' She was feeling her way down the first flights of stairs while Leandros walked a few steps ahead of her.

'That depends on who is the most stubborn,' he replied, and turned his dark head to offer his first wide white grin. He was talking about them, she realised, not the strikers or the government.

Opening her mouth to make some tart reply, she missed her footing and let out a frightened gasp as she almost toppled. But he was right there to catch her. His hands closed around her slender waist and her body was suddenly crushed against his. Her stifled expression of fright brushed across his face and, on a soft oath, he trapped her up against the wall then lifted her up until their faces were level.

'I want you back in my life, my home and in my bed,' he declared with deep, dark, husky ferocity. 'I don't want us to fight or keep hurting each other. I want us to be how we used to be before life got in the way. I want it *all* back, *agape*. Every sweet, tight, glorious sensation that tells me that you are my woman. And I want to hear you say that you feel the same way about me.'

With her body crushed between the wall and the wonderful hardness of his body, and their eyes so close it was impossible not to see that he meant every passionate word, offering him anything but the truth seemed utterly futile. 'Yes,' she whispered. 'I want the same.'

In many ways it was a frighteningly naked moment. In other ways it was a relief. The truth was now out in the open and the only thing being held back were those three little words that would make exposure complete.

His dark eyes flared with the knowledge of that. She held her breath and refused to be the first one to say the words. 'Ruthless little witch,' he muttered thickly then his mouth found hers.

They actually shared, on that dim stairwell, the most honest kiss they had ever exchanged. It contained emotion, real emotion, the kind that rattled at the heart and dug its roots deep into that place where the soul lay hidden—along with those three small words.

When they were disturbed by the sound of someone else coming down the stairs, neither came out of the kiss breathing well. When Leandros levered his body away from her, he did so with a reluctance Isobel shared. She couldn't look at him, she was too busy trying to deal with the inner spread of those greedy roots of that oh-so-fickle thing called hope, that said yes, I want to take a risk on this. It is what's been missing for all of these years.

They continued their way downstairs into the foyer. The profusely apologetic manager listened as Leandros issued curt instructions about the packing of possessions and where to send them. The other man tried not to appear curious as to why the wife of Leandros Petronades had been staying in his hotel in the first place.

'He thinks we are very odd,' Isobel remarked as they stepped outside into a pink-glow sunlight.

'I feel very odd,' he came back drily—and caught hold of her hand.

Life suddenly felt so wonderful. Leandros's car was parked fifty feet away. It was low and sleek and statement-red and so much the car for a man of his ilk. Opening the door to the Ferrari, he guided her into the passenger seat, watched her coil her long legs inside, watched her tug her skirt down, filled her up with all of those sweet, tight sensations he had been talking about on the stairs, then closed the door to stride round the long bonnet and take the seat at her side.

The air was electric. He turned the key in the ignition and brought the car alive on a low, growling roar. The nerve-ends between her thighs flicked in tingling response to the car's deep vibration. The man, the car—it was like being bombarded by testosterone from every possible source, she thought breathlessly.

Did he know she was feeling like this?

Yes, he knew it. She could see his own tension in the way his long fingers gripped the squat gear stick, and the way his sensual mouth was parted and his breathing was tense as he looked over his shoulder so he could reverse the car in the few inches available to him to ease them out of the tight parking place. There was a hint of red striking along his cheekbones; his eyes glittered with that strange light that told her she was sitting beside a sexually aroused male. When he turned frontward again, she was showered with static. He changed gear, turned the steering wheel with one of those smooth fingertip flourishes that said the man controlled the car and not the other way around.

With a blaring of car horns he eased them out into the stream of traffic. The low sun shone on her face. She reached up to pull down the sun-visor and found her hand caught by another. The way he lifted it to his mouth and kissed the centre of her palm stifled her ability to breathe for long seconds. As he drove them through the busy streets of Athens, they communicated with their senses. He refused to release her hand, so when it became necessary to change gear it was her hand that felt the machine's power via the gear stick, with his hand holding it there.

It was exciting. She could feel sparks of excitement shooting from him, could feel the needle-sharp pinpricks attacking her flesh. Beneath the dress her breasts felt tight and heavy, between her thighs it was as if they were already having sex.

When they were forced to stop at a set of traffic lights he turned to look at her. His eyes filtered over her face then down her front. The dress was short, but not as short as she had used to wear three years ago, when glances like this used to be accompanied by a frown. This time her thighs were modestly covered but still he made her feel as if she were sitting there naked. The inner tingling turned into a pulsing. She tried pressing her thighs together in an effort to contain what was happening to her. His eyes flicked up, caught the anxiety in her eyes, the way she was biting down on her soft lower lip.

'Stop it,' she protested on a strangled choke of breathless laughter.

'Why?' was his devastatingly simplistic reply.

Because I am going to embarrass myself if you don't stop, she thought helplessly, but suspected that he already knew that.

The lights changed and he turned his glance back to the road again. She managed to win her hand back and tried to ignore what was passing between them. But the bright white of his shirt taunted her with what hid beneath it. If she reached out and touched him she knew she would feel the tension of muscles held under fierce control, and she could see a telling pulse beating in his strong brown neck that made her heart thump madly with the urge to lean across the gap separating them and lay her moist tongue against his throat. The way he moved his shoulder said he'd picked up on the thought and was responding to it.

They began to climb out of the city where the mishmash of buildings gave way to greener suburbs and breathtaking views over Athens to the sunkissed waters of the Saronic Gulf. Eventually they began to pass by the larger properties, set in their own extensive grounds and built to emulate classical Greece. Leandros's mother had a house here, though further up the hill. They drove past the Herakleides estate, where his Uncle Theron lived with his granddaughter Eve, who had been perhaps the only person in the family Isobel felt at ease with.

But then Eve was of a similar age and she was also half-English. She might be the very spoiled and the worshipped grandchild of a staunchly Greek man but she had always determinedly hung on to her British roots.

'Eve is married now,' Leandros broke their silence to inform her.

'Married?' Isobel turned disbelieving eyes on him. The girl she remembered had been a beautiful blonde-haired, blue-eyed handful of a creature who'd constantly foiled her grandfather's attempts to sell her into bondage—as Eve had called it.

'It's a long story,' he smiled, 'and one I think you will enjoy more if I let Eve tell it to you.'

The smile was rueful and turned her heart over because it reminded her of when he'd used to offer her sexily rueful smiles all the time. Rueful smiles which said, I want you. Rueful smiles which said, I know you want me but we will have to wait.

This smile was rueful because he knew what she was thinking about his precocious cousin Eve. But Isobel didn't smile back because she was remembering that, for all her staunch Englishness, Eve was adored by her Greek family. It was Eve's mother who had never made the grade. As Eve had once told her, 'They accept me because I do have their blood in my veins, even if I like to annoy them all by pretending I don't. But my poor mother was looked upon with suspicion from the moment she came here with my father. Thankfully, we spent the first ten years of my life living in London so the family didn't have a chance to put any spanners in the works of my parents' marriage. When they died and I was sent here to live with Grandpa they felt sorry for me so I got the sympathy vote. But that doesn't mean I don't know what they can be like, Isobel. Just do me one great favour and don't let them win.'

But they had won in the end. And, although Isobel remembered that Eve's grandfather had always been pleasant to her, she had never trusted his genial manner. Because like his much younger sister, Thea Petronades— Leandros's mother—Theron had no real wish to see the Herakleides blood-line further diluted with yet more English blood.

'Who did she marry?' she asked Leandros. 'Someone from a great Greek family no doubt?'

'Eve, meet Theron's expectations?' He grinned. 'No, she married a tough British bulldog called Ethan Hayes. And I don't think he is ever going to recover from the shock.'

'Who, Theron?' she prompted with just enough cynicism to wipe the grin from his face.

'No, Ethan Hayes,' he corrected. 'And your prejudice is showing, *agape*.'

Her prejudice? She opened her mouth to protest about that accusation then closed it again when she realised that he was right. She was prejudiced against these people. The knowledge did not sit comfortably as he turned the red car in through a pair of gates that led to the house that had once been her home.

This house was not as grand as the Herakleides mansion—or the Petronades mansion further up the hill. Leandros's mother still occupied the other home along with the rest of the Petronades family. But still, this building had its own proud sense of presence and made no secret of the fact that it belonged to a very wealthy man. Leandros had bought it just after they were married in an attempt to give them some private space of their own in which to work out the problems they were already having by then. His mother had taken offence, said it was not the Greek way, and if Isobel could not live with the family then maybe it should be Thea and the rest of the family who should move out, since the Petronades home had belonged to Leandros since his father's death.

Problems—there'd been problems whichever way she'd turned back then, Isobel recalled with a small sigh. Leandros heard the sigh, pulled the car to a stop in front of the neat entrance, switched off the engine then turned to look at her.

Her expression was sad again, the flush of sensual awareness wiped clean away. He wanted to sigh too, but with anger. Was the sight of their home so abhorrent to her? He glanced at the house and recalled when he'd bought it as a desperate measure in the hope that it would give them some time and space to seal up the cracks that had appeared in their relationship. He'd even got a friend in to refurbish the whole house before he'd brought Isobel down here to surprise her with his new purchase.

But all he had achieved was yet another layer of discontentment. For she'd walked in, looked around and basically that was all she could do. He had realised too late that to have the house decorated and furnished ready for occupation by some taste-sensitive interior designer had been yet another slight to Isobel's ability to turn this house into a home for them.

Home being an awkward word here, he acknowledged bleakly. For it had never become one—just a different venue for their rows without the extra pairs of ears listening in. He had still worked too many hours than were fair to her. She had still walked away from him down this sunny driveway each morning without a backward glance to see if he cared when he watched her go.

It was her one firm statement, he realised now, as they sat here remembering their own history of events. Because his working day had begun later than Isobel had been used to in England, she had left him each morning with her best friend, her camera, when really she knew he would much rather have been lingering over breakfast with her—or lingering somewhere else. If he came home at siesta time, she had rarely ever been here to greet him. After he'd burned the midnight oil working, she had been very firmly asleep when he'd eventually joined her in the bed. If he'd woken her she'd snapped at him and the whole circus act had begun all over again. Stubbornness was her most besetting sin but his had been gross insensitivity to the lonely and inadequate person she had become.

Strange, he mused now, how he did not move back into the big family house after she had left him for good. Strange how he'd preferred to leave Athens completely, having continued alone here for almost a year.

Hoping that she would return? he asked himself as he climbed out of the car and walked around its long, shiny red bonnet to help her alight.

Long legs swivelled out into the sunlight, cased in sheer silk; he caught the briefest glimpse of lacy stocking tops before the dress slid back into place. Classically styled and an elegant blue, the dress was not dissimilar to the one Diantha had been wearing the day he'd made his decision to break his marriage link to Isobel. But as she took his hand to help her to rise upright, there was nothing else about this woman or the dress that reminded him of any of those thoughts he'd had back then. In fact he could not believe his own thick-skinned arrogance in believing he could prefer Diantha's calming serenity to this invigorating sting of constant awareness that Isobel never failed to make him feel.

She was beautiful, stunningly so. As she came to stand in front of him he watched the loose fall of her shining hair as it slid silk-like across her slender shoulders, the curving shape of her body moving with innate sensuality beneath her dress. The length of her legs would make a monk take a second look but, for him, they made certain muscles tighten because he could imagine them wrapped tightly around his waist.

He was just contemplating that such a position might not be a bad idea with which to make the transition from here into the dreaded house, when he noticed a familiar car parked beneath the shade of a tree. His brows came together on a snap of irritation. Drawing Isobel towards him, he made do with dropping a kiss to the top of her head as he closed the door to the Ferrari and wondered how he was going to explain this away.

There was no explanation, he accepted heavily. He was in deep trouble and the only thing to do was to get it over with.

CHAPTER SIX

WALKING towards the house took more courage than Isobel had envisaged. The moment Leandros swung the front door open her stomach dipped on a lurching roll of dismay. The late-afternoon heat gave way to air-conditioned coolness in the large hallway, with its white glossed banister following the graceful curve of the stairs to the landing above. The walls were still painted that soft blue-grey colour; the tiles beneath her feet were the same cool blue and grey. To the left and the right of her stood doors which led into reception rooms decorated with the same classy neutral blend of colours and the kind of furniture you only usually saw in glossy magazines.

This house had never felt like home to her but instead it was just a showcase for this man and a bone of contention to everyone else. She had been miserable here, lonely and so completely out of her depth that sometimes she'd used to feel as if she was shrinking until she was in danger of becoming lost for good.

A strange woman dressed in black appeared from the direction of the kitchens. She was middle-aged, most definitely Greek, and she offered Isobel a nervous smile.

'This is Allise, our housekeeper,' Leandros explained, then introduced Isobel to Allise as *my wife*.

Wondering what had happened to Agnes, the cold fish his mother had placed here as housekeeper, Isobel smiled and said, '*Hérete,* Allise. It's nice to meet you.'

'Welcome, *kiria*,' the housekeeper answered politely.

'Your guests await you on the terrace. I shall bring out the English tea for everyone—yes?'

It felt odd to Isobel to be referred to for this decision while Leandros stood beside her. Agnes used to look to Leandros for every decision, even those simple ones regarding pots of coffee or tea. 'Yes—thank you,' she replied in a voice that annoyed her with its telling little tremor.

'What happened to Agnes?' she asked as Allise hurried back to her kitchen.

'She left not long after you did,' he replied, and there was something in his clipped tone that suggested it had not been a friendly parting of the waves.

But this was not the time to go into domestic issues. Isobel had a bigger concern looming forever closer. It came in the shape of her mother, and how Silvia was going to take the news that, having watched her daughter go off this morning ready to end her marriage, Isobel was now agreed to trying again.

Indeed, the marriage had again been consummated, as Leandros had so brutally put it.

They took the direct route to the terrace, treading across cool tiling to a pair of French doors at the rear of the house that stood open to the soft sunlight. They didn't speak. Isobel was too uptight to talk and she could feel Leandros's tension as he walked beside her. Was he worried about her mother's reaction? she wondered, and allowed herself a small, wry smile, because if she were in his shoes she would be more worried about his own mother's response when she found out about them.

The first person Isobel saw was her mother, sitting on one of the comfortable blue-covered cane chairs, looking a bit happier than she had done the last time she'd seen her. Lester Miles was there too, but he was wearing a brooding frown and he jumped to his feet the moment he saw them step outside.

Her mother glanced around; a welcome smile lit her face. 'Oh, there you are,' she greeted brightly. 'We were just wondering where you'd both got to!'

The *we* didn't register as meaning anything special until someone else began to rise from the depths of another chair. She was small, she was neat, she was dark-haired and beautiful. Even as she turned to them, Isobel knew who it was she was about to come face to face with. She had met her just once during a hastily put-together dinner party meant to celebrate Leandros's surprise marriage. The dinner party had been a complete disaster, mainly because everyone was so very shocked at the news, none less than Diantha Christophoros.

'I've just been explaining to Diantha how kind it was of you to put us up here after our dreadful experience at that awful hotel, Leandros,' Isobel's mother was saying with all the innocence of someone who had no idea whom it was she was giving this information to.

Leandros allowed himself a silent oath, and decided that if lightning could strike Silvia dumb right now, he would lift his eyes in thanks to the heavens. As it was, even the older woman had to feel Isobel stiffen and see the faintly curious expression Diantha sent him that had a worryingly amused and conspiratorial gleam about it.

He tried to neutralise it with an easy smile. 'Diantha,' he greeted mildly. 'This is a surprise. I don't think I recall that you were expected here today.'

Wrong choice of words, he realised the moment that Isobel took a tense step away from him.

'I know, and I am sorry for intruding like this,' Diantha replied contritely. 'Allise should have warned me that you had guests arriving unexpectedly, then I would not have made myself quite so at home.'

'Oh, you've been a great help,' Silvia assured in her innocence. Lester Miles was standing there looking distinctly ill at ease. 'We hope you don't mind, Leandros, but with stairs being a problem for me Diantha has arranged for your handyman to set up a bed in that nice little annexe you have attached to the main house. I think I will be very comfortable there until we catch our flight back to London.'

'It was my pleasure, Mrs Cunningham.' Diantha smiled a pleasant smile. 'I hope you will enjoy the rest of your stay in Athens. Leandros,' she turned back to Leandros without pause in her smooth, calm voice, 'I need a private word with you before dinner this evening. Your mother—'

His mother. 'Later,' he interrupted, feeling very edgy due to Isobel's silent stillness. What was more apparent was the way Diantha was ignoring Isobel. Did she believe she had a right to do that?

Had he allowed her to believe she had that right?

'Isobel, darling, you look very pale,' Silvia inserted. 'Are you feeling OK?'

No, Isobel was not OK, Leandros thought heavily. She believed Diantha was his lover. She had believed Diantha was the woman he had been about to put in her place. Her chin was up and her eyes were glinting. It was payback time for the way he had treated her Adonis and he did not for one moment expect Isobel to behave any better than he had done. But for all that he might deserve the payback, Diantha was innocent in all of this. He could not afford an ugly scene here, and turned urgently to face his statue of a wife.

'Isobel...' he began huskily.

'Oh, you do look pale!' Diantha exclaimed gently. Then

she was smiling warmly as she walked forward with a hand outstretched towards Isobel, and Leandros was at a loss as to how to stop what he knew was about to take place. The air began to sing with taut expectancy; he felt the sensation attack his loins. 'I don't suppose you remember me, Isobel,' Diantha was saying pleasantly. 'But we met once, at...'

Isobel turned and walked back into the house, leaving the horrified gasps echoing behind her and the sound of Leandros's urgent apologies to his mistress ringing in her head!

Striding back down the hall with the heels of her shoes tapping out a war tattoo against hard ceramic, she opened a door that led to one of the smaller sitting rooms at the front of the house. She stepped inside the room and slammed the door shut.

'Get out of here,' she lanced at Leandros when he managed to locate her several seething minutes later. 'I have nothing to say to you, you adulterous rat!'

'Back on form, I see,' he drawled lazily.

She turned her back to him and continued to glare out of the window that looked out on the front of the house. Her arms were folded beneath her heaving breasts and she could actually feel the fires of hell leaping inside.

The door closed with a silken click. A shiver chased down the rigid length of her spine. He hadn't gone. She could feel him standing there trying to decide how best to tackle the fact that his wife had just come face to face with his mistress!

'You were very rude.' He began with a criticism.

Typical, she thought. Attack instead of defence. 'I learned from an expert.'

'I suppose you are referring to me?'

Got it in one, she thought tightly. 'I hate this house.'

'As you hate me?'

'Yes.' Why bother denying it? She hated him and she could not believe she had let him seduce her into coming back here. She had to have gone temporarily insane. The whole day had been one of utter insanity, from the moment she'd got into that cab this morning with Lester Miles!

She heard his sigh whisper across the room, then felt the smooth, steady vibration of his tread as he began to walk towards her, her fingers curled into two tight fists. Suddenly she was having to fight a blockage in her throat.

'As soon as my luggage arrives I'm leaving,' she muttered.

He came to a stop an arm's reach away; she could feel his presence like a dark shadow wrapping itself around her shivering frame. If he touches me I won't be responsible for my actions! she told herself shrilly. If he dares make excuses I'll—

'Is that why you're staring out of the window?' He issued a soft, deriding laugh. 'It is just like you, Isobel, to cut and run in the face of trouble. I now have this great image of you walking up that driveway dragging your suitcase behind you. It looks so pathetically familiar that it makes me want to weep!'

His angry sigh hissed; she spun around to face him. She was shocked by how pale he looked in the deepening glow of the evening light. His clothes had lost their normal pristine smoothness and he needed a shave. Sinister was the word that leapt up to describe him. Sinister and frustrated and so angry it was pulsing out of every weary pore.

How could a man change so much in a few short minutes? It was this house, she decided. This hateful, horrible house. And that image of her that he had just conjured up was dragging on her chest and tugging out the tears.

'Don't you dare compare this with my life here before!' she cried.

'*Our* life!' he barked at her. 'Whatever happened here before happened to *both* of us! But we are not discussing the past.' His hand flicked out in an irritable gesture. 'We are discussing here and now, and your propensity to run instead of facing what threatens to hurt you!'

'I am not hurt, I'm angry!' she insisted. His mouth took on a deriding twist. The flames burning inside her leapt to her eyes.

'Diantha—'

'Is so comfortable here she instructs your staff on what to do!'

'She is a natural organiser,' he sighed out heavily.

He was daring to stand here defending his mistress? 'Just what you need, then,' she said. 'Because I can't even organise a pot of tea!'

He laughed; it was impossible not to. Isobel turned away again and managed to break free.

'I did not marry you for your organisational skills,' he murmured huskily.

Sex; they were back to the sex, she noted furiously.

'I married you because you are gorgeous and sexy and keeping my hands off you is like having an itch I cannot scratch.'

Her spine began to tingle because she knew her husband and he had just issued fair warning that he was going to touch.

'Get your mistress to scratch the itch,' she suggested.

'Diantha is not my mistress.'

Scornful disbelief shot from her throat. 'Liar,' she said.

The light touch of his fingers feathered her bare arms. Excitement shivered across every nerve-end. He was standing so close now her body was clenching in defence against that sensational first brush with his thighs.

'She is a close family friend, that is all.'

Isobel's second huff of scorn sent those fingers up to gently touch her hair. She was suddenly bathed in a shower of bright static.

'This conversation is developing a distinct echo to it,' he then tagged on ruefully.

He was comparing it with their row about Clive. 'The difference here being that I *know* about Diantha. You just jumped to conclusions about Clive because you have that kind of mind.'

'He was *raw* with desire for you,' he growled close to her earlobe.

'Whereas she only wants you for the prestige of your money and your exalted name.'

His low laugh of appreciation brought his lips into contact with her skin, at which point she was about to turn, deciding that braving eye contact had to be easier to deal with than the assault Leandros was waging on other parts. But a noise beyond the window caught her attention. Leandros straightened when he heard it too, and both of them watched a van come trundling down the drive bearing the name of the Apollo Hotel on its side.

Her luggage was about to arrive. Her heart began to thud. It was decision time. Did she stay or did she go?

'I stayed, *agape mou*,' Leandros said gruffly. 'Despite the suspicions I still have about you and the Adonis, I am still here and fighting for what I want. Don't you think it is about time that you stood still and fought for what you want?'

Fight the mistress? She did turn and look at him. 'Are you challenging me to go and throw her out of this house?'

A sleek black eyebrow arched in counter-challenge. 'Will it make you feel better about her if you did?'

No, it wouldn't, she thought bleakly, because throwing Diantha out of this house would not be to throw her far enough. 'You hurt her once before by marrying me in her place. Are you really prepared to do that to her again, Leandros?'

'I don't know what you're talking about.' He frowned.

Isobel's sigh of irritation was smothered by the sound of the van coming to a shuddering stop outside the window. 'I do know about your old romance with her,' she told him heavily. 'If an ordinary high-street lawyer like Lester Miles can find out about your present relationship, then we are talking about a serious breach of Greek family ethics here, of which—'

'Just a minute,' he cut in, and the frown had darkened. 'Back up a little, if you please. What old romance am I being accused of having with Diantha?'

He was going to make her spell it out. 'The way your sister Chloe told it, you virtually jilted Diantha at the altar when you married me.'

'Chloe?'

'Yes, Chloe,' she confirmed and could not stand still a moment longer looking into the clever face of confusion. Stepping round him, she put some distance between them. Outside a van door gave a rattling slam. 'Within days of you producing me as your wife, Diantha's family were shipping her off to Washington, DC and away from the humiliation you caused her.'

He was following her tense movements with increasingly glowering eyes. 'And my sister Chloe told you this?' he demanded. Her shrug confirmed it. 'When—when did she relay these things to you?'

'Does it matter?'

'Yes, it matters!' he snapped. 'Because it is not true! Nor is this—rumour, which seems to be everyone else's property but mine, that I am about to divorce you to marry her! I do not know who began it, and I can positively tell you that Diantha has received no encouragement from me—at either time—to believe that I have a marriage between her and me in mind!'

'Are you saying you have never considered marrying her?' Her challenge was etched in disbelief. But when he released a hard sigh then turned *his* back to *her*, Isobel knew the truth.

'Stop playing with people, Leandros,' she snapped and walked towards the door.

'I am likely to do a lot more than play, Isobel, if you try to walk through that door before we have finished this line of discussion.'

A threat. She stopped. Somewhere beyond these four sizzling walls a doorbell gave a couple of rings. She turned to face him. He was furious, she saw. Well, so was she! 'It was one thing playing the interloper here four years ago but to hell with you if you think I am going to go through all of that again!'

Her eyes were bright, her mouth trembling. If he dared to, he would go over there and...

And what? Leandros asked himself angrily. Force her to believe that which he could not deny outright? 'I had no such relationship with any other woman before I met you,' he announced thinly. 'Diantha did not leave Athens nursing a heart broken by me,' though he could tell who had broken her heart. 'Before Diantha arrived on my yacht in Spain as a hurried substitute for Chloe, who was needed here by my mother, I had not set eyes upon her in four years. During the two weeks Diantha stayed with me, we neither kissed nor slept together and very rarely touched.

But I did find her easy company to be with,' he admitted. 'And on an act of pure arrogance I made a decision that maybe—just maybe—she would eventually make a wife for me. The one I had did not, by that time, have much use for me, after all!'

'So it's my fault that you gave everyone the impression that you were divorcing me to marry her. Is that what you're saying?'

'No,' he sighed. 'I am saying that I was arrogant, but only within my own head!'

'But she uses this house as if she belongs here because *she* is arrogant.' If Isobel fizzed any more she was going to pop like a champagne cork, Leandros noted frustratedly.

'She is a friend—that is all,' he gritted. 'A *good* friend, who has been helping me out by liaising between myself and my mother, who is a neurotic mess because of Nikos's big wedding next week!'

'Liaising,' she scoffed. 'That's a good one, Leandros. Now I'm hearing repeated lies!'

Oh, to hell with it, he thought, and began striding towards her. Someone rattled the handle on the door. It flew inwards, forcing Isobel to leap out of its way and bringing him to a stop almost within reach of his aggravating target.

Isobel's mother appeared in the opening, propelling herself in her wheelchair. She looked cross—everyone was cross!

'Would you like to explain to me, young lady,' Silvia flicked sternly at her daughter, 'what happened to the good manners I taught you? How could you be so rude as to turn your back on that nice Miss Christophoros and walk away? I have just had to spend the last half an hour covering up for you!'

'That *nice* Miss Christophoros you have been happily *liaising* with happens to be *my* husband's mistress!'

Silvia's furious daughter replied, and, having silenced her mother, she then stalked away, hair flying like a warning flag, long legs carrying her out of the room and—

Leandros went to go after her...to stop her from leaving, then halted again when he saw her take to the stairs. A grin appeared. The minx might want to take his head off right now, but she was not going to leave him.

'What was she talking about?' Silvia demanded.

'She's jealous,' he murmured. 'She does not know what she's saying.'

'It sounded pretty clear-cut to me,' Silvia countered. 'Is that woman your current mistress?'

Current? He pondered on the word while he listened for that old familiar sound of a door slamming somewhere. Rear bedroom, not his, he calculated when, as predicted, the sound came.

Diantha, he noticed, had gone from being *that nice Miss Christophoros* to *that woman*. Silvia was nothing if not loyal to her own. Which brought forth another thought. 'Where is Diantha?' he asked sharply.

'She left just as the luggage arrived. Didn't you hear her car pull away?'

No, he had been too busy fighting with Silvia's witch of a daughter. 'Silvia,' he said, coming to a decision, 'you may not like what I am about to tell you, but I suggest you come to terms with it. Isobel and I are not getting a divorce,' he announced. 'We are, in fact, very much a re-united couple.'

He had to give it to his mother-in-law—she was not slow on the uptake. Her eyes went round. 'In just half a day?'

He smiled; it was impossible not to. 'It took less than half a day the first time we met,' he admitted candidly.

'That was before you broke Isobel's heart and sent her

home to me in little pieces,' Silvia said brutally. Eyes as fierce and contrarily vulnerable as her daughter's glared at him. 'I won't let you do it to her again.'

'I have no intention,' he assured. 'But I warn you again, Silvia,' he then added seriously, 'Isobel is still my wife and is staying that way.'

Isobel's mother studied his grimly determined expression. 'I think you should try telling her that,' she advised eventually.

'Oh, she knows it.' His eyes narrowed. 'She is afraid of what it is going to mean, that's all.'

'And the mistress?'

He mocked the question with a grimace. 'Is a mere friend.' The sooner certain other people recognised that the quicker he could settle down to convincing Isobel. 'Where is the lawyer?' he then asked thoughtfully.

'Still on the terrace looking slightly poleaxed by high-society living.'

Nodding, Leandros went to walk past her then paused and instead bent his dark head to place a kiss on her cheek. Her skin felt as smooth as her beautiful daughter's. But then Silvia was still a very attractive woman, even sitting here in this wheelchair. She had her daughter's eyes and beautiful mouth, and, though her hair might not be as red as Isobel's any more, it was still luxuriously silken.

'I am happy to see you back here again, *ee peteria*,' he told her huskily. 'But I am not happy to see you confined to this thing.'

'It won't be forever,' Silvia replied firmly. 'I am getting stronger by the day and don't usually spend so much time sitting here.'

'Would it be too much for you to explain to me what happened?'

Ten minutes later he was going to find Lester Miles,

with his head so filled with his new insight into Isobel and Silvia's last few years while they'd fought Silvia's battle together, that he didn't notice Isobel sitting on the top stair, where she'd listened in on the whole illuminating conversation.

When he'd gone she came down the stairs and brushed her mother's cheek with a silent salutation. She'd had no idea how tough her mother had found the last two years until she heard her confiding in Leandros.

'Come on,' she said softly. 'Let's go and check out your new accommodation.' And, taking charge of the wheelchair, she turned it round to face the hallway.

'You OK?' Silvia asked.

'Yes,' Isobel answered.

'You still love him don't you?'

'Yes,' she answered again; there was really nothing more either of them could add to it.

Together they checked over everything and found nothing to complain about. The rooms had used to be a fully self-contained study added on by a previous owner of the house who was a writer and liked his own space when he was working, so most of the necessary facilities had been built into the annexe. When the designers moved in they'd converted the whole thing into a state-of-the-art office for Leandros. But he'd rarely used it, preferring to use the conventional study in the main part of the house. Isobel had taken it over to use as a photo studio, where she'd developed her photographs and played around with them via the computer sitting in the corner on its state-of-the-art workstation.

With Diantha's famed organisational skills, a bed had been added along with a couple of armchairs and a huge TV set. Reluctant though Isobel was to admit it, the place looked great.

'I'll want for nothing here,' her mother announced with satisfaction. Even her luggage had been carefully unpacked and put away.

Now she must go and check on their other guest, she realised. 'Where's Lester Miles?' she asked her mother.

'Ask Leandros,' she suggested. 'He went looking for him a few minutes ago.'

But Lester Miles was being driven away from the house even as Isobel went to search him out. 'What have you done with my lawyer?' she demanded when she met Leandros in the hall.

'He's just left.'

Her very expressive eyes began to flash. 'Don't tell me you've sent him back to rough it at the Apollo!'

'No.' His mouth twitched. 'He had to go back to England with some urgency. My driver is taking him to the airport.'

'He won't get a flight,' Isobel stated confidently.

'Oh?' he murmured curiously. 'Why not?'

'Because all the flights to London are full—I already checked,' she drawled.

'How enterprising,' he commended. 'Were you hoping to escape *before* we made it to the bed or afterwards?'

Refusing to answer that, she turned and started up the stairs. Leandros arrived at her side.

'I am flying your lawyer home—along with the Adonis. There,' he smiled. 'Am I not a graciously accommodating man?'

Refusing to rise to that bit of baiting, she kept her gaze fixed directly ahead.

'Where are we going?' he enquired lightly.

She was on her way to find her own luggage; where he was going did not interest her one little bit.

He smiled at her again. She wanted to hit him. 'Is your mother comfortable?' he enquired.

'Perfectly, thank you,' she answered primly.

The sound of low laughter curled her insides up. They arrived on the upper landing, where six doors led to elegant bedroom suites. Isobel made for one door while Leandros made for another. With their hands on the door handles they paused to glance at each other, Isobel with the light of defiance in her eyes, because the room she was about to enter was not the one they'd used to share. Leandros simply smiled—again.

'Dinner,' he said, 'eight-thirty,' and disappeared from view, leaving her standing there seething with anger and a sense of frustration because, by refusing to comment on the fact that she was clearly not intending to share a bedroom, he had managed to grab the higher ground.

Dinner was a confusing affair. Silvia was tired and had decided to eat in her room then watch a video film before going to bed. Isobel came down, wearing the same dress—since it was her only dress. Though she had taken a shower, pinned up her hair and added some light make-up.

Leandros on the other hand was wearing full formal dinner dress. He looked handsome and dashing and her heart turned over. 'A bit over the top for an informal meal in, isn't it?' she remarked caustically.

'I have to go out later,' he explained. 'My mother is expecting me, and, since I have been strictly unavailable to anyone today, either I turn up or she will come here to find out what I am playing at.'

Isobel wished she knew what he was playing at. There were undercurrents at work here that made her feel out of control. Yet she didn't know why, because it wasn't as if she hadn't known about the dinner tonight. Diantha had mentioned it, being so efficient. What she had expected was that Leandros would make some concession for once in his important existence and have remained here with her.

Which was telling her what? she asked herself. She didn't like the answer that came back at her, and that revolved around dear Diantha and his preference for where he would rather be!

They walked into the smaller of the two dining rooms that the house had to offer, like two strangers on their first date. Leandros politely held out a chair for her. Allise, she saw, had pulled out all the stops for this cosy dinner for two and the table had been dressed with the best china and candles flickered softly instead of electric lights.

She sat down. Leandros helped her settle her chair. By the time he'd moved away without so much as touching her even by accident, she was feeling so incensed she felt she was living within her own personal battle zone.

He sat down opposite. Candlelight flickered over lean, dark features completely stripped of his thoughts. He was beautiful. It wasn't fair. The black of his jacket and the white of his shirt and the slender bow-tie gave sophistication a whole new slant. He reached for a napkin, shook it out then took a bottle of champagne out of its bucket of ice. The napkin was folded around the bottle. Long brown fingers deftly eased out the cork. It popped softly but did not dare to explode—not for this man who had learned how to open a bottle of champagne in his crib. Frothy gold liquid arrived in the crystal goblet in front of her without him so much as spilling a drop. He filled his own glass. She considered picking up hers and tossing the contents at him.

But the suspicion that he was already expecting her to do that held her hands tightly clenched on her lap. If he didn't say something to ease this tension, she was going to be the one to explode...like the champagne cork should have done.

'You can come with me, if you want.'

She sat there staring at him, unable to believe he had just said that—and as casually as he had done!

'Thank you,' she said coolly. 'But I am watching a film with my mother.'

His grimace said—fair enough. He picked up his fizzing crystal goblet and tipped it in a suave toast to her. 'Welcome home,' he said, then drank.

If Allise hadn't arrived with the food at that point, maybe—just maybe—Isobel would have reacted. But wars like this required nerves of steel and she had them, she told herself.

They ate in near silence. When she couldn't push her food around her plate any longer, Isobel drank some of the champagne, which instantly rushed to her head. Her mouth suddenly felt numb and slightly quivery. She put the goblet down. Leandros refilled it. Allise arrived with the second course. When the last course arrived, Isobel refused the delicious-looking honey-soaked pudding and asked for a cup of black coffee instead. She'd drunk two glasses of champagne like a woman with a death wish because she knew as well as Leandros knew that she had no head for the stuff.

When the dreadful meal was finally over, she got up on legs that weren't quite steady. Leandros didn't get up but lazed back in his chair, studying her without expression.

'Goodnight, then,' she said.

He gave a nod in acknowledgement. She walked out of the room. She suffered watching the film with her mother out of grim cussedness, then escaped to her self-allotted bedroom, got ready for bed, crawled beneath the crisp white sheets, pulled them over her head and cried her eyes out.

He was with her, she was sure of it. He was standing in some quiet corner of his mother's house, gently explaining the new situation. Would she beg, would she cry? Would he surrender to the liquid appeal in her dark eyes and stay with her tonight instead of coming home?

She drifted into sleep, only to be consumed by visions she did not want to see. It wasn't fair. She hated him. He was tying her in emotional knots just like the last time. A pair of arms scooped her off the bed and jolted her out of sleep.

CHAPTER SEVEN

'GET off me, you two-timing brute!' she spat at him.

'Well, that isn't very nice,' he drawled.

'Where do you think you are taking me?'

'You did not really think that I was going to let you sleep in any other bed than our own, did you? Foolish Isobel,' he mocked as he lifted up a knee then swung her down onto another bed.

The knee stayed where it was, the rest of him straightened so he could remove his robe, his eyes glinted dark promises down at her, and because she was too busy trying to cover her dignity by tugging her ridden nightshirt over the shadowy cluster of golden curls at her thighs she missed her only chance to escape. He came down beside her in a long, lithe stretch of male determination. One hand slid beneath the fall of her hair while the other made a gliding stroke down her side from breast to slender thigh. Then it came back up, bringing her nightshirt with it.

He stripped it from her with an ease that left her gasping. She aimed a clenched fist at him, he caught it in his own hand, then his mouth was coming down to cover her mouth. She groaned out some kind of protest but it wasn't enough to bring this to a halt. It was dark, it was warm and, as he subdued her, her senses were already beginning to fly. Seconds later she was lost in the hungry, driving intensity of the kiss.

Her fingers unclenched out of his grip on them, lifted then buried themselves in his hair. The kiss deepened. She could feel his heart pounding, felt the thick saturation of

121

his laboured breath. Her body, her limbs, every sinew moved and stretched on wave after wave of desperate delight. He dragged his mouth away and looked down at her, no smile, no mockery, just heart-stunningly serious desire.

'Did you go to her?' she whispered painfully.

'No,' he replied.

'Was she there?'

His eyes darkened. 'Yes.'

Her fingers tugged at his hair until he winced. 'Did you speak to her—touch her?'

'No,' he grated. 'I had no reason to.'

The black ferocity of his gaze insisted that she had to believe that. Her mouth slackened into a wretched quiver. 'I imagined all sorts,' she shakily confessed to him.

'I am with the only woman who has *ever* done this for me,' he answered harshly. 'Why would I lust after less?'

'Three years, Leandros,' she reminded him painfully. 'Three years can make a man accept less.'

'Were you unfaithful?' He threw the pain right back at her.

'No—never.'

'Then why are we talking about this?'

They didn't talk any more, not after his mouth claimed hers again and his hands claimed the rest of her with a grim, dark, fierce concentration that robbed her of the will to do anything but feel with every single sense she possessed.

She was possessed, Isobel decided later, when she lay curled in the secure circle of his arms. Her cheek rested in the hollow of his shoulder, her fingers were toying with the whorls of hair on his chest. There wasn't another place she would rather be, but knowing it made her feel so very vulnerable. She didn't think she was any better equipped now than she had been three years ago to deal with what loving a man like Leandros meant.

She released a small sigh. The sigh aggravated the muscles controlling Leandros's steady heartbeat. She might be lying here in his arms but he knew she had problems with it. Did he take a leap of faith and force those problems out into the open so they could attempt to sort them out?

He trapped his own sigh before it happened. He didn't want to talk. His eyes were heavy, his body replete and content. Her hair lay spread across his shoulder, her soft breathing caressed his chest and the darkness soothed him towards sleep.

She moved just enough to place a kiss on his warm skin, then followed it up with another pensive sigh. Contentment flew out of the window. He moved onto his side and flipped her onto her back then came to lean over her with his head supported by his hand.

'What?' she said and she looked decidedly wary.

'Why the melancholy sighs?' he demanded.

'They were not melancholy.'

He arched an eyebrow to mock that little lie. She lowered dusky eyelashes until they brushed against skin like porcelain. Her mouth looked small and cute when he knew that the last thing you could ever call Isobel was *cute*.

'I have this urge to stand you up against the nearest wall and shine a bright light in your eyes,' he murmured drily. 'We have just made love. You cried out in my arms and clung to me as if I was the only thing stopping you from falling off the edge of the earth. You told me you loved me—'

'I did not!' The desire to deny that brought her lashes upwards.

'You thought it, then,' he amended with a shrug meant to convey a sublime indifference to semantics. Then he reached out to gently comb her hair from her face, and was suddenly serious. 'We need to talk, *agape mou,* about why we parted.'

Without the gentleness she might not have caught on to what he was actually daring to broach here. But he saw the light in her eyes change, saw them flood with horror then with tears. 'No,' she said, then was leaping out of the bed and racing from the room.

By the time he had grabbed his robe and gone after her she was standing in the other bedroom, huddled inside the blue robe. His chest ached at the sight of her, at the sight of that robe that said so many things about the real Isobel, like the look of pure anguish whitening her face.

'Will you stop running?' he ground at her. 'Just stop running from this,' he repeated almost pleadingly. 'If we do not face the past together, how are we supposed to move on?'

Isobel stood and shook and remembered why she hated him. If she could take back the last mad day then she would. Her heart hurt, her throat hurt; just seeing him standing there looking as if he was experiencing the same things made her want to wound him as he had once almost fatally wounded her. How could she have forgotten what he had done to her? How could she have lain in his arms and let herself ignore the kind of man she knew him to be?

'You didn't want our baby,' she breathed. 'Is that facing it?'

He winced as if the tip of a whip had just lashed him. 'That is not true…'

'Yes, it is,' she insisted. 'By the time I was pregnant I don't think you even wanted me!'

'No…' He denied that.

'I was the irritation you just didn't need, and you made

sure I knew it.' But he was right; she could not run from this! It had to be faced before they made the same mistakes a second time and turned lust into love, which then turned into regret filled with frustration and bitterness. 'You married me when you didn't need to, we both knew that—you'd already enjoyed what was on offer after all! You lifted me out of working-class drudgery into wealth and luxury beyond compare then expected me to show eternal gratitude. But how did I pay you back for this generosity and goodness? I refused to conform. I refused to smile weakly and say "Yes, thank you, Mama," when your mother lectured me on how I should behave.'

'She was attempting to advise you.'

'She was cold and critical and so dismayed by me that I don't know how she managed to stay in the same room with me half the time!'

'So you played up to that criticism, is that it?' he bit out. 'Or should I say you played down to it just for the hell of watching her squirm?'

'I stayed *away* from it!' she corrected. 'Or didn't you notice?' She was aching and throbbing as it all came rushing back. 'I went out and found my own kind of people.' Her hand stretched out to encompass the view of Athens lying beyond the window.

'Like Vassilou.'

'Did your mouth flatten like that in distaste, Leandros?' she challenged the expression on his grim face. 'If you can't see the difference between *"Do you really need to wear those terrible trousers, Isobel?"* and *"Ah,* Kyria, *you look so cool and fresh today!"* well, I certainly can. Or—*some babies are ill-judged and ill-timed, Isobel.'*Her eyes began to sting. She swallowed thickly. 'Words like that when spoken by the mother of your husband rarely shore up an ailing marriage. They help to shatter it.'

'My mother could not have said such a thing to you,' he denied, but he'd gone pale. He knew she was telling the truth. 'She would not be so—'

'Cruel?' she finished for him when the word became glued to his tight upper lip. '*"Maybe it was for the best."*' Hoarsely she quoted his own choice of words back at him. '*"We were not ready for this."*'

He swung his back to her and walked over to stare out of the window. The desire to leap on that back and pummel it to the ground sang in her blood. If she shook any more fiercely she would have to sit down.He had lifted the lid on black memories, and now she was standing here being consumed by them.

'I was ashamed of myself when I said that,' he uttered.

'Good,' she commended. 'I was ashamed of you too.' With that she walked over to the chest of drawers and withdrew a fresh nightshirt then went into the bathroom. She didn't shut the door because she was *not* running away this time. Not from this—not from anything *ever* again.

He came to stand in the doorway. With her back firmly to him she dropped the robe and replaced it with the clean nightshirt. 'You were inconsolable and I did not know how to cope with your grief,' he said huskily.

'No, you were busy and had to be pulled out of an important meeting,' she gave her own version of events. 'And if it wasn't bad enough that you didn't want me to get pregnant in the first place, you then found yourself having to deal with an hysterical woman who didn't appreciate '*"Maybe it is for the best."*'

'All right,' he rasped. 'So I did not want us to have a baby at that time!'

She swung round to look at his face as he dared to admit that! No wonder his skin looked grey!

'We were both too young. Our marriage was in a mess!

You were miserable; *I* was miserable! We had stopped communicating on any level—'

'Especially between the sheets.'

'Yes, between the bloody sheets!' he grated, and suddenly he was swinging away from the door and gripping her upper arms. 'I adored you. You fascinated me! You sparkled and sizzled and took on all-comers with a courage that took my breath away. When you were in my arms it was like holding something powerfully special. But our marriage had not had the time to grow beyond that all-consuming physical obsession before you were presenting me with a red stop light. I resented having to stop!'

'I didn't ask you to.'

'You did not need to.' His sigh took the anger out of him; dropping his hands, he moved away. 'You did not see how fragile you looked, as if you would shatter if I so much as touched you.'

He walked back into the bedroom. This time it was Isobel that followed him. 'Couldn't you have just told me that instead of turning cold on me?'

'Tell you that I was such a selfish swine that I did not want half a lover in my bed?' He released a self-derogatory laugh. 'Tell you that I did not want to share your body with anything?' An oath was thrust out from the cavernous depths of his chest. 'I despised myself. I did not know what was happening inside my own head! When you lost the baby I believed I had wished it to happen. I still believe that. My punishment was to lose you, and I was willing to take it. I was willing to take any punishment so long as I was not forced to face you with what I had done.'

'So you let me walk away.' She understood him now.

'You tied me in so many knots I was relieved to see you go.'

'And broke my heart all over again,' she said with painful honesty. 'Didn't it occur to you that I needed you to come for me?'

His shook his head; his shoulders were hunched, his gaze grimly fixed on his bare feet. 'I despised myself. It was easy, therefore, to convince myself that you despised me too.'

'I did.'

Silence fell. It came with a heavy thud. Isobel looked at the spacious bedroom with its cool floors and lavender walls and purple accessories, and wondered how silence could hurt so much.

'It wasn't your fault,' she murmured eventually. 'The baby, I mean,' she added, then had to swallow tears when he lifted his dark head to send her an agonisingly unprotected look. 'The statistics for losing a first baby in the first three months of pregnancy are high. It was simply bad luck.'

She tried a shrug to punctuate her absolute belief in that, but it didn't quite come off and she had to turn away in the end, wrapping her arms across her body and clutching at her shoulders with tense fingers that shook. A pair of arms arrived to cover her arms; long fingers threaded tensely with hers. It was so good to feel him hold her that she couldn't hold back the small sob.

'I had my own guilt to deal with,' she thickly confided. 'I felt I had failed in every way a woman could. I had to leave because I couldn't stand everyone's pitying expressions and the knowledge that they thought the loss of our baby more or less summed up our disaster of a marriage.'

He remained silent but his arms tightened, offering comfort instead of words. On a small whimper she broke the double arm-lock so she could turn and give back some comfort by placing her arms around his shoulders and pressing her face into the warm strength of his neck.

'Tomorrow we begin making a better job of this second chance we have given ourselves,' he ordained gruffly.

She nodded.

'We talk instead of fighting.'

She gave another nod.

'When people say things you do not like you tell me about it and I listen.'

She agreed with another nod.

He shifted his stance. 'Don't go too meek on me, *agape mou*,' he drawled lazily. 'It makes me nervous.'

'I'm not being meek,' she informed him softly. 'I'm just enjoying the feel of your voice vibrating against my cheek.'

With a growl, she was lifted up and kissed as punishment. The kiss led to other things, another room and a familiar bed. They slept in each other's arms and awoke still together, showered together and only separated when Isobel had to go back to the other bedroom to find something to wear.

They met up again on the terrace. The first cloud that blocked out her sunlight came when she saw Leandros was dressed for the office in a dark suit, blue shirt and dark tie. Handsome and dynamic he may look, but she needed him to stay here with her.

'For a few hours only,' he promised when he saw her expression, getting up to hold out a chair for her.

'It is reality, I suppose.' She smiled.

'And some unfortunate timing,' he added. 'I have been back in Athens for only a few weeks after a long stay abroad. Nikos's marriage is like a large juggernaught racing down a steep hill and taking everyone else along with it for the ride.'

Was he talking about his time in Spain as his long stay abroad? Isobel wondered. But didn't want to think about that right now when she was trying hard not to think of anything even vaguely contentious.

'So, when is the wedding?' she asked brightly.

'Next week.' He grimaced as he sat down again. 'In my father's stead I have been slotted into the role of host for the many pre-wedding dinners my mother has arranged, and also as to escort her to those that the Santorini family are having. Hence my having to leave you last night.' He paused to pour her a cup of coffee. 'Tonight I must do the same—unless I can talk you into coming with me?'

Body language was one hell of a way to communicate, Leandros mused as he watched her smile disappear and her eyes hide from him while she hunted for an acceptable excuse to refuse.

It came in the shape of Silvia Cunningham, who appeared on the terrace then. She was walking with the aid of a metal frame, and even to him it was a worthy diversion.

He stood up and smiled. 'What a delightful sight!' he exclaimed warmly. '*Ee pateria*, those beautiful legs look so much better when viewed upright.'

'Get away with you,' Silvia scolded, but her cheeks warmed with pleasure at the compliment. 'You know, I can't make up my mind if it is the fierce heat or the relentless sunshine, but I feel so much stronger today.'

Isobel got up to greet her mother with a kiss then pulled out a chair for her and waited patiently while Silvia eased herself into it. As he watched, Leandros saw the tender, loving care and attention Silvia's daughter paid to her comfort without making any kind of fuss.

He also noticed the look of relief on her face because their conversation had been interrupted. Stepping across the terrace to where the internal phone that gave a direct line to the kitchen sat, he ordered a pot of tea for Silvia then came to sit down again. He listened as mother and daughter discussed what kind of night Silvia had had while thoughts of his own began to form inside his head.

Allise arrived with the pot of tea. There was a small commotion as room was made on the table and an order for toast and orange juice was placed. Biding his time, he sipped at his coffee, watching narrowly as Isobel used every excuse she could so as not to look at him.

She was wearing the green trousers teamed with a white T-shirt today. The hair wasn't up in a pony-tail, which had to mean that she was not about to run. But, beautiful though she undoubtedly was, fierce and prickly and always ready for a fight, she was also a terrible coward. It had taken him a long time to realise that, he acknowledged, as he watched her bright hair gleam in the sunlight, her green eyes sparkle as they smiled at Silvia and her very kissable mouth curve around her coffee-cup.

He waited until both ladies had put their cups safely down on their saucers before he went for broke. 'Silvia,' he aimed his loaded bet directly at Isobel's weakest point, 'Isobel and I must attend a party tonight. We would be very honoured if you would accompany us.'

He had chosen his bet well, for he could remember Silvia before her accident. She might have spent her working hours stuck behind the window as a teller in a high-street bank but her social life had used to be full and fun.

'A party, you say?' Eyes so like her daughter's began to sparkle. 'Oh, what fun! And you really don't mind if I come along with you?'

From across the table, barbs began to impale him. He made eye contact with a brow-arching counter-challenge that gave no indication whatsoever to what was beginning to sizzle in his blood. This woman could excite him without trying to. She brought him alive.

'We didn't come to Athens equipped to attend parties,' Isobel reminded *both* of them.

Silvia's face dropped in disappointment. Isobel saw it happen and looked as if she had just whipped a sick cat.

'No problem,' he murmured smoothly. 'It is an oversight that can be remedied within the hour.'

'Of course!' Silvia exclaimed delightedly. 'We have time to shop, Isobel! It's about time we treated ourselves to something new!'

I hate you, the other pair of eyes informed him. The sulky mouth simply looked more kissable.

'Whose party is it?'

With the smoothness of a born gambler, he turned his attention to his mother-in-law and explained about his younger brother Nikos's wedding next week and how tonight's party was being held at Nikos's future in-laws' home, which was a half-hour's drive out of the city towards Corinth.

'You don't play fair,' Isobel told him in flat-toned Greek. 'You know I don't want to go.'

'What did you say?' her mother demanded.

'She said she didn't think it was fair to expect you to shop and spend the evening partying,' he lied smoothly. 'So we will solve the problem the rich man's way, and I will have a selection of evening gowns sent out here for you to peruse at your leisure.'

The *rich man* part was said to tease yet another smile from Silvia. The daughter didn't smile. But he did get a flashing vision of retribution to come. 'Try anything stupid just to get back at me, and I will retaliate,' he warned in Greek.

'What did *he* say?' Silvia wanted to know.

'He said choose something outrageously daring,' Isobel responded defiantly.

He laughed. What else could he do? He knew he had asked for that. It was fun having a wife that spoke his language, he decided.

But it was also time to cut and run, before she decided to corner him somewhere private and he did not get any work done today. Rising to his feet, he bid Silvia farewell and stepped round the table to kiss his wife's stiff cheek, then strode away, still feeling those wonderful barbs that had launched themselves at him.

'Don't you want to go to this party, Isobel?' her mother asked when she saw the way she glared at Leandros's retreating back.

Isobel turned her head to look at her mother, who had known about her problems with Leandros three years ago, but who had never been told about the problems Isobel had had with his family. 'I'm just a bit nervous about meeting people again,' she answered. 'It's too soon.'

'When you fall off a horse the best thing to do is get right back on it,' was her mother's blunt advice—while thoroughly ignoring the fact that mounting the dreaded horse had come about three years too late. 'And if I can see that you two looked so happy you have to be right for each other, then give other people the chance to make the same discovery,' she added sagely.

Isobel was about to open her mouth and tell her mother the hard facts about those other people, then changed her mind, because what was the use in stirring up trouble before it arrived? She was here—though she still wasn't sure how it had happened. She was staying—though she wished it didn't fill her with such a nagging ache of uncertainty.

Silvia sat back in her chair and released a happy sigh. 'Gosh, I feel reborn today,' she said. 'It makes me want to sing.'

She did sing—all morning. She loved every gown that

arrived—within the hour—complete with every accessory she could require. By the time Silvia went off for her afternoon siesta, Isobel was glad to escape to her room and wilt. But she couldn't wilt completely because she was expecting Leandros to walk in at any moment and she wanted to be ready for him.

However Leandros was running late. The few hours he had intended to spend at work had gone smoothly enough. Time began to get away from him when he went to the boot of his car to put away the briefcase he had left in his office the day before, and discovered that the jacket he had been wearing still lay where he had placed it before chasing after Isobel.He saw the edge of the envelope straight away. It was sticking out of one of the pockets but it was only when he reached down to slide it free that he remembered what it contained.

Two minutes later he was heading into the city, not out of it. A few minutes after that and he was striding into the bank with his wife's safety deposit box key and her letter authorising him to open the box. His curiosity was fully engaged as to what Isobel's idea of *family heirlooms* actually consisted of...

By the time he did eventually arrive home it was to find Isobel sitting cross-legged upon the bed, wearing what looked like one of his own white T-shirts—and nothing else from what he could see. She must have just come from the shower. Her hair was wet, and she was sitting with her head thrown forward while she combed the silken pelt with slow, smooth strokes, allowing the excess water to fall onto a white towel she had laid out in front of her.

'If you want a shower, I suggest you use a different bathroom,' she advised without lifting her head. 'Otherwise I might decide to murder you while you're naked and vulnerable in this one.'

He started to grin as he stood leaning in the doorway. In truth, after the trick he'd pulled this morning he had expected her to show her protest by refusing to come near this room.

'Not you, my sweet angel,' he denied lazily. 'You would see my quick death as being too kind to me.'

'Don't bank on it.'

'OK. I will live dangerously, then.' With that he levered away from the doorframe, came into the room and closed the door.

She still did not deign to lift her head as he walked across the room and placed two black velvet jewellery cases into the top drawer of a chest. Studying her as he removed his jacket and tie, he tried to decide whether to simply jump on her and give her no chance to defend herself, or whether to annoy her by ignoring her as she was ignoring him.

The former was tempting, but the latter should win since the shower seemed the best venue for the both of them. Her hair was wet already. The T-shirt belonged to him, and, having issued the threat, she would not, he knew, be able to remain sitting there passively without being drawn to carry out it out.

With a click and a scrape he undid his trousers and heeled off his shoes. Isobel's comb continued its smooth strokes while he removed his socks, then his under-shorts, which left only his shirt to conceal the fact that he was already very much aroused by this little game. He needed a shave so he strode into the danger-zone of the bathroom, paused long enough to reach in and spring the showerhead to life before he picked up his electric razor and began using it.

She arrived at the door as he had predicted, looked disconcerted to find him standing by the bathroom mirror, then mulish when she realised she had been outwitted by him.

'Choose your weapon,' he invited without allowing his eyes to leave the mirror, where his own reflection showed him a man who had changed a lot in the last twenty-four hours. Gone were the harsh lines of cynicism he had watched increase over the previous three years. Now he saw a pretty good-looking guy with a decent pair of shoulders and sexily provoking promise about him.

She did this for him, he acknowledged. This moody woman with the slicked-back wet hair and the sensationally smooth white skin.

She leapt without warning. Dropping the razor into the washbasin, he swung round in time to catch her against his chest. Green eyes glittered, her mouth quivered, her arms wrapped tightly around his neck.

'I don't want to go tonight!' she cried out plaintively.

She chose her weapon well. Anger he could deal with—a physical attack. But true tears and fear were different things entirely. 'Don't cry, *agape mou*. That isn't fair.'

'Can't we wait a few days before you toss me to the wolves again—please?' she begged.

The *please* almost unmanned him. He recovered while carrying her back to the bed. 'If anyone so much as glances at you wrongly I will strike them down, I promise you.'

'They can still think what they like about me, Andros!'

Andros; she was the only person to ever get away with calling him that, so when she did it, it turned his senses over, it tied possessive ropes around his heart. Vulnerable, cowardly, beautiful Isobel—the Isobel she let no one else ever see.

With grim intent he sat down on the bed then, as she still clung to him, he rolled them both backwards until they lay on their sides. 'Do you truly believe that we two are the only ones to regret what happened before?' he demanded. 'My mother had to watch me go to pieces. Within the year after you left I left here also and rarely ever came back again.'

'Where did you go?' She was diverted. He almost laughed at the irony. He revealed weakness and she suddenly became the strong one! 'To Spain,' he replied. 'To a place called San Estéban. I ran my companies from a stateroom on my yacht and learned to live with myself by pretending Athens didn't exist.'

'You should have come to me!' Her fist made contact with his shoulder. He trapped her beneath him on the bed. Her legs still clung though. She was not letting go of him and she was wearing nothing beneath the T-shirt.

'I did come to you,' he growled. 'Every night in my dreams!'

'Not good enough.'

'Then we have a lot of time to make up for,' he gritted and entered her—no preliminaries. Her cry was one of pleasure because she was ready to receive him. She clutched his head and brought his mouth crashing down onto hers. They rode the hot wind of raging passion. When it was over and he felt his strength return to him he got up as still she clung and walked them both beneath the shower, where he began the whole exhilarating ride all over again.

Getting ready to go out was not easy when he was feeling laid-back and slumberous. Fortunately, Isobel had wisely disappeared to the other bedroom so at least the temptation to forget tonight's party and remain lost in her was removed—in part. He was all too aware of that soft, pulsing sense of continued possession. He had only to think of her and he could imagine her crawling all over him in her desire to lay claim to every exquisitely receptive inch of his skin.

He grimaced as he retrieved the black jewellery cases from the chest of drawers, then went to find his red-haired tormentor. If she launched another attack on his defences, they would not be going anywhere, he promised his impatient senses.

CHAPTER EIGHT

HE ENTERED the room with a light tap to warn of his arrival. Isobel turned to the mirror to take one last look at herself and could not decide if she liked what she saw.

Nervous fingers fluttered down the short, close-fitting lined straight dress she had chosen to wear. It was made of a misty-jade silk-crêpe that clung sensually to her slender figure without being too obvious—she hoped. Her make-up was light and natural, her kitten-heeled lightweight mules matched the colour of the dress. But had she struck the note she had been striving for, in a different key to the old downright-provocative Isobel, without appearing as if she had conceded anything to the Greek idea of what was good taste?

'What do you think?' She begged his opinion while anxiety darkened her eyes and she wished to goodness that she'd worn her hair down—it had not occurred to her before that she liked to use her hair to hide behind and now she felt very exposed.

Leandros didn't reply, so she turned to gauge his expression, only to go breathlessly still when she found herself looking at a man from any warm-blooded woman's dreams. He'd discarded the conventional black dinner suit in favour of a white dinner jacket, black silk trousers and a black bow-tie. He looked smooth and dark and so sexually masculine that those tiny muscles inside her that were still gently pulsing from their last stimulation began to gather pace all over again.

His darkly hooded eyes moved over her in a way she

recognised only too well. Mine, the look said. 'Stunning,' he murmured. 'Nothing short of perfect.'

So are you, she was going to say, but as he walked towards her she noticed the black velvet jewellery cases in his hand and recognised them instantly.

Nervous fingers feathered the front of her dress again. 'S-so you got them back,' she said.

'The heirlooms?' His mouth twitched. 'As you see,' he confirmed easily.

With the neat flick of a finger he opened the flat case, gave her a few seconds to stare down at the platinum scrolls pierced with glowing emeralds and edged with sparkling diamonds that she had thought so beautiful when first she saw them. But that was before his sister's scornful, *'He's given you those old things? Mother always refused to wear them. Though they are definitely wasted on you,'* had taken their beauty away.

Now those same long fingers were lifting the necklace from its bed of velvet. 'Turn around,' he commanded.

'I...' Reluctance to so much as touch any of the pieces lying in that case was crawling across her skin. 'I gave you them back,' she pointed out edgily. 'I don't really want—'

'It has been a few eventful days filled with many second chances,' he replied in a light tone filled with sardonic dryness, 'for here I am, giving them back to you. They will be perfect with this lovely dress, don't you think?'

Maybe they would. 'But...' The necklace sparkled and glittered across the backs of his fingers. She lifted wary eyes to his and instantly felt as if she was drowning in a thick, dark sea of lazy indulgence. Let's go back to bed, she wanted to say. I feel safe there with you. 'Don't you think my wearing them tonight would be like slapping your family in the face with the fact that I am back? M-maybe I will wear them another time.'

'But you are back,' he pointed out with devastating simplicity. 'You are my beautiful wife. I gave these beautiful things to you and *I* want you to wear them. So turn around...'

She turned around, taking that sudden gleam of determination in his eyes with her. The necklace came to lie against her skin, circling the base of her throat as if it had been specially made to do so.

'A new beginning for you and I also mean a new beginning for everyone, *agape mou*,' he said deeply as she felt the warm press of his lips to her nape.

Then he was gently bringing her round to face him. With a neat flick the matching bracelet arrived around her slender wrist. Her stomach began to dance when he reached up to gently remove the tiny gold studs she was wearing in her ears. She could not believe there was another man alive who knew how to thread the fine hooks, from which there were suspended matching emerald-and-diamond-studded scrolls, into the piercing of a woman's ears without hurting.

He was standing so close—close enough for it to take only the slightest movement from her to close the gap. She stared at the sensual shape of his mouth and wanted badly to kiss it. Her breasts began to ache, her breathing shallowing out to hardly anything at all.

Flustered by her own crass lack of control around him, she turned away to stare into the mirror again. He was right about the jewellery looking perfect with the dress, she conceded reluctantly.

Her eyes flicked up to catch his in the mirror. He stood a head and the white-covered width of his shoulders taller than she did. She saw dark and light, frailty and strength.

They contrasted in every way there was, yet fitted together as if it had always meant to be this way.

'I still think that wearing these is like a slap in the face to your family,' she insisted.

Reaching up with a hand, he ran the gentle tip of a finger around the sparkling necklace. 'I think I am going to enjoy myself not too many hours from now.'

He was talking about sex on a bed draped with his wife wearing nothing but diamonds and emeralds. He was conjuring up enticing visions with which she didn't need any help to remember for herself. He laid a kiss upon her shoulder; she quivered, he sighed—then stepped away to pick up the other velvet box he had brought into the room with him.

She had forgotten all about it until he flicked up the lid. Her stomach was not the only thing to dance with fine flutters as he took a ring between finger and thumb. Ridding himself of the box, he slid the ring onto her finger until it came to rest against her wedding ring.

'This stays where it is,' he said very seriously.

The huge central stone seemed to issue a proclamation as he lifted it to his mouth. The diamonds framing the emerald almost blinded her beneath the overhead light. She might not know much about precious stones but she could recognise quality when she saw it.

'Who did these belong to—originally, I mean?' she asked curiously.

A mocking look appeared along with a lazy grin. 'The emeralds once belonged to a Venezuelan pirate who wore the one in the ring set into his front tooth.'

She laughed; it was irresistible not to at such an outrageous fairy tale. 'He would have had to have huge teeth!' she exclaimed.

'A swashbuckling, dark giant of a man with a black

velvet patch worn over one eye,' he embroidered shame-
lessly. Then, so unexpectedly it took her breath away, he
bent to kiss her full on the mouth.

He stole her lipstick; she didn't care. He stole her every
anxiety about tonight by reminding her of what really mattered. They left the bedroom hand in hand and walked
down the stairs, meeting her mother, who was just making
her way down the hallway, looking so lovely in her blue
dress threaded with silver that her daughter stopped and
sighed, 'Oh, Mum...'

The nerves returned when they turned into the driveway
of a mansion house set in beautiful gardens lit to welcome
its guests. Isobel's mother refused the use of her wheelchair, waving it away when their driver attempted to help
her into it. Dignity and pride came before common sense
tonight, though Silvia could not dismiss her need of her
walking frame, no matter how independent she would prefer to be. However she was feeling buoyant and determined to enjoy herself.

Her daughter wished she could find the same motiva-
tion. Leandros's hand resting against her lower spine instilled some reassurance but the line-up of people waiting
at the entrance was so daunting that Isobel was glad they
were forced to take their time by matching their pace to
her mother's slower steps.

She was introduced to Mr and Mrs Santorini and their
daughter Carlotta, who was a lovely thing with dark hair
and even darker liquid, smiling eyes. All three welcomed
Isobel graciously but they were obviously curious about
her, no matter how they tried to hide it. Nikos reminded
her of Leandros when she had first met him, before life
had got around to honing his handsome face. Nikos's smile
was rueful as he greeted her with a lazy, 'Happy to see

you here, Isobel.' As he bent to place a kiss on her cheek he added softly, 'And about time too.'

It was a nice thing for him to say, and helped to ease the next moment when Isobel had to face Leandros's mother. Thea looked stiff and awkward as she greeted the daughter-in-law who had been such a big disappointment to her. She was kind to Silvia, though, showed a genuine concern about her accident and promised to spend time with her later, catching up on what had happened.

'See, it wasn't so bad,' Leandros said quietly as they moved away.

'Only because you'd obviously primed them,' she countered.

The click of his tongue told her she had managed to annoy him. 'The chip on your shoulder must be very heavy, *agape*,' he drawled caustically, and the hand at her spine fell away. Feeling suddenly cast adrift as they stepped into a large reception room, Isobel then had to stand alone to deal with something like a hundred faces turning her way.

Some stared in open surprise, others glanced quickly down and away. Her skin began to prickle as the nerves she had been keeping under tight control broke free. Leandros could prime his family but he could not prime everyone, she noted painfully as the hiss of soft whispers suddenly attacked her burning ears.

It was awful. She felt that old familiar sensation as if she was beginning to shrink. With a lifting of her chin she stopped it from happening. Damn you all, her green eyes flashed.

Like the old times—like the old times, she chanted silently.

Her mother arrived at Leandros's other side, thankfully drawing some of the attention her way. Silvia, too, stopped to stare in surprise at what was taking place. 'Are we the star turn, Leandros?' she asked him. She wasn't a fool; her mother knew exactly what was going on here.

One of his hands went to cover one of Silvia's hands where it gripped the walking frame, the other arrived at Isobel's waist. Then he lifted his dark head to eye the room as a whole, and with a few economical movements he silenced whispers.

It came as a small shock to Isobel to see how much command he seemed to have over such an illustrious assembly. He had not warranted this much respect the last time she'd been here. Their three years apart had given him something extra she could only describe as presence. She had noticed it before in other ways but had not suspected that he could silence tongues with a single lift of his chiselled chin.

People went back to whatever they had been doing before they'd arrived to interrupt. Without uttering a word Leandros guided them towards a low sofa set against the nearest wall to them and quietly invited Silvia to sit. She shook her head. Like mother like daughter, Isobel mused ruefully. Neither of them was going to allow themselves to shrink here.

A waiter appeared to offer them tall flutes of champagne. Beginning to feel just a little bit nauseous, she allowed herself a tiny sip. 'OK?' Leandros murmured huskily.

'Yes,' she replied but they both knew she wasn't.

'I apologise for my earlier remark.' It was an acknowledgement that the chip-on-the-shoulder taunt had not been fair. 'I think I should have anticipated this. But, in truth, I did not expect them to be so...'

Rude, she finished for him. And—yes, he should have

expected it. But this was no time to jump into a row with him. That would come later, she promised herself.

'Isobel!' The call of her name brought her head up and the first genuine smile to widen her mouth. A diversion was coming in the shape of Eve Herakleides, who was bearing down upon them with her daunting giant of a grandfather and another man Isobel presumed must be Eve's new husband.

'Oh, this is just too good to be true!' Eve exclaimed as she arrived in front of them. Suddenly and intentionally, Isobel was sure, friendly, warm faces were surrounding them.

She and Eve shared kisses. Leandros was greeting Eve's grandfather—his uncle Theron—and introducing Theron to Silvia. Then Eve drew her husband forward and proudly presented him as her gorgeous Englishman. Ethan Hayes grimaced at being described in this way, but his eyes were smiling and his hand made its possessive declaration where it rested on Eve's slender waist.

Tensions began to ease as shifted they positions to complete introductions all round. Isobel found herself confronted by the great Theron Herakleides, who looked nothing like Leandros's mother. But then, they had been born several decades apart to different mothers. 'I am very happy to see you here,' he announced quite gravely, and bent to make the traditional two-kiss greeting.

Someone else arrived within their select little circle. It was Leandros's beautiful sister, Chloe, wearing an exquisite long and slinky gown of toreador red that set off her tall, dark, slender beauty to perfection. Her actions were stilted, the greeting she offered Isobel filled with the same awkward coolness as her mother's had been. Chloe was the youngest of the three Petronades children. All her life she had been adored and doted on by all the Petronades males, which in turn had made her spoiled and selfish, and she resented anyone who threatened to steal some of that adoration away from her.

She'd seen Isobel as one of those people. It still remained to be seen if Nikos's lovely Carlotta was going to be treated to the same petulant contempt. But, for now, Isobel was prepared to be polite and friendly—just in case Chloe had changed her attitude in the last three years.

Leandros saw his sister differently. Spoiled and selfish though she undoubtedly had been three years ago, she had gone through a very tough time after their father died. She'd worshipped him above all others, and losing him had left a huge gap in her heart that she'd looked to him and Nikos to fill. When he'd married Isobel, Chloe had taken this as yet another devastating loss and had fiercely resented Isobel for being the cause.

Chloe had changed over the last three years though. Grown up, he supposed, and was less of a spoiled little cat. Though he understood that Isobel didn't know that— which was why he felt her fingers searching for the secure comfort of his hand as Chloe levelled her dark eyes upon her and said, 'Welcome home, Isobel,' then concluded the greeting with a kiss to both of Isobel's cheeks with a very petulant mouth.

He was about to offer a wry smile at this bit of petulance, when something else happened to wipe out all hint of humour. As she drew away Chloe's gaze flickered down to the jewels flashing at Isobel's throat and a faint flush was suddenly staining her elegant cheekbones as she looked away in clear discomfort.

He had his culprit, he realised grimly.

The ever-sharp Eve also noticed Chloe's fleeting glance at Isobel's throat—and her ensuing discomfort. The little minx made a play of checking out Isobel's necklace. 'Oh, how lovely,' she declared. 'Are they old or are they new?'

'Most definitely new,' Leandros answered smoothly. 'I had them specially commissioned for Isobel just after we were married,' he explained. 'As far as I recall Isobel has only worn them once before—isn't that so, *agape mou*?'

'I... Yes.' He watched her fingers jerk up to touch the necklace. She was trying to hide her shock at what he had said, while his sister had turned to a block of stone.

'We like to call them the family heirlooms.' Oh, cruelty be mine, he thought with grim satisfaction as he soothed Isobel with the gentle squeeze of her hand and smiled glassily into his sister's unblinking eyes. Chloe realized that he now knew the kind of unkind rubbish she had fed to his wife. She also now realized that she was in deep trouble the next time he got her alone. He was looking forward to it, Chloe certainly wasn't.

The buffet dinner was announced. Maybe it was fortunate because it gave his darling sister the excuse to melt away. People shifted positions as the slow mass exodus to the adjoining room began. Eve strolled away with her husband. Theron was gallantly offering to escort Isobel's mother. They went off together, Theron matching his long strides to Silvia's smaller steps while talking away to her with an easy charm.

Which left them alone again. 'I think Theron has taken to your mother,' he observed lightly.

'Just don't speak,' his wife told him stiffly. 'I'm too angry to listen to you.'

He looked down into glinting eyes. 'Why, what have I done?' he asked innocently.

'You don't have to do anything to be a horrible person,' she answered. 'It must be in the genes.'

'Then you understand why my sister is the way that she

is,' he countered smoothly, and when she went to stalk away from him he stopped her by tightening his grip on her hand. 'We do not run away any more, *agape mou*,' he reminded her.

'Sometimes I can hate you.' Her chin was up. 'All the time you were dressing me up in these, you were laughing at me!'

He laughed now, low and huskily. She was beginning to sizzle. He loved it when she sizzled. 'The Venezuelan pirate was pure inspiration.' Another flash sparked from her eyes and he should have been slain where he stood. 'Now tell me the fairy tale Chloe fed to you.'

Her mouth snapped shut in refusal to answer. 'Loyalty from the witch for the cat?' he drawled quizzically. 'Now, that does surprise me.'

Isobel had surprised herself. She had a suspicion her silence had something to do with the pained look she'd seen on Chloe's face as Leandros taunted her, and the fact that Chloe had flicked her a glance of mute apology before she'd slipped away.

'I'm hungry,' she said, which could not be less true since she knew she would not be able to swallow a single thing tonight. But the claim served its purpose in letting him know that a discussion about his sister was not going to happen. Not until she understood where Chloe was coming from these days. It was Leandros who wanted her to give his family a chance, after all.

'Why Venezuelan?' she asked suddenly. 'Why not French or Spanish or—?'

His laughter sent his dark head back. People turned to stare as if they weren't used to hearing him laugh like this. He deigned not to notice their disconcerted glances, kissed her full on her mouth then led her to join the crush around the buffet table.

The evening moved on. With a quiet determination, Leandros took her from group to group and pulled her into conversation in a way that she could only describe as making a statement about the solidarity of their marriage. As he did this he also exposed yet another secret, by always making sure he made some remark to her in Greek. By the time a couple of hours had gone by there wasn't a person present who had known her before who did not know now that she understood their native tongue.

And he had done it with such ruthless intention. Leandros was making sure that people thought twice before discussing his wife in her presence. Some looked uncomfortable at the discovery; some simply accepted it with pleased surprise. The uncomfortable ones were logged in his memory; Isobel could almost see him compiling a list of those people who would not be included in their social circle in the future.

Other people made sure they kept their distance, which spoke even greater volumes about what they were thinking. Takis Konstantindou was one of those people. Chloe, of course, was another one. She could understand Chloe's reasons for steering clear of them but the lawyer's cool attitude puzzled her.

Then there was Diantha Christophoros. If Isobel glimpsed her at all it was usually within a group that contained either Chloe or Leandros's mother. In a way she could find it in herself to feel sorry for Diantha, because it couldn't have been easy for her to turn up here tonight knowing that everyone here was going to know by now that old rumours about Leandros wanting to divorce his wife to marry her had to be false.

'Don't you think we should go and speak to her?' she suggested when she caught Leandros glancing Diantha's way.

'For what purpose?' he questioned coolly.

'She has got to be feeling uncomfortable, Leandros. The rumours affect her as much as they do you.'

'The best way to kill a rumour is to starve it,' was his response. 'Diantha seems to have my sister and my mother to offer all the necessary comfort.'

Which said, more or less, what Isobel had been trying *not* to think. The family preference could not be more noticeable if they stuck signs on their backs saying 'Vote Isobel out and Diantha in'. It was Eve Herakleides who put it in an absolute nutshell when she came to join Isobel out on the terrace, where she'd slipped away to get some fresh air that did not contain curiosity and intrigue.

'Word of warning,' Eve began. 'Watch out for Diantha Christophoros. She may appear nice and quiet and amiable but she has hidden talents behind the bland smile. She has a way of manipulating people without them realising she's doing it. It was only a few weeks ago that she convinced Chloe that she should remain here to help her mother with Nikos's wedding arrangements, while Diantha went to Spain in Chloe's place to help Leandros with a big celebration party he threw in San Estéban. Chloe puzzled for ages afterwards as to how it had actually come about that she'd agreed, since she had been so looking forward to spending two weeks with her brother. Then, blow me if Diantha isn't back in Athens for less than a day when the rumours were suddenly flying about Leandros filing for divorce from you so that he could marry her. She wants your husband,' she announced sagely. 'And her uncle Takis wants her to have him.'

'Takis and Diantha are related?' It was news to Isobel.

Eve nodded. 'They're a tightly knit lot, these upper-crust Greeks,' she said candidly. 'Thank goodness for women like you and my mother or they'd be so inbred they would have wiped themselves out by now.'

'What a shocking thing to say!' Isobel gasped on a compulsive giggle.

'And what shocking thing is this minx saying now?' Leandros intruded.

A pair of hands arrived at Isobel's slender waistline, the brush of his lips warmed her cheek—the lick of his tongue against her earlobe as he pulled away again sent her wretched knees weak.

'Woman-talk is for women only,' the minx answered for herself. 'And you, dear cousin, have had a lucky escape in my opinion.' With that provocatively cryptic remark, she walked away.

They both turned to watch her go, an exquisite creature dressed in slinky hot pink making a direct line for her husband, who sensed her coming—his broad shoulders gave a small shake just before he turned around and grinned.

'She hooked him in against his will,' Leandros confided. 'I think he still finds it difficult to believe that he let her do it.'

'Well, I think he's a very lucky man,' Isobel stated loyally because she liked Eve and always had done.

'Mmm,' he murmured, 'so am I...'

'No—don't,' she breathed when he began to lower his dark head again. 'Not here; you will ruin what bit of dignity I have managed to maintain.'

His warm laughter teased as he used his grip on her waist to swing her round until her hips rested against the heavy stone balustrade behind her. His superior bulk was suddenly hiding her from view of everyone else. Eyes like molasses began sending the kind of messages that forced her to lower her gaze from him.

'I like you in this,' she murmured softly, running her fingers beneath the slender lapels of his white jacket.

'Tell me I look like a Greek waiter and I will probably toss you over this balustrade,' he warned.

Her smile appeared wrapped in rueful memories of the time she had once said that to him in an attempt to flatten his impossible ego. 'I was such a bitch,' she confessed.

'No,' Leandros denied that. 'You assured me at the time that you had a hot thing for Greek waiters. I think I was supposed to feel complimented,' he mused thoughtfully.

It was irresistible; she just had to lift her laughing eyes upwards again. It was a mistake. She just fell into those eyes filled with such warm, dark promises. Her breath began to feather, a new kind of tension began circling them like a sensual predator circling its two victims while inside the house, beyond the pair of open terrace doors, a party was taking place. Music was filtering out to them on the warm summer air along with laughter and the general hum of conversation.

'I love you,' she said. It came out of nowhere.

He responded with a sharp intake of breath. His shoulders tensed, his whole body stiffened, his grip tightened on her waist. 'Fine time to tell me that!' he snapped out thinly. But he wasn't angry, just—overwhelmed.

She began to tremble because it had been such a dangerous thing for her to say out loud. It committed her, totally and utterly. It stood her naked and exposed and so vulnerable to hurt again that her throat locked up on a bank of emotion which threatened to turn into tears.

He was faring no better. She could feel the struggle he was having with himself not to respond in some wildly passionate way. A verbal response would have been enough for Isobel. A simple, 'I love you too,' would have helped her through this.

'I'll take it back if you like,' she shot out a trifle wildly.

'No,' he rasped. 'Just don't speak again while I...'

Deal with this; she finished the sentence for him. It was silly; it was stupid. They were grown-ups who were supposed to have a bit more class than to put each other through torture in public. She couldn't stop herself from flicking a glance at his face. As she did so he looked down. A wave of feeling washed over both of them in a static-packed blowback from just three little words.

They could have been alone. They *should* have been alone. Her breasts heaved on a tense pull of air. His hands pulled her hard against him. 'Don't kiss me!' she shot out in a constrained choke.

'The balustrade is still very tempting,' he gritted. 'I thought Eve was the biggest minx around here but you knock her into a loop.'

Heat was coursing through her body; the shocking evidence that he was on fire for her was shutting down her brain. The music played, the laughter and hum of conversation swirled all around them. In a minute, she had a horrible suspicion, she was going to find herself flattened to the ground with this big, lean, suave and sophisticated man very much on top.

'All sweetness and light,' he continued, thrusting the words down at her from between clenched teeth. 'All smiles and quiet answers for everyone else. The hair is up, so neat and prim—since when did you ever give way to such convention? Everyone back there sees the beautifully refined version of Isobel but I have to get the tormenting witch!'

'Keep talking,' she encouraged. She was beginning to get angry now. 'If you do it for long enough maybe you will wear yourself out!'

'I am not wearing out.' He took her words literally. 'I

am just getting started. From the moment you strode back into my life on those two sensational legs of yours you've had me standing on pins like some love-lost fool with no idea what is happening to me.'

'Did you dare use the love word then?' she taunted glacially.

'I've *always* loved you!' he thrust out harshly. 'I loved you when we flirted across the top of a Ferrari. I still loved you when you left me pining for three damn years!'

'Three years of pining,' she mocked unsteadily. 'I didn't see any evidence of it.' But he'd said it. He had actually said it.

'We've been through that already,' he snapped out impatiently.

'You brought me back here to divorce me.'

'It was an excuse. Anyone with sense would have realised that.'

'You had your next wife all picked out and ready.'

'I am arrogant. You know I am arrogant. Can you not cut a man a bit of slack?'

'Which is why I had to say it first, I suppose.'

The air hissed from between his teeth. If an electric cable had been fitted to them, they could have lit up the night there was so much static stress.

'I think the *both* of us are about to go over this balustrade,' he gritted furiously.

'You will go first,' Isobel vowed. 'And I hope you break your arrogant neck!'

A sound behind them brought them swinging round in unison. Isobel's heart sank to her shoes when she saw her mother-in-law hovering a few yards away. What did they look like? What did she see? Two people locked in a row that probably brought back a hundred memories of similar rows like this? She looked wary and anxious, her black eyes flicking from one to the other. Oh, God, please help me, Isobel groaned silently.

'I am sorry to intrude,' Thea said stiffly, and her gaze finally settled upon Isobel's blushing face. 'But I am concerned about your mama, Isobel. Theron has her dancing with her walking frame and I am afraid his enthusiasm is tiring her out.'

A single glance through the doors into the house was all that was needed to confirm that Thea's concerns were real. The seventy-year-old Theron was indeed dancing with her mother, who was using the walking frame as a prop. The man was flirting outrageously. Silvia was laughing, enjoying herself hugely, but even from here Isobel could see the strain beginning to show on her face.

'I'll go and...' She went to move, but Leandros stopped her.

'No, let me. She will take the disappointment better if I do it,' he insisted. At Isobel's questioning glance, 'Two men fighting over her?' he explained quizzically, then dropped a kiss on her lips and strode off, pausing only long enough to drop a similar kiss on his mother's cheek.

Suddenly Isobel found herself alone with a woman who did not like her. Awkwardness became a tangible thing that held them both silent and tense.

'My son is very fond of your mother.' Thea broke the silence with that quiet observation.

'Yes.' Isobel's eyes warmed as she watched Leandros fall into a playful fight with Theron for Silvia's hand. 'My mother is fond of him, too.'

She hadn't meant it as a strike at their cold relationship but she realised that Thea had taken it that way as she stiffened and turned to leave. 'No, don't go, please,' she murmured impulsively.

Her mother-in-law paused. An ache took up residence

inside Isobel's chest. This was supposed to be a time for fresh starts and for Leandros's sake she knew she had to try to reach out with the hand of friendship.

'You were arguing again.' Once again it was Thea who took up the challenge by spinning to face her with the accusation.

'You misread what you saw,' Isobel replied, then offered up a rueful smile. 'We were actually making love.' Adding a shrug to the smile, she forced herself to go on. 'It has always been like this between us. We spark each other off. Sometimes I think we could light the whole world up with the power we can generate...' Her eyes glazed on a wistful float back to what Thea had interrupted. Then she blinked into focus. 'Though I understand why you might not have seen it like that,' she was willing to concede.

Her mother-in-law took a few moments to absorb all of this, then she sighed and some of the tension dropped out of her stiff shoulders. 'I understand that you learned Greek while you were here the last time.'

'Yes,' Isobel confirmed.

'I think, perhaps, that you therefore heard things said that should not have been said.'

Lowering her gaze. 'Yes,' she said again.

Another small silence followed. Then Thea came to stand by the balustrade. 'My son loves you,' she said quietly. 'And Leandros's happiness is all I really care about. But the fights...' She waved a delicately structured hand in a gesture of weariness. 'They used to tire me out.'

And me, Isobel thought, remembering back to when the sparks were not always so lovingly passionate.

'When you left here, I was relieved to see you go. But Leandros did not feel the same. He was so miserable here that he went to Spain on a business trip and did not come back again. He missed you.'

'I missed him too.'

'Yes...' Thea accepted that. 'Leandros wants us to be friends,' she went on. 'I would like that too, Isobel.'

Though Thea's tone warned that she was going to have to work at it. Isobel smiled; what else could she do? Her mother-in-law was a proud woman. She was making a climb-down here that took with it some of that pride.

Taking in a deep breath, she gave that pride back to her. 'I was too young four years ago. I was overwhelmed by your lifestyle, and too touchy and too rebellious by far to accept advice on how best to behave or cope.' Lifting her eyes to Leandros's mother's eyes, 'This time will be different,' she promised solemnly.

Her mother-in-law nodded and said nothing. They both knew they had reached some kind of wary compromise. As she turned to go back to the party Thea paused. 'I am sorry about the baby,' she said gravely. 'It was another part of your unhappiness here, because kindness was not used to help you through the grief of your loss.'

It was so very true that there really was no ideal answer to give to that. Her mother-in-law seemed to realise it, and after another hesitation she walked back into the house.

Leandros appeared seconds later and Isobel had to wonder if he had been leaving them alone to talk. He searched her face. 'OK?' he asked huskily.

She nodded, then had to step up to him and, sliding her arms inside his jacket and around his back, she pressed herself against his solid strength. 'Don't ever let me go again,' she told him.

'I won't.' It was a promise.

They left the party soon after that, making the journey home without speaking much. The talking was left to

Silvia, who chattered away about Theron and the plans he had to take her out tomorrow for the day.

'I can't believe it,' Isobel said to Leandros as they prepared for bed. 'My mother has caught the eye of the wealthiest man in Greece!'

'His roving eye,' Leandros extended lazily. 'My uncle Theron is an established rake.'

'But he's got to be seventy years old! Surely he can't be looking at my mother and seeing…'

Her voice trailed away in dismay as a dark eyebrow arched. 'I share the same blood.' He began to stalk her with a certain gleam in his eyes. She was wearing nothing but the family heirlooms. 'Do you think you will be able to keep up with me when I reach seventy and you will be…?'

'Don't you dare tell me how old I will be!' she protested.

But, as for the rest, well, she was more than able to keep up with him throughout the long, dark, silken night. This time it was different, like a renewal of vows they made to each other four distant years ago. There were no secrets left to hide, just love and trust and a desire to hold on to what they had found.

The morning brought more sunshine with it and breakfast laid out on the terrace for two. Silvia was taking breakfast in her room today before she got ready for her date. When it came time for Leandros to go and spend a few essential hours in his office, he left her with a reluctance that made her smile. Theron arrived. A big, silver-thatched, larger-than-life kind of man, he was polite to Isobel, flirtatious with her mother and somehow managed to convince Silvia that her wheelchair was required today, which earned him a grateful smile from Silvia's daughter.

Left to her own devices, Isobel asked Allise for a second

pot of tea, then sat back in her chair and tried to decide what she wanted to do with the few hours she had going spare while Leandros wasn't here.

She was wearing the green combat trousers and a yellow T-shirt today. The sum total of the wardrobe she had brought with her from England had now been exhausted and she was considering going out to do a bit of shopping, when Allise arrived with the promised pot of tea and an envelope that she said had just been delivered by hand.

Maybe Isobel should have known before she even touched it that it could only mean trouble. Everything was just too wonderful, much too perfect to stay that way. But the envelope did not come with WARNING printed on it, just her name typed in its centre and the fizz of intrigue because she could think of only one person who would do this, and he had been gone only half an hour.

He was up to something—a surprise, she decided, and was smiling as she split the seal.

But what fell into her hands had her smile dying. What she found herself looking at had her fingers tossing the photographs away from her as if she were holding a poisonous snake and she lurched to her feet with enough violence to send crockery spilling to the ground. Her chair toppled over with a clatter against the hard tile flooring, her hand shot up to cover her shaking mouth. Her heart was pounding, eyes that had been shining were now dark with a horror that was curdling the blood.

She stepped back, banged her leg on the upturned chair. She was going to be sick, she realised—and ran.

CHAPTER NINE

ALLISE found Isobel sitting on the floor of the bathroom which lay just off the terrace, her cheek resting against the white porcelain toilet bowl. On a cry of dismay the housekeeper hurried forward. '*Kyria,* you are ill!'

It was a gross understatement. Isobel was dying inside and she didn't think she was going to be able to stop it from happening.

'I get the doctor—the *kyrios.*'

'No!' Isobel exploded on a thrust of frail energy. 'No.' She tried to calm her voice when Allise stood back and stared at her. 'I'm all right,' she insisted. 'I just need to— lie down for a wh-while.'

Dragging herself to her feet, she had to steady herself at the washbasin before she could get her trembling legs to work. Stumbling out of the bathroom, she headed for the stairs, knew she would never make it up there and changed direction, making dizzily for the only sanctuary her instincts would offer up as an alternative—her mother's room.

Back to the womb, she likened it starkly as she felt the housekeeper's worried eyes watch her go. She was going to ring him; Isobel was sure of it. Allise would feel she had failed in her duty if she did not inform Leandros as to what she had seen.

But Leandros didn't need informing. At about the time that Isobel received her envelope, he was receiving one himself. As he stared down at the all-too-damning photographs the phone began to ring. It was Diantha's father;

161

he had received an envelope too. Hot on that call came one from his mother, then an Athens newspaper with a hungry reputation for juicy gossip about the jet set. It did not take a genius to know what was unfolding here.

Leandros was on his way home even as Isobel paused at the table where the photographs lay amongst the scattered crockery. His mobile phone was ringing its cover off. With an act of bloody, blinding frustration he switched it off and tossed it onto the passenger seat with the envelope of photos. Whoever else had received copies could go to hell because if he was certain about anything, then it was that Isobel had to be looking at the same ugly evidence.

His car screeched to a halt in the driveway, kicking up clouds of dust in its wake. He left the engine running as he strode into the house. Watching him go, the gardener went to switch off the engine for him, his eyes filled with frowning puzzlement. Allise was standing in the hall with her ear to the telephone.

'Where is my wife?' he demanded and was already making for the stairs when the housekeeper stopped him.

'Sh-she is in her mama's rooms, *kyrios*.'

Changing direction, he headed down the hallway. He lost his jacket as he hit the terrace. His tie went and he was about to stride past the debacle that was the breakfast table and chairs, when he saw the envelope and scatter of photographs, felt sickness erupt in his stomach and anger follow it with a thunderous roar.

Pausing only long enough to gather up the evidence, he continued down the terrace and into the rooms allotted to his mother-in-law. He had not been in here since Silvia took up residence and was surprised how comfortable she had managed to make it, despite the clutter of Isobel's photographic equipment still dotted around. Not that he cared about comfort right now, for across the room, lying curled on her mother's bed like a foetus, was his target.

His heart tipped sideways on a moment of agony—then it grimly righted again. Snapping the top button of his shirt free with angry fingers, he approached the bed with a look upon his face that promised retribution for someone very soon.

'Isobel.' He called her name.

She gave no indication that she had even heard him. Was she waiting for him to go down on his knees to beg for understanding and forgiveness? Well, not this man, he thought angrily and tossed the photographs down beside her on the bed.

'These are false,' he announced. 'And I expect you to believe it.'

It was a hard, tough, outright challenge. Still she did not even offer a deriding sob in response. It made him want to jump inside her skin so that she would *know* he could not have done this terrible thing.

'Isobel!' he rasped. 'This is no time for dramatics. You are the trained photographer. I need you to tell me how they did it so I can strangle the culprit with their lies.'

'Go away,' she mumbled.

On a snap of impatience, he bent and caught hold of her by her waist, then lifted her bodily off the bed before firmly resettling her sitting on its edge. Going down on his haunches, he pushed the tumble of silken hair back from her face. She was as white as a sheet and her eyes looked as if someone had reached in and hollowed them out.

'Now just listen,' he insisted.

Her response was to launch an attack on him. He supposed she had the right, he acknowledged as he grimly held on to her until she had finally worn herself out. Eventually she sobbed out some terrible insult then tried scrambling backwards in an effort to get away. Her fingers made contact with the photographs. On a sob she picked them up.

'You lied to me!' she choked out thickly. 'You said she meant nothing to you but—look—*look*!' The photographs shook as she brandished them in his grim face. 'You, standing on your yacht w-wearing nothing from what I can see, h-holding her in front of you while she's just about covered by th-that excuse for a slip!'

'It never—'

The photograph went lashing by his cheek, causing him to take avoiding action, and by the time he had recovered she was staring at the next one. 'Look at you,' she breathed in thick condemnation. 'How can you lie there with her, sleeping like an innocent? I will never forgive you—'

She was about to send the images the way of the other when he snaked out a hand and took the rest from her. 'You will believe me when I say these are not real!' he insisted harshly.

Not real? Isobel stared at him through tear-glossed eyes and wondered how he dared say that when each picture was now branded on her brain!

'I believed you when you said you hadn't—'

'Then continue to believe,' he cut in. 'And start thinking with your head instead of your heart.'

'I don't have a heart,' she responded. 'You ripped it out of my body and threw it away!'

'Melodrama is not helping here, *agape*,' he sighed, but she saw the hint of humour he was trying to keep from showing on his lips.

That humour was her complete undoing, and she began wriggling and squirming until he finally set her free to stand.

'I'm leaving here,' she told him as she swung to her feet.

'Running again?' he countered jeeringly. 'Take care,' he warned as he rose up also, 'because I might just let you do it. For I will *not* live my life fearing the next time you are going to take to your feet and flee!'

Isobel stared at him, saw the sheer black fury darkening his face. 'What are you angry with me for?' she demanded bewilderedly.

'I am not angry with you,' he denied. 'I am angry with—these.' He waved a hand at the photographs. 'You are not the only one to receive copies…' Then he told her who else had. 'This is serious, Isobel,' he imparted grimly. 'Someone is out to cause one hell of a scandal and I need your help here, not your contempt.'

With that he turned and began looking around the room with hard, impatient eyes. Spotting whatever it was he was searching for, he strode over to her old computer system and began checking that everything was plugged in. 'You know how to do this better than I do,' he said. 'Show me what I need to do to bring this thing to life.'

'It hasn't been used for three years. It has probably died from lack of use.'

'At least try!' he rasped.

It was beginning to get through to her that he was deadly serious. Moving on trembling legs and with an attitude that told him she was not prepared to drop her guard, she went to stand beside him. With a flick of a couple of switches she then stood back to wait. It was quite a surprise to watch a whole array of neglected equipment burst into life.

'Now what?' she asked stiffly.

'Scan those photographs into the relevant program,' he instructed. 'Blow them up—or whatever it is you do to them so we can study them in detail.'

'A reason would be helpful.'

'I have already told you once. They are fakes.'

'Sure?'

He swung on her furiously. 'Yes, I am sure! And I would appreciate a bit of trust around here!'

'If you shout at me once more I will walk,' she threatened fiercely.

'Then stop looking at me as if I am a snake; start using a bit of sense and believe me!' Striding off, he recovered the photographs—yet again. Coming back, he set them down next to the computer screen.

'Fakes, you say,' she murmured.

'Do your magic and prove me right or wrong.'

The outright challenge. Still without giving him the benefit of the doubt, she opened the lid on the flatbed scanner and prepared to work. Her mouth was tight, her eyes were cold, but with a few deft clicks of the mouse she began to carry out his instructions. If he was lying then he had to know she would find him out in a few minutes. If he was telling the truth then...

Her stomach began to churn. She was no longer sure which alternative she preferred. It was one thing believing that your estranged husband had been involved in an affair during your separation but it was something else entirely to know that someone was willing to go to such extremes to hurt other people.

'Why is this happening?' she questioned huskily. 'Who do you think it is that took these? It needs a third party involved to take photographs like these, Leandros. Someone close enough to you to be in a position to catch you on film like this.'

He was standing to one side of her and she felt him stiffen; glancing up, she caught a glimpse of his bleak expression before he turned away. 'Chloe, of course,' he answered gruffly.

Chloe? 'Oh, no.' She didn't want to believe that. Not Chloe, who adored her brother. 'She has nothing to gain by hurting both you and her best friend!'

'She gains what she's always wanted,' he countered tightly. 'Work—work!' he commanded as the first photograph appeared on the screen. Turning back, she clicked the mouse and the picture leapt to four times its original size. 'All her childhood she fantasised about one of her brothers marrying her best friend,' he continued darkly. 'Nikos and I have ruined those fantasies, so now she is out for revenge.'

'I don't want to believe it.'

'She has also been cleverer than I ever gave her credit for,' he added cynically. 'She damns me in your eyes. Damns both Diantha and me to Diantha's father, who honoured me with his trust when he allowed her to stay on my yacht with me. I saw a man taking photographs of the yacht from the quay. This one,' he flicked a finger at the screen, 'Shows exactly how I was dressed that day.'

'In nothing?'

'I have a pair of shorts on, you sarcastic witch!' He scowled. 'He had to have been paid by someone. Scheming Chloe is the logical person. Her ultimate aim is to see you walking off with a divorce and me being forced into marrying Diantha to save her reputation!'

'All of that is utterly nonsensical!' Isobel protested. 'No one goes to such drastic extremes on someone else's behalf.'

'Who else's behalf?' he challenged. 'Diantha's? She is being manipulated here just as ruthlessly as we are,' he insisted. 'Look at the evidence. Chloe sends Diantha in her stead to San Estéban. These photographs were taken there. I actually saw the guy taking this one!'

'And the one in your bedroom?' she prompted. 'How did he get in there?'

He paused to frown at the question. Then the frown cleared. 'He has to be a member of my crew,' he decided. 'He was too far away for me to recognise him.'

He thought he had an answer for everything. But Isobel was recalling a conversation with Eve Herakleides the night before, and suddenly she had a very different suspect to challenge Leandros's claims.

Flattening her lips and concentrating her attention on the screen, she took only seconds to spot the first discrepancy. Within a few minutes she had circled many—a finger missing, a point on the yacht's rail that did not quite fit. With the mouse flying busily, she copied then pasted each detail onto a separate frame, increased their size then sent them to print.

Through it all Leandros watched in silent fascination as the whole photograph was broken down and revealed for the fraud that it was. 'Do you want me to do the same to the rest of them?' she asked when she'd finished.

'Not unless you need to assure yourself that they are all fakes,' he responded coolly, gathering up his precious evidence.

It was a clean hit on her lack of trust. Isobel acknowledged it with a sigh. 'I suppose you want me to eat humble pie now.'

'Later,' he replied. 'Humble pie will not come cheap.'

But neither smiled as he said it. Fakes or not, the photographs had stolen something from them and Isobel had to ask herself if they were ever going to get it back again.

'Leandros...' He was striding for the door when she

stopped him. 'Chloe knows what I do for a living; remember that when you confront her.'

'Meaning what?' He glanced at her.

Isobel shrugged. 'Just go there with an open mind, that's all,' she advised. It wasn't up to her to shatter his faultless image of Diantha. And, anyway, she wasn't sure enough of her own suspicions to make an issue out of it.

But she was as determined as he was to find out.

He had been gone for less than two minutes before she was printing off her second lot of copies. His car was only just turning off the driveway when she was calling a taxi for herself. The Christophoros mansion was much the same as most of the houses up here on the hill. She was greeted by a maid who showed her into a small reception room, then hurried off to get the daughter of the house.

Diantha took her time. Needing something to do, Isobel reached into her bag to search out a hair-band and snapped her hair into a pony-tail. Leandros would see this as her donning her tough-lady persona, but she didn't feel tough. Her nerves were beginning to fray, her stomach dipping and diving on lingering nausea. She didn't know if she had done the right thing by coming here, wasn't even sure how she was going to tackle this—all she did know with any certainty was that Diantha had to be faced, whether guilty or innocent.

The door began to open and she swung round as Diantha appeared looking neat in a mid-blue dress and wearing a thoroughly bland expression that somehow did not suit the occasion, bearing in mind that Isobel could be a jealous wife come here to tear her limb from limb.

Indeed Diantha looked her over as if she were the marriage breaker in this room. 'We will have to make this brief.' There was a distinct chill to her tone. 'My father is on his way home and he will not like to find you here.'

Then she really took the wind out of Isobel's sails when she added smoothly, 'Now you have seen the truth about Leandros and myself, can we hope that you will get out of our lives for good?'

Isobel's fingers tightened on the shoulder strap to her bag. 'So it was you who sent the photographs?' she breathed.

Diantha's cool nod confirmed it. It seemed a bit of a let-down that she was admitting it so easily. 'Though I must add that anything I say to you here I will deny to anyone else,' she made clear. 'But you are in the way, and I am sick of being messed around by Leandros. Two weeks ago he was promising me he would divorce you and marry me, then I am being sidelined—for business reasons, of course; isn't it always?'

'Business reasons?' Isobel prompted curiously.

'The lack of a pre-nuptial agreement between the two of you put Leandros in an impossible situation.'

It was like being in the presence of some deadly force, Isobel thought with a shiver. Diantha was calm, her voice was level and Isobel could already feel herself being manipulated by the gentle insertion of the word pre-nuptial. Before she knew it Lester Miles' warnings about the power of her own position came back to haunt her. She was seeing Leandros's sudden change from a man ready to sever a marriage to a man eager to hang on to that marriage.

'I have to say that I am seriously displeased at being forced to lie about our relationship while he sorts out this mess,' Diantha continued. 'But a man with his wealth cannot allow himself to be ripped off by a greedy wife. Nor can he afford to risk our two family names being thrown into the public arena with a scandal you will cause if you wish to turn your divorce ugly. But you mark my words, Kyria Petronades, a contract will appear before very soon, mapping out the details of any settlements in the event of your marriage reaching a second impasse.'

'But you couldn't wait that long,' Isobel inserted. 'So you decided to cause the feared scandal and get it out of the way?'

'I am sick of having to lie to everyone,' she announced. 'It is time that people knew the truth.'

'About your affair in Spain with my husband,' Isobel prompted.

'A relationship that began long before you left him, if you must know the truth.' Her chin came up. 'He visited me in Washington, DC.'

Isobel remembered the Washington trips all too well.

'Our two weeks spent in Spain were not the first stolen weeks we managed to share together. I have no wish to hurt your feelings with this, but he was with me only yesterday, during siesta. We have an apartment in Athens where we meet most days of the week.'

'No photographic evidence of these meetings?' Isobel challenged.

'It can be arranged.'

'Oh, I am sure that it can.' And she removed the printouts from her handbag and placed them down on the table that stood between them. Believing she knew exactly what she was being presented with, Diantha didn't even deign to look.

'You are nothing but a lying, conniving bitch, Diantha,' Isobel informed her. 'You manipulate people and *adore* doing it. Chloe was manipulated to get you to Spain. My mother-in-law has been beautifully manipulated by your ever-so-gentle eagerness to please and offer her up an easier alternative to me as the daughter-in-law from hell.'

'You said it,' Diantha responded, revealing the first hint that a steel-trap mind functioned behind the bland front.

Isobel laughed. 'Leandros extols you for your great organisational skills—not a very appetising compliment to the woman he loves, is it?' she added when Diantha's spine made a revealing shift. 'Apparently you know how to put together a great party.' She dug her claws in. 'As for me, well, I struggle to organise anything, but he calls me a witch and a hellion and claims I have barbs for teeth. When we make love he falls apart in my arms and afterwards he sleeps wrapped around me. Not like this.' She stabbed a finger at the photograph. 'Not with him occupying one side of the bed while I occupy the other.'

Black eyelashes flickered downwards, her face kept firmly under control. Now she had drawn her attention to the photographs, Isobel slid out the other one, and its enlarged partners in crime. 'Thankfully, Leandros still has *all* his fingers.' She stabbed one of her own fingers on the missing one splayed across Diantha's stomach. 'If he stood behind you like this, the top of your head would reach no higher than his chest, not his chin. You are short in stature, Diantha—let's call a spade a spade here, since you wish to talk bluntly. You are not quite this slim or this curvaceous. And when you cut, shave and paste with a computer mouse it is always advisable to make sure you fill in the gaps you make, like the yacht rail here, which seems to stop for no apparent reason. A good manipulator should always be sure of all her facts and you forgot to check one small detail. This is my job.' She stabbed at the printouts. 'I am a professional photographer. I dealt with computer photography almost every day of my working life. So I know without even bothering to enlarge the bedroom scene that the folds of the sheet don't quite follow a natural line.

The slight shrug of Diantha's shoulders and indifferent expression surprised Isobel because she should have been feeling the pinch of her own culpability by now. But she just smiled. 'You are such a fool, Isobel,' she told her. 'I have always known what you do for a living, and these photographs were always meant to be exposed as fakes. Indeed it is essential that I did so to allay a scandal. I merely intended to expose them myself for what they are, then suggest that you probably did these yourself as a way of increasing your power in a divorce settlement. For who else is better qualified?'

She believes she has everyone tied up in knots, Isobel realised in gaping incredulity. She is so supremely confident of her own powers of manipulation that she has stopped seeing the wood for the trees!

'There is only one small problem with your plan, Diantha,' Isobel said narrowly. 'These photographs may be fakes, but I have no reason to want a divorce.'

'But does he want you or is Leandros merely protecting his business interests?'

'Oh, yes, I want her,' a smooth, deep voice replied.

The two women glanced up, saw Leandros standing there and looking as if he had been for quite a long time.

'Every minute of every waking moment,' he added smoothly. 'Every minute of every moment I spend lost in my dreams. You have a serious problem with your dreams, Diantha,' he told her sombrely, then without waiting for a reply he looked at Isobel. 'Shall we go?'

She didn't even hesitate, walking towards this man who was her life, with her eyes loving him and his loving her by return.

But Diantha was not about to give up so easily. 'Just because these photographs are not real, it does not mean we did not sleep together,' she threaded in stealthily. 'Tell her, Leandros, how we spent the nights upon your yacht. Tell her how your mama thinks she is a tart and your sister Chloe despises every breath that she takes. Tell her,' she persisted, 'how your whole family knew she was having an affair with some man while she was here last, and how you tried to discover who he was and even believed the child she was carrying belonged to this other lover!'

Isobel's feet came to a shuddering standstill. Her eyes clouded as she searched his. She was looking for sorrow, for a weary shake of the head to deny what Diantha was saying! For goodness' sake, she begged him; give me anything to say that she's still manipulating me here!

But he'd gone as pale as she'd ever seen him. His fingers trembled as he lifted them up to run through his hair. Most damning of all, he lowered his eyes from her. 'Come on,' he said huskily. 'Let's get out of here.'

Someone else was standing just behind him, and as Leandros moved Isobel saw Chloe looking white-faced. 'Diantha, stop this,' Chloe pleaded unsteadily. 'I don't understand why you—'

'You don't understand.' Diantha turned on her scathingly. 'What has it got to do with you? Your brothers used me and I will not be used!'

Brothers? Each one of them looked at her when she said this. She was no longer calm and collected, Isobel noticed. The veils of control had been ripped away and suddenly Diantha was showing her true cold and bitter self.

'All my life I had to watch you, Chloe, being worshipped by your family of men. You have no idea what it is like to be unloved and rejected by anyone. My father rejected me because I was not a desired son. Your brother rejected me because I was not what he wanted any more.'

'Diantha, I never—'

'Not you,' she flashed at Leandros. 'Nikos! Nikos rejected me four years ago! He said we were too young to know what love was and he did not even want to know! But I knew love. I waited and waited in Washington for him to come for me. But he didn't,' she said bitterly. 'You came instead, offering me those pleasant messages from home and not one from Nikos! So I came back here to Athens to make him love me! But when I arrived he was planning to marry Carlotta. I was out in the cold and there you were, Leandros, hiding in Spain with your broken heart! Well, why should we not mend together? You were thinking about it, I know you were. You can lie to her all you like, but I know that it was for me that you told Uncle Takis to begin divorce proceedings with her!'

His eyes narrowed. 'So Takis has been talking out of line,' he murmured silkily.

'No!' she denied that. 'I have discussed this with no one.'

'Then how did you know there was no pre-nuptial agreement?' Isobel inserted sharply.

Diantha floundered, her mouth hovering on lies she could not find.

'I think this has gone far enough,' yet another voice intruded. It was Diantha's father. 'You have managed to stop the photographs being printed in the newspaper, Leandros?' he enquired. At Leandros's grim nod, he nodded also. 'Then please leave my house and take your family with you.'

Mr Christophoros had clearly decided that his daughter had hurt enough people for one day.

The journey away was completed in near silence. Chloe sat sharing the passenger seat in Leandros's Ferrari with Isobel, her face drawn with shock and dismay. Leandros took his sister home first, pulling up outside a house that was three times the size of his own. As she climbed out of the car, she turned back to Isobel.

'I'm sorry,' she whispered urgently. 'I never meant—'

'Later, Chloe,' her brother interrupted. 'We will all talk later but now Isobel and I have to go.'

'But most of this is my fault!' she cried out painfully. 'I encouraged her to believe that she was meant for one of my brothers—'

'Childhood stuff,' Leandros said dismissively.

'I let her know how much I disliked Isobel!'

Isobel's chin went down on her chest. Chloe released a choking sob. 'I confided everything to her and she took it all away and plotted with it. I can't tell you how bad that makes me feel.'

Isobel could see it all. The two girls sighing over Leandros's broken heart—as Diantha had called it. The two of them wishing that Isobel had never been born.

'But I never knew a thing about her and Nikos,' Chloe inserted in stifled disbelief.

'It was nothing,' her brother declared. 'They dated a couple of times while you were away at college, but Nikos was made wary by her tendency towards possessiveness. He told her so and she took it badly. He was relieved when her family went to live in Washington—and I would prefer you not to mention this to him, Chloe,' he then warned very seriously. 'He will not appreciate the reminder at this time.'

He was talking about Nikos's coming marriage. Chloe nodded then swallowed and tentatively touched Isobel's arm. 'Please,' she murmured, 'can you and I make a fresh start?'

A fresh start, Isobel repeated inwardly, and her eyes glazed over. Everyone wanted to make fresh starts, but how many more ugly skeletons were going to creep out of the dark cupboard before she felt safe enough to trust any one of them?

She lifted her face though, and smiled for Chloe. 'Of

course,' she agreed. But the way her voice shook had Leandros slamming the car into gear and gunning the engine. His sister stepped back, her face pale and anxious. Isobel barely managed to get the car door shut before he was speeding away with a hissing spin of gravel-flecked tyres.

'What's the matter with you?' she lashed out in reaction.

'If you are going to cry, then you will do it where I can damn well get at you,' he thrust back roughly.

'I am not going to cry.'

'Tell that to someone who cannot see beyond the tough outer layer.' He lanced her a look that almost seared off her skin. 'I did not sleep with her—*ever*!' he rasped, turned his eyes back to the road and rammed the car through its gears with a hand that resembled a white-knuckled fist. 'I *liked* her! But she has poison in her soul and now I can feel it poisoning me.' His voice suddenly turned hoarse. 'Did I give her reason to believe what she does about me? Did I offer encouragement without realising it?'

His hand left the wheel to run taut fingers through his hair. It was instinctive for Isobel to reach across and grab the wheel.

'You don't need to do that,' he gritted. 'I am not about to drive us into a wall.'

'Then stop acting like it.'

The car stopped with a screech of brakes. Isobel had not put on her seat belt because Chloe had been sharing her seat and the momentum took her head dangerously close to the windscreen before an arm shot out and halted the imminent clash with a fierce clenching of male muscle.

Emotions were flying about in all directions. Stress—distress! Anger—frustration. He threw open his door, climbed out and walked away a few long strides, leaving

Isobel sitting there in a state of blank bewilderment as to what it was that was the matter with him.

It was her place to be this upset, surely? She had been the one who'd had to place her trust on the line ever since she came back here! She got out of the car, turned and gave the beautiful, glossy red door a very expressive slam. He spun on his heel. She glared at him across the glossy red bonnet. They were within sight of their own driveway but neither seemed to care.

'Just who the hell do you think you are, Leandros?' she spat at him furiously. She was still responding to the shock of almost having her head smacked up against the windscreen; her insides were crawling with all kinds of throbs and flurries. He was pale—*she* was pale! The sun was beating down upon them and if she could have she would have reached up and grabbed it then thrown it at his bloody selfish head! 'What do you think her poison is doing to me? You want a divorce then you don't want a divorce. Rumour has it that you have your next wife already picked out and waiting in the wings. Pre-nuptial agreements are suddenly the all-important topic on everyone's lips! And I am expected to trust your word! Then I am expected to trust your word again when those photographs turn up. I even face the bitch with her so-called lies!'

'They are lies, you know that—'

'All I know for certain at this precise moment is that you have been working me like a puppet on a string!' she tossed at him furiously. 'I've been insulted in your board-room—*stalked* around Athens—which appears is not the first time! I've been seduced at every available opportunity, teased over family heirlooms, paraded out in front of Athens' finest like a trophy that was not much of a prize!'

He laughed, but it was thick and tense. She almost climbed over the car bonnet to get her claws into him! 'Then I am forced to stare at those wr-wretched ph-photographs.' Her throat began to work; grimly she swallowed the threatening tears. 'Do you think because I could prove them to be fakes that they lost the power to hurt?'

'No.' He took a step towards the bonnet.

'I haven't finished!' she thrust at him thickly, and the glinting green bolts coming from her eyes pinned him still. '*I* faced the poison—while you went chasing off to the wrong place!' she declared hotly. 'I listened to her say all of those things about you and *still* believed in you. My God,' she choked. 'Why was that, do you think, when we only have to look back three years to see that we were heading right down the same road again?'

'It is not the same!' he blasted at her.

'It has the same nasty taste!' she cried. 'Your mother is prepared to *try* and like me for your sake and now your sister is prepared to do the same. Do I care if they like me?' Yes, I do, she thought painfully. 'No, I don't,' she said out loud. 'I don't think I care for you any more,' she whispered unsteadily.

'You don't mean that—'

She flicked his tight features a glance and wished to hell that she did mean it. 'Tell me about the pre-nuptial thing,' she challenged. 'Then go on to explain about this other man I am supposed to have fathered my child to. And then,' she continued when he opened his mouth to answer, 'explain to me why I have just had to listen to you bemoaning the poison that wretched woman has fed into you!'

Silence reigned. He looked totally stunned by the final question. A silver Mercedes came down the road. It stopped beside Isobel. 'Is something wrong?' a voice said. 'Can we be of assistance?'

Isobel turned to stare at Theron Herakleides. Beside him in the passenger seat, her mother was bending over to peer out curiously. 'Yes,' she said. 'You can give me a lift.' With that, she climbed into the back of the Mercedes.

'What about Leand—?'

'Just drive,' she snapped. Theron looked at her in blank astonishment. He had probably never been spoken to like this before in his life! Then she put a trembling hand up to cover her equally tremulous mouth. 'I'm sorry,' she apologised, and tears began to burn her eyes.

'Drive, Theron,' her mother murmured quietly. Without another word, Theron did as he was told, his glance shifting to his rear-view mirror, where he saw his nephew left standing by his car looking like a man who had just been hit by a car.

Watching his uncle Theron drive away with Isobel, Leandros was feeling as if he had been hit—by an absolute hellion with a torrent that poured from her mouth.

How had she done it? How had she managed to leave him standing here, feeling like the most selfish bastard alive on this planet?

Because you are, a voice in his head told him. Because there was not a word she'd said that did not ring true.

Ah. He spun around to stare blankly at his native city spread out beneath him and shimmering in a late-morning haze, and instead saw a jigsaw of words come to dance in front of his eyes. Words like, insulted, stalked, seduced— trophy. He uttered the same tense, half-amused laugh then wasn't laughing at all because she believed it to be the truth.

Just as she believed that he suspected their baby could have belonged to another man. His heart came to a stop, thudding as it landed at the base of his stomach as he joined that new belief with her old belief that he was glad when she miscarried. And what had he done? He'd sat beside her in his car and voiced concerns about his behaviour towards Diantha.

Was he mad? He turned around. Did she accuse him of possessing the sensitivity of a flea? Because if she did not then she should have done. Where the hell had his head been? he asked himself furiously.

What was he doing standing here when there was every chance she was packing to leave him right now?

Damn, he cursed, and climbed into his car. The engine fired; he pushed it in gear. If her suitcase was out then he was in deep trouble, he accepted as he covered the fifty yards to his driveway at breakneck speed.

Theron's car was already parked outside the front door and empty of its passengers. Striding into the house, he didn't think twice about where to look for her and took the stairs three at a time, arriving outside their bedroom before he paused then diverted to the room next door.

Thrusting the door open, he stepped inside. His instincts had not let him down. She was standing by the window, facing into the room with her arms folded.

Waiting for him, he noted with grim satisfaction, and closed the door. 'I did not believe you had been unfaithful to me,' he stated as he strode forward. 'The only marriage contract that you and I will ever have will have to be written in my blood on my deathbed since I have no intention of letting you go before I die. I do not think of you as a trophy, a puppet or a thing of mockery. And I don't *stalk* you, I *follow* you like some bloody faithful pet dog who does not want to be anywhere else but where you are.'

He came to a stop in front of her. Her eyes were dark, her mouth small and her hair was stuck in a pony-tail. She was wearing combat trousers and a tough-lady vest top but there were tears sliding down both smooth cheeks.

'If I loved you any more than I do already they would have to put me away because I would be dangerous,' he continued huskily. 'And if I sounded bloody insensitive back there then that is because I was hurt by those photographs too.'

She stifled a small sob. He refused to reach for her. He would answer all charges and *then* he would touch.

'Diantha has been a part of my family since she and Chloe were giggling schoolgirls. I believed Nikos had hurt her four years ago, I thought he had deliberately set out to turn her head and when she became serious left her flat. I even felt sorry for her so I visited whenever I was in Washington. But Nikos now tells me that he recognised her need to manipulate even then. I was wrong about her and now I am sorry—and don't think those tears are going to save you,' he added, 'because they are not.'

'Save me from what?'

'Retribution,' he answered. 'For daring to believe I could question the parentage of our child.'

'Your face—'

'My face was pained, I know,' he admitted. 'There is only one person who could have put such a filthy idea in her head and that is Takis. And how do I know that? Because he once dared to suggest such a thing to me.'

'Takis...?' Her eyelashes fluttered, tear-tipped and sparkling.

He rasped out a sigh that fell between anger and hurt. 'I was miserable, you were miserable,' he reminded her. 'We were living within a vacuum where we did not communicate. Takis was the closest thing I had to a father back then. He asked about our marriage, and when I stupidly said in a weak moment that I was worried about you because you were forever going missing he suggested that maybe I should find out where you go.'

He clamped his mouth shut over the rest of that conversation. What it contained did not matter here. What did was that his most trusted friend and employer had been passing on confidential information. 'Now I find he has been disclosing confidential information about pre-nuptial contracts and the lack of.'

'Did he set up the photographer too?'

He sighed and shook his head. 'I am hoping he did not. I am hoping that the photographs were all Diantha's idea. Has it occurred to you that she had taken those things before she knew that you and I would get back together? Which means she always planned to use them whether or not you were still on the scene. A safeguard,' he called it. 'In case I did not come through with the marriage proposal. How do you think it makes me feel to know I was open to such manipulation?'

'An idiot, I guess.' She offered him a shrug that said she believed he deserved it. Insolence did not begin to cover the expression on her beautiful face.

His eyes narrowed. Challenge was suddenly back in the air. Then without warning she issued a thick sob then fell into his arms—because she belonged there.

'I've had a h-horrible day,' she sobbed against him.

'I can change that,' he promised, picked her up and took her to the bed. They could make love—why not? It was the most effective cleanser of poison that he knew of.

Afterwards they went downstairs to find their home overrun by people who wanted to make amends for all the ugliness. His mother was there, his sister, Chloe, even Nikos had come with Carlotta pinned possessively to his side. Silvia and Theron were looking shell-shocked because someone had run the whole sequence of events by them.

No Takis Konstantindou though, he noticed, and felt a short wave of anger-cum-regret flood his mind. Takis was out, and he probably knew it by now. Diantha's father would have seen to it. He was a man of honour despite what his daughter was.

Eve arrived with Ethan Hayes, carrying a crate of champagne. 'To welcome Isobel back into the fold,' Eve announced, but they all knew that she'd heard about today's events too.

'You don't need jungle drums up here,' Isobel whispered to Leandros. 'The rumours get round on a current of air!'

But her cheeks were flushed and she was happy. The doorbell sounded and two minutes later another visitor stepped onto the sunny terrace. 'My God, I don't believe it,' Leandros gasped in warm surprise—while everyone else was thrown into silence by the sight of the dauntingly aloof Felipe Vazquez, while he appeared taken aback by so many curious faces. 'When did you get into town?'

'My apologies for the intrusion,' he murmured stiffly.

'No intrusion at all,' Leandros assured and took him to meet his beautiful wife, who stared up at his friend as if what she was seeing lit a vision in her head.

Leandros grinned as he watched it happen. 'No,' he bent to murmur close to her ear. 'Felipe is Spanish, not Venezuelan.'

'Oh,' she pouted up at him. 'What a terrible shame.'

The afternoon took on a festive quality. By the time everyone drifted away again, Isobel was looking just a little bewildered. 'We seem to have become very popular all of a sudden,' she said.

'Too popular,' he answered. 'After Nikos's wedding you

and I are flying to the Caribbean to gatecrash his honey-moon,' he said decisively.

'But we can't do that!' Isobel protested.

'Why not?' he countered. 'He intends to cruise on my yacht. I intend that we stay so stationary that it will be an effort to move from the bed to the terrace. But for now,' he began to stalk her, 'you owe me something I am about to collect.'

'Owe you what?' she demanded.

'Humble pie?' he softly reminded her.

THE BRAZILIAN'S
BLACKMAILED BRIDE
MICHELLE REID

CHAPTER ONE

THERE was an old-world elegance about the walnut-panelled room that somehow scorned the idea that anyone would be tasteless enough to raise their voice in anger in here. Under normal circumstances Anton Luis Ferreira Scott-Lee certainly would not have dreamt of doing it.

But there was nothing normal about this situation, and the anger was certainly here, pulsing away in the background, even if it was safely encased in ice right now.

'I will have to resign,' he announced, effectively throwing the two people in the room with him into a frozen state of horror and dismay.

His mother was too young, at fifty, and much too beautiful to be a widow—but apparently *not* too young, after marrying at the youthful age of nineteen, to have clocked up a murky past which had now come back to haunt her.

'But—*meu querido*...' She recovered first to speak shakily. 'You cannot possibly resign!'

'I don't think that I have a damn choice.'

Maria Ferreira Scott-Lee flinched, her liquid brown eyes wrenching down and away from her son's hard expression.

'Don't be crazy, boy,' Maximilian Scott-Lee thrust out impatiently. 'This has nothing to do with the bank! Let's try to keep some perspective here.'

Max wanted perspective? Switching his gaze from his mother to the man he had lovingly called Uncle for all of his life, Anton felt a sudden rushing urge to smash a fist into his beloved face!

No perspective there, he thought as he swung away to

5

aim his bitter black mood at the view beyond one of the long casement windows that lined the beautifully appointed study of this, the Scott-Lees' Belgravia home.

It was a lousy day out there. The rain, lashing down from an iron-grey sky, was battering what leaves were left clinging to the trees down onto the square below. Anton knew how those leaves felt. Two hours ago a bright, calm winter day had been shining on London and he had been attending a board meeting, supremely confident in his place as chairman of the old and prestigious Scott-Lee Bank.

Now look at him, cast adrift like those storm-battered leaves out there.

A muscle flicked at his clenched jaw, emphasising the stubborn cleft in the centre of his chin…a cleft he had not thought to question until today, just as he had not thought of questioning many things about himself that were now staring him hard in the face.

And why should he have? Born the adored only child of Brazilian beauty Maria Ferreira and wealthy English banker Sebastian Scott-Lee…or so he'd believed until today…he'd naturally taken it for granted that he'd inherited his lean dark Latin looks from his Brazilian mother and his shrewd business mind from his late and still deeply missed English father.

At first, when he had read the letter from a Brazilian called Enrique Ramirez who was claiming to be his real father, he'd thought it was some kind of sick joke. It had taken this confrontation with his mother and his uncle to have his joke theory crushed right out of him. Now he was having to come to terms with the ugly fact that not only was this Ramirez guy telling the truth, but the man he'd always believed to be his real father had known about his mother's affair with Enrique and that Anton was not his real son! A very hush-hush adoption had secured his legal place in Sebastian Scott-Lee's life, along with the abiding wish that Anton should never find out the truth.

'You know as well as I do that without you the bank will collapse,' Max pushed into the thickened silence. 'You *are* the bank, Anton. If you resign people will want to know why you've gone. The truth will inevitably come out, because juicy stuff like this always does, and the family name will be—'

'This truth didn't come out,' Anton said harshly.

'Because my brother was careful to make sure that it didn't,' the older man said. 'Who the hell expected Ramirez to come along with his kiss-and-tell last will and testament?'

Kiss and tell, Anton echoed silently, hot, spitting bitterness rolling around inside him and spinning him about.

'Did it never occur to you that *I* had a right to know?' he fired directly at his mother.

Maria tensed, slender fingers mangling the handkerchief she held on her lap. 'Your father did not want—'

'Enrique *bloody* Ramirez is my father!' Anton thundered with explosive force.

The words bounced around the room like the aftershock from an earthquake.

'No.' Maria quivered as she shook her head. 'Enrique w-was a terrible mistake in *my* life, Anton! You did not need—'

'—to know that I've been living a lie for all of my thirty-one years?'

Maria subsided, lifting the handkerchief up to cover her trembling mouth. 'I'm sorry,' she whispered.

'Hearing you say that does not particularly help.'

'You do not understand…'

'You can say that again,' he uttered. 'I thought I was the son of a man I loved and revered above all men. Now I find out I'm the result of an extra-marital affair you enjoyed with some globe-trotting Brazilian polo-playing stud!'

'It wasn't like that.' Maria was going paler by the second. 'I was…with Enrique before I married your f-father.'

'So let me get this right,' Anton said, seeing the red mist of his growing fury swim up across his eyes. 'You had an affair with this guy. He left you pregnant, so you looked around for a gullible substitute to take his place, found Sebastian, and simply foisted me on to him? Is that it?'

'No!' For the first time since this had begun his fine-boned slender mother showed some of her Brazilian fire by shooting to her feet. 'You will not speak to me in this insulting tone, Anton! Your father knew. He *always* knew! I was *honest* with him from the start! He forgave me—and he loved *you* as his own son! *His* name is on your birth certificate. *He* raised you! He was proud of your every achievement and not once did he treat you as anything but the shining light in his life! So don't you *dare* hurt his memory now by turning it into a thing to speak of with contempt!'

Anton flung himself back to the window, seething inside with an eruption of feeling that was crucifying him with anger and bitterness and now tinged with a remorse that placed a sting in his eyes. He'd loved his father, looked up to him in every way a loving son could. When Sebastian had been killed in a freak road accident, Anton had lived for months in a black hole filled with inconsolable grief.

'I always knew I looked nothing like him.' The words arrived hoarse and uneven, pulsing with a deeply felt emotion that forced poor Maria to muffle a sob.

'My brother knew he could not have children, Anton,' Max filtered in huskily. 'He was already aware of that when he met and fell in love with Maria. When she told him about you he saw your coming birth as a gift.'

'A gift he insisted must be kept secret.'

'Don't deny him the right to some pride,' his uncle sighed.

But Anton couldn't think of anyone else's pride right now. 'I'm the son of a Brazilian,' he muttered. 'That makes me about as un-English as I can get. I live like an Englishman, I speak, think, *behave* like an Englishman and—*hell!*' A second explosion of emotion sent his clenched fist pounding into the window's wood casement, because he'd just remembered something. Something he'd spent the last six years trying to forget!

Now a face swam up in front of him—an excruciatingly lovely face, with dark eyes and a lush red mouth. *'But I cannot marry you, Luis, My father will not allow it. Our Portuguese blood must remain pure...'*

'Is Ramirez a Portuguese name?' he demanded roughly.

Still quaking from her son's sudden burst of violence, his mother breathed out a quavering, 'Yes.'

Anton tried for some air but didn't make it. That burst of blistering rage was now pooling inside his head as he replayed once again that unforgettable moment when five feet four inches of Latin scorn had told him that he wasn't good enough for her.

His teeth came together, accentuating that cleft in his chin. Not good enough—*not good enough!* No one before or since had ever dared say such a thing to him.

And he was damned if he was going to give her the chance to say it to him again.

It was then that the ice took over—an ice that those who knew him recognised with dread. Turning to face the room, he saw his mother was trying to fight back the tears still. His uncle just looked old. Maximilian's health wasn't good. He'd suffered his first heart attack which had forced him to retire from the bank, only weeks after his brother's death.

His words to his then grief stricken and shock-battered nephew had been, 'Take the reins, boy. I have every confidence in you to make this family proud.'

That word again—proud.

The muscles around his heart contracted. To be really proud of someone you had to accept them as they were, warts and skeletons alike. These people who claimed to love him only loved a lie they'd constructed to protect their own pride.

Anton stepped back to the desk that had been Sebastian's before he had died leaving everything he possessed—including this house in Belgravia, the family estate near Ascot and the major share in the Scott-Lee Bank—to the person he had been *proud* to call his son.

Well, Anton didn't feel proud of them right now. He felt angry and cheated in too many ways to count.

On the desk lay the documents that had been delivered to him from the lawyer attending to the Ramirez estate. Splintering emotions threatening to take him over again, he sent long blunt ended fingers flicking through the papers until he found the one he was searching for.

'There is more to this,' he clipped out, and saw from beneath his lowered eyelashes his mother and his uncle tense up. 'I am not the only poor swine Ramirez is laying claim to. There are two more like me out there somewhere. Two more sons...'

Two half-brothers with their own lying mothers? His top lip curled in contempt.

'Considering the globe-trotting lifestyle Ramirez enjoyed, they could be anywhere...'

'You mean he does not say?'

'No, not exactly,' Anton drawled cynically. 'How much amusing mileage would he get from making it as simple as that?'

He was already getting to know Ramirez, he noted, and didn't like it—hated it, in fact.

'But he's dead—'

'Yes,' he nodded. 'But still thoroughly enjoying himself at my and my half-brothers' expense.' He heaved in a taut breath. 'You see, he's been keeping tabs on all three of us for years.'

It was like being invaded—spied upon by some faceless stalker. Ramirez knew things about Anton that made the hairs on the back of his neck stand on end. What schools he'd attended, his academic success. He knew about every damn trophy he'd won on the sports field, every major deal in business he'd pulled off. He even knew about all those other trophies he'd notched up in that other sporting arena—his bed.

'He sees us as three sex-obsessed chips off the old block,' he summed up with a white-toothed razor slice. 'So, in his wisdom, he means to teach my brothers and me a lesson in life that apparently he did not grasp until he was too old and it was too late to change what he was.'

He saw his mother wince at the intimacy already honing his tone when he referred to his brothers. Odd. A nerve flicked in his jaw. But he *felt* that intimacy in some deep place inside him, like a newly formed artery feeding the blood link, and it was hungry for more.

'Ramirez was loaded,' he continued. 'And we are not talking about a few paltry million here. He owned diamond mines, emerald mines, some of the richest oil fields in Brazil...' The fact that he could see from their lowered expressions he was telling them things they already knew did not make him feel any better about this. 'We—his three sons—get to share the booty,' he explained with sarcastic bite. 'So long as we fulfil several conditions our dear departed sleazy coward of a father has set out in his will.'

'Enrique was not sleazy,' his mother protested.

'What was he, then?' Anton asked.

'N-nice, h-handsome—like you—charming...'

His mother was still fond of the bastard! Another explosion began to gather.

Maximilian shifted in his seat. 'What kind of conditions?' he questioned.

Anton fought the explosion back down again.

'I can only speak for myself, because that's all that's referred to here,' he said. Then a strange kind of smile hit his mouth. 'I am to mend my philandering ways,' he enlightened. 'Get responsible, find a wife, settle down, produce legitimate progeny—'

'Good God!' Max expelled. 'The man's brain must have been addled by the time he popped it!'

Coming from a confirmed bachelor, his uncle's attitude made sense.

'It makes me wonder what my brothers need to do before they win the right to meet me.'

'You don't need to do anything, *querido*,' his mother inserted. 'You don't need his money. You don't need any of—'

'I don't want his damn money; I want to meet my half-brothers!' Anton lashed out, and watched his mother flinch, despised himself for it, despised Ramirez for doing this to them all. His mother was right, he didn't *need* to do anything. But, knowing that did not alter the fact that he felt bloody cheated—denied of the right to know so many things about himself.

He would *not* be denied this chance to know his own flesh and blood—no matter what the cost!

The cost.

His gaze flicked back to the papers spread out in front of him, green eyes glassing over as he re-read the paragraph in which Ramirez accused him of running out on a woman six years ago, leaving her in dire straits. He was insisting that Anton make reparation and was giving him six months in which to do it. He was then expected to turn up at some lawyer's office in Rio with this woman as his wife, ripe with his child, or he would never know his brothers and Anton's share in his birthright would go to *her* instead.

'So w-what are you going to do?' his mother questioned.

Anton didn't hear her. He was too busy staring at the name typed in bold print that was leaping at him off the page—along with a vision of waist-length black hair with a sexy loose spiral twist framing a small heart-shaped face with a pointed little chin, a lush red provocative mouth, and a pair of she-devil fiery dark eyes that had a habit of turning into burning rubies when she was—

'Anton…?'

His eyes lifted automatically at that appealing note in his mother's voice, but he wasn't seeing her because he was seeing that other woman who had been so instrumental in the making of him. His body was burning, filling with the deep grinding pulse of uncontrolled sexual power that had always been his response whenever he let—

'Anton, please tell us what you intend to do about this!' his mother begged.

'Carry out his wishes,' he heard himself utter, as cold and hard as death.

'What—get *married* at some dead man's behest?' his uncle Max gasped in horror. 'Are you crazy, boy?'

Stark staring mad—but up for it, Anton thought as the heat in him grew and grew. He was going to hunt down, trap and then marry the lying little tramp called Cristina Marques and make her life a sexual hell…

* * *

The old and sadly neglected book-lined room that had used to be her father's sanctuary rang to the sound of raised voices and the fierce-eyed fury of one of its two occupants.

'For goodness' sake, Cristina, will you listen to me? If you—'

'No, *you* listen.' A small clenched fist made angry contact with the desk. 'I said no!'

Sheer frustration threw Rodrigo Valentim back into his seat. 'If you will not take my instruction,' he sighed out impatiently, 'then what am I doing here?'

'You are here as my attorney to find a way to get me out of this!'

'And I keep telling you,' he enunciated tightly—but then this had been going on for ages now, and the longer it did the more angry both of them became— 'I cannot do that!'

Cristina straightened, her fine-boned slender figure giving no hint to the strength of the woman within. With a proud toss of her head she sent her long black tresses flying back from narrow shoulders. Eyes like flashing devils pierced Rodrigo Valentim with a defiant glare.

'Then I will have to find myself a lawyer who can, will I not?'

Another loaded sigh and Rodrigo's forty-years-in-the-business jaded expression suddenly gave way to a rueful smile. 'If I believed it could make the difference then I would take you to one myself. Do you not understand, *minha amiga*?' he pleaded. 'Santa Rosa is all but bankrupt. If you do not agree to this offer it will die!'

It was like taking a whip to a wounded animal. Cristina's pained little whimper crucified the tough lawyer's ears. She turned away, tense fingers jumping up to burrow into the sleeves of a well-used sweater as she paced away from the desk. The window beckoned, drawing her hopeless gaze to

the open pampas, where the gauchos roamed free and machismo still ruled.

Out there, where most of the other large estates had
turned their land over to soya or wine, Santa Rosa was one
of the few traditional working cattle ranches left functioning in this part of Brazil. A Marques had ruled here since
her Portuguese ancestors had claimed the land and built this
house she was standing in.

And here she stood, Cristina thought bleakly, the last
Marques in a long invincible line—and a female, of all
things.

A female who was being forced to face the demise of
the Marques land, name and pride.

'Your father should have let you run things years ago,
then you would not be in this mess,' Rodrigo gruffly pronounced. 'He was a stubborn old fool.'

That word machismo echoed again, and Cristina's lovely
mouth stretched into a bitter, wry smile. The men in these
parts did not defer to their women. Her father had preferred
to turn a blind eye to what was happening around him and
wait to die rather than hand a single decision about Santa
Rosa over to her.

'You need big investment to put this place back on its
feet again,' Rodrigo continued. 'And you need it urgently.
The Alagoas Consortium offer is more than generous for
your purposes, *querida*.'

'At an *impossible* price.'

The consortium wanted to scythe off a whole section of
Santa Rosa, which would give them access to part of a sub-
tropical forest that was of particular natural beauty—not
that this was what interested them. The forest blocked the
rest of the world from mile upon mile of white sandy
beaches, making them impossible to reach by land at present. They aimed to buy the tract of land, then bulldoze the

forest and build a road link to the Atlantic, where they planned to build skyscrapers along a beautiful and rare stretch of untouched coast.

'When is there never a price?' Rodrigo posed sadly. 'You of all people should know this.'

Because she had paid a heavy price once before to save Santa Rosa. That 'price' was dead now, thank goodness. Along with the man who had been content to sell his daughter to gain a few extra years of comfort in his blindness to what was happening. Now here she stood with her eyes wide open, seeing all too clearly who must pay the price this time around. If she did accept the offer, the land, the people who lived on it and the forest would become the sacrifice.

'How long do I have to make a decision?' It stuck in her throat to ask the question and it showed in the husky tone of her voice.

'They want the deal badly enough to wait only a little while,' Rodrigo answered.

Cristina turned and nodded. 'Then keep them hanging on for their—little while,' she instructed. 'And I will make one last plea to the banks for help.'

'You have done this several times already.'

'And I will do it as many times as it takes until time runs out for me.'

'It is running out, Cristina,' Rodrigo said heavily. 'The wolves are already baying at your door.'

'I must still keep trying.' Dark eyes and soft mouth firm in their stubbornness, Cristina turned back to the window. Behind her, Rodrigo studied her too-slender figure with a kind of pained exasperation tinged with genuine but useless respect.

She was beautiful—exquisite—the kind of woman who at only twenty-five years old should have had the whole world lying at her feet. Indeed, she had once been that favoured person.

Then something had happened in this house to make her run away, and she had not been heard of again for over a year. When she eventually had come back she'd been a different person, hardened and cold, as if someone had snuffed out the burning light that had made her the wildly beautiful creature she had once been. She'd walked back into this house and within weeks out of it again, as the wife of Vaasco Ordoniz, a man as old as the father who had happily sold her to him.

For the next year she had lived in Rio as a rich old man's beautiful ornament. She'd outfaced her critics and their bitching cruelty without a hint of her true feelings showing on her face. When Ordoniz had taken sick and retired from society to his isolated ranch he'd taken Cristina with him, and neither had been seen or heard of for the next two years. Then Ordoniz had died, and the mocking laughter had truly been heard when it had come to light that he'd been quietly gambling his wealth away, leaving his fortune-chasing wife so penniless she'd had to move back to her father's house to become unpaid servant and nurse to yet another sick, money-squandering old man.

Yet her stubborn chin had never faltered. Those beautiful eyes had always looked out on life with defiance and pride. Rodrigo admired her for those things and respected her refusal to give up on life no matter how many bad things it threw at her.

'Okay, we will give it one more try,' he heard himself utter, and wondered straight away if he was being cruel to offer her a small chink of light? 'I think we will enlist some help this time. Gabriel knows all the right people.' He did not add that his son had already been approached by some anonymous businessman looking for new investment in

Brazil. Rodrigo did not want to raise her hopes. 'Gabriel just might be able to get you a hearing with those who would not listen to you before.'

Still, when Cristina turned to look at him, her hopes were already rising in the new shine in her eyes.

Rodrigo heaved a sigh. 'Gabriel might run in the right circles, Cristina, but money men are notoriously ruthless. They will not invest in you without demanding something solid back in return.'

CHAPTER TWO

ANTON saw him as he was crossing the hotel foyer, and on a single heavy thump of a heartbeat he came to an abrupt halt.

It had been happening a lot since he'd been told he had two half-brothers out there. He would glimpse a man with dark hair, or with something about his physical appearance that reminded him of himself, and this thump at his heart would stop him in his tracks.

It was the not knowing that made it impossible to deal with—the deep-boned fear that he could be standing right next to his own flesh and blood and not have a single clue.

He hated it. He hated this sudden leap his heart would make just before the thick sinking rush that paralysed him.

And the need—he hated feeling this need he hadn't known was there until he'd received that damn—

'Anton...?'

Kinsella's questioning prompt jolted him back to his surroundings. The stranger had gone, disappearing into one of the lounge bars and out of Anton's sphere of temptation to just go up to him and ask outright if his father had been a rich polo-playing Brazilian who'd left bastard byeblows in just about every port!

Anger set him moving again, though it did not show on his face. They hit the lifts, four of them in all, the two junior executives looking limp with jet-lag while Kinsella, his new personal secretary, who had only recently been promoted through the Scott-Lee ranks, still looked as smooth and fresh as she had all day.

Anton glanced at her and she thoroughly jolted him by offering him one of those smiles that said *I'm available if you want me*. She was a great-looking blue-eyed blonde, with the kind of figure guaranteed to fire up most men's heat. Until now she'd been good to have around because she was easy on the eye and her secretarial skills were unquestionable—but sex with the boss as a sideline?

He lowered his eyes and pretended he had not noticed the invitation—or the sudden tension that leapt around the confines of the lift. Apart from the unbroken rule that he never bedded his employees, he hadn't wanted to touch a woman since the day when his life as he'd known it had been put to death.

The lift doors slid open. His two junior executives quickly stepped out into the corridor, eager to find their rooms, but Kinsella left it a couple of telling seconds longer before she did the same.

Once again Anton ignored the little hesitation. Eyes half hidden behind the low sweep of his eyelashes he said, 'Get some food inside you, then sleep off the jet-lag. I'll see you all for breakfast in my suite at seven-thirty prompt.'

The boss playing the boss, he noted wryly, as three heads nodded, getting the message, one looking faintly flushed now. Serves you right, Kinsella, he thought, without a twinge of regret.

'Goodnight,' he said, and the lift doors slid shut across their three murmured replies.

Anton yawned, stuffed his hands into his trouser pockets and leant back against the lift wall as it took him up to the penthouse suite on the top floor, where not only did he get the best in accommodation that was available, but he also got adjoining offices and a conference room in which most of his business day would be spent.

He preferred working from his hotel when he made

an unannounced spot-check on one of his international branches. That way he could sweep into the bank and take everyone by surprise, so that they did not have time to pull any cover-ups. He would then put every department head through a major grilling before sweeping out again, with his entourage in tow, and returning to his hotel to hold his post mortem, leaving his quivering staff to recover from the fallout of his unexpected invasion. They would call him a few tasty names to each other, enjoy a collective sigh of relief that he'd gone. Then they would start urgently boning up on what they'd thought they knew inside out but, after one of Anton's interrogating sessions, had now realised they knew nothing at all.

Ruthless but necessary methods to keep his multinational army of employees on their toes, he judged without a qualm.

The lift doors slid open again. Levering himself upright, he crossed the private foyer and unlocked the door. The suite was much like any other hotel suite he had used over the years, with luxurious living space, two bedrooms with *en suite* bathrooms, and a connecting door which led directly into the all-singing, all-dancing working environment business tycoons expected from their accommodation these days.

His luggage had arrived. Ignoring it, Anton made directly for the drinks cabinet to check that the hotel had provided him with a bottle of his favourite Scotch whisky. He poured himself a measure, added some bottled water to the mix, then took it with him to a pair of French doors which led out onto a terrace beyond.

The moment he stepped outside, the sights and sounds of Rio hit his senses, stirring them to a quickened rhythm only someone with Latin blood running through him would understand.

That quickened rhythm should be filling him with pleasure, but it wasn't. In fact he resented the hell out of it. It
was six long years since he'd last looked out on the Bay
towards Sugarloaf, and if he'd had his way it would have
been another six years before he'd look out on it again—
if ever.

He took a sip of the whisky, the shape of his sensually
moulded lips barely altering their grim tilt as they parted
to receive the drink. Heat rolled over his tongue and fired
up his increased pulse-beat. He'd used to love Rio de
Janeiro. This beautiful, exciting city had once been like a
home from home to him during his childhood, when he'd
used to visit here regularly with his mother, and later, when
he'd spent a full year working at the Scott-Lee Bank branch
here.

With hindsight, he mused, he would have been better
staying put in England, then he would not have met Cristina
and spent that whole year in love with a lie.

Another lie.

That hot surge of anger he'd been nurturing for weeks
now began to pump through his system. Going back inside,
he closed the door on the sights and sounds of Rio, chose
a bedroom at random to use, then set about removing his
clothes. Ten minutes later he was shutting down the taps
gushing water into a huge sunken bathtub.

The tub needed to be big to accommodate a man with
his impressive framework. He stood six feet two in his bare
feet, and every inch was made up of hard muscled bulk.
And lean, he was very lean, but that leanness did not take
anything away from the fact that, stripped to his natural
golden skin, he presented the kind of masculine sight that
could make women gasp. Wide shoulders, long torso, narrow hips, the lot supported on long and powerfully corded
legs. Then there was the pelvis that cradled one of the ma-

jor weapons in his sexual arsenal. He was built to seduce, built to guarantee hours of untold pleasure. He knew it— just as his women knew it.

Not that he cared about any of that right now as he stepped into the bath and sank down into its hot steamy depths. He was tired and fed up and still wishing himself elsewhere. Easing his wide shoulders back against the bath, he closed his eyes on a sigh.

If it wasn't enough that he'd seen the interior of too damn many transit lounges as he'd criss-crossed the world to get here, he'd spent most of that time obsessively studying every tall dark guy that ventured into his vicinity, hunting for signs that one of them might be related to him.

He hated the not knowing.

He more than hated Rio.

If he'd been given the luxury of choice he'd rather be anywhere else on this earth than here. But choice was something snatched away from him by the simple insertion of a name.

Cristina Marques...

The satin gold muscular formation of his wide shoulders shifted, black silk bars for eyebrows drawing together across the bridge of his nose. Parting the grim tension holding his lips together, he gritted his teeth and wished to hell that other parts of his body would stop responding to that name.

Another sigh had him lifting a wet hand to swipe it over his tired face. The refreshing sting of hot water made his skin tingle, but did nothing to ease the discomfort of a twelve-hour beard growth. He should have shaved before he got in here, he mused grimly. He should have cleaned his teeth.

The second thought sent his hand reaching out in search of the glass of whisky he'd had enough sense to replenish before he climbed in here. Sipping the Scotch was a darn sight tastier than any toothpaste, and did a whole lot more to ease the tension from his aching muscles—though not from other parts.

What he needed was a woman—any woman. He hadn't had one in way too long. He'd been too busy losing himself in work and bad temper and setting up this trip. A woman right now might just be the medicine he needed to effect the cure for the one woman he did not want to want.

Maybe he should have broken his own rule and taken Kinsella up on her offer, he mused idly. Maybe a slender, sleek, blue-eyed blonde would be the perfect cure for what was ailing him. But—

No. He might have closed the door on the sights and sounds of Rio, but its innate beat was still vibrating through his blood, and the only woman who would satisfy it would have to be one of the warm, dark, passionate kind. One who would know instinctively that all he wanted her to do was to climb naked into this bath with him and seduce him to one of those exquisite near death experiences.

A half smile touched the edges of his mouth, his shoulders beginning to relax as he let his weary mind drift. She would have a pair of decent-sized breasts that would weigh heavy in his hands but still be firm enough to pout. Dark nipples…he loved dark nipples…and a silky, slippery golden body that would arch over him in pleasure as he suckled to his heart's content.

His mouth received attention from the whisky. It wasn't nearly the same as the glorious sense-tugging taste of a woman, but he savoured it all the same while behind closed eyelids his fantasy woman began to take real shape.

Dark eyes…she'd have sultry dark eyes the colour of hunger, and sweeping black eyelashes that would half hide the glow of sensual relish she would experience as she aroused him while he lay back and enjoyed. Ebony hair, he decided, with a sexy hint of a twist to it that would trail over his chest and shoulders as she leant down to offer him a kiss from her gorgeous, greedy, voluptuous mouth, practised in the art of pleasing as she took him inside her with the…

'Hell—'

The curse raked his throat and he sat up so abruptly he spilled whisky into the bath. He'd been describing Cristina. He'd been lying here flirting with fantasy and building himself the perfect replica of the one woman he was supposed to be blocking out!

Tell that to your body, he thought darkly, and rid himself of the glass, then rubbed his wet hands over his face again. Tension had hold of him in a manacle. Standing up, he dripped water from taut rippling muscles as he stepped out of the bath. As he hooked up a towel to dry himself, it accidentally brushed across that part of him that was an aching agony of untamed want. With an indrawn quiver of cursing contempt, he tossed the towel aside and headed for a cold shower instead.

He didn't want to want Cristina. He did not want to remember how she was. He wanted to be utterly turned off by reality, and hoped that when he eventually came face to face with her she'd have turned into a complete hound dog!

And he would come face to face with her, he vowed as he stepped out of the shower cubicle feeling more like a man in control of himself. The wheels to make it happen were already turning, and very soon he would have his confrontation with Cristina Marques.

The telephone began ringing as he was finishing shaving. Walking naked out of the bathroom, he picked up the receiver.

'I have tracked her to Rio, *senhor*,' a distinctly Brazilian male voice informed him. 'She is residing with Gabriel Valentim. He will be escorting her to the charity gala tomorrow evening, as hoped.'

She was hooked; the sting was on. The hot burn of satisfaction that flung itself down his body excited a sexual arousal he had thought he'd brought under control.

'Good,' he said, as cold as an English winter. 'Tell me the rest tomorrow.'

'Before you go there is something I have discovered that I think you should know, *senhor*!' Afonso Sanchiz put in hurriedly. 'It was not mentioned in the profile you sent to me—but six years ago the lady in question married a man called Vaasco Ordoniz. She is widowed now, and has reverted to using the Marques name, but...'

Cristina did not want to be here. Partying while her life was tumbling down around her placed a very bad taste in her mouth. But Gabriel insisted it was the only way. The best deals were struck in the social arena, not across a desk in some bank.

So here she was, standing in the foyer of one of Rio's top hotels, dressed to kill in sparkling black silk. Her hair was up in an elegant twist and her late mother's diamonds sparkled at her ears and throat.

She would have sold the diamonds if they'd been worth anything, but she'd found out the hard way that they were not. They were fakes—very good fakes, but fakes all the same. She did not know when her father had cashed in the genuine articles and replaced them with paste, but she had little doubt that he had done so. In fact, she'd discovered over the months since he died that there was very little left in Santa Rosa that was not a copy of its original. She now lived with the hope that when Lorenco Marques met his art-collecting ancestors on his way up to heaven they'd give him a swift push in the other direction.

And, yes, she told that shocked part of her that did not like what she was thinking, she felt that bitter and that bad.

Gabriel was guiding her towards a pair of doors beyond which the charity gala they were about to attend should be in full flow. Two smiling lackeys jumped to open the doors for them. The smooth background sound of a bossa nova song drifted out towards them as the foyer gave way to a vast reception room set against a backcloth of wall-to-wall glass, offering breathtaking views towards a night-lit Sugarloaf.

People glittered and sparkled beneath overhead lighting, the warm tones of their conversations floating towards her on richly perfumed waves. Cristina's stomach lurched, then rolled, and for a moment her courage completely failed her, pulling her to a trembling halt.

From the other side of the room Anton watched as she entered on the arm of just about the most attractive man here. She was still unutterably beautiful, he noted, allowing himself a small grimace at his unanswered hound dog prayer. The hair was too neat for his liking, and the dress might be glamorous, and sexy enough to knock most men's eyes out, but he'd never liked to see her wearing black. She suited bright colours, colours that flagged her hot-blooded temperament. But the face, the wide-spaced almond-shaped eyes, the mouth...

Ah, the mouth, he observed darkly. It was still as lush and red and kissable as he remembered it. A mouth that instinctively knew how to—

Her escort murmured something to her. As she looked up to smile at him sudden tension was bathing Anton's body in a fine layer of sensual heat. It was the smile of a born seductress. A smile she had once used to keep exclusively for him. It was the deceit in that smile that had ruined all other smiles every woman had offered him since.

Did she sleep with Gabriel Valentim? Had the handsome lawyer got to share a steamy hot interlude in a bath with the widow of Vaasco Ordoniz before they'd set out here?

'Anton, your glass is empty…'

Looking down, he saw it was, frowning slightly because he didn't remember drinking the champagne. He must have been sipping it while observing Cristina with her latest lover. Now he became aware of the tension in the fingers that held the glass and the angry fizz of champagne in his mouth.

'Here, let me replace it…'

Reaching out, Kinsella took the empty glass from him. As she did so her body brushed against his. She was wearing no bra beneath the slip dress she was wearing. He'd felt the button-tight brush of her nipple against the back of his hand.

Yet another sexual message from his secretary? Irritation hit, then was instantly lost when he caught sight of Cristina's escort lowering his handsome head to brush a kiss to her cheek.

'Stop worrying,' Gabriel softly chided her, feeling the tension in the stiff set of her spine beneath the resting palm of his hand. 'No one is going to eat you.'

No? Cristina would question that. Six years ago she had scandalised these people by marrying a man old enough to be her father. She had become a gold-digging freak worthy of derision and scorn from that moment on. Discovering that Vaasco Ordoniz had left her virtually penniless would not have altered their opinion of his widow.

A waiter appeared, carrying a silver tray of drinks.

'Here.' Hooking up two fluted glasses frothing with

champagne Gabriel slotted one into her hand. 'Remember why you are here,' he said firmly. 'Get some of this fortifying champagne inside you and stop looking so tragic.'

'I am not in any way tragic,' Cristina denied, trying hard to ignore the hectic thrum of her pulse. 'I just dislike the prospect of having to be pleasant to people I no longer like.'

'Does that include me?'

Glancing up into the lean golden face of the man she had known since childhood, Cristina saw the wry glint of amusement in his soft amber eyes and couldn't help but smile.

'Thank you for doing this for me,' she said softly. 'I know that your father had to push you into it.'

'I don't need pushing to be with a beautiful woman, *querida*.' Reaching out, he covered her fingers and lifted the glass to her lips, then held it there until she took the first sip. 'And you should know better than to think that I am one of those who believed the gold-digging rumours about you.'

Her smile faded. 'Would it make a difference if I told you that those rumours were true?'

'To my escorting you?' Gabriel's mouth assumed a small grimace. 'Look at these people, Cristina,' he prompted. 'Do you think none of them have skeletons to hide? I am a lawyer, like my father. Such a profession allows access to privileged information that would make the hair on the head of the good father in the confessional box stand on end. Take my advice and look upon them all as crooks and you will begin to feel much better about yourself.'

Her eyes widened in fascination. '*Are* they all crooks?'

'No.' Gabriel laughed. 'But it helps a great deal to see them like that.'

Someone came up to greet Gabriel then, a perfect

stranger to Cristina, so she was able to relax a little as Gabriel made the introductions and even managed to smile as she sipped at her glass of champagne and listened to the two men converse. A few minutes later the stranger had moved off again, and they began to circulate.

Gabriel's hand was always light on her waistline. He was well known and well liked, his good looks and his naturally friendly manner drew people to him, and she wanted to kiss him for the way he was carefully manoeuvring them around the room so that she was not forced to come face to face with any of the old crowd—though she had glimpsed many of them here.

It was then that it happened. Just as she was beginning to relax in the company she picked up the sound of a dark-timbred very English voice, speaking in such beautifully fluent Portuguese that she had twisted around without giving herself a chance to think.

By then it was too late. Her swift movement had caught his attention. The next instant she found herself welded to the spot as a pair of darkly hooded glinting green eyes fixed on her shocked face.

Luis, she thought. *Meu Dues*, it was Luis...

He was standing less than ten feet away, a tall, lean, solid, dark force backed by the night view of Rio. Her legs turned to water, her head swirling so dizzily that for a horrible moment she was afraid that she was actually going to faint. No one else was in the room suddenly. No voices sounded. No slow and sensual bossa nova beat. All she could hear was the blood pumping heavily through her body as those hooded eyes looked at her and took everything, stripping away six long miserable years to leave her standing there feeling so exposed and vulnerable that she just could not bring herself to look away.

And he wasn't going to do it, she realised as she watched

those eyes begin a slow, slow glide over her face. Her shock-blackened eyes. Her shock-whitened cheeks. He let his gaze linger on every telling detail until finally fixing it on her helplessly parted lips.

Those lips quivered as if he'd touched them. A knowing smile stretched the contours of his. It was electric, dynamic, so overwhelmingly sexual and intensely familiar she was nailed by it, drenched in sensation that slithered and danced across her skin. They had been lovers for twelve months more than six years ago, yet for these few breathtaking seconds those years just did not exist.

She trembled—all over. He watched that happen too, and swung his gaze up to clash with hers again. Mockery lanced through those glinting green eyes and he lifted his glass, tilting it towards her in a salute that was so dryly cynical it sucked her back through those six years with a painful, dizzying whoosh.

He hated her. It was there for her to see it. And she could not even blame him for feeling that way. She had encouraged him to hate—worked at it like an actress putting on an Oscar-winning performance. She'd mocked him and cursed him and died a little more inside with each slaying remark she had thrown at his face.

Tears began to gather, hot, like acid burning in her chest and her throat. She loved him, would always love him for as long as she had left to draw breath, but she'd wished—oh, how she had wished—never to set eyes on him again.

Someone shifted beside him, forcing her gaze to flicker sideways in time to watch a woman step in close to murmur something to him. She was beautiful, a reed-slender blonde wearing aquamarine silk. Whatever it was that she said to Luis, it lost Cristina her contact with his eyes as he turned to the woman with a lazy, sensual smile on his lips.

And Cristina knew that smile, recognised it with every sensory nerve she possessed. They were lovers. Jealousy roared up like a snarling, spitting wild animal inside her, and on a choked little whimper she spun away.

Trembling like mad, she moved in so close to Gabriel that she earned herself a curious glance as his arm accommodated her, though his attention did not falter from the discussion he was involved in.

'The problem has been global,' he was saying smoothly. 'But the industry is showing signs of recovery, and we have a plan in place to get in first where this growth is happening. People will pay a high price for a flawless pedigree. Santa Rosa can give them that—hmm, Cristina?' He prompted some input from her.

Gabriel was into his sales pitch, and she had to fight a gigantic battle with herself to find sensible words to speak.

'S-Santa Rosa stock is conceived born and raised on the land on which it roams free,' she heard herself say, as if from down a long dark tunnel. 'We are proud that we still farm by traditional methods where quality always takes precedence over quantity.'

'But quantity is what makes the big profit, *senhorita*,' Gabriel's companion wryly pointed out.

'*Sim.*' She nodded, battling to keep herself together. 'We know this, which is why we want to diversify a little...turn Santa Rosa into a showcase where people can come and stay for a while, experience what it is like to live in a genuine Portuguese mansion house, and spend time with the gauchos learning of the life and true traditions of a working ranch. But such plans require investment—'

'At great risk to the investor, I would say,' a smooth-as-silk voice put in.

Both Gabriel and his companion turned to face the newcomer. Cristina didn't—not again, she told herself as her pounding heart increased its crazy beat.

'Most worthy investments require a certain amount of risk, *senhor*,' Gabriel countered easily.

'The knack for the successful investor is to pick out those investments that have at least a starting chance to earn him some profit.'

'With commitment to hard work and true dedication we can certainly promise our investors their profit,' Gabriel declared without hesitation, at the same time making out that he had a big stake in the project himself, when in truth he was simply playing the machismo rule to the hilt for her sake. 'Let me introduce myself,' he then offered affably, releasing Cristina to hold out his hand. 'I am Gabriel Valentim, and this is—'

'I know who this is...' Anton smoothly put in, and the instant that Gabriel's hand left the base of her spine his replaced it, fingertips moving in an all too familiar stroke that sent shock waves stinging up her spine.

His warm breath brushed her nape as he moved in closer. 'Cristina, *meu querida*,' he greeted with husky intimacy. 'Surely you must remember me?'

It took every ounce of will power she could muster to turn and face him. Her insides were dipping and diving even before she lifted her chin and looked directly into his face.

'Luis,' she responded, with very shaky coolness.

'But you're mistaken,' a cool English voice intruded. 'This is Anton—Anton Scott-Lee.'

Anton Luis Ferreira Scott-Lee, to give him his full title, Cristina corrected silently. Anton to most people, but always Luis to her. A man with two faces—his English face and his Brazilian face.

And she was seeing his Brazilian face right now, as he

smiled one of his slow, sensual smiles at her and reached out to take a light grasp on her hand. 'Don't look so shattered,' he softly admonished. 'I will answer to Luis if it still pleases you to use it...'

The air in her lungs ceased to be of any use to her. This close up he was everything she remembered about him—everything. Her lips parted, trembling again as she tried desperately to find something light to say.

'This is some kind of joke, yes?' Gabriel asked curiously, as a set of slender white fingers claimed Cristina's attention by coiling possessively around Luis' sleeve.

The fingers belonged to his beautiful blonde companion. Cristina glanced into a pair of gentian-blue eyes and blinked at the amount of ice she met with. Was this the kind of woman Luis preferred these days?

'No joke,' the man himself was denying, bringing Cristina's eyes slewing back to his face. 'Cristina and I are very old friends—hmm, *amante*?'

Lover.

Her senses went haywire. She had to fight to pull in some air, unaware of the silence slowly thickening around them, unaware of everything but those eyes and that smile and that *word*, playing like a silken caress across her skin.

A thumb-pad stroked against the skin of her palm and she looked down at it, staring blankly at the way his long fingers coiled so easily around the fragility of hers.

'Cristina?' Gabriel prompted an answer from her, because she was taking too long to speak.

She looked up at him next, not seeing him—not seeing anything. Not even the flash of venom that hit Luis's companion's eyes. Her heart had stopped beating. The thick curdling slurry of so many old feelings was churning inside her, leeching the last of the colour from her skin. She couldn't think. Even as she tried very hard to find the right response that would defuse the tense moment a thick whooshing sound in her head stopped her from being able to think.

His thumb stroked her palm again and she looked back at her hand, still caught in his. She felt a strange lethargy creep over her, and on a shivered gasp tugged her hand free.

'I—please excuse me,' she heard herself mumble in stifled constriction. 'I n-need to—use the bathroom…'

And on that crass, stupid and utterly unsophisticated exit line she turned and fled, leaving a stunning silence in her place.

On legs that felt dangerously like cotton wool she made it into the foyer. A passing waiter had only to take one look at her face to quickly direct her to the nearest private bathroom. Closing the door behind her, she leant back against it. She was shaking all over, locked in the kind of hard shock that turned flesh to ice. Lurching unsteadily across the room, she sank down onto the toilet seat.

Luis was here in Rio. *'Meu dues,'* she whispered.

Why was he here? Why now, after all of these years? Why should he want to acknowledge her at all?

It came then, that final damning scene they'd had six years ago, swimming up through her mind to send her hands up to cover her face. She saw Luis standing there, stunned and bewildered, staring at her as if she had grown a forked tail and hooves.

'What's wrong with you? You love me. Why are you doing this? We lived here together for a year before I had to go back to England to attend my father's funeral. That year must have meant something to you—told you that I was serious about us!'

'Things change—' He'd been too angry to notice her deathly pallor, or the agony etched into her face.

'In three months? No, they don't,' he'd denied harshly. 'You made me promise to come back for you and here I am as promised, with a rock-solid marriage proposal and plane tickets to a whole new life! For goodness' sake, Cristina—' his voice had roughened '—I love you. I want you to be my wife, I want to have children with you and grow old with you, watch those children grow into adults and have their own children!'

Cut to death inside by his vision of the future, she'd tossed her head at him. Sitting here in this room lined in glaring white marble, Cristina winced as she remembered the way she'd tossed her head at him that day. 'I will never marry you, Luis. I will never have your children. There, I have said it. Will you accept it now?'

Oh, yes, he'd accepted it. Cristina had seen it happen as she'd watched the bitter look that overtook his face. 'Because you don't want to spoil that perfect body of yours?'

'That is exactly it,' she'd agreed. 'I am selfish and heartless and incurably vain. I am also a Marques, with three centuries of pure Portuguese blood running in my veins. Diluting my blood with your half-English blood would be a sin and a sacrilege that would turn my ancestors in their—'

The brief knock on the door was the only warning she received before it was swinging open. Cristina lifted her face out of her hands, and froze yet again.

CHAPTER THREE

LUIS was not so afflicted. He shut the door and shot home the bolt she had stupidly forgotten when she'd come in here. Then he turned, leant his wide shoulders back against the door, pushed long-fingered hands into the pockets of his well-cut trousers, fixed his steady gaze on her agonised face and simply waited for her to make the next move.

Dressed in a dark lounge suit and white shirt he looked big and hard and absolutely in control. The room was too small, too brightly lit, and he was too close for comfort, the electric charge vibrating from every pore of him so violently sexual it grabbed her attention and refused to let go.

Mouth running dry, she took in every hard, honed inch of him like someone seeing the chance of life restoring water after a six year drought. Nothing about him had changed—nothing. His hair was still short black and silky, his skin still golden and smooth. Eyes the colour of a sensual green ocean glowed at her from between half lowered eyelashes, and the unsmiling shape of his mouth did nothing to spoil the passionate promise it made.

'When you fled in here like a frightened rabbit I knew you would forget to lock the door, because you always did forget to lock doors, so I thought—why not join her and relive some of the good old times?' he drawled.

Her insides quivering madly, Cristina lurched unsteadily to her feet, fingers searching for and clutching tensely at the sink behind her for support. 'W-what do you want?' she demanded shakily.

'Now, there's a good question.' The twist of his mouth was dryly sardonic as he sent his mocking gaze around the room. 'We could fill the room with hot steam, if you like, strip off our clothes and get down to some really physical reacquainting?' he suggested. 'I can see by the way you look at me that you're up for it, *querida*, and I'm certainly up for it. So what the hell?' He gave a shrug of his wide shoulders. 'We could do it against the bath, *in* the bath, in the shower, or right where you were sitting just now. Or you could coax me down flat on the cold marble floor like an offering and crawl all over me. You used to like crawling all over me, Cristina, do you remember? You used to love to make me beg, then laugh in my face as you took me inside you. *Got you, Luis,* you used to purr in that greedily possessive, husky, triumphant voice of yours. *Mine,* you used to say.'

'Shut up!' she gasped out shrilly. 'How dare you speak to me like this? Get out of here, Luis—*get out!*'

He did the opposite, pushing those muscled shoulders away from the door and striding forward so purposefully that Cristina found herself pressing back hard against the sink. It was like being trapped in a cage with a lean, dark green-eyed predator. She had never felt so afraid.

'No,' she breathed as a set of long fingers closed over a bare shoulder.

The other set lifted to curl around her nape. As she arched her back in an effort to put space between them he stepped in close. The solid bar of his hips made contact with her stomach. She quivered. He smiled—then stopped smiling. His eyes glittered, his lips parted, then he tugged her head forward and captured her mouth.

The predator—the predator—the *hungry* predator. She was devoured without mercy, lips prised apart and her mouth invaded by the kind of kiss that locked every muscle tight with shock. Her mouth filled with the taste of him, sensitive tissue untouched for too long pulsing with pleasure and crying out for more. He explored her teeth, the excruciatingly sensitive roof of her mouth, her fiercely retracted tongue.

Long fingers stroked across the satin skin of her shoulder, then slid to her back, to begin a slow gliding down the length of her spine. She was quivering all over by the time he heaved her tight up against him. The heady scent of him, the sensual knowledge of his touch, the unholy eroticism of his kiss wiped away six years without having to try hard, and as her arms lifted up and around his neck she marked her surrender to him with a pained little moan.

After that they were kissing like sex-starved wild things, hotly, deeply. It was mad. Moving against each other, heaving and panting, gripping and clawing—or she was. Anything—*anything*—to keep this from stopping. The heels of her shoes were screeching against marble, her fingers clutching at his silk dark head. Her skirt had rucked up round her hips, aided by the seeking slide of his hand, and he was touching with the intimate familiarity of a passionate lover—her thighs, the tight curve of her bottom—pressing her legs that bit wider to accept the taut, probing thrust of his manhood, straining against the zip of his trousers, while she tasted him, clung to him, moved and invited him.

It was desire gone rocketing out of control. She was hot, yet shivering, appalled with herself, yet desperate for more.

'Now?' he posed softly. 'You want it right here and now, *viuva de Ordoniz*?'

The widow Ordoniz. It was an icy douche that brought her gasping back down to earth.

Opening her eyes, she found he was standing there studying her through eyes that were cynical and cold. Oh, he was aroused. She could feel the power and strength of that arousal pushing against her. But the man himself was in complete control.

Unlike her.

His hand still claimed the heated dampness of her arousal. Shame had her push it away, only to release a revealing shudder at its removal. He found it so easy to let go and take a step back that she wanted to die where she stood.

'Who do you think you are to treat me this way?' she choked out, desperately tugging at the hem of her dress.

'The bit of rough you are clearly still partial to,' he answered, watching her go pale as his cutting reference hit home. Then he turned away. 'Now, pull yourself together.' It was hard and cold. 'We need to talk and we don't have much time.'

He glanced at his watch as he said that, not a crease on him, not a hair out of place. While she was a sizzling, quivering wreck he was a man so completely contained that tears of self-disgust stung at the backs of her eyes.

'We have nothing to talk about.' She just wanted him to get out of here.

'Oh, we do,' he turned to insist. 'You are in deep trouble, Cristina, not least because I am back in town. But we will deal with that some other time. I have a proposition to put to you.'

'I want nothing to do with you.'

'But you will by the end of this evening,' he assured her with cool confidence. 'And stop looking at me as if I'm some kind of snake because you find that you're still hot for me. It's in your favour that you do feel like that, or I would be leaving you to the hungry wolves out there.'

'I don't know what you are talking about.'

'Yes, you do. And sticking that defiant chin up to me

and firing contempt from those eyes won't cut it,' he sliced at her deridingly. 'You always were a skilled little liar— and you do know what I am talking about now, I see...'

His eyes raked her face as it paled with understanding.

'Yes.' He smiled. 'You made a big mistake six years ago when you tossed me aside with your lies and then trotted off to marry an old man with one foot already in his grave. You should have listened more closely to me when I told you how much I was worth. Even my unworthy half-English blood has a sweet taste to it when it comes wrapped in billions, *amante*. Now look at you,' he mocked. 'A pariah in your so-precious Portuguese society. And look at me, the half Englishman, holding the only chance you will have to save your Marques pride.'

'You are not the only rich financier here tonight,' Cristina hit back, wanting to sink weakly back down on the toilet seat and keeping herself upright only with the help of that Marques pride he'd just tried to crucify.

Beautiful, Anton thought. Sensational—exciting. Even while she stands there still trying to kill me with her eyes. And, yes, I'm up for it, he reaffirmed angrily. Whatever the lying sob story that was fed to Enrique Ramirez about our relationship six years ago, I am willing to fulfil his conditions and marry the Ordoniz widow. I'll fill her up with my seed and I will make reparation to *myself*, by never telling her how that seed is as Portuguese as her own.

Revenge, he decided, will taste sweet.

'By all means spend the rest of the evening taking your begging bowl round the present company,' he invited. 'You never know—you might get lucky and snag some other old man willing to bail you out in exchange for the use of that perfect body of yours. But if the bowl remains empty, then call this number...' Taking a business card out of his pocket, Anton handed it to her. 'It has my private line via the hotel switchboard,' he explained as she stared down at the card embossed with the logo of a top hotel in Rio. 'And remember, *querida*, when you do use that number, to ask for *Anton* Scott-Lee—not *Luis*.'

With that cutting stab at the other intimacy they had shared, he turned and walked to the door, unbolted it and walked out, leaving Cristina staring numbly after him as the door slid quietly back into its housing.

Silence clattered down. She began shaking all over, shock overlaying the skin-burning residue of his touch, holding her still as she listened to the sound of his deep voice as he began speaking to someone in the foyer, advising them to find another bathroom because this one was broken.

'Believe me, you really don't want to go in there,' she heard him say in smoothly amused cultivated English which brought forth a fluttering flirtatious female laugh that for some silly reason flooded her eyes with hot tears.

When he turned on that voice he could charm anyone, she remembered. He'd charmed her into his life and into his bed without having to try very hard.

For an impressionable young woman up from the country used only to meeting the dow old friends of her father or solitary gauchos out on the plains, Luis had been like a fairytale figure to her—young, handsome, light-hearted, passionate, and so exciting to be with he'd turned her escape to Rio into the most magical time of her life.

And she'd loved him totally. Still loved him like that, she admitted as a second wave of pained tears burnt her eyes. When she'd thrown Luis away so callously she'd thrown her heart away with him, and lived the last six years without one.

The shared laughter on the other side of the door grew

quieter as they moved away, then there was silence. With an effort Cristina pulled herself together, turning to check her hair and her make-up in the mirror and hurriedly trying to cover the swollen evidence of his kiss with a layer of red lipstick. It was not successful—how could it be when her lips continued to pulse, her eyes shone too brightly and her skin wore a flush that was not all to do with humiliation and shame?

She looked away, turned away, then took in a deep breath and made herself go back to the party—to hear from a disgruntled Gabriel that Luis had already left with his beautiful companion.

'Where do you know him from? How did you meet him?' he demanded to know. 'Do you know *who* he is? He owns big stakes in just about every banking house between here and the moon, and if I had known you knew him we could have used the connection. But the way you just walked away has probably blown that opportunity.'

'Sorry,' she murmured, not sorry at all. 'I felt ill suddenly. I thought you would prefer it if I didn't embarrass you by throwing up on his shoes.'

The begging bowl remained empty. By the time Gabriel saw Cristina into his car, the mood between them had turned very grim. As he drove them towards his apartment the silence grew like a heavy weight around both of them.

Then he told her why. 'The word is out, Cristina. You are untouchable. Most of the people there tonight have a stake in the Alagoas Consortium. They *want* you to surrender and sell.'

Strangely enough, she was not surprised—though she did wonder how big a stake Luis was holding.

It was the first question she asked him when she rang him from the privacy of the bedroom Gabriel had loaned her for her stay in Rio. She'd left Gabriel stretched out on a chair in his living room, brooding about the evening over a glass of brandy before going out again to meet up with his lover.

'Is it relevant?' Luis countered.

'If you want to see me fail as much as everyone else does, then yes,' she said. 'It is relevant.'

'Be here at my suite at twelve o'clock sharp,' was all he said. 'And don't bother to bring the lover along with you.'

'Lover?' she echoed blankly.

'The handsome blond with the very white teeth,' he extended with a sarcastic bite from his own white teeth.

'You mean Gabriel?'

'Yes, I mean Gabriel,' he mocked her.

'But he is—'

'Out, *querida*,' Anton said coldly. 'And I mean right out—of your life *and* the business loop. If you want me to save your precious Santa Rosa then from now on you deal only and exclusively with me.'

The line went dead. Anton let the receiver fall onto his naked chest and released a surprised laugh.

She'd cut him off, the reckless little witch!

The laugh changed into a smile as he relaxed back on to the pillows to stare at the ceiling while he imagined the way her eyes would be flashing with fury right now. He might have her cornered, shocked and frightened, but he had not scared her enough to make her behave herself when she was angry.

Nobody told Cristina Marques what to do. The moment anyone attempted to lay down the law with her she turned into a she-devil with bite. She got fiery and feisty and sometimes totally, excitingly unmanageable. They'd had rows in their twelve months together that had made Rio shake. She'd slammed doors, spat insults and all but lit up with defiance—while he had remained so laid back and cool about everything it had used to send her wilder still.

He'd used to love her wildness. He'd used to stand back and calmly goad her on, then wait for the moment when she would fly at him with her angry claws drawn. Fielding her with the ease of a man virtually born on an English rugby field had been a delight and a provocation in itself. She would kick, she would bite, she would scratch—or try to, without a hope of wounding him. And he would urge her on with taunts from his eyes and provoking comments while he went looking for the nearest horizontal surface on which to safely drop her.

And himself. Of course himself. A wide naked shoulder gave a shrug as if that was a given. You didn't catch yourself a wild thing without enjoying all of that fire and passion. You tapped into it. You provoked it further. You let it drive you crazy until that defining moment arrived when—

The phone rang again, vibrating against the smattering of dark hair on his chest. He lifted it to his ear.

'You will not dictate to me, Luis!' Her voice came shrill, packed with those sensationally sexy vowel sounds that littered her English. 'This is business, and in business anyone would be a complete fool to meet with you without their lawyer present also!'

'Did I say we would be discussing business?' he questioned. He listened to the sudden silence that clattered down the line at him, then added, *'Boa noite, amante,'* in husky dark Portuguese. *'Sonhos doas.'*

And he broke the connection.

Cristina stood taut, seething with anger and frustration—and fear. *That Goodnight, lover* had landed its message. The *Sweet dreams* had told her exactly what he expected her to go through for the rest of the night.

He was not going to give an inch. He had her hooked and he knew it. Just as he knew that the dreadful kiss in the white marble bathroom had ignited things inside her that were going to haunt her sleep. If she ever slept again, she thought with a shudder, when just thinking about that kiss drenched in her tight, stinging, sensual heat.

She did not want to want Luis again. She did not want to feel so out of control like this!

The knock at the bedroom door was hardly a warning before it swung open—just as she was about to do something stupid like throw herself down on the bed to weep her aching heart out. Gabriel stood there, big and strong, jacket and tie gone, amber eyes still brooding.

'You were lovers,' he announced, like an accusation.

She threw herself on Gabriel instead, landing with a sob against his wide, white-shirted front, and just cried her eyes out while he stood, maybe shocked but silently supportive, until it was over. Then he quietly sent her off to the bathroom to wash and change for bed. When she came back he had folded back the bedcovers. Without a single word passing between them he watched her lie down, then curl up like a defenceless child.

The covers were folded over her. Gabriel sat down on the edge of the bed. A gentle set of fingers reached out to brush her loosened hair from her cheek.

Her stupid eyes filled with yet more tears.

'It was there in the way you called him *Luis*,' he explained gently. 'And in the sexual tension that flashed like static around you both. But I stupidly did not realise it until a few minutes ago. When you ran he followed, like a man with a purpose—a sexual purpose—and earned you an enemy in his lovely companion.'

'Are *they* lovers?' The words shot right out of the sudden burn of acid jealousy clawing at her breast.

'Well, she certainly wants them to be,' Gabriel said dryly. 'And she did not like it when you snatched him literally right out of her grasp.'

'She can have him with my blessing.' And she meant it—she did!

'So tell me about it,' Gabriel invited.

Cristina closed her eyes and refused to speak—then was almost instantly flicking them open again. 'What do you think you are doing, Gabriel?' she demanded as she watched him heeling off his shoes.

'Getting more comfortable.' To her further consternation he stretched out on the bed beside her, then reached for her and drew her against him. 'Be calm,' he said lazily, when she went to push away. 'You are as safe here in my arms as you will ever be in a man's arms, and you know it. But I am not leaving here until you tell me everything. You understand me, Cristina? I want to know it all.'

'We had an affair six years ago.' The words left her reluctantly.

'Ah. Would this be the year of the mysteriously missing Cristina Marques?'

'I ran away,' she admitted. 'My father would not let me go to college, so I went without his permission.'

'And angered him greatly.'

'Do you think I cared about that?' A slender shoulder gave an indifferent shrug to her father's feelings. 'He believed a woman's place was in the home, playing slave to her men.' She did not add that he had also believed he had the right to marry her off to whoever would pay him a large injection of cash.

'He was a bullying tyrant.'

'*Sim,*' she agreed. 'I thought you were going to go out again?'

'My lover can survive without me for one night,' he said.

'This is much more interesting than sex. How many people would love to know what happened to the beautiful Marques heiress during the year she went missing?'

'Some heiress.' She laughed bitterly, thinking that the only thing she had inherited was the useless Marques pride, while Gabriel closed his eyes and envisaged his beautiful gold-skinned lover sulkily awaiting his arrival and understanding nothing.

'Continue, please,' he said. 'You ran away from home and went to college…?'

'No.' Cristina frowned. 'I had to earn the money to pay for college first, so I managed to find a job working in a bar on the Copacabana and slept in a little cupboard of a room on the floor above…'

It had been a hot and airless little room, and the hours she'd worked in the bar had been long. She had just begun to wonder if fate at her father's hands might not be better than what she had landed herself in, when Luis had strolled into the bar.

Tall, dark, handsome Luis, with the beautiful English accent and the sensational smile. Her heart gave a pained little throb, and, curling up against Gabriel, she told him everything—almost everything—from their instant attraction to each other to her moving into his apartment to live with him.

Her missing year had been a wonderful year, filled with love and passion and laughter, an introduction to the kind of world she had never believed really existed outside the pages of romantic books. His apartment on the Copacabana had been a haven in which they'd lost themselves.

'…then his *papa* died in a car accident and he had to go back to England,' she concluded.

'End of story?'

End of them, Cristina thought bleakly. '*Sim,*' she said.

'You simply waved this passionate lover farewell, then went back to Santa Rosa?'

That came three months later, Cristina remembered bleakly. 'We did not part—pleasantly,' was all she said out loud.

'He wanted you to go with him?'

No answer to that one.

'But you preferred to marry Vaasco Ordoniz instead?'

No answer to that one either. But he felt her fine shudder of revulsion when he mentioned her dead husband's name.

'And now your passionate ex-lover is back?'

'*Sim.*' She did answer that one. No use denying it. Luis was back. Bigger than she remembered him to be, leaner and harder, and colder than she remembered him to be, and so much more potently desirable than she remembered him to be—and the memories had been potent enough.

'He has offered to bail me out,' she admitted.

'And the price?'

Cristina moved restively. Sex was the price. Retribution was the price. Last time he had offered her marriage. This time she would be offered—something else. She could deal with *something else*. In fact, she was truly shocked and terrified by how much she wanted to have something else with Luis again.

'I will find that out tomorrow, when I meet with him.'

'You have already arranged this?'

'*Sim.*'

Gabriel sat up. 'And when were you going to get around to telling me of this meeting?' he demanded.

'I'm only just getting used to the idea for myself!'

He made a sound of impatience. 'You had better give me the time, so I can free myself up. I have a very busy schedule tomorrow, and if Senhor Scott-Lee is moving this quickly then we will—'

'No, Gabriel,' Cristina cut in softly, placing a hand on his arm. 'I want to thank you from the bottom of my heart for coming to my aid tonight, but from now on I will deal with this by myself.'

'Don't be foolish, Cristina.' He frowned down at her. 'The man is a shark beneath that smooth cloak of English sophistication. And he's hungry. I saw it in his eyes when he looked at you. He wants to eat you, *querida*. If he is about to offer you a rescue package then he means to play with you a little first.'

And he is powerful enough to play with you too, if I let him, she thought sadly. 'No,' she repeated. 'I know him. I can deal with him better if I do it by myself.'

CHAPTER FOUR

IT WAS all right to be brave, and determined to go it alone like this, but from the moment Cristina stepped into the hotel lift that would take her up to the top floor suite she knew that she wasn't feeling brave at all.

Gabriel was right. She had to be a complete fool to come here alone. She was just asking for trouble—begging for it.

The lift came to a stop. Her insides began to tingle, but what worried her most was that the tingle was not entirely to do with fear. As she stood facing the doors, waiting for them to open, those tingles went chasing down her arms and her legs in tight anticipation of—what?

Seeing Luis waiting for her dressed in one of those white bathrobes he'd always used to favour? Luis with his long tanned legs peppered with crisp black hair on show, and the triangle of hair that used to curl temptingly around the lapels of the robe?

An otherwise naked Luis. A man making a statement— a *You are here to please me or else* kind of statement.

Would he be that obvious, that crass, that—?

The doors began to move. Suddenly she lost the ability to breathe. Then her chin was lifting in the automatic response of a woman who'd learnt to meet trouble with defiance. If Luis was thinking he could march her into the nearest bed then he was going to have a—

A woman stood there. The same blonde woman Luis had been with the night before.

'Mrs Ordoniz?' she enquired in coldly cultured English,

giving no hint whatsoever that she had so much as set eyes on Cristina before in her life. 'I am Kinsella Lane, Mr Scott-Lee's personal secretary. If you will follow me, please, I will take you to him...'

No Luis to greet her personally—dressed or undressed. No threatening intimacy of a hotel suite with a bed very much on show. Just a private foyer, with several closed doors leading from it, and a woman who called herself Luis's personal secretary—but only a fool would believe that. Why else would she be here, in Luis's private suite? Did she share the accommodation with him? Did they share his bed as well as his suite?

Anger rose, fizzing on the edge of jealousy as she followed in Kinsella Lane's blue-suited wake. She knocked briefly on a door, then swung it inwards and was gliding forward on her long model's legs.

'Mrs Ordoniz to see you, Anton,' she announced in a low, intimate voice.

Several things struck Cristina hard at the same moment, the name *Anton* being the hardest strike, tugging her to a stop as the man himself came into view. He was leaning against the edge of a long conference table that spanned almost the full width of a room made up almost entirely of pale wood.

Two other men were with him. Cristina didn't see them. She only saw Luis, but not Luis, wearing a steel-grey business suit with a waistcoat that hugged his front like a piece of finely tooled armour worn over a bright white shirt and silver tie. His neat black hair, his golden features, even the long-fingered hands he used to add expression to whatever he was saying placed an aura around him that trapped the breath in her chest. And he was speaking in English, laying out instructions in clean, crisp, deep-bodied tones laced with authority that held his audience captive and mute.

This man was not the magical warm dark Luis she'd used to know. He was *Anton*, the ruthless banker, a gladiator of business, wearing the suit of armour of a man used to and comfortable with power in a way he had not been six years ago.

He turned his head to look at her then, and with the light coming in from a window behind him his eyes appeared even darker than hers. Two disturbingly black spaces set between slumbrous eyelashes that began lowering as he made a slow study of her from the neatly contained hair and conservative black suit to the unremarkable style of her low-heeled shoes.

She looked as if she'd come here to attend a funeral, Anton was thinking, and felt a wave of anger shoot through him, followed by a twinge of something else that he did not want to analyse.

He'd spent long enough analysing the grim state of Cristina's finances to know she owned hundreds of square miles of top-quality grazing land, thousands of heads of pedigree beef. She owned a whole mountain and a lush, fertile valley between it and a strip of rainforest that stood between the developers and a prime stretch of Atlantic coastline. But she'd had to borrow the money to make the flight to Rio.

It was no wonder she'd come here wearing unflattering black. The last time she'd worn that terrible suit had probably been to her wastrel of a father's funeral, and before that the funeral of her lousy gambler of a husband. Today had to feel like yet another funeral to her.

The death of the Marques pride.

That twinge tightened its grip on him. Pity? his mind suggested anyway. But what was there to pity about Cristina? She'd turned her back on him to marry for money.

For the thoroughbred continuance of the Marques blood-line. You didn't pity that, you derided it.

And where was the brood of pure-blood child stock?

Nowhere. Vaasco Ordoniz had died childless, and if any-one knew why then it had to be himself. So, no, he did not pity Cristina, he informed that uncomfortable twinge across his chest.

But he did still desire her—more so when she dared to lift that chin to him, as if to say *To hell with what you think of me. I am what I am and you will not change that.*

Well, that remained to be seen.

Kinsella demanded his attention then, by touching his arm and saying something softly to him. Forced to drag his eye away from Cristina, Anton found that his secretary was standing a bit too close. He said something curt—he didn't know what. Then he took a moment to dismiss all three employees while his attention fixed itself back on Cristina's defiant stance.

What he did not notice until the three shifted into motion was that the electric current running through the room was so strong it had removed the ability to breathe. His two young executives were curious. They'd never seen him this distracted by anything—especially by a woman they be-lieved he was about to indulge in a perfectly ordinary busi-ness meeting with. Kinsella, on the other hand, had picked up on the sex sparking through the tension, and he noticed the hostile flash her blue eyes gave Cristina. That look alone told him that she was piqued.

If she did not watch out, his super-efficient secretary was going to have to take a move sideways, out of his orbit, he decided.

Then forgot all about Kinsella as the door closed behind her.

They were alone.

Silence fell.

Was her heart beating as rapidly as his? Was she standing so still because, like him, she was afraid that if she moved all this sexual static would ignite and explode in a glorious barrage of untamed want?

And those eyes...

Those wide-set, almond-shaped, luster-dark eyes were looking at him as if they would dearly love to put a curse on him but were too busy trying not to eat him alive.

The look hit him where he'd expected, hard between his legs, pouring those warm pleasurable hormones into his bloodstream as his sex began to swell. She'd done this to him the first time he'd ever set eyes on her, turning him back into a sex-charged schoolboy unable to control the urge. That she could still do it to him now, dressed as she was and looking at him as she was, should be surprising him. But, having spent the night before in a state of high arousal on her account, he'd had to come to terms with the unarguable fact that this woman did it for him all the time, like no other woman—still.

Then she did surprise him, breaking the tension gripping both of them by dragging her eyes away and moving across the room to stand staring out of one of the side windows at the view. It wasn't the same spectacular view he got from the windows in the private part of his suite, but then this was a conference room, and conference rooms were designed for business not to give people a riveting vista of Rio. Nor were rooms like this designed for seduction. But in his private suite—

He grimaced, deciding not to let his mind go there—yet.

'You could at least say *Hello, Luis*,' he prompted dryly.

'You are not Luis, you are Anton,' she coolly replied.

Another grimace worked its way across his mouth, because he knew exactly who he felt like.

Hell, he knew that.

'I suppose this means that you expect me to call you Senhora Ordoniz?' he countered.

She turned to look at him. 'I am a Marques,' she announced, in that proud way she had of saying that name. 'I always have been and I always will be a Marques. I never used the Ordoniz name, so I would therefore appreciate it if you would stop using it and inform that—Kinsella Lane person of this, so she will not make the same mistake again.'

Kinsella? A black satin eyebrow arched in curiosity. 'Jealous of her already?'

The taunt earned him a flash from her eyes. But she remembered as well as he did what a naturally jealous and possessive little witch she'd used to be.

'She is your paramour—don't bother to deny it.' She dismissed the way he opened his mouth to do just that. 'I saw it in her face when she looked at you. I heard it in that silly husky voice she used to speak to you when all I received from her was a chill.'

'Paramour?' Anton repeated. 'What an old-fashioned word to use.'

'Mistress, then.' It made no difference to Cristina.

'A mistress is reliant solely on the generosity of her benefactor for her pampered existence. Kinsella holds down a good job and relies on no man for anything—unlike some.'

He meant herself. Cristina stiffened. 'I was never your mistress.'

'I housed you, clothed you, fed you and bedded you— good definition of a mistress.' He shrugged.

She ignored that. 'Paramour suits her better—the way she flutters around you like some silly fluffy moth.'

'But she is so beautiful, and so very willing, *meu*

querida.' He smiled tauntingly. 'She also comes with no strings attached. How is a man supposed to resist?'

'Then enjoy her.' Cristina turned her face back to the window.

'The position is yours if you want it.'

'I don't want it.' She added a toss of her head.

'Then that,' he said, 'concludes our business.'

Unimpressed by the shocked face she swung round to show him, Anton levered his long frame upright from the desk, his mood swapping from teasing to deadly serious with a speed that took her by surprise.

'You know why you are here, Cristina,' he said grimly. 'If you are being foolish enough to let yourself think that you're in a position to bargain with me, try thinking it through again.'

'I will not share your bed with another woman!' she tossed at him tautly.

'You will do as you are damn well told!' he lanced back.

And it was there, just like that—his contempt for her, the cold anger that froze her where she stood.

Cristina pulled in a deep breath. 'I don't understand how you can want me when you feel such hate for me,' she said as she breathed out again.

'Strange, that.' He grimaced. 'I've been puzzled by the same thing myself. I hate you, but you can still turn me on faster than any other woman of my acquaintance—and that, *querida*, is your only bargaining chip,' he warned. 'So be sensible and use it to your advantage instead of questioning it. Now, come and sit down.'

He swung out one of the black leather club chairs that lined the length of the table, then calmly reached out to hook up a phone.

'Coffee, please, Kinsella,' he instructed. 'Brazilian, and make it strong…'

Cristina hadn't moved a muscle by the time he turned back to her. His eyes turned a darker shade of green. Tension leapt as he began striding towards her like a lean, sleek hunting cat. One glance at the set of his face and alarm bells were ringing, sending a shot of adrenalin shooting down her spine. She knew that smouldering expression—recognised it from the evening before. Sparks began flying. Sexual sparks. That dreaded familiar heat began to pool between her thighs. On a short breath of air she took a wary step backwards, met wall and window, and put out her hands.

'Anton—'

'Luis,' he corrected, bypassing her hands to coil long fingers around her elbows and used them to tug her against his chest. There was a moment's stifled stillness between them as his eyes held her eyes and then he lowered his head and claimed her mouth.

It wasn't a pleasant kiss, or even that deep a kiss, but still by the time he lifted his head again there wasn't much of her that wasn't quivering.

'Okay, we have a choice at this juncture,' he said coolly. 'We can attempt to behave like civilised people, and sit down over there to discuss our business. Or we can go in the other direction, through that door you can see over there...' he indicated '...which leads to the very private part of this apartment, find the nearest bed and conclude this side of our business first. Now, which is it to be? Your decision.'

Her decision? Cristina thought dizzily. She let the tip of her tongue trace the pulsing contours of her lips and stared fixedly at the knot of his tie while she tried to find the strength to speak.

His hands still had possession of her elbows; her hands lay splayed across his chest. She could feel the muscular tightness of his body beneath the fitted waistcoat, feel his heart pumping to an accelerated beat that was telling her which option he would prefer.

And she was tempted. It appalled her to realise just how much she was tempted to throw business to one side and just take the rest.

'Tough choice?' he prompted when she took too long to answer. 'Need a little help?'

Before she realised what he meant he'd lowered his head again, touching his lips to the corner of hers. A sigh feathered her throat as instinct sent her head turning in a hunting move to capture that mouth, but it had already moved on, brushing her flushed cheek to send a fine quiver of pleasure running through her when he found her earlobe and gently closed his teeth on the tender soft flesh. Her breath feathered again and she moved that bit closer, fingers shifting in a tense little movement upwards, to the wide spread of his shoulders, then compulsively into the silk dark hair at his nape.

The soft sound of his laughter barely registered as derision until he released her lobe and murmured, 'Business should always come before pleasure, *querida*, as any street hooker should know.'

It took a full second for it to sink in that he was likening her to a street hooker. Cristina tugged herself free. Humiliation surged up from the quivering mess her senses were in and, without saying a word, she stepped around him, walked on cotton wool legs to the chair he'd pulled out for her and sat down on it.

Behind her, she felt his cruel amusement reaching out to her. In front of her lay nothing but more glass, set too high in the wall for her to see anything but uninterrupted blue sky. Her eyes burned, her heart hurt, inside she could feel herself coming to pieces—sitting tensely on the part of her

anatomy that was twisting and twirling with the heated excitement one kiss had fed into it while the rest of her
crawled with self-loathing.

Because he was only telling it as it was. She *was* little
more than a street hooker, here to sell the only commodity
she had that he was interested in.

The silence between them throbbed like a struggling
pulse-beat. If he said one more word to her Cristina knew
she was going to further humiliate herself by breaking
down to weep. Maybe he knew it. Maybe he still possessed
enough sensitivity in his hardened soul to recognise it.
Because all he did was take up his previous position against
the table, dominating everything within her fixed vision,
even the patch of blue sky. Crossing his long legs at the
ankles and folding his arms across his chest, he waited in
silence for her to calm down.

He'd shattered her, Anton could see that. Blank, hurt-
blackened eyes were standing out on her pale face. The
knowledge should be filling him with satisfaction but,
oddly, it was doing the opposite. Six years ago she had
shattered him, crucified everything he'd believed they felt
for each other, then calmly walked away. If revenge for
that moment had been his motive for doing this to her then
he was discovering that he did not like what it made him
feel.

Suppressing the urge to issue an apology, he moved his
gaze to the contours of her mouth. It looked so tiny, held
under control despite the evidence of his kiss still pumping
blood into the lush lower lip. The delicate heart shape of
its upper partner had a deeply vulnerable look to it that
made him want to…

His eyes drifted lower as he imagined that beautiful skin
stripped naked for him to see and touch. Was the rest of it
still as smooth as her face was? Did her skin still shine like

golden silk? He saw his hands drifting over her, felt the pleasure in stroking such perfection, then frowned as a different pair of hands took the place of his. Old hands, gnarled and withered hands, belonging to the man she had married in his place.

Anger leapt up inside him, growing on a wave of bitter, bloody disgust and contempt.

'Let's talk about your marriage,' he said abruptly.

She stiffened as if he'd shot her, and something flashed across her eyes—gone before he could catch it.

'My husband is dead,' she stated coldly. 'And I will not discuss him with you.'

'Not even to throw in my face how you married him within a month of turning me down?'

She sent him a silent icy stare in reply.

'Ordoniz left you destitute. So perhaps I can understand your desire to pretend he did not exist.'

No response again.

'And your own father was no better,' he continued. 'He squandered everything of any worth to that Marques pride you try so hard to hang onto. So take my advice and try not to say the name as if it should mean something of respect to me, because it doesn't. Okay?'

Okay... He was after her blood now, ruthlessly diminishing her to nothing in a few well-chosen statements.

'Do you feel better for saying all of that?' she asked stiffly.

'Hurt, did it?'

'*Sim.*' No use in pretending that it had not.

He nodded, but did not actually voice the *Good*. It hung there in the space between them all the same. He wanted payback for every cruel thing she had ever said or done to him. Making her swallow the truth about the Marques pride

was only the beginning. There was, she was sure, much
more to come.

'What does Enrique Ramirez mean to you?' he asked
next.

Cristina almost shot from the chair in shock. Never in
million years had she expected *that* name to come up in
conversation with anyone! It took every bit of control she
had in her to keep her voice level when she said, 'Enrique
who?'

But Luis had noticed her first reaction. His eyes narrowed. Her skin began to crawl with heat.

'Ramirez,' he repeated, very dryly. 'A man of about your
father's age—a good-looking guy when he was in his
prime…' His mouth turned down as he said that. 'He was
a favourite with the ladies…got rich by marrying diamonds
and oil. Played polo for Brazil and was a bit of a celebrity
here for a—'

'Polo?' Cristina looked up, her breathing fracturing.

'That means something to you?'

'M-my late h-husband used to train polo horses,' she told
him, looking away again. 'It was a major part of his life
until…'

Her world tilted into silence as a far-distant memory replayed itself in her head. She was seeing a small child,
breaking free of her career to run towards the paddock,
unseeing of the dangers—how could she see them? She was
too young, and she loved horses. Scooting under the fence
was the quickest way to get closer to them. She heard a
horse galloping towards her, turned to face it, then froze.
Wide-eyed, she watched it try to stop short of her, snorting
and skidding and in the end rearing up high while its rider
tried to stay on its back.

'Go on,' Luis prompted, unaware of what she was seeing
in her head. 'Your husband trained polo horses until—?'

'H-he had an accident,' she breathed unsteadily. 'He was trampled beneath one of the horses and was badly injured. He never went near a horse again afterwards, but—'

Her world tilted again, turning her face quite white as she sat there, seeing Vaasco hitting the ground, then the lethal power of the horse's hooves pounding into him. The horse was confused, scared as it tried to disentangle itself. It reared up again, huge, like a great roaring giant to the small child, then came thundering down with—

Cristina leapt to her feet, gasping sharply—she just couldn't stop herself.

'What the hell—?' Luis was suddenly grasping her arms in support.

It took another shaky breath to pull herself together. 'I have remembered that I have heard that name before,' she breathed, lowering her eyes from him and fighting to keep the tremor out of her voice. 'Enrique Ramirez was the name of the man who pulled the horse away from Vaasco, at great risk to his own safety. I—V-Vaasco owed his life to him.'

'You added a *but* before you went as white as a sheet.'

'Did I?' The sheet-white face turned perfectly blank.

'Were you there, Cristina?' Luis questioned narrowly. 'Did you witness your husband's accident?'

An odd kind of smile touched her pale mouth. 'It happened years ago. I was only a very small child.'

'Your husband told you about it?'

'Oh, yes,' she replied, with strange bitter smile.

'And also mentioned Ramirez by name?'

'Why are you interested in Enrique Ramirez?' She threw in her own question.

'Nothing important.'

It could have been the imminent arrival of the ordered coffee that made him let go of her so abruptly, but somehow Cristina did not think so—because she might have been economical with the truth just now, but she had a suspicion that so had he been, with his 'nothing important' throw-away.

Then again, the way he'd moved away from her like that could have more to do with Kinsella Lane being the person carrying the coffee tray, she decided, as she watched him stride across the room to meet the other woman halfway.

The fact that Kinsella had picked up on the tense atmosphere was clear in the look she sent Cristina before she carefully lowered her gaze.

Anton had seen the look also, and frowned as he reached out to take the tray.

'A Senhor Pirez has called several times to speak to you,' Kinsella informed him stiffly.

'No calls,' he instructed as the tray changed hands.

'Senhor Pirez was very insistent.'

'And you know the drill, Kinsella,' he responded. 'When I say no calls, I mean no calls.'

Cristina watched the other woman's blue eyes glint beneath her lashes before she turned and walked stiffly out of the room. Clearly she did not like his censure.

Had they had a lovers' spat? she thought nastily. But that was how she felt—nasty and mean and bitter and—

'You should be careful. She knows why you have brought me here,' Cristina heard herself snipe as he walked towards her with the tray.

'Meaning?'

'She is dangerous, that one. You think I was a jealous cat, but she will scratch your eyes out if you dare to take another woman to your bed.'

'Whereas you will grin and bear it for the sake of the money I can offer you.'

'I have told you once.' Cristina's chin came up. 'I do not share a man's bed with other women.'

'What about another man?'

The question confused her. She frowned at him and he smiled as he placed a cup in her hand.

'Gabriel Valentim,' he enlightened her. 'Did you share his bed last night?'

She was tempted to lie and say *Yes—passionately*, but there were already too many lies between them. 'I am not involved with Gabriel,' she said coolly.

'Lover without the loving?' He took a sip from his cup.

'Gabriel is just a friend.' She took a sip of coffee too.

'*Just* a friend?'

'A long-standing friend,' she extended. 'His father has been our family lawyer for ever. It is just your nasty mind that wants to make our relationship more intimate than that.'

'He's a good-looking guy. He's reasonably well-heeled. You need money.' A lazy shrug of a wide shoulder said the rest.

'Not as rich as you,' she hit back. 'And he is also *gay*,' she added, 'So you will please keep your unwanted thoughts to yourself.'

Gay.

Anton stared at her for a moment, then threw back his dark head and laughed. He'd spent the whole of last night lying wide awake in his bed, tormenting himself with visions of the handsome swine locked in Cristina's eager arms, when all the time—

'I don't know what you find so amusing in hearing that.'

'I don't suppose you do,' he replied, still smiling as he rid himself of his cup.

Cristina did the same at that exact moment, and their arms brushed. It was like making contact with a live wire.

Sparks shot through his body, then gathered at his loins. Anton sat back very slowly. Cristina simply froze. It was getting worse. Maybe the bed option before the business one was the right way to go, he considered wryly.

Cristina pulled in a deep breath. What was the matter with her? Why was she feeling like this? For six years she had kept all her emotions firmly under wraps. Then Luis walked back into her life and suddenly she was finding she could not control anything.

'Anton—' she burst out. 'Can we—?'

'Small hint, *querida*,' he interrupted. 'When the only thing you've got going for you is the intimacy of a name, then use it. Anton is a ruthless bastard. You really do need to keep him out of this as much as you possibly can.'

'And who is Luis? Anton's nice, *kind* alter ego?'

'His *sexual* ego,' he enlightened her. 'Luis is sitting here aching to strip you naked and sink himself so deep inside you he will never find his way out. Anton aches to see you stripped of everything but the clothes on your back.'

'A no-win situation, then.' She sank back into the chair in a helpless gesture.

'That depends on what you want out of this.'

I want you to look at me with those eyes lighting with the flames of love like they used to, Cristina thought helplessly.

'Your help,' was what she said. 'I want you to help me save my home.'

'That's it?'

Pressing her lips together, she nodded.

'At any price?'

'Almost any price,' she modified, with a nervous touch of her tongue to her suddenly dry upper lip.

He said nothing for so long that Cristina was forced into looking at him. He was staring at her mouth. Her heart gave a thump; lips he'd brutally kissed not that many minutes ago began to reheat. She wanted to look away but she couldn't. She wanted him to say something but he still didn't speak. The heavily laden silence began to weave around her like a silken web. He was so beautiful, her Luis. So—

'Okay.' He nodded. 'Then let us see if we can find the ceiling on your *almost any price*.'

Hooking out another chair from beneath the table, he lowered his long frame into it. 'This is how things stand for you, Cristina, and it isn't good,' he warned. 'The Alagoas Consortium have decided to fight dirty. They are in the process of trying to buy your mortgages, plus all the other debts you've managed to incur. If they succeed they will turf you out of Santa Rosa without giving you a chance to catch your breath.'

'You said you would help.'

'But on my terms, *querida*. And non-negotiable terms at that.'

The *almost* test. She could hear it coming. 'What kind of terms?' she asked huskily.

'A large stake in Santa Rosa.'

Cristina nodded, having expected to hear him say that.

'Full control over how the money I invest is spent.'

That brought her chin up. 'You know nothing about farming!'

Green eyes glinted. 'But my future wife does.'

Future *wife*—? It had not occurred to her that he might be getting married! Jolted into a reaction, she felt her backbone tense and jumped to her feet.

'You will not bring another woman into Santa Rosa, Luis!' she spat at him angrily. 'I would rather take my chances with the Alagoas Consortium than let you!'

His hand closing around her wrist silenced her. 'Your

tantrums used to turn me on, Cristina. Now they do not. You are badly used goods, *querida*, wearing a badly used suit which makes you even less appealing. So try at the very least to find a little dignity. Sit down again and listen,' he instructed icily.

Cristina sat, slaughtered by his brutal opinion of her. Letting go of her wrist, Anton sat back.

'Now, this is what happens,' he continued, as if the incident in the middle had not taken place. 'My bank will buy you out of trouble. It will keep Santa Rosa ticking over until such time as you fulfil your part of the deal.'

'Which is what?' she asked bitterly.

There was a pause—a carefully constructed pause that held Cristina completely trapped. Then it came—smoothly, calmly, quietly.

'I need a wife,' he announced. 'And I need one quickly. You, *meu querida* are in the fortunate position of suiting my requirements.'

CHAPTER FIVE

SHEER disbelief had Cristina twisting to stare at him. 'You are asking *me* to marry you?' The words arrived gasping from her lips.

Anton's face hardened, his whole demeanour turning to ice. 'Take note, Cristina, that at no point in this discussion am I *asking* you to marry me,' he said, very clearly. 'This is a business arrangement. I need a wife,' he repeated. 'You happen to fit the bill. You are young, presentable, and still desirable.'

'Even for badly used goods?' she quavered.

'As you say.' He nodded. 'You also need my money *more* than I need you.'

'*Why* do you need a wife?'

'That's my business.'

'You want a *silent* wife?' She was unable to stop the slicing sarcasm from coming out.

'You could say that—though I think it might be stretching my luck.' He smiled in spite of the ice.

'I wonder you are not putting your secretary in the role, then.'

'She does not suit my requirements.'

'But she would not say no to you.'

'Are you thinking of saying no to me?'

Cristina was too busy trying to grapple with it all to say anything.

'Maybe you would rather let Kinsella suffer my English touch than be forced to suffer it for yourself again.'

That did it. She turned on him, swivelling in the chair to

69

burn him with a look. 'I *never* once said I did not enjoy making love with you, Luis!' she said hotly. 'And stop throwing my six-year-old words back at me!'

'Strong words, though, Cristina. Hard words from a proud Marques mouth.'

'As you have already pointed out, what pride is there now in being a Marques?' she countered, then had to heave in a deep, unsteady breath. 'The name, like my reputation, is demolished. Do you think I am too stupid and too *proud* to have realised that for myself, long before you came back into my life?'

'My apologies,' he said.

She looked away from him and said nothing. An apology only meant something if it carried regret.

'Am I allowed to ask what my role as *wife* to you is supposed to entail?'

'Of course you may ask,' he answered, so smoothly it was like a slap in her face. He was sitting there—*relaxing* there now—as if the anger of before had never been, while she…

Was hurt and fighting not to show it.

And afraid of what was going to come next.

'Your role will be the same as any other wife,' he told her. 'You will keep my house, be my hostess and sleep in my bed. You will also make yourself available to me for sex whenever I desire it…' He sat forward then, so he could look into her face. 'And here is the bad one, Christina, so prepare for it because you are not going to like this,' he warned. 'We—as in you and I—are going to have to go all-out for a fast and probably furious attempt at conceiving a baby. I need you to be pregnant, you see, within a few months…'

Having shot his final past-avenging dart into her useless little heart, Anton watched, totally riveted—because it actually was like witnessing a murder take place. She seemed to die right there in front of his eyes.

'Too much to ask?' he prompted.

She didn't answer.

'Still protecting your gorgeous figure at all costs?'

She still made no response.

Something vicious tightened inside him. 'Or perhaps you still cannot face the prospect of my half-English blood mixing with your blood?'

She breathed then—blinked. One of those very slow lowerings of fine-veined eyelids over terrible blank eyes. As they lifted again so did Cristina, rising out of the chair like a zombie. Then she just turned and walked towards the door, leaving Anton sitting there, stunned and so damn angry that she could do this to him—again!

He threw himself to his feet. 'I see that we have found your ceiling price,' he fed harshly after her. 'But know this, Cristina. The deal remains in place only until you reach that door!'

She stopped walking, trembling from hair root to toe tip.

'I *hate* you, Luis,' she whispered painfully.

'I am so gutted by that, *querida*,' he drawled in return. 'Do you go or do you stay?'

She spun on him then, her beautiful face blanched of its warm golden colour, dark eyes shot through with a kind of agony that had him folding his arms across the sudden tightness trying to band his chest.

'Stay for what?' she cried out shrilly. 'So that you can take more revenge for that precious ego that I bruised so badly once?'

'Did you bruise it? I don't remember.'

'I battered it!' she spat at him. 'I crushed it in my fist and flung it to the ground! You want more of the same from me, *querido*? You want to feel the same rejection again?'

'Reject me, then. Use the door,' he invited. 'You never know—if you spread your net wide enough you might catch another withered old man willing to buy his way into that sensational body of yours.'

She flew at him then. It did not surprise him. He'd been goading her towards it since she'd first walked through the door. The tied hair, the grim suit—as a disguise they were useless where he was concerned. With every flash of her eyes and every smart-mouthed comment he'd seen the real Cristina lurking there. Now she was out, and he was going to make sure that she stayed out.

He fielded her arrival without having to do very much other than catch her as she arrived at his chest, wrap his arms around her and lift her clean off the ground. Their faces came level—hers whitened by stark fury, his as ungiving as rock. She hit out at him with her fists. He laughed—once—harshly, then treated her angry mouth to a totally carnal flat-tongued lick.

All hell broke loose with that one action. She quivered from wetted lips to slender thighs. A whimper broke from her—a sobbing, cursing protest. He did it again, only this time he took the lick inwards and turned it into a full-blown deep and devouring assault. Her angry protest vibrated through both of them. As he levered himself away from the table and started walking her fingers clawed into his hair.

Did those fingers attempt to pull his mouth away from her mouth? Not this woman. She held him down, held him right there, where she was greedy for him. He knew her. He knew what made her explode sexually—and what made her *his*!

When he reached the door that would give them access to his private suite, he flattened her against it with his body, so he could use his hand to seek out the handle. As the door swung open, with the weight of their bodies as impetus, he had to use his hands against the heavy wood to cushion the moment when it hit the wall behind and they followed it. Her feet found solid ground again, but she didn't let go of him. So they remained there, pressed against the door, kissing like hungry maniacs for long lost minutes. Time in which he managed to rid her of her jacket. The skirt was too big. He had only to release the zip for it to fall in a heavy whisper to the floor.

Did she let go then? Did she come to her senses? Did she even *know* this wasn't six years ago? Not this hot, greedy, sexually hungry woman who pushed his jacket from his shoulders with impatient fingers and sent it dropping to the floor with her own clothes.

Her hair came next, pins flying as he loosened that glorious mass of twisting ebony and let it tumble over his fingers. She was working free the buttons on his waistcoat when he lifted her up again. She wrapped her legs tightly around his waist, took his bottom lip between her teeth and bit.

It hurt. She had meant it to. When he winced out a curse she did it again. When he attempted to pull his head back she imprisoned it in her hands, then she was the one to instigate the next mouth and tongue-devouring kiss.

She was wild for him. He loved it. Exhilaration ran through him as he made the move to the bedroom by pure instinct. She clung. He pulsed. She moved against him. His hands gripped her bottom and she felt like satin, warm, too slender, too delicate to be real. He dropped her on the bed, then came down with her, the heat of need pounding through his body and scoring streaks across his hard taut cheeks.

His mouth ached, his jaw, his warring tongue. He broke

the kiss to look down at her and watched as she gasped and panted for air.

'Are you staying or going?' he demanded in a voice as cold as an English winter. The stark contrast between his physical self and his mental self was so acute that she stared at him for a full ten seconds before reality finally sank in.

'You want your pound of flesh!'

'I want more than that,' he responded. 'I want your thankless little soul gift-wrapped and handed to me with a rock-solid guarantee that this time it belongs to me!'

Cristina looked into the hard, cold, face of this man she loved so much and had hurt so much, and wished there was a tiny molecule of hope for them.

But there wasn't. 'You will come to regret it,' she told him honestly.

'Are you staying?'

'You will learn to hate me all over again.'

'You are not here because I adore you, *querida*. You are here because I still want you.'

It should hurt to hear him say that, but it didn't. How could it hurt when she did not deserve more than he was offering?

'In your bed?' She demanded confirmation.

'Yes.'

'As your obedient little sex slave?'

His green eyes began to gleam. 'Most certainly that.'

A strange smile touched the corners of her hot pulsing mouth. 'Gift-wrapped?'

'*Sim.*' He swapped languages so there could be no mistaking the answer.

'You can have me like that without marrying me.'

'I had you like that once before. Didn't like it. So the marriage thing stays. It comes with the package.'

As the baby did? She wanted to weep all over him—but she didn't.

'The gift-wrapping?' she asked.

'The rock-solid guarantee of a marriage certificate—written in blood if need be. I will not compromise,' he warned huskily.

Take it or leave it. Take this man when you know that you should not. Take everything he wants to dish out to you in the name of revenge when you know you will end up having to walk away.

Again.

Eventually.

'So, are you staying?'

She made no answer, her beautiful eyes so painfully, hauntingly bleak that something too close to fear grabbed at the muscles in Anton's chest. He did not want to be hooked by her again. He wanted Cristina firmly hooked by him.

'Answer or leave,' he ground out roughly.

She looped an arm around his neck and drew his mouth back down to hers.

Was it an answer?

He was going to take it as one. Choice was something ripped away from him the moment her tongue made a sliding caress over the top of his. She lifted a long silken leg to loop it around his hips in one of her old, uninhibitedly sensuous and possessive moves, and on a surrendering growl he let himself fall prey to the whole wild experience that was Cristina Marques, the enemy of his once bitten ten times shy heart.

Mouths open, hot and fused. Her fingers back at his waistcoat. She all but ripped it from his body, setting the tight satin muscles in his shoulders rippling as she tugged it down his arms. His tie came next—an impatient yank at the slender knot and silver silk slithered apart—and she was already opening the buttons on his shirt. Eager, needy, her fingers made familiar contact with the whorls of dark hair covering his thundering breastplate, curling, then scoring into his flesh to make him shudder with pleasure as he brought his own impatient fingers to the hem of the cotton T-shirt she wore.

They had to break the kiss so he could strip the T-shirt over her head. Separation brought with it a moment of sanity as he felt the thinness of the fabric. Well washed and well-worn, he saw, and made a mental note to buy her a new wardrobe as he tossed the scrap of cotton aside.

Then he saw them. Proud, unfettered, full and firm. Two golden globes tipped by long dark nipples standing up in bold and brazen demand. On a growl he pounced, sending her slender spine arching on a high-pitched quivering cry as he took possession in an open-mouthed, wet-tongued, hungry claim.

His shirt hung open. Her fingers crawled all over hard muscle and taut male flesh. When he sucked, she writhed beneath him, and he ground out a soft curse as electric sensation shot to his thighs. As if she knew, she located the fastener for his trousers and began an urgent attempt to strip him of those.

It was no use. He was forced to help because there was no way she was going to succeed while he still wore his socks and shoes. Sitting up with a growl of impatience, he reached down to remove the obstructing articles while her hands slid beneath his shirt and began a sensual exploration of his satin-smooth back.

His shoes hit the floor, followed by his socks, then he stood up to remove the trousers. She watched him, her eyes like burning rubies, coveting each new piece of hard male flesh he revealed.

No other woman had ever looked at him the way Cristina looked at him.

'Greedy,' he muttered as she reached out to touch him, brushing feather light worshipping fingers along his full length. He throbbed and swelled and hardened so fast it was almost an agony. He had to fight with uncoordinated fingers to release cufflinks so he could remove his shirt.

Stripped naked he was beautiful. *'Bonito,'* Cristina murmured.

Still beautiful…*always* beautiful. Her Luis, she thought helplessly as she drifted her eyes over his tall dark stance, with its arrogant masculine pride in his own prowess.

He came down beside her, stretching out along her slender length, then sliding an arm beneath her shoulders and lifting her towards him. He held her like that, with her hair rippling behind her and her passionate mouth parted, ready for the hungry onslaught of his.

Eyes like glowing emeralds looked deep into her eyes. He didn't speak. She didn't want him to. If he did they would fight, and all she wanted to do was make love. Would he know, afterwards, that he had been her only lover ever? Could men tell these things?

He moved then, claiming her mouth with a hot, deep, probing assault that pressed her back against the pillows so he could cover her with his warm naked weight. After that it was a voyage of rediscovery, hot and intense and achingly poignant. Neither bothered to look for restraint.

And six years was a long time to starve a fever. It was hungry and it wanted feeding. They fed it. Oh, yes, they fed it. The rest of the world might have come to an end and they would not have noticed or cared.

Neither heard the quiet footsteps making their way across the living room. Neither recalled that they'd left the doors to the conference room and bedroom hanging wide open.

Kinsella Lane stood in the bedroom doorway. She had been there for a long time, watching like a voyeur and listening to everything they said, with the cold blue eyes of hate.

She wanted Anton. She had always wanted him, from the moment she'd first seen him when she was only a very junior secretary at the Scott-Lee Bank, much too low in the ranks for him to notice her. She'd worked long and hard to gain entry into his select circle. She'd made a careful study of all the different women who'd floated in and out of his life. He liked blondes. She'd become a blonde. He liked them slender and neat, supremely elegant and sophisticated. She'd learnt how to achieve that elegance and sophistication. She'd honed and pruned and sculpted herself to meet the specifics of his sexual criteria. And he had begun to notice her. She'd seen the warmth grow in his eyes when he looked at her—felt the telling sting of his attraction towards her begin to catch light.

When he'd brought her along on this trip to Rio she'd thought it was because he was ready to deepen their relationship. His rejection of her in the lift the other day had hurt. But then two other employees had been present, so she'd understood and learnt yet another lesson—get your timing right. Or so she'd thought.

Now look at him, locked in the arms of the complete opposite from everything he had ever been attracted to. She was dark, she was small; she wore ugly clothes. Her hair was a mass of wild black twists and her breasts were too big. And there was no sophistication in the way she kissed him or touched him or taunted him or even spoke to him. Yet he was mad for her!

It was there in the way he shuddered when she caressed him. No finesse. No smooth, slick seduction. Just animal hunger and hard, hot sexual feast. Even the way he was covering her now and reaching round to wrap her legs around him showed an animal with no grace.

His lean golden flanks rippled as he made that first lunging thrust into her body. Her cry of pleasure echoed round the room.

Turning away in disgust, Kinsella left as silently as she had entered, stepping over discarded clothes and touching nothing, not even bothering to close those doors.

As soon as she gained the privacy of her office she opened the safe and took out the file Anton had placed there that morning, after his private meeting with a man called Sanchiz. Ten minutes later and she was replacing the folder in the safe, then picking up the telephone and dialling London.

'Mrs Scott-Lee?' she said. 'I think you should know that your son is intending to marry a Brazilian woman. A young widow—Cristina Ordoniz.'

There was a long silence, then a faint, slightly tremulous question. 'Ordoniz, you say? Are you sure of that name?'

'Yes,' Kinsella confirmed.

'And young, you said? How young?'

'About my own age, Mrs Scott-Lee,' Kinsella answered. 'I understand that her husband was an old man when she married him for his fortune. Not quite the person you'd want as a wife for your son, I would think.'

Anton's mother made no response to that. And there was another one of those silences before she said, 'I will be catching the next flight to Rio. Thank you for helping me with this, Miss Lane...'

He'd forgotten what it was like to have her breathe his name all over him. Forgotten too much, Anton realised as she blew six years of other women to absolute Hades and

rolled him up, tied him up and packaged him with a label—
Belonging to Cristina Marques.

Did he care? The hell he cared, he thought as he made
that first driving thrust inside her, then stopped, watching
in dark eyed fascination as she tensed, then cried out in an
echoing response to their first time together, when she'd
given him her virginity without bothering to warn him that
it was there.

'Long time, *querida*?' he questioned huskily.

'*Sim,*' came the gasping reply.

Her fingernails were scoring deep grooves into his shoulders, and the slender arch of her body was an instinctive
attempt to fight off his invasion. For a short, frowning second he thought of withdrawing, but she opened her eyes
and looked directly into his.

Her mouth shook, but she said, 'Don't you dare, Luis.'

He smiled then, amused by how well she too was remembering that first time, when he had tried to withdraw
only to have her stop him. And, like that first time, he
reached up to brush her hair from her face, then lowered
his mouth to gently soothe her with soft kisses while he
waited for the tension to ease.

Familiarity should breed contempt, but not in this case.
Familiarity was everything when she lifted up her hands to
cup his face, then began whispering soft words of love
against his lips. In one way he did not want to hear them
spoken; in another way he lapped them up with true macho
arrogance as she told him everything she was feeling, everything she wanted to feel, and eventually, as the tension
eased from her body, everything she demanded he give.

And he gave it all. He gave everything. They matched.
They'd always matched—in hunger, in passion, in what
they wanted and demanded and made sure they received.
They kissed, they touched, they rolled, they built it. It was

hot and it was fevered. Each surging thrust overpowered
the previous one; each coiled-spring meeting of their bodies
drove them closer to the edge. He kissed her mouth, her
breasts, her fingers when they came back to his face. When
he felt the first ripples of her growing climax he lost it
completely and quickened the pace. She came as she'd always come—wildly, noisily, gasping and shuddering and
tugging him with her over the edge.

Afterwards they lay in a heap of tangled limbs and
sweat-slicked skin and shuddering senses. He could feel the
thunder of her heartbeat and the quiver of her lips against
his throat.

'Well, that was worth the six-year wait,' he murmured
eventually.

'Don't talk,' she said, and he grimaced.

Maybe she was right. Talking was bound to spoil everything. Rolling onto his back, he took her with him so she
lay along his length with their bodies still joined and no
desire on either side to separate.

Her hair was stuck to his face and he reached up to brush
it away, then gently rearranged her into a more comfortable
position, with her cheek in the damp, cushioning crook of
his shoulder and her boneless legs resting along the sides
of his.

He was sated, he realised, then thought, Strange, that.
Because the feeling had nothing to do with the sex but with
this—having Cristina lying on top of him like a warm,
sleek, sleepy cat.

Reaching for one of her hands, he lifted it to his mouth
and began idly tasting each slender finger while he attempted to work out why he was feeling like this.

Cristina, on the other hand, was trying to work out how
she'd break it to him that marriage was out of the question,

no matter what slant he wanted to put on what they had just done.

Why did he need a wife, anyway?

Or a baby?

The thought of the latter addition made her start to tense up. He instantly soothed her with the featherlight brush of his fingers down the length of her spine.

Luis was always like this after making love, she remembered. Wide awake, but relaxed, content to keep her this close. Any minute now he would start to instigate a second loving. She knew it because she could feel him inside her, still a bold, probing force, even though he was not quite fully erect. And this time it would be slow, more deeply intense and sensually exploring.

Did she let it happen? Did she give in and steal just one more escape from reality before she told him that his deal was not going to happen?

'You told me you still love me,' he remarked idly.

'I did not!' she denied, lifting her head up from his shoulder so that she could glare that denial into his impassive face.

He was so beautiful her heart turned over. His slumbrous eyelids lowered as he sucked her index finger into his mouth and wrapped his tongue right around it, then began a slow mimic of a different act that set him hardening and swelling inside her.

Her soft gasping quiver had him releasing the finger.

'You did,' he insisted, then reached up and brought her mouth down on his before she could answer. A few seconds later and she had forgotten what they were talking about as it all began again in a slow deep mutual loving—just as she had predicted.

Just this one more time, Cristina told herself as she let him take her over.

*   *   *

Back in London, Maria Ferreira Scott-Lee was standing by her dressing table. In her hand she held a small package from Estes & Associates, Advocates of Law, Rio de Janeiro. The package had arrived the same day that her son had flown out to Brazil. Inside it was a jewel box and a letter. The jewel box held an exquisite, priceless diamond-encrusted emerald ring. The letter was personal—deeply personal—handwritten by Enrique himself.

Don't mess with what you do not yet understand, Maria, Enrique had written as a warning footnote. *Our son will marry the widow of Vaasco Ordoniz and you will forget that you ever knew that name if you value our son's love for you.*

But she could not forget Vaasco Ordoniz. She could not forget that Anton would have been Vaasco's son if Enrique had not got in the way.

Ah, the tangles life could throw at you, she thought on a sigh that had her lowering herself onto the dressing stool. Enrique was the most handsome man she had ever encountered. Meeting him at Vaasco's ranch had turned into the ruin of her life. Betrothed to Vaasco, in love with Vaasco, she had still fallen for Enrique's charm and into his bed. When she'd fallen pregnant with Enrique's child she'd had to tell Vaasco. It was natural that he'd thrown her out of his life.

'Back to the gutter where you belong,' he'd said.

Sebastian had come to her rescue. It had been Sebastian who flew her back to Rio and eventually brought her to England with him. Dear Sebastian, who had been in Brazil to buy horses from Vaasco. He'd come back with a broken-hearted, shamed and pregnant woman instead.

Now here was life making a tangling full circle, and the

Ordoniz name was haunting her again. Who was this woman? How did Enrique know about her? Why had he sent their son to her? Who was playing a game with whom?

She was young, Kinsella Lane said. Vaasco had been a very wealthy man. He had trained horses for the polo field as a hobby, not to earn a living. Who was this—person who would marry an old man if she was not some kind of cynical fortune-hunter? And, having managed to inherit Vaasco's money, was she looking to get her hands on Anton's money as well?

Maria looked down at the ring box sitting on her dressing table, then at the words in Enrique's note.

For you, Maria, in sincerest gratitude for the son you gave me and as a token of my regret for the life you had taken away from you on my account. Our son grew in my image. He deserves to know this. He deserves his share in my inheritance. Vaasco turned out badly. One day you will perhaps thank me for saving you from him. Think on that when you meet his widow. She is not what she seems and deserves your pity.

'I pity no one who means to hurt my son,' she murmured.

Maria's son wasn't hurting. He was sleeping the sleep of the thoroughly sated.

Lying beside him, Cristina watched him—just watched, as she'd used to love watching Luis sleep. He had a way of sprawling on his front across three-quarters of the bed, leaving her one quarter to curl herself into. She never minded. When he awoke, her quarter would become his quarter too, leaving the rest of the bed to grow cool.

Or it would if she intended to be here when he awoke.

She had already delayed her departure for much longer than she should have.

But for now—for a few more precious seconds—she was content to reacquaint herself with the way his hair flopped over his forehead and how his face wore the relaxed expression of sleep.

Her tummy muscles quivered, her heart squeezing out a tight, painful ache. He was beautiful, her Luis. Passionate, demanding, insatiable—and the low-down pulse of just how insatiable still played its pleasure across the sensitive muscles where she loved to feel Luis most.

How had she lived six years without being with him?

How was she going to manage without him all over again?

They'd got up at one point between bouts of wild passion, gathering up clothes and closing doors. It had made her blush and him grin when they realised how they had left them standing wide open for anyone to come in and catch them.

'My staff know better than to intrude on my privacy,' he had stated with arrogant confidence.

Still, they'd been—noisy. She was blushing again now just remembering some of the gasps and cries she'd emitted in the throes of her pleasure. Or those tense little curses he'd rasped out as his control snapped, and the resulting driving sound of his breathing when he finally gave in.

He was no silent lover, this cool-headed half-Englishman she loved so much, Cristina thought with a smile. The desire to reach out and gently stroke that floppy lock of hair away from his forehead almost got the better of her.

But it was time for her to get up and go...

Stay a little longer, urged a soft voice inside her. See out the rest of the day, then the long dark night with him. Leave tomorrow.

No. The time to go was now…while she could.

Her heart gave that painful little squeeze in protest. At the same moment a pair of ink-black eyelashes lifted upwards and eyes the colour of a dark ocean focused on her face. It was as if he'd sensed what she was thinking, the way a set of long fingers reached up to brush a gentle caress across her cheek.

'You're still here,' he said softly. 'I was dreaming you'd left me.'

'No,' she whispered

Tomorrow, Cristina thought. I will leave tomorrow. 'Kiss me, Luis,' she begged.

CHAPTER SIX

IT WAS into the afternoon by the time Cristina let herself into Gabriel's apartment.

'Where have you been?' Gabriel demanded, almost before she had managed to close the door. 'It was bad enough that the rushed message you left with my answering service last night said almost nothing, but did you have to go missing today too?'

Having spent most of the day trawling through the banks and financial houses of Rio, it was all she could do to utter a weary, 'Sorry.'

'Not good enough, Cristina,' Gabriel censured. 'I was worried about you. When I rang Scott-Lee to find out what was going on, all I got was some cold Englishwoman claiming that she had never heard of Cristina Marques!'

The lovely Kinsella, Cristina thought dryly. 'I was there,' she said, then explained about the mix-up in names.

Gabriel shoved his hands into his trouser pockets. 'I was beginning to think he'd abducted you,' he said gruffly. 'I had this image of him bundling you into a sack and shoving you in the boot of his car, then driving off to some unknown location to have his evil way with you.'

'Not very English of him, Gabriel,' she mocked, though Luis had bundled her into bed pretty effectively, she allowed.

'He does not look very English…just sounds it.'

He makes love in English, Cristina thought, then had to turn away before Gabriel could see the look in her eyes.

Too late, though. 'You look like death, *quérida*,' he observed gruffly.

Feel it too, Cristina thought. 'I need a shower,' she said, and walked down the hall towards her allotted bedroom.

Gabriel followed. 'You want to explain why you look like death?'

Not particularly, Cristina thought as she crossed the bedroom to open a drawer that held the bits of underwear she'd brought with her.

'I spent the day visiting the banks,' she told him, shifting to the wardrobe to rifle through the few items of clothing she had. Just two good dresses worthy of the kind of social events like the gala last night—both black. Vaasco had only allowed her to wear black.

'Scott-Lee's offer was not good enough?'

Her shoulders ached with the strain of trying to appear normal. 'It was not the right one.'

'As in…?'

As in I would be his willing mistress for the next fifty years even if he married another woman and had twenty children with her. But that was not what Luis wanted.

'He wanted your body,' Gabriel derived from her silence. 'Since you spent the night with him, I conclude that he *had* your body?'

A strained laugh escaped past the lump in her throat.

'I cannot believe that you were stupid enough to give him his reward before he'd handed over the money, Cristina,' he muttered.

It was so like advice for a street hooker that she swung on him angrily. 'Don't speak to me like that, Gabriel!'

But he was angry too. 'What did he do? Seduce you with a load of promises, take what he wanted, then throw you out on the street this morning?'

No, I sneaked away when he wasn't looking, Cristina

thought heavily. 'Can we leave the lecture until after my shower, please?' she requested.

'Sure,' Gabriel replied, and stormed out, leaving Cristina to wilt down onto the end of the bed, recalling how she had left Luis.

She'd pretended to be perfectly content to lie curled in his bed while he got dressed for a business meeting at his bank. She'd even smiled when he'd kissed her farewell and let that kiss cling enough to send him away with a rueful smile upon his face. The moment he'd left the suite she'd been out of that bed and racing for the shower.

Coward, she thought now. Weak little coward.

It was probably appropriate that she should have met Kinsella Lane in the hotel lobby, wanting to come into the lift as she was leaving it. The blonde had taken one look at her and said, 'Bitch,' shocking a neatly dressed young man standing to one side of the lifts. When she'd tried to walk away Kinsella had grabbed her wrist and spat the kind of venom at her that was still turning her stomach. 'Don't kid yourself that I will stand back and let you take my lover away from me, because I won't. It was my body he drowned in the night before you fell into bed with him, and it will be me he will return to London with.'

Odd how the truth had the power to hurt so much, Cristina thought now. Because Luis *would* be returning to London with Kinsella, and she—

She spied her suitcase, sitting at the bottom of the wardrobe, and on a sudden burst of urgency pulled it out and tossed it onto the bed. She did not want to think about what she would be doing when Luis returned to London. She did not want to think of anything other than packing her case and catching the first flight to Sao Paulo she could get a seat on, and to hell with—

The door swung open. Gabriel stood there. Big and lean

and endearingly handsome, even with that look of contrition on his face. 'I did not mean to insult you,' he apologised gruffly.

'I know that.' And, strangely enough, she did. Gabriel had been her friend for too long for her to take any real offence because he gave it to her as he saw it.

'I was worried about you.'

'*Sim.*' She understood that too.

'I was concerned that you were desperate enough to snatch at any rescue package placed on the table if it stopped the Alagoas Consortium from raping your land.'

'You know what, Gabriel?' Her shoulders sagged suddenly. 'I thought so too…'

'But it did not work out like that?'

No, it didn't. Luis had found her ceiling price without even knowing it.

'I'm going home,' she said quietly.

'Since I am watching you pack, *minha amiga*, I have managed to make that assumption,' Gabriel drawled. 'But then what will you do?'

The answer to that was frighteningly simple. 'I don't know.'

And neither, by his silence, did Gabriel.

'Get your shower,' he advised, after one of those dull, throbbing moments. 'I will see if I can get you a seat on a flight to Sao Paulo tonight.'

The shower went part-way to lifting her flagging spirits, aided by her refusal to let herself think. She spent time blow-drying some of the wetness from her hair, then left it to do its own thing while she applied a light layer of make-up, then put on fresh underwear, followed by the jeans and a white T-shirt. All she had left to do was to finish packing.

Placing the case ready by the front door, she made her way along the hall towards the kitchen, following the aroma of freshly made coffee. Pushing open the door was the simple part. Taking in the sight that met her eyes was not simple at all.

Her heart ceased to beat, robbing her of the ability to do anything other than stand there and stare at the two men casually propping up the kitchen units, drinking coffee like old friends. Both were wearing dark business suits, their jackets hanging carelessly open over white shirts and dark ties as they sipped coffee from white porcelain mugs. Only one of them had the power to hold her so thoroughly trapped like this.

'Luis...' She breathed his name.

'Does she always call you Luis?' Gabriel asked curiously.

'Unique to Cristina,' Anton replied, eyes like green granite as he flicked them over her loose hair and her casual T-shirt and jeans.

'W-what are you doing here?' she demanded stupidly.

'Treading in the shadow of your stubborn path.' A black eyebrow arched. 'Did you really expect me not to come after you?'

'Cristina has always been stubborn,' Gabriel put in conversationally. 'You have an English saying I cannot quite bring to mind that describes this stubbornness perfectly...'

'Cutting off her nose to spite her beautiful face?'

'Ah, *sim*.' Gabriel nodded. 'She also hates to admit it when she is wrong...'

Dragging her gaze away from one man, Cristina looked at the other. It did not take many brain cells to read the message in Gabriel's tone. While she had been showering he and Luis had talked. Gabriel now knew that the rescue package was not only rock-solid but that it came with a very respectable offer of marriage as well. The dream solution, in other words, for not only did she get the money she needed to save Santa Rosa from the wicked developers, she got herself a good looking, filthy rich husband willing to save her miserable, empty little soul at the same time!

Cristina pulled in a breath. Her chin went up. 'I see,' she said as she breathed out again. 'From hating each other, the two of you have now become firm allies over a friendly cup of coffee. Well, forgive me if I don't bother to join you.'

With that she turned and walked out—*escaped* was a more honest word. Inside she was trembling and shaking, shocked to find Luis here and truly afraid of what it was going to mean. She'd seen the anger burning in the green granite. She'd heard the warning threat threading his smooth silken voice. And even as she hurried down the hall towards her suitcase she knew she was running scared.

The hand that reached for her suitcase before she could pick it up told her everything. The strong arm that became a manacle around her middle said a whole lot more.

'Packed already?' Luis said lightly. 'Good. Then we can leave.'

'I am not going with you,' she told him, standing like a wooden plank in the crook of his arm.

'You are,' he returned without compromise. 'We made a deal.'

'I changed my mind.'

'Before or after the sex?'

'Before,' she declared. 'I took the sex because it came free.'

'You think?'

'I know.'

'Nothing comes free in this world, sweetheart,' Anton mocked. 'So, say thank you nicely to Gabriel, for letting you stay with him, and then set your treacherous little backside moving out of the front door or I will throw you over my shoulder and carry you out!'

Cristina heaved in a hot breath as she twisted round in his grasp with the intention of fighting herself free. Only it didn't work out that way. His arm banded her closer, and she found herself inhaling the clean, washed smell of him, and the much more disturbing scent of very angry male. Looking up into his face, she caught the flare of green in his eyes just before she heard her case hit the ground. Then his other hand was taking control of her nape, and all she managed was a husky, quavering, 'Don't...' before she received the full force of his mouth on hers in a punishing, plundering act of pure vengeance that left her shocked, shaken and shamefully desperate for more.

Feeling like a boneless quivering wreck, it was all she could do to subside weakly against him, her face pressed into his shirt front while he held her there and talked over the top of her head to Gabriel as if the kiss had been nothing at all.

Just the fact that Gabriel had witnessed it was a further humiliation she had to contend with. When she heard him say, 'I will leave the small print to you, Anton,' Cristina felt as if she'd lost her only friend in the world.

Anton retrieved her case and pushed her towards the door. She went quietly after that. The lift took them downwards. Neither spoke. A chauffeur driven black Mercedes waited at the kerb. The moment they were both encased in its plush leather interior the car moved off. She sat staring out of the window. He sat staring directly ahead. He was angry...she was angry.

'I suppose you told Gabriel that I am the love of your life?' she said tightly.

'I told him what he needed to hear to let you walk away with me.'

'Lies.'

He released a dry laugh. 'You fell apart in my arms over one short kiss, so don't blame him for believing what his own eyes could see,' he charged. 'And we are both good at lying, Cristina, so you can drop that reproof from your voice. It cuts no ice with me.'

'Does anything?' She sighed.

'No.'

'Gabriel—'

'Is no fool,' he incised. 'He knows I make a better friend than I would an enemy. Let him believe he allowed you to come with me because it's what you really want. It's safer for him.'

She turned her head to look at him then. 'You are so powerful these days?'

He didn't even bother to look at her. 'Yes,' he said.

He made her shiver. He made her truly fear the man he had become.

'Leave Gabriel alone,' she whispered.

'If you possessed a modicum of sense, *querida*, you would be worrying about your own situation more than your friend.'

He turned his head to look at her for the first time since they'd left Gabriel's apartment then, and Cristina's heart gave a wary little squeeze in her breast when she looked at him. Everything about him was hard, coldly angry, intimidating.

'I don't know where you get the arrogance to think you can play games with me a second time,' he delivered coldly.

'I was not playing a game,' Cristina replied. 'I just needed—'

'The sex,' he cut in. 'So you thought, Why not get it from Luis since he's so damn good at it?'

Her cheeks flushed. 'We did not have sex, we made love,' she corrected.

The expression of derision in his eyes as they glinted at her made her want to crawl away inside her own skin and hide. She knew on one level that she deserved his anger. She knew that in the way she had sneaked out of his suite while he slept she had taken the coward's way out. But—

'You were bullying me, Luis!' she hit back accusingly. 'You backed me into a corner and gave me no room to think! I left because I needed some time to consider what you were proposing!'

'I'm sorry to tell you this, *querida*, but you don't have the luxury of time or choice.'

Something landed on her lap. Cristina stared down at it for several long seconds before reluctantly picking it up. By the time she'd finished scanning the sheets of legal jargon tears were clogging up her throat.

'When did you acquire these?' she asked in a stifled whisper.

'Before I stepped foot in Brazil,' he replied. 'As you can see, *I* own you, Cristina. Not various banks and loan companies. I own the power to decide what happens to your precious Santa Rosa. And if I decide to foreclose on your debts and sell out to the Alagoas Consortium, I can promise you that it will happen—the very next time you attempt to walk out on me.'

It was such a brutal, totally unequivocal statement of intent that she shuddered. Luis owned her. He all but owned Santa Rosa by taking on the never ending length of her debts—the bottom line total of which, when laid out in black and white, actually made her feel ill.

They arrived at his hotel. Anton got out of the car and came around to her door, then took hold of her hand and pulled her out.

She came without protest, and it was crazy but that annoyed the hell out of him. He didn't want her beaten and subdued. He wanted her out here fighting—because when she was fighting he could fight back.

And he wanted to fight with her. He wanted to build it and build it until it progressed to a different kind of fight. She was in his blood again, like a fever. The sexual fever that was Cristina Marques.

His hand trailed her into the hotel foyer. The concierge saw them enter and attempted to catch Anton's eye but he pretended not to notice. He did not want to talk to anyone, be pleasant or polite. He made directly for the bank of lifts, cursed silently when they were forced to share it with a pair of young lovers who couldn't keep their hands off each other. They laughed and teased and touched and kissed all the way up to the floor below his own. Standing rigid beside him, Cristina stared unblinkingly at the lift console. He stared grimly at the floor.

The moment they reached the privacy of his hotel suite Cristina twisted her hand free and walked away from him. Anton made for the bedroom to deposit her suitcase. When he came back she was standing in the middle of the room, staring at an empty wall.

His chest made that tightening clutch at him. Grimly ignoring it, he crossed to the drinks cabinet.

'Why?' she fed unsteadily after him.

He did not attempt to misunderstand the question. 'Call it payback for six years ago,' he answered. 'You owe me for six years. For my inability to believe what any other woman says to me—for not daring to believe what my own senses are telling me about them.'

'I never meant to do that to you.'

He swung round. 'Then what did you intend?'

Exactly what she had achieved, Cristina thought bleakly,

which had been to make him hate her enough to leave her and never come back.

Only he had come back, and now here he stood—hard, coldly angry, still hating her for which she had done to him. Though now the hate had sexual desire to feed his determination to carry this through to its bitter end.

'So all of this is for revenge,' she murmured emptily.

Glass in hand, Anton offered a shrug. 'And to solve the immediate problem I have that demands I get married and produce a child.'

Those words cut so deep that Cristina actually quivered, dark pain clouding her eyes. 'Then you have chosen the wrong woman for this—quest you are bent on,' she told him, and had to pull in a breath to steady herself before she could go on. 'B-because I cannot give you that child, Luis. I am not able to—'

It was like watching ice explode. The way his face altered as he slammed down the glass and then made a grab for her set her whimpering in surprised shock.

'Don't *ever* utter that lie to me again—understand me?' he rasped down at her.

Cristina lifted her pale face. 'It was not a lie—'

'You lie every time you open that lush red kissable mouth!' he bit out. 'You lied six years ago when you told me you loved me, then enjoyed watching me squirm as you put that particular lie to death!'

'No!' she cried brokenly. 'It wasn't like that! It—'

'It was exactly like that!'

Meu Dues, Cristina closed her eyes—because he was right, it had been just like that. 'If you will just listen to me for a moment, I can explain—'

'You know what?' He unclipped his fingers from her shoulders. 'I don't want you to explain. Your reasons no longer interest me. You owe me. I'm collecting—on my terms.'

He turned back to his drink.

'Terms I cannot deliver.'

He twisted round again. 'My terms,' he repeated hardly. 'As in you as my wife, my willing sex slave and the mother of my child.' He spelled it out yet again. 'In return you get your precious Santa Rosa, gift-wrapped, with all debts cleared. Fair exchange, in my view.'

'Or a choice that is no choice,' she murmured indistinctly.

'Which means...?'

Which means... She was feeling so very cold now that she had to wrap her arms around herself. 'I will marry you,' she said.

There was a single second of total silence. A long, sharp needlepoint second when he stared at her as though he could not believe she had surrendered at last.

Then, 'Say it again,' he instructed. 'And this time say it much clearer, so there can be no more misunderstanding. Because this is it, Cristina. Your last chance. I am not playing any more games here. So say it loud and clear so I know that you mean it.'

'You will regret it,' she whispered.

'Say it,' he repeated.

'All right!' she flashed at him, and in true Cristina style she rose to her surrender with the proud lift of her chin. Silky black hair went spiralling back from her narrow shoulders, her eyes flashing his coldly ruthless and unremitting face a look of burning contempt.

'I will hate you, Luis, for treating me like this and making me behave like a whore,' she told him. 'I hate you already, for your threats and your blackmail and your thirst for revenge that makes you want to treat me this way. But

I *will* marry you,' she repeated clearly, as instructed. 'I will sell myself to you like a whore in the marketplace in exchange for Santa Rosa—and when you discover how empty your revenge cup will be I will stand like this in front of you and laugh in your face!'

Luis moved without warning. She was trembling and panting so badly by the time she had finished that she just didn't see him coming, and before she knew it she was somehow plastered to his front.

Her stomach flipped. 'No,' she protested.

'Say that again in thirty seconds,' he challenged, and delivered his mouth to hers with a lip-crushing deep-tongued kiss.

Cristina did not need those thirty seconds. She did not need even ten to reduce to such a melting, boneless mass of quivering compliance that she couldn't think of anything else. She was useless, lost, his eager plaything. Her mouth clung to his mouth; her fingers clung to his head.

Then it stopped. Why it stopped she had no comprehension. It took more seconds than it had taken her to sink into it to float back out of it again.

'Great way to hate, *querida*,' his husky voice taunted. 'It excites the hell out of me, anyway...'

It was like being smashed when he'd already broken her. On a pained little whimper she pulled herself free and ran for the bedroom.

Anton winced as the door landed in its housing. He spun around and snatched up his drink, downed it, then went to pour another one—only to stop himself when he realised what he was doing, and stare grimly into the bottom of his empty glass instead.

He'd got what he wanted from her, so why wasn't he feeling better about it? Why was he standing here feeling as if he'd just lost something vital instead?

Her face. It had been the look on her face when she'd finally accepted there was no other way out for her. She called it hate; he called it—pain.

Why pain? He slammed the empty glass down, because he suddenly remembered that he had seen that look once before—six years ago, when she'd sliced him to pieces with her rejection. Had the scorn she'd used to do it been masking pain then, only he had been too blind to see it?

Oh, stop looking for excuses for her, he told himself angrily. He did not understand her. Thinking about it, he never had understood what really made Cristina tick.

What was it about her that she could make out that she despised him with all she had in her, yet fall apart in his arms without much of a sign that she had any control over what she did?

The buzz words were Santa Rosa, he reminded himself. Not him. Not the sex. Santa Rosa.

The bedroom door suddenly flew open. Cristina was standing there like a wild thing. He felt his body respond with enough heat to set him on fire.

'You can tell that manic secretary that your affair with her is over!' she tossed at him.

'You are in no position to bargain,' he threw back. 'Just think of Santa Rosa and I'm sure you will get over her presence in my life.'

The door slammed shut again. On a tight curse Anton turned and poured himself that second drink. Then he laughed—he *laughed*!

God, there was no other person alive on this earth who could arouse him to just about every emotion going.

He put down the glass because he discovered that he suddenly did not need the whisky. Still trying to control the smile, he headed for the conference room instead, where a full day's business awaited his attention. Where the hell he had got the idea that he could come to Brazil and play the hotshot banker *and* deal with Cristina he would never know.

While Anton was trying his best to lose himself in business matters, in a very sedate, very upmarket office in another part of Rio, an old man with white hair and immaculate grooming sat carefully filing his nails while he listened to the report being relayed to him by an unassuming young man with the unassuming name of José Paranhos.

Until now Senhor Javier Estes had been quietly satisfied with the information being relayed to him. All, it seemed, was going to plan. Senhor Scott-Lee had taken up the challenge, and the object of that challenge was making it difficult enough to keep him dancing on his toes. He'd even smiled when he heard that Cristina had spent the night with Scott-Lee in his suite.

It was the next part that lost Senhor Estes his smile and sharpened his attention. 'Say that again?' He prompted confirmation. 'This woman accosted Senhorita Marques as she was exiting the elevator?'

José nodded. 'Senhorita Lane was very angry and very unpleasant,' the younger man expressed. 'She claimed that she and Senhor Scott-Lee are lovers and that they had slept together only the night before. Naturally, Senhorita Marques was upset.' He went on to relay what else the secretary had thrown at Cristina.

Frowning now, Senhor Estes dropped the nail file to pick up his pen and scrawl a few terse notes on the file open in front of him. The indication that those few notes represented a black mark against Anton showed in the way with which the words were underscored.

'*Obrigado*, José. You will maintain your observation and keep me informed.'

With a nod, José left the office, and Senhor Estes withdrew a sealed envelope from the file. The envelope was addressed to Cristina Ordoniz.

Cats set among pigeons, Javier mused, invariably caused mayhem…

CHAPTER SEVEN

LUIS was sitting at the conference table, attempting to concentrate on the information being fed to him. His two executives kept looking at him oddly when they constantly had to repeat themselves. He didn't blame them for the odd looks. He felt odd, enlivened and distracted, too damn sexually aware that Cristina was on the other side of that door over there.

The telephone by his elbow began to ring. Remembering that Kinsella was not in the outer office to intercept all calls because he'd sent her to the bank to pick up some documents, he reached out and picked up the phone.

'Scott-Lee,' he announced himself briskly.

'At last!' Maximilian rasped down the line at him. 'Where the hell have you been, Anton? I've been trying to contact you all damn day!'

Tensing up at the urgency in his uncle's voice, Luis flicked a quick frowning dismissal at the two other men. 'Why? What's wrong, Max? Has something happened to my mother?'

'You could say that,' the older man answered dryly. 'She's on her way to Rio,' he warned his nephew. 'Should be setting down at the airport as we speak.'

'Coming here? What for?'

'To put a stop to this crazy marriage you are planning, of course. What else?'

His marriage? 'How the hell did she find out about it so quickly?' he demanded incredulously.

'Far be it from me to want to put a spoke in Maria's

plans, Anton—I adore that woman like she was my own sister, *and* I have no wish to see you throw yourself away on some gold-digging widow—but—'

Anton stiffened like a board. 'Watch your mouth, Max,' he warned thinly.

'You mean this woman is *not* the widow of Vaasco Ordoniz?'

Anton did not answer that. Something else far more disturbing had grabbed his attention. 'You know Vaasco Ordoniz,' he declared in a driven undertone. It had been right there in Max's tone.

'I'm not getting into that one,' Max refused. 'That's up to your mother.'

His *mother* knew Cristina's late husband?

'But I will tell you this,' Max continued. 'There is something going on within the ranks of your team that quite frankly stinks. And, love Maria though I do, I refuse to stand back and watch while you are stitched up by some jumped up little secretary who is paid to keep her mouth shut about your movements, not ring up your mother with all the gory details. I mean, how can a man have a private life if some—?'

'What are you talking about, Max?' Anton thrust furiously into this bewildering tirade.

There was a moment's silence while his uncle absorbed that fury. Then he said, very seriously. 'Kinsella Lane rang your mother yesterday to inform her of your intention to marry the Ordoniz widow. Your mother reacted like a demented chicken and caught the next flight she could get on to Rio.'

Anton swore soundly.

'Maria has taken a suite on the floor below yours, Anton. And the very helpful Miss Lane arranged it.'

Kinsella had done all this behind his back? Anton was stunned and shattered.

'I've been ringing you on and off all day, trying to warn you about this—did the secretary tell you? I bet she didn't. I can read the tone of a machinating woman from thousands of miles away, and that one is dangerous. Do yourself a big favour and get rid of her. She's a risk to your security.'

Anton eventually put down the phone on a string of tight curses. His mind was whirling at the flood of information his uncle had just fed into it. Kinsella had been passing on personal information about him to his own mother of all people? How had she got that information? Nobody attached to his entourage knew anything about his plans to marry Cristina! *How* had she heard, seen, picked up anything? Unless—

He remembered the file from his investigator, which he'd placed in the safe yesterday. Kinsella had been irritating the hell out of him since they'd arrived here in Rio, and Cristina had accused him of keeping Kinsella around as a lover within minutes of clapping eyes on her. He'd flicked the remarks away as unimportant when any man with sense knew he should never dismiss the uncanny power of the female instinct when it sensed a rival in its presence.

Had his not very private secretary been snooping where she should not look? Found out all she needed to know about Cristina and then calmly called up his mother to relay the information to her?

His mother.

His mind flipped to the next pending crisis. Reaching out, he snatched up the phone to ring down to Reception and find out the expected time of arrival of Maria Scott-Lee. The inner curses became progressively more colourful as that conversation was concluded.

Then he pulled himself together and stood for a few

minutes, grimly sorting his priorities into some kind of order. By the time he'd done that he'd turned into the ice man.

As Cristina was the first to see.

He entered the bedroom like a bullet, strode up to where she was standing, staring out of the window, caught hold of her hand before she barely had a chance to turn round, and just hauled her out of the suite.

'What do you think you are doing?' she demanded as he tugged her inside the lift.

Swinging her into the far corner, he pinned her there with a hand pressed against the wall at either side of her startled face.

'Why did you marry him?' he delivered.

Cristina blinked, taken aback by the question. Then her eyes hooded over. 'I have told you before. I will not discuss that with you.'

'Why not?'

Folding her arms across her front, she stared down at her shoes and pinned her lips shut.

'He was wealthy when you met him,' Anton persisted. 'He only started gambling the money away after you came into his life. Could the gambling have had something to do with the fact that you conveniently failed to give him a son?'

Cristina went as white as a sheet, but still refused to react in any other way.

He moved in closer. 'Was the need to keep your gorgeous figure perfect worth what it cost you in the end, Cristina? When you finished up a poor widow who had to go back begging to her miserable father? Did *he* hold it against you that you had not produced a male grandson for him to leave Santa Rosa to? Or was that always your goal?' he pushed on relentlessly. 'Was the only way you could own your beloved Santa Rosa by making sure you would never produce a son?

'Well, I've got news for you,' he continued, when she still said nothing. 'You will have *my* child whether or not you want it. Son or daughter. I have no preference. And Santa Rosa will be placed in trust for that child to inherit, because it will give me such pleasure to watch you lose the one thing that you covet the most!'

He kissed her then, using his hand in her hair to tug up her face and laying the kiss on her like a brand of hate. Tears were sparkling in her eyes by the time he straightened, her burning mouth working on the desire to just break down and weep. Luis looked at her as if he would love to strangle her right here in the lift—but the doors opened and he was grabbing her hand instead.

The lobby was busy. People everywhere—standing, sitting, moving about, checking out or checking in. Cristina blinked the hurt tears from her eyes and looked up at the hard-as-nails profile of this man she knew she would never forgive for saying what he just had.

And she would never forgive herself for giving him reason to say it.

'Where are we going?' she asked unsteadily.

'Shopping,' he answered.

Shopping... For a few short seconds the meaning of the word just refused to register in her bemused head. Then it did register. Luis had just destroyed her and now he was walking her into the swish shopping mall attached to the hotel as if it was perfectly acceptable to knock her down then take her on a shopping trip.

Cristina bit her teeth together and said nothing.

Anton was wishing he could take back what he'd said in the lift.

But he was angry—still angry—about many things. Not

least the amount of interference and manipulation that was taking place in his life. Ramirez, his mother, Kinsella—he could go right back to the day of his birth!

And that crack by his uncle Max about his mother knowing Vaasco Ordoniz was niggling the hell out of him. It was just one more thing other people had knowledge about and he did not. If he had any sense he would just drop this whole crusade, go back to England and—

It was then that it happened. As if Ramirez himself was listening in on his angry thoughts, Anton came smack up against a heart-leaping thump that stopped him dead in his tracks.

He was standing in front of a jeweller's window. Tall, dark hair, Latin profile, and a way of resting his hands in his pockets that was so familiar it completely locked Anton up where he stood.

Was it? Could it be? What if it was? The desire to go over there and ask the man outright if he'd heard of Enrique Ramirez vibrated like an engine in his blood.

'Luis…?' Cristina prompted warily.

He barely heard her. He could barely hear his own thoughts above the humming going on in his head. The man turned, as if drawn by the mental energy he was generating. The moment Anton looked into his face he knew he was looking at a perfect stranger. No green eyes, no cleft chin— no hint anywhere on that solid-shaped face that he could reflect back to himself. The rushing sinking feeling shot through him.

'Luis, you're hurting my hand…'

He looked down at the woman beside him. Saw the expression in her face and relaxed his grip. His half-brothers—his *half-brothers*, he repeated, and felt his mind swoop into full focus on his main goal in all of this.

Whatever it took, he told himself fiercely. Money, blackmail, seduction—threats. This woman, who was looking up at him through rich, dark, warily questioning eyes, was going to be his wife as soon as he could make it happen. She was going to grow ripe with his child. And to achieve those two aims he was prepared brush aside anything and anyone that attempted to run interference.

In fact he was more than ready to run some interference of his own.

And it began right here, in the first shop he pulled her into.

An hour later and they were standing in the spare bedroom surrounded by designer bags containing the designer clothes that he had chosen because she would not.

'Put on the red dress,' he instructed. 'You have—' he glanced at his watch '—about an hour and a half.'

With that dictatorial announcement he strode out of the bedroom and closed the door, leaving Cristina to sink down onto the end of the bed, where she sat staring at the array of bags spread around her. Even with the confused mixture of anger, hate and total bewilderment she was feeling, there was a tiny dark corner of her that wanted to dive with a shriek of delight into the lot.

There were bags containing sensuous floaty skirts and filmy tops by Nina Ricci, evening dresses from Valentino, day suits from Armani and Chanel. She could see the Gucci logo, Prada, Jimmy Choo… In a short, breathtaking hour Luis had trailed her through a wonderland of purchases without once letting go of her hand. He'd perused, selected and thrown casually at hovering assistants. If Cristina had not responded when he'd asked for her opinion, he'd used their clasped hands to lift up her chin, then kissed her full on the mouth.

He'd charmed, he'd smiled, he'd tossed off light, teasing comments. The assistants had been starry-eyed with hero-worship by the time he paid his account—while she must have looked like a spoiled and petulant over-indulged lover by the frozen look on her face.

But those starry-eyed assistants did not know what was going on behind the charm he ladled out for their benefit. They could not know that those smiling green eyes were laced with anger, or that the kisses he laid on her lips were hard and cold with contempt.

Luis, she had realised very quickly, was functioning to his own agenda. Be nice to the future wife in public, but treat her like dirt beneath your feet when not.

His real agenda had been fed to his mother via the telephone, while Cristina sat miserably on the end of the bed. Yes, he was surprised to hear she'd arrived in Rio. The concierge had told him, of course—who else? No, he did not have time to share a pot of tea with her, but dinner would be nice. Eight o'clock in the Mezzanine restaurant? He was sorry he would not be able to collect her from her suite, but he had some business to attend to first, so would it be all right if they met in the lounge bar?

Kinsella arrived back from the bank looking her usual smooth, immaculate self in a cream roll-neck sweater that skimmed her figure and a pencil-slim skirt to match. Anton watched through hooded eyes as she moved around the conference room, clearing away the day's business. Cool and calm, super-efficient—not a single hair or carefully curled eyelash out of place. There was no way from looking at her that anyone would know the danger that lurked beneath that efficient façade.

'Join me for dinner tonight,' he invited, in a low, soft, husky tone of voice, and saw her catch her breath before she turned to offer him a carefully composed smile.

'I...' She went for female hesitation.

'My mother has just arrived from England,' he added. 'I thought we could turn her first dinner here into a special night.'

'And Mrs Ordoniz?'

He did not correct the name. 'Let's leave her out of this for now, shall we?' he suggested, with just enough intimacy to make Kinsella blush.

He could turn them on without batting an eyelash. Anton had always known he could do it, but would never have believed himself capable of using the gift so cynically.

'Dinner would be lovely...thank you,' she accepted.

She thought she'd got her man in her pocket at last.

She thought she had an ally in his mother.

She thought she was about to break into the inner circle of his close family, consolidate the two and end up with happy-ever-after. Having had his eyes opened wide by Max, Anton was seeing everything with such crystal clarity it actually shook him cold.

The dress was most definitely red, Cristina dryly confirmed as she followed its smooth and sensuous lines, cut to mould every curve she possessed and show off her long slender legs. The fact that she had not tried on a single one of Luis's purchases in the shop said a lot about his unfailing eye for size and style. The dress had long sleeves that began at her wrists and hugged like a second skin all the way up to the under-curve of her arms, leaving her smooth shoulders bare. And the bodice shot straight across her chest, just low enough to show a shadowy cleavage and the gentle slopes of her breasts.

Sexy, she thought as she viewed herself in the long mirror. Definitely very thought-provoking, without revealing too much naked flesh. Her mother's fake diamonds sparkled at her ears and her throat, and she'd put her hair up because she knew that Luis would not like to see it like that. But then she'd gone for compromise by teasing a few glossy twists free to fall around her neck and her face. Her make-up was heavy—the dress seemed to demand it—dark and sultry shaded eyelids, a double lick of black mascara on her curling eyelashes and of course a matching red lipstick that enhanced the passionate shape of her mouth.

And because it was a long time—more than six years— since she'd worn anything so openly gorgeous and sexy, she could not resist striking a flirty come-and-get-me pose and adding a lush-lipped pout.

'Now, that is the woman called Cristina Marques,' a deep voice murmured in appreciation.

On a soft gasp Cristina spun around so quickly that she almost fell off her new backless high stiletto shoes, a hectic blush mounting her cheeks at being caught girlishly playing up to the mirror.

Luis was leaning in the bedroom doorway looking ev-erything he was in a black dinner suit and bright white dress shirt. All long lean lines of laid-back sartorial elegance, with that ever-present tummy-tingling underlying vibration of latent, purring, sexual male.

'I was beginning to think she had been banished for ever,' he went on in the same low lazy attitude. 'But here she is, beautiful and exotic in her new fine feathers, viva-cious and sexy and loving it.'

The last two razor-tipped words pinned his mood. He was still angry. Cristina's chin came up, challenging, de-fiant. If her hair had been loose it would have been flying back from her shoulders.

'Even *viuva de* Ordoniz can enjoy dressing up on occa-sion,' she retaliated.

The relaxed lines of his face hardened. 'You claim never to have used that name. Don't use it now.'

Straightening away from the door, he moved across the room with the grace of a prowling panther. Arriving a short foot away from her, he came to a stop, overwhelming her with his height and his masculine presence, fluttering her heart muscles and turning her knees weak when she did not want to feel like that.

Reaching up to flick a fingertip at the diamond droplet dangling from her ear, he then hooked the same finger beneath the matching necklace she wore at her throat.

'Diamonds?' he murmured.

Opening her mouth to tell him they were paste, her pride stopped her—what bit she had left after the way he had been scraping her clean of such a vice.

'They were my mother's,' was all she said.

'Ah,' was all he said, and he gently withdrew the finger, leaving her to wonder if he would have ripped them from her if she'd told him that Vaasco had given them to her.

'I don't want to fight with you, Luis,' she heard herself say in a husky whisper, and wished she knew why she did.

'Who's fighting?' he said, dipping his hand into his jacket pocket.

Cristina shivered out a sigh. 'What happened between us six years ago was—'

'Six years ago,' he inserted. 'Forget it, Cristina. It is what's going to happen in the future that counts now.'

But for her the past and the future were as indelibly linked as night following day. 'You cannot—'

'I can do anything I like while I'm in the driver's seat.'

'Will you let me speak one full sentence before you interrupt?' she flashed.

'Not right now.' His hand came out of his pocket. 'Give me your left hand...'

She sucked in a tense breath. 'What for?'

'Just give...'

He took possession of the hand without bothering to wait for her to yield it. Cool fingers with a thumb pressing lightly against her palm dragged her eyes downward. It did not occur to her that he meant anything ground-shaking by the gesture. Even when he stroked a light touch across the base of her ring finger she still did not catch on.

'No mark,' he observed.

'No.' The mark that Vaasco's wedding ring had placed there had long gone.

'Good,' he murmured. 'I like that...'

It was then that she saw it, catching a fleeting glimpse just before the ring slid smoothly into place. Bright flickering diamonds clustered around a burning dark ruby set on a band of gold. Her heart ceased to beat, her throat closing over the thick lump that formed in her throat.

'Do you like it?'

Of course she liked it—she loved it! 'But—Luis...' She drew in a deep breath. 'We have to talk about—'

'Try to think of it as my stamp of pending ownership,' he described. 'Soon a wedding ring will have joined it.'

'Soon?' She looked up questioningly.

'Yes, soon,' he repeated. 'As soon as can be arranged.' Then he bent and lightly kissed the anxious shape of her mouth. 'And you *will* use *my* name, *querida*,' he vowed as he raised his head again. 'Cristina Scott-Lee has such a staunch Englishness about it, don't you think?'

The barbs were really flying. Head lowering again, so that he could not see her face, Cristina said nothing. What was the use when it was clear he was going to lash out at her whatever she did try to say?

Anton waited, still holding her hand, wishing he had not said that in the cold, nasty way that he had. It was not going to help his cause if he made her hate him enough to walk away—again.

But that wasn't the point, and he knew it wasn't what was really eating away at him. When he'd walked in here and seen her posing in front of the mirror, just as the younger Cristina would have done, his heart had clattered straight through his body to land with a thump at his feet.

Why? Because it had suddenly hit him that he was still in love with her—with that beautiful, vivacious creature flirting with the mirror anyway. He wanted her back, but he couldn't have it like that, and wishing for the impossible was not going to change a single thing. Cristina was still the woman who'd scorned him for an older man six years ago, and he was still the man who wanted revenge.

He dropped her hand.

She lifted her head to look at him. 'Luis—'

No.

He turned away from whatever that look in her eyes was trying to convey to him. 'If you're ready, let's go.'

Cristina stood staring after him. One small peek out of her hiding place and he'd jumped on her, crushed her in his cold iron fist, then stuck a ring on her finger that staked ownership.

In the foyer he stabbed the lift call button. There was a full-length mirror attached to one of the foyer walls and Cristina found her attention caught by it. What she saw was the profile of a tall, dark, excruciatingly handsome and sophisticated man with the inherent cool and classy bearing of an Englishman mixed with the exotic gold tones of a warm-blooded and tempestuous Brazilian.

'I wish you had never come back.' It was out before she could stop it.

He glanced down, saw her eyes were fixed on the wall and turned his head. It was like clashing head-on with an electrified fence. The green eyes darkened slowly, pouring a heat into her body that dried up the inner surface of her mouth.

What Luis was seeing was beyond Cristina's comprehension, but he came to stand right behind her, hands coming up to clasp her slender upper arms right at the rim of the red sleeves, where they met with the narrow curve of her shoulders. Then he shifted their position until they were facing the mirror full on.

They fitted. They always had fitted together, she thought painfully as she looked at the way the top of her head reached the bow tie at his throat. In every way she was fine-boned delicacy to his muscular dominance. The slenderness of her legs, the fragile curve of her figure in the clinging red dress, even the silken cups of her shoulders, hovering there just above his hands, said *vulnerable woman in the possession of a tall, dark, dominant male*.

He moved—it was hardly anything, but she suddenly felt the jut of erection against her and fell foul of a soft stifled gasp. Her lips parted, red, lush, inviting. Her eyes turned decidedly black. He sent his fingers gliding down the smooth red sleeves to her wrists, then gently pleated them with her own fingers. Cristina watched, held breathless by shimmering sexual tension as he moved their hands to the narrow slopes of her hips then began a slow, slow exploration of her whole body coming to a stop only when both sets of hands were covering her breasts. Eyes fixed in fascination, she felt her nipples tighten against her own palms. It was such a thrilling experience being made to feel the sensual stirring of her own body, that she stood totally breathless, unable to push out a single protest. He moved in that bit closer, and his desire for her was without restraint. Awareness spread like a fine veil across every sense she possessed.

Anton wondered if he was going mad, doing this to them

when they were about to go downstairs and into the public domain, but—

'Look at you,' he rasped out softly. 'You are the most exquisite creature I have ever held this close to me.'

'And you hate yourself for wanting to hold me.'

The two black satin edges of his eyebrows came together across the bridge of his nose. 'Not hate,' he denied, holding her dark eyes with his own disturbingly perplexed ocean green. 'Worried,' he provided. 'If I don't watch out I think you could seriously get me again, and I don't think that would be good for my—'

'Plans?'

He sent her a smile through the mirror—it was like being lit up from inside. 'I was going to say something really soppy—like heart,' he confided, watching her breasts move as her breath caught. Then he added softly, 'But I think that would be just a bit too honest, so we will stick to your word—for now.'

The lift arrived then. Maybe it was fortunate. Any more of this and she would be dragging him back into the suite.

The lift carried them downwards. Cristina stood in front of him, with their clasped hands now pressed to the tiny pulse beating in the flat of her stomach. His mouth arrived to brush a featherlight caress across her throat where it met her shoulder. With a sinuous stretch of fragile muscle she gave him greater access and lost herself in a cloud of sumptuous desire. There wasn't a part of her that had not quickened, not a single inch that did not want to feel the warm brush of his mouth. She moved against him, felt his inner pulse like a living entity.

'Luis.' She breathed his name in the wispy voice of an aroused woman.

That was how their waiting party saw them when the lift doors opened to reveal a tantalisingly beautiful creature dressed in red, lost to the sensual desires of her tall, dark, handsome lover.

CHAPTER EIGHT

CRISTINA, took in the gathered assembly staring at them and felt an icy barb of shock hit her chest. Kinsella was there, dressed in a tube of pale blue fabric that showed off every perfectly neat curve of her long slender shape. Her creamy face was cold, her blue eyes split by a fury she could not contain.

'How could you?' Cristina gasped out accusingly, and tried to stiffen away from him.

He kept her right where she was. 'Listen,' he murmured in what must have looked like a lover's whisper. 'That lady you see standing next to Kinsella is my mother. She is the most important person in the world to me so you will behave like the totally besotted bride-to-be. Understand me?'

Understand? Pulling her gaze away from the angry Kinsella, Cristina looked at the woman who had once been betrothed to Vaasco, and understood so much more than Luis could ever appreciate that the consequences of that understanding were already threatening to squeeze the life out of her sinking, sickly dipping heart.

Maria Ferreira was a beautiful woman of indefinable years, dressed in a beautiful smoky blue silk evening suit that made her look as delicately structured as a fragile rose yet contrarily regal, though she was unable to hide her shocked dismay.

Cristina had not expected this. In the last mad forty-eight hours her mind and her body had been so engrossed in Luis that she just had not once considered the possibility of coming face to face with the one person Vaasco had hated above anyone.

And Vaasco had hated.

Swallowing tensely, she tried to turn within Luis's embrace, needing to stop this before it exploded in their faces. But he was not in the mood to listen.

'Behave,' he repeated, kissed her pale cheek, then straightened, releasing only one of her hands as he moved to her side so they could exit the lift.

And it was not by accident that he retained her left hand, bringing two pairs of eyes dipping down to stare at the diamond clustered ruby adorning her finger. It was making a huge statement, Cristina realized, with a growing awareness of the disaster about to descend on their heads.

Recovering her poise first, his mother took a couple of steps forward.

Did she know? Cristina wondered anxiously.

'*Querida*,' Anton greeted her warmly, lowering his dark head to brush his mother's smooth cheek with his lips.

'*Querido*—' his mother responded, returning his embrace.

'You look tired,' he observed as he straightened again. 'Perhaps we should have left this until tomorrow, to give you time to sleep off your jet-lag.'

'I am fine; do not fuss,' his mother said with quiet impatience. 'Although I did assume you and I would be sharing a private dinner, Anton,' she scolded. 'I needed urgently to talk to you, but—'

'You will contain your impatience for another time?' her son suggested with a gentle amusement that made his *mamma*'s eyes flutter—because, like Cristina, she had heard the censure threading through his tone.

'*Meu querida...*' His hand tightened its grip on Cristina's hand to draw her closer. 'Let me introduce you to my mother, Maria Ferreira Scott-Lee—Mother…this beautiful creature is Cristina Vitória de Santa Rosa…Marques…'

The pause, staged for effect, certainly had its reward, Anton noted as he watched his mother's spine rack up in shock.

'You are the daughter of Lorenco Marques?' Maria asked Cristina sharply.

'Y-you knew my father?' Cristina returned, her voice small and very wary.

'We met once—many years ago,' Maria replied in a slightly dazed way. Then her lovely liquid brown eyes narrowed. 'But I was led to believe—'

'You knew Cristina's father?' Anton smoothly took back control. 'Well, this unexpected surprise makes what I have to say next all the more special.' He smiled. 'Mother, you can be the first to congratulate us because the astonishingly beautiful daughter of Lorenco Marques is about to become my wife…'

It was like living in a kind of nightmare after that, one in which people talked and behaved in one way when their body language said entirely something else.

'Well, this is a—surprise.' Luis's mother used dignity to hide behind as she tried not to go pale. 'Congratulations, my dear.' And she even managed to kiss Cristina on both cheeks, when surely she would rather be demanding answers to all the questions that must be whirling around in her head.

Was it Kinsella who had mentioned the Ordoniz name to Luis's mother? Cristina only had to meet the venom in the blue eyes as she politely offered them her congratulations to know that she had.

Only Luis appeared not to notice the undercurrents weaving around them. He smiled, he charmed, he pretended to be the happiest betrothed on this earth. They toasted their coming nuptials with champagne drunk from tall fluted glasses. They moved from the lounge into the restaurant. They discussed food and ordered their individual courses. Luis chose the wine.

And through it all either his hand or his eyes or his mouth were in contact with Cristina somewhere. He toyed with her fingers. If she snatched them beneath the table his followed, captured and tangled with hers, then lifted them up to receive the brush of his mouth before he placed them back on top of the table again. It was like being paraded naked for everyone to stare at, because he was making absolutely no secret of what they would be doing right now if they were not sitting here.

The first course arrived with a flourish from four waiters eager to impress. Cristina looked down at her salad starter and wondered how she was ever going to manage to place a single forkful into her mouth. Her stomach had knotted, the tension in her stretched across every muscle she had. Letting her gaze slip around the table, she saw across the flickering candlelight how difficult his mother was finding it to keep the conversation pleasant and polite.

Kinsella ate sparingly and kept her eyes carefully lowered, but it was what was going on behind the lowered eyelashes that worried Cristina. How could Luis do it to her? How could he make his lover sit here and endure this when only recently she had still been sharing his bed?

He was ruthless. He gave way on nothing, she decided. Did his *mamma* know she had raised this kind of man?

'May I look at your ring, Miss Marques?' Maria Scott-Lee requested.

'Cristina,' her son corrected softly.

Biting her lip in annoyance with him, because his mother was at least *trying* to be nice, Cristina stretched out her hand to display the ring.

· Mrs Scott-Lee gazed down at it for a long time before she glanced up at Cristina. 'I have one just like it,' she said with a tense little smile. 'Instead of your beautiful ruby mine has an emerald in the centre—to match the colour of my son's eyes…'

Those eyes belonging to her son narrowed for some reason. His mother refused to look at him. Tension whipped around them all like barbed wire stretched to its optimum. The waiters arrived to remove plates.

While they waited for their main course to arrive, it was Luis's mother who surprised Cristina once again, by mentioning Santa Rosa.

'I visited your home once—a long time ago,' she said. 'It is such a beautiful place.'

Cristina blushed. *'Obrigado,'* she murmured, thinking bleakly, *You would not find much beauty there now.*

'Have you seen Santa Rosa, Anton?' Luis's mother asked her son. 'The ranch sits on the edge of the pampas, with fertile pastures and valleys dramatically backed by the rise of the mountains and the most awe-inspiring sub-tropical forest acting like a barrier to hold back the ocean beyond…'

She went silent for a moment, eyes lost to some distant memory. Then she blinked. 'I may be mistaken, because it was more than thirty years ago when I was there, but I seem to recall that the house itself resembles a Portuguese mansion house?'

Cristina nodded, wetted her dry lips with a sip of wine. 'My ancestors built the house over three hundred years ago. It was not unusual for Portuguese settlers to reproduce the style of house they were used to living in Portugal. The area has many similar-styled houses.'

'But few were built and furnished to the grand style of Santa Rosa, I suspect.'

Cristina lowered her eyes, thinking about the home she

had left only a few short days ago, where grandeur had lost out to peeling paint and damp walls.

'Do you think I might know your mother?'

Cristina shook her head. 'My father met and married my mother when he was visiting Portugal. She died a year later, giving birth to me, so I doubt you would have met.'

'It is a shame, then, that your father could not join us this evening.'

Her tone had taken on a subtle alteration. Everyone noticed it. Luis tensed. Kinsella reached for her wine glass. Cristina waited a moment before she lifted her eyes.

'Both my parents are dead, Senhora Scott-Lee,' she provided, as calmly as she could.

'Ah, my sympathies.' Mrs Scott-Lee tilted her head. 'But surely your father must have married again? Provided you with a brother, perhaps, to inherit Santa Rosa?'

'I am an only child. I inherited Santa Rosa.'

'Then my son has indeed made a fortunate choice in bride,' his mother said. 'Your children will be truly blessed on both sides of the family—unless you have children from your first marriage, who will naturally inherit from you?'

It was like taking a double punch in the stomach. Cristina didn't answer, could not answer. More tension leapt around the table. Kinsella sent her a cold, sly, malicious little smile that chilled Cristina's blood.

'Is there a point to this line of questioning?' Anton intervened at last.

Maria looked at her son. 'I was led to believe that your— betrothed had previously been married.'

'Interesting,' Anton murmured. 'Who exactly led you to believe this?'

She didn't bat an eyelash. 'Miss Lane and I were discussing the interesting fact that you had a—guest staying with you, just before you arrived, *querido*.'

'Miss Lane—' Anton did not so much as cast a glance in Kinsella's direction '—should know better than to discuss my private business with anyone.'

'Even with your mother?'

'I apologise if you feel I've overstepped my working brief, Anton.' Kinsella came in on a contrite little rush. 'But I assumed your mother must already know about—'

'And why should information relayed to you by my secretary make you jump on the first plane out of London to Rio?' Anton continued, right over Kinsella's breathless little rush.

His mother stiffened as she stared at her son. 'Max?' she whispered.

Anton nodded grimly. 'I would also like to know why the fact that Cristina has been married before is of any interest to anyone but Cristina and I, and why you feel it is necessary to interrogate her like this.'

Maria flushed. 'I was merely trying to ascertain—'

'What I was up to?'

'You hardly know the woman, *querido*!' his mother suddenly sparked. 'You met her for the first time barely twenty-four hours ago. She is not what she seems. She is—'

'The widow of Vaasco Ordoniz,' Cristina herself placed into the erupting tension.

'Cristina—'

Ignoring the husky warning in Luis's tone, she looked directly at his mother instead. 'Since you say you knew my father, I must assume that you also knew my husband, Vaasco?'

'He was—'

'I know what he was, Senhora Scott-Lee. I married him; you did not,' Cristina said, and watched as the older woman caught her meaning, then went pale. 'It is therefore perfectly understandable to me, if not to Luis, that you should wish to know why I was willing to marry a man who was more than twice my own age.'

'You misunderstand me—'

'Not at all,' Cristina said. 'I understand you perfectly.'

Luis mother was staring at her with a kind of pained plea glowing in her eyes. She was terrified of what Cristina was going to say next. Kinsella was utterly captivated, and Luis was too calm for her to suspect that he had any idea what was threatening to come out into the open.

But Cristina was not going to be the one to tell him. Let his *mamma* confess her own sins, she thought as she rose to her feet. 'I think I will—'

Her hand was closed inside a male fist. 'Sit down,' Luis instructed.

'Anton—' his *mamma* said on a hushed warning breath. The altercation at their table was beginning to attract attention, other diners were turning to stare.

A man appeared at Cristina's side. Young, slight and immaculately dressed. 'Excuse me for interrupting your dinner, *senhora*,' he murmured politely. 'I have been instructed to give this to you...'

He handed Cristina a white envelope. Amidst the rest of what was happening around her it made the whole scene take on a surreal quality as the young man bowed politely, then melted away again.

'What the hell was that about?' Anton demanded.

His guess was as good as anyone's—except for Cristina's. She took one glance at the envelope, went as white as a sheet, then turned on a muffled, 'Excuse me,' stepped around her chair and fled.

Anton shot to his feet to go after her. His mother was on her feet too. 'No, Anton,' she said quickly. 'I think Miss Marques needs to read her letter alone.'

Not while I'm here to stop her, Anton thought grimly, and went to go after her.

'You cannot enter the Ladies' Room, darling!' his mother said anxiously.

'I will go if you like.'

It was enough to make Anton's head whip around. 'You will remain right where I can see you, Miss Lane!' he lanced at his so called private secretary.

Kinsella blanched at his tone. His mother gasped. They were all on their feet now and people were openly staring.

Frustration bit into him. This had all gone wrong. How had he let it go so wrong?

His mind shot back to the call from Max. Until then he had been firmly focused on what he was doing and why he was doing it. Everything had been running smoothly and under his control. Then Max's call had arrived to muddy the waters, and the arrival of his mother had muddied them some more. The machinations of Kinsella, the burning leap of angry jealousy that had come with Max's wisecrack about the Ordoniz widow—and seeing the stranger in the shopping mall when he thought he'd sharpened his focus. In truth, that was the moment he'd lost what bit of focus he'd had left.

This dinner was supposed to have been a trial by demonstration, aimed to show his mother and Kinsella Lane that, no matter what they thought or wanted or hoped to the contrary, he and Cristina were an inseparable item. Whatever else needed to be said should have taken place in private. Why would he want to turn it into a public scene? Why would he want to embarrass Cristina in front of anyone? She was the woman he was going to marry, the woman he—

Dear God. It hit him then, the one thing he had been carefully skirting around without actually grasping with both hands. It had been there staring at him from the moment he saw her across the crowded reception room. Further back, when he'd stood staring at her name typed in bold on a document and felt himself coming alive. He'd even fooled himself into thinking he was still in love with a memory when he'd watched her pose in her red dress, but it was no distant memory. It was here and now and so potent he could actually taste it!

He must have looked strange because his mother placed a hand on his arm to capture his attention, and when he looked at her he saw concern there, a mother's instinctive understanding wrapped in dark-eyed remorse.

'I will go and see if Cristina is all right,' she said gently.

The letter. His mind spun. What was in the letter? Who was it from? Why would one look at the envelope make Cristina turn and run? His chest grew tight, as if a steel band was trying to squeeze down a searing hot desire to explode into panic. But there were other issues here that had to be dealt with—Kinsella Lane being the most pressing one.

He caught his mother's hand as she went to follow Cristina. 'She is the most important thing in the world to me, so you treat her with respect—understand?'

His mother pressed her lips together and nodded while the words he'd just uttered played a taunting echo inside his head.

Anton took in air, and by the time he had released it again and turned his attention to Kinsella he had himself back in control.

'Right, let's make this more formal, Miss Lane,' he enunciated with ice-tipped authority. 'We will take our business upstairs to the conference room, I think.'

Then he turned to stride across the restaurant, ignoring all the curious looks he was receiving and pausing by the *maître d'* to sign a hastily produced bill for their ruined dinner. As he moved on towards the lifts he took out his cellphone to call his two executives to the conference room. He wanted witnesses to what was coming next.

'Anton, please listen to me.' Kinsella's hand arrived on the sleeve of his jacket, the soft, slightly pleading tone in her voice making his skin start to creep. 'You don't understand. Your mother made it impossible for me to—'

'You would be wise to keep your mouth shut until we gain privacy,' he bit right across her, thinking Cristina was right; she did flutter around him like a fluffy moth. He swatted her hand away, then walked into the lift.

Cristina was sitting in a chair, staring at the unopened envelope she clutched in her fingers. It was addressed to Cristina Ordoniz, which was enough to turn her stomach, but what was really choking her of any ability to open the letter was the logo neatly printed on the corner of the envelope.

Javier Estes and Associates, it said. *Advocates of Law.*

Vaasco's lawyers. How many of these awful white envelopes had she received in the months after Vaasco's death? Each one of them had carried only bad news. Each one had turned her into this trembling, shaking person she was now.

But the letters had stopped a long time ago—long before her father had died. Why start again now? And why receive it hand-delivered right in the middle of a busy restaurant?

The only way to find out was to open it, she told herself, then swallowed and made her fingers break the seal and draw out the single sheet of paper that was inside.

Shock hit then—the kind of totally bewildering stunning shock that twisted her brain into complete knots. The letter was not to do with her late husband's estate at all. Senhor

Estes had more than one client—of course he did, she told herself. But—Enrique Ramirez?

Her stomach rolled and kept on rolling as she read in growing disbelief what it was she had been handed.

A bequest, it said, and named a figure that scrambled her brain all the more. Enrique Ramirez had bequeathed her just enough money to save Santa Rosa.

Just enough to pay off her debts.

Dared she believe it? The letter had been delivered in a very unconventional manner. Maybe it was a joke—a very sick joke. Maybe she would be wise checking out the source before she—

The door suddenly opened and she looked up just to stare as Luis's mother walked in.

'Are you all right?' Mrs Scott-Lee questioned warily.

'No.' It was no use pretending she was when she wasn't.

'You feel ill? The letter—distressed you?'

The letter, Cristina thought, is a dream come true.

Except for one unattainable dream. 'I think I need to go to my room,' she whispered.

'Of course,' Luis's mother said, walking towards her. 'I will take you there—' Then she stopped, hesitation in every line of her slender, elegant frame. 'You know about Vaasco and me, don't you?' she thrust out suddenly.

Cristina nodded. 'You were betrothed to him, but you had an affair with another man. This man.'

Cristina held out the letter. Pale as herself now, hands as unsteady as her own hands, Luis's mother took the letter, lowered her eyes and began to read.

'Ramirez again,' she breathed after a long silence, then on a heavy sigh she folded into the chair next to Cristina's.

Cristina did not know what to say to her. When you possessed the knowledge that a woman of Luis's mother's stature had had some wild affair beneath the very roof of her then betrothed, words just refused to come.

'You knew Enrique well for him to leave you this money?'

The money. Cristina sucked in a deep breath as her stomach rolled again. She knew why it kept doing that. She understood exactly why she was feeling sickly instead of jumping for joy.

'I met him only once,' she replied. 'He—he saved my life when I was very little... Why did Luis mention his name to me?'

'Anton,' his *mamma* corrected absently.

For some crazy reason, in this mixed-up situation, Cristina heard herself laugh. 'I know his name, *senhora*,' she said dryly. 'I have known his name for a long time— for six years, in fact, since we first met and fell in love and then—' *Lost each other,* she tagged on silently

'You mean—*you* are the one?' Maria Scott-Lee was staring at her oddly.

'The one?' Cristina frowned.

So did Luis's mother. 'Nothing.' She looked away. 'Forget I mentioned it.'

Silence tumbled. And, in the way that everything had been happening in its own peculiar way tonight, the silence was not tense or tight or hostile, as it should have been. It was just—silent.

'You love my son?' Mrs Scott-Lee asked suddenly.

I refuse to answer that, Cristina thought. 'I will not be marrying him, if that is where this is leading.'

'But why not? What is wrong with Anton that you turn him down not once but twice?'

'Who said that I turned him down twice?' Cristina asked sharply.

'No one. My mistake.' His mother was frowning again. 'Why are you saying you will not marry him?'

For a million unutterable reasons, she thought hollowly—but named only one. 'Well, he's a womaniser, if you must know.'

'Of course he enjoys the company of women,' his *mamma* defended loyally. 'He is young and handsome and possesses a perfectly healthy sexual appetite. However, when Anton marries he will have the good manners to stay faithful to his wife!'

The good manners? Cristina released another of those laughs. It would take more than good manners to make Luis keep the zip on his pants shut!

'He spent the night before last in the arms of another woman.'

'I do not believe you.'

'His secretary informs me that she and Luis have been lovers for months.'

'Miss Lane?' For some reason Luis's mother sounded thoroughly shaken. 'I sincerely hope that you are wrong about that,' she murmured unsteadily.

'Well, I'm not.'

The threat of tears came then. Cristina got up, the fool inside her giving way to a heartbreaking bout of common sense.

'Give this to Luis and show him the letter,' she said huskily, removing the ring and dropping it gently on his *mamma*'s lap. 'He will understand.'

Then she turned to leave.

'He will not let you go,' Mrs Scott-Lee fed after her.

'That is no longer his choice to make!' Cristina choked.

'Anton does not have a choice!' Maria stood up—letter and ring clasped in one hand, the other closing on Cristina's arm. 'He has to marry you, Cristina, or he will not inherit from his father.'

His father? Cristina twisted round. 'What are you talking about? His father has been dead for six years!'

'I don't mean—' Mrs Scott-Lee stopped herself, then uttered a soft, unladylike curse. 'He will not forgive me for this,' she whispered. 'He is not going to forgive me for my interference anyway, but...' She looked at Cristina. 'Please sit down again,' she invited unevenly. 'I need to explain some things to you...'

Anton's face-off with Kinsella was not a pleasant one. Having been cornered by her own machinations, his loyal secretary gave it to him hook, line and spitting venom. Then, with his two young executives standing by as witnesses, he went on to formally dismiss her from his employment on the grounds of gross misconduct.

'Do you think you can do this to me when I've devoted the last six years of my life to you?' she attacked. 'From the day that you stepped into your dead father's shoes I have been working hard to turn myself into everything you could possibly want!'

'But I don't want what you are,' Anton denounced brutally.

'No.' Kinsella quivered in disgust. 'You prefer a black-haired witch who was more than willing to fall into bed with you the first chance she was handed!'

How Anton kept his hands from closing around her throat he had no idea. 'You see, Miss Lane,' he responded icily, 'the difference between you wanting to fall into my bed and my wanting *any* other woman there is that *they* are desirable and *you* are not.'

'And *she* is so good at playing the whore, isn't she?' Kinsella spat back. 'But then she is a woman who is willing to do anything to get what she wants, even marry a fat and withered old man! I wonder if she crawled all over him like I watched her crawling all over you!'

White now, knocked back on his heels by that last venomous spit, Anton glanced at the connecting door, securely shut at the moment whereas yesterday it had been left swinging wide open. An icy sensation crept down his spine as his mind replayed a sequence of events that should have been private to him and Cristina.

But Kinsella had walked into this conference room and coolly followed the trail of discarded clothing to the bedroom. His skin began to crawl as he imagined her standing in the bedroom doorway watching them and listening, like some sick bloody voyeur, before quietly walking out again to go and snoop in his private files before calling up his mother.

He felt sick. *She* was sick. He turned his back on her. 'Get her out of here,' he rasped at the two other men.

Striding into his suite five minutes later, he found his mother sitting tensely on the edge of a chair. She jumped up. 'Anton—'

'Where is Cristina?' he demanded.

'I—we need to talk first,' his mother said, her eyes pleading with him in a way that locked up every single bone he possessed.

'Where is she?' he bit out, and spun towards the bedrooms. He wanted to know what was in that damn letter. He wanted to know what it was that had made her run like that!

'She's gone!' His mother's shaking voice froze him. 'Sh-she has gone home to Santa Rosa, *querido*. She—'

All his life he had loved this woman, without exception, but when he turned on her now Anton understood why his mother took a jerky step back.

'If you've talked her into leaving me I will never forgive you,' he grated.

'She left of her own volition, I promise you,' Maria vowed painfully. 'I might be a foolish woman, Anton, but I—' She stopped to swallow thickly. 'She said for me to tell you that she will be in touch with you to explain when she feels that she can.'

'Feels that she can *what*?' he bit back as an old bitterness began to well up inside him.

Then it sank in. Cristina had gone. The tension holding him released its grip and he turned from his mother as a violent shudder racked his frame.

Gone—again. Left him—*again*.

'She claims that Miss Lane is your lover,' Maria explained unsteadily. 'Anton, has learning about your real father meant a thing to you? Enrique flipped from woman to woman! He enjoyed them—yes! But he died an unhappy and lonely man!'

'I don't want to hear about him,' he gritted.

'Yet it is because of him that you are here!'

'What a joke.' He laughed, swinging back round again. 'You know, *querida*, I never so much as clapped eyes on Enrique Ramirez but I think he knew me better than you do or even than I know myself!' He took in a deep breath. It hurt to do it. 'I am here for Cristina. I'm in love with Cristina. I have always—damn *always* been in love with Cristina!'

A hand shot up to cover his mouth.

It was an act so unfamiliar to both of them, 'Oh, *Meu Dues*,' his mother choked, and sank down into the chair.

Anton dragged the hand away again. 'I'm going after her—'

'No, Anton, please wait!' She shot up again. 'There are some things I need to explain to you before you do that...'

CHAPTER NINE

CRISTINA was busy by the main barn when a sound made her look up to watch a helicopter fly overhead. It circled the homestead a couple of times before deciding to drop down into an empty paddock out of her field of sight.

It had to be Luis. She did not do much as even consider the possibility that it could be anyone else. He would be arriving for their last big confrontation, though she had not expected him to get here quite so soon.

A frisson slid through her. She had to give her determination a hard tug not to react to the sting of electric excitement and, tightening the softness of her mouth, she returned to what she had been doing. But she felt his approach like long icy fingers curling themselves around her until she could not take in a single breath.

Anton came to a halt several feet away, watching in silence as she hefted bales of hay from the barn to the truck while Pablo, her helper, eyed them both warily from beneath the brim of his hat. She was wearing work-faded jeans and a check shirt. Heavy work gloves protected her hands. Her hair was lost beneath a red spotted headscarf and her face was bare of everything but its smooth golden skin. She looked too delicate to touch, yet she hefted those bales of hay like a man.

Clenching his body across the rush of anger that hit it, he stepped closer, flicked the helper a look that sent him scuttling away, then turned his attention to Cristina.

'Look at me,' he commanded.

Her response was to bend, with the intention of hefting

136

up yet another bale, and in biting frustration Anton stepped forward and placed his foot down on it. He watched her go still, watched her eyelashes flicker when she took in his black leather hand-stitched shoes and the cut of his black silk trousers. The tension between them heightened the higher those eyes drifted, taking in the black silk dinner jacket hanging open to reveal the fine white dress-shirt he still wore beneath.

If looks could paint a picture then the expression on her face was a masterpiece of a woman totally riveted by what she was seeing.

'Impressed?' he said, bringing her eyes up that bit further, to the open collar of his shirt, where the rich golden skin at his throat was glossed with the sheen of sweat. His bowtie still hung there, like a trailing piece of black ribbon.

'It took hours of negotiation to get the helicopter charter company to let me fly myself,' he supplied, with hard, harsh, husky bite. 'Before that I had to get to Sao Paulo—and I was right on your stubborn tail until then, *meu querida*,' he informed her. 'Count yourself lucky that I was delayed, or you might have found yourself prostrate by now on this bale with my fingers wrapped around your slender throat. Instead I find I don't have the energy. I'm hot, I'm tired, and I'm in dire need of a shower and a shave—'

Her eyes flicked to the stubble covering the cleft in his chin. Her lips parted, that vulnerable upper lip just begging—begging for it.

His own lips flexed.

'I need a drink so badly my throat thinks it's been cut, and some food inside me would be pleasant, since you effectively ruined dinner last night...'

Then, just to make sure that his next point went home,

he bent low enough to bring his eyes into full contact with her darker than black eyes, vulnerable, wishful—sad.

His teeth came together. 'In other words, sweetheart, what you see here is a man at the end of his rope. So be warned that ignoring me right now is a very—very dangerous thing to do.'

She blinked, she swallowed, and her lips quivered as she took in a small breath. He nodded, held her eyes for a moment longer, and thought about kissing her utterly, totally—*punishingly* breathless, but then straightened up and took his foot off the bale.

It was then that she saw his overnight bag, dumped on the ground. He watched her look at it, then pull in a breath. 'Luis—'

'Anton,' he corrected, turning his back on her to take an interest in his surroundings. 'I don't feel much like Luis right now.'

He could almost hear her lips snapping shut before they opened again.

'I will not marry you.'

'Fine.' He shrugged. 'Now, show me round this heavy investment I've bought into.'

'Will you listen to me?'

He swung back, everything about him hard like iron. 'Only when you have something to say that I want to hear.'

'I don't need your money any more! Did your mother not tell you?'

'About my father's bequest to you?'

'Father—?' She stared at him.

Anton returned the look with an inscrutability that said he was not going to play that game. 'You know that Enrique Ramirez was my father because my mother told you. Now that we have that attempt at yet more deception out of the way, will you show me around—please?'

Please. Cristina looked at this tall, dark, arrogant man, with his beautiful accent and his beautiful manners and the hard crystal eyes that warned her to beware. She felt that oh, so helpless, *I do so love you, Luis* lump form in her throat, and—

'I can pay my debts.' She stuck to her guns, chin up, eyes defiant.

'You can try,' he invited with a thin smile. 'But the moment you so much as attempt to pay me off, I will sell all your debts on to the Alagoas Consortium so fast your head will spin. They will not be so easy to please as I am.'

He would do it too. Cristina could see the cold intent cast like armour on his face.

'You are not easy to please.' She sighed wearily, then turned away from him to remove her gloves so she could toss them down onto the bale of hay.

Without looking at him again she walked over to the hand pump beside the barn and set cool water flowing to wash her hands, then pulled the scarf off her head and wet it to use to cool her sweat-sheened face and throat.

If Luis thought he'd had a bad day then he should have lived hers, she thought tiredly. Three ranch hands had walked off the job the moment she'd left for Rio, leaving Pablo alone to do the jobs of four—five, if she counted herself. They had not been paid in months, so how could she complain about them walking away? And when she'd entered the house she'd found Orraca, the housekeeper, on her hands and knees mopping up the kitchen which had flooded due to a burst pipe. Orraca was too old to be on her hands and knees, so Cristina had taken over the mopping while Pablo fixed the leaky pipe. Then she and Pablo had come out here, to start catching up on the jobs that had not been done. Now it was two o'clock in the afternoon, the sun was at its hottest, and all she wanted to do was to take that shower Luis had mentioned, crawl into her bed and sleep…for a hundred years if she could.

A hand came out to take the wet scarf from her. It was stupid for her lips to start quivering, but they did. Luis drenched the scarf again, folded it carefully, then placed it carefully around her neck.

A sob rolled in her throat. 'Don't be nice to me,' she protested, having to blink the tears back.

'You'd prefer my hands there instead of the scarf?' he quizzed. 'Or maybe you would like it better if I just turned round and left again.'

Cristina's mouth opened but nothing came out. His hands dropped to her shoulders, and it just was not fair that he pulled her close. Before she knew what she was doing two sets of fingers had crept up in between them and were toying with the black ribbon edges of his bowtie, which were dangling either side of the tantalising V of damp skin exposed at his glistening throat.

'I'm in your blood,' he murmured huskily. 'You are in mine. Why keep fighting it?'

Because I have to, she thought, and moved away from him, lifting her chin and taking in a deep breath.

'Do you want some refreshment?' she asked then.

'Or something?' he drawled by return.

Her eyes gave a warning flash. 'Do you?' she persisted.

His turn to utter a sigh as he glanced at his watch, then gave a shake of his head. 'If you're going to show me around the place then we don't have time for food and drink. There's a weather front coming in,' he explained. 'I would rather use the helicopter to see Santa Rosa from the air while we can…'

It was a complete refusal to give in to anything, Cristina noted. Standing here, looking at him, stubbornly willing to continue the fight, she caught the signs of tiredness around his eyes, and for the first time the hint of strain playing with the corners of his mouth.

And she surrendered—for now.

Time later to be stubborn again, she told herself, as without another word she turned to seek out Pablo, who was still standing in the shadow of the barn, and ask him to take Luis's bag into the house.

With a very hooded look at Luis, and a nod of his head to her, Pablo complied. Cristina knew that by the time they arrived back here the whole of Santa Rosa would know that she had been steamrollered by a man.

Luis took off his jacket and with a polite 'Thank you' handed it to Pablo to take inside with his bag. By then Cristina had unearthed a bottle of water from the chiller she kept in the truck. Silently she handed the bottle to Luis, and he drank thirstily on the way to the helicopter. Ten minutes later they were in the air, and Cristina was quietly explaining what they could see while he sat beside her, listening, asking shrewd questions and controlling the helicopter as if he had been born to do it.

Which he probably had, she thought ruefully.

Anton listened to the way her voice began to soften as she described what lay beneath them. And he understood why her voice did that. Santa Rosa was a stunning place of breathtaking contrasts.

They flew over wide open plains scattered with cattle and the occasional gaucho, then on to the first change in scenery as they swept over rich green meadows threaded with gushing streams not quite wide enough to be called rivers but impressive nonetheless. She directed him to fly over a hill and into a valley dotted with small neat whitewashed houses, each surrounded by their own small plot of land.

'This is part of Santa Rosa?'

Cristina nodded. 'The valley beneath us is the land the Alagoas Consortium wants to turn into a spur from the highway to the forest,' she explained, and Anton did not need telling what the people who lived in the whitewashed houses down there would be losing if the developers had their way.

Then she directed him to fly over the other side of the valley. Almost instantly Anton saw exactly why she had instructed him to come this way. Even before they rose above the valley rim he saw the forest rising up like a huge dark wall in front of them. Majestic, invincible...or so you would like to think. But from up here it didn't take words for him to see what was so valuable to the developers. A natural fault in the earth's crust had carved a deep groove in the forest that stretched for miles and miles towards what he saw in the misted distance was the sea.

'This is it?' he said, as they tracked along the fine vein of water that threaded the base of the groove.

'*Sim.*'

'What happens to the river when the rains come?'

'It floods.'

'So what do they intend to do with the flood when they build their road?'

Not if but when, Cristina noted with a shiver. 'They plan to run their road along either side of it, above the flood line.'

Her eyes scanned the area of forest that would have to be demolished to achieve such an aim. Beside her she could feel Luis doing the same thing.

'The banker in me says what a goldmine you're sitting on. The human in me says what a sick, criminal waste,' was his only comment.

Cristina said nothing. And that was how it remained between them as they made the journey back the way they had come. They landed back in the paddock behind the house, but not before Anton had circled the two-storeyed plaster-walled mansion house. He said nothing about its poor state of repair, but his mouth maintained a flat line as he settled them back down to earth again.

The heat of the afternoon was intense, and the silence between them all the more so—growing as they walked towards the house, passing the collection of ageing barns and paddocks as they did. The house itself was surrounded by a low whitewashed wall which sectioned it off from the rest of Santa Rosa. An open archway took them into gardens that would once have been beautiful but had, like the house itself, fallen into decay.

They hadn't seen a single living soul since they landed. 'It's very quiet,' he remarked.

'Siesta time,' Cristina murmured.

Now, there's an idea, Anton mused, but kept the thought to himself.

The tension between them grew even stronger when they entered the coolness of the house itself. Without another word passing between them Cristina led the way across a high-ceilinged hallway and up a wide, gracefully curving flight of stairs. Anton looked around him at the once elegant but now scuffed and chipped tiled floor, and the walls hung with heavy-framed oils that looked as if they'd seen much better days.

Mentally crossing her fingers that Orraca had instructed Pablo to place Luis's bag in the only useable guest bedroom out of twelve, Cristina pushed open the door.

His bag sat, on the heavily carved ottoman, she saw with relief and stepped aside to allow him to precede her inside.

'There is a bathroom through the connecting door,' she told him, in a cool level tone that just did not reflect what was trying its best to erupt inside her. 'I will organise something to eat and drink for when you come back downstairs.'

He did not say a single word, just stood inside the room looking around him. Cristina closed the door with a quiet, dignified click and then swung herself back against the nearest wall. Eyes tight shut, heart dipping and diving, breasts heaving beneath her damp and sticky shirt, she refused, absolutely, to look at why she was feeling like this.

Then, right on the back of that refusal, she was pushing away from the wall and running like a crazy woman down the stairs, across the hall and into the kitchen, situated at the rear of the house. She still did not allow herself to think about what she was doing as she snatched up a tray and laid it on the kitchen table. Two minutes later she had added a small freshly baked loaf of crusty bread, fruit conserve, a pitcher of chilled lemonade from the refrigerator, and the plate of sliced fresh fruit she'd spied in there. Then, as a last impulse she flew down into the wine cellar and plucked at random one of her father's bottles of wine and added it, a bottle opener and two glasses to the tray.

Sad, weak, pathetic, she castigated herself when she eventually picked up the tray and made her way back to the stairs again. *'Triste, fraco, patético,'* she repeated beneath her breath, just to make sure she got the point.

In the bedroom Anton was experiencing a similar overload—of the masculine kind which translated into tight-chested, gut-gripping anger beneath his own sweat-soaked shirt.

This place was like some cracked and crumbling forgotten museum. How long had she been living here on her own, rattling around it like the resident ghost with no life worth speaking of? Where did she get off, preferring this to marriage and a full life with him?

He yanked his shirt off over his head and used it to wipe the sweat from his face, then tossed it angrily to the ground. It landed in a float of expensive silk on top of a worn Persian carpet that must have once cost the earth.

Well, not any more, he thought grimly as the rest of his clothes joined the shirt. The carpet, like the faded satin coverlet on the bed and the matching curtains at the windows, needed a hasty burial—along with the rest of this time-locked place.

Unzipping his bag, he hunted down his toilet bag and headed for the connecting door. Half expecting to find a cast iron tub with a pitcher of water standing beside it, it did not mollify his feelings one iota to discover a fully functional if old-fashioned set of sanitary units waiting for him. He turned on the shower suspended over the white bathtub and grimaced his surprise when it gushed clear water into the bath. Then, with a sigh, he turned his attention to removing the growth from his face.

He did not know what was coming next—hell, he did not want to think about what was coming next if it meant yet another battle to get her to see some damn sense. But his insides were already revving up for it, stinging and tensing and—girding, he thought with yet another tight grimace.

Cristina was functioning on a different level by the time she'd carried the tray upstairs and arrived outside the bedroom door. Balancing the tray on one arm, she grabbed her lower lip between her teeth, then gave a knock on the door before twisting the handle and pushing it open.

Luis was not there. Her tummy muscles twisted with what might have been relief, though she wasn't sure. As she placed the tray down on a table by the window she could hear the shower running, and that was when she saw his clothes lying in a heap on the floor.

Was she going to do it?

Those muscles twisted again. Her heart did the same nervous trick because—yes, she *was* going to it. *Just* this once—just this once she was going to do what she really wanted to do and act out a dream that had haunted her for six long years, which involved Luis, this house and that bed.

Her clothes landed on the top of his clothes. With trembling fingers she released her hair from its topknot, then on impulse bent to snatch up Luis's bowtie and used it to loop her loosened hair back from her face.

The knock sounded as Anton was drying his face with a threadbare but spotlessly clean towel. He turned to stare as the door opened, then went completely still when a perfectly naked Cristina stepped inside, closed the door again, then turned to look at him.

She just looked. He just looked. Both of them held in tight stasis that knew exactly where to centre itself. Her chin was up and her dark eyes were defensive, her soft, lush, beautiful mouth quivering and as vulnerable as hell.

Now she had come this far Cristina did not know what to do or say next to make something happen. If he rejected her she would die where she stood. Water hissed from behind the plastic curtain drawn across the bath, steam swirled and eddied, to say that the ancient boiler had not let her down as it often did.

He recognised his bowtie holding her hair back and his eyelashes flickered across the darkening green of his eyes.

'I thought we could share the shower,' she heard herself say in a breathless little voice. 'Do you mind?'

Did he mind? Anton mocked. For the first time in six

years she had come to him, and it did not need words on his part to tell her how he felt about that. She only had to dip her eyes to the cluster of black curls surrounding his sex to know whether he minded her coming to him like this.

The pink tip of her tongue appeared as she looked at him. The physical response his body gave brought her eyes flickering back to his face. Without uttering a single word he reached out with one hand and swept back the plastic curtain, watched the tight little pull of air she took before she could peel herself away from the door.

Suddenly stupidly shy, Cristina slewed her eyes away from him and turned to put out a hand to test the heat of the water spraying out of the shower head. It was too hot; she adjusted it. His hands arrived on her hips as she did so, the jut of his sex making its bold statement against her while he waited for her to be very practical and get the water temperature just right. For some reason the situation caught her with a compulsive giggle, and from behind her she heard his low, deep, husky laugh.

The tension broke, just like that, and he was lifting her up against him to latch his teeth to her shoulder while he stepped into the bath. Water poured down her front, the curtain was swept shut, steam fogged her vision and Luis fogged up everything else.

He touched, he stroked, he moulded her to him, following the streams of water. She responded by lifting up her arms to curve them around his neck and turned her face so she could claim his mouth. When that was no longer enough she twisted to face him, and that was when the really serious kissing and stroking began.

He filled her hands and she stroked him gently. His hand slipped between her thighs. They made love to each other with their mouths and their fingers until both were barely on the planet, but he was not going to let this be over as quickly as that, because once it was over neither knew what was waiting beyond, and they didn't want to know.

So he soothed things down by locating the soap, and began washing her all over while she stood gazing up at him with heavy, dark, love-drugged eyes. *'Luis, Luis,'* she kept on saying. He wondered if she was aware at all that she said his name like a whispered call to a lost lover. I'm here, he wanted to say, but was too afraid of breaking into the spell that was holding them both.

Instead he handed her the soap and then stood and just enjoyed while she washed him, caressed him, until he could stand it no longer and he switched off the shower and stepped out of the bath. He wrapped a towel each around them, then lifted her into his arms to carry her into the bedroom.

His eyes blazed when he saw that the covers had been stripped back from the bed. She'd planned this, had known they were going to end up here. This beautiful, stubborn contrary woman, who was her own worst enemy, pushed him away with one hand and hooked him right back to her with the other.

They fell on the bed in a spray of clean water droplets, rough towelling and deep, hungry kisses. They made love while the afternoon sun dropped lower in the sky. And when it was over it wasn't over, because they still touched, kissed, drew out the after-loving like a trailing silken thread, until hunger and thirst sent her leaping off the bed to pick up the tray.

She'd forgotten nothing. Anton smiled as she placed the tray on the flat of the bed between them, then gave him the wine bottle to open while she knelt beside him, golden, slender, totally carefree in her nakedness, as she broke off chunks of bread and smeared them with conserve, offering him a piece, then smiling at him as he handed her the wine to pour while he bit into the bread. His bowtie had managed to stay in her hair, though he didn't know how it had, considering what they had been doing. She looked loved and lovely, lips soft and swollen from his kisses, the swing of her nipples dark and tight.

She offered him a glass of wine. He took it and drank, then his face instantly contorted at the harsh, brackish taste.

'My God, you're trying to poison me,' he gasped.

To his shock, huge glistening tears filled her eyes.

'What did I say?' he demanded in bewilderment, then saw the way she was staring at his glass of wine. 'Christina…' He sighed. 'Don't be such a baby. I was joking! Here—try the wine,' he invited. 'I can guarantee it will knock your eyes out.'

She shook her head, mouth small now, and trembling, those tear-filled eyes too big in her face. Anger roared up like a monster inside him. Who the hell had knocked the spirit out of her to the extent that she could almost fall apart over a glass of poor wine?

That bastard Ordoniz?

He tossed the rest of the wine to the back of his throat and swallowed, then slammed the glass back down on the tray.

'All right,' he said then. 'Let's talk about this. Since when did you get this upset over a lousy glass of wine, instead of just tossing your own glassful into my face for being so insensitive?'

'I wanted it to be perfect.'

'Wanted *what* to be perfect?'

'This…' She stared at the bed, the tray—him. 'You, me, here—our last time together,' she whispered.

Our last time…

The rumbling beginnings of their next major battle began

to roll around the room. Anton tried to hold it back by clamping his lips together and clenching just about every muscle he could. But it was not going to happen. Anger six long years in the fermenting, it was filling with a bitterness that by far outstripped the taste of the wine.

'So this—' he flicked a hand at the tray '—the surprise visit to the bathroom and the rest—was just for the sex, was it?'

'No—'

'A last good old frolic with your Englishman before you kicked him out of your life again?'

'Y-you—'

'I've had it,' he announced, and launched himself right off the bed.

'Luis—no!' she cried. The look he sent her had her scrambling off the bed. 'You don't understand!'

'What's to understand? I've noticed the pattern here. Have you noticed it?' he rasped. 'You run; I follow. You take the sex. You run again—or in this case you kick me out.'

'I don't mean it to be like that—'

'No?' He released a hard laugh, dragged on a pair of pale chinos and zipped them up. 'I've offered to marry you—again,' he delivered. 'I've offered to save this bloody awful place. I've *given* you the sex! Who is the fool here, do you think? You or me?'

This time she didn't answer. Reaching out, he picked up a white T-shirt and dragged it on over his head.

'And of course I must not forget that you have other options now,' he continued bitterly. 'Enrique Ramirez has seen to that.'

'Y-you said—'

'What did I say?' he lanced at her, ignoring—refusing—to see the way she was standing there naked, shivering, face as white as the worn sheet on the bed. 'That I would sell you out to the Alagoas Consortium if you tried to pay me back? Do I really come over to you as the kind of bastard who would do that to you?'

Without wanting a reply, he ripped out a sigh and went hunting for a clean pair of socks in his bag. He came out with another folded white T-shirt and tossed it at her.

'Cover yourself,' he said, as if he hated the very sight of her body now—and turned his back on the next pained look that crossed her face and sat down on the bed to pull on his socks. 'You married a man old enough to be your father to save all of this once. I would love to know why you could not bring yourself to do the same thing with me.'

'You are not old.'

'So you've come to *prefer* older men, is that it? Does their lined and sagging flesh turn you on?'

If only you knew, Cristina thought painfully as she pulled on the T-shirt, emerging from its clean white folds to have her breath catch in her throat at the sight of him. Fully dressed now, and standing at the end of the bed grimly stuffing clothes into his bag, his height and the lean muscle power beneath the casual clothes hit her harder than the sight of him in one of his smart business suits had ever done.

'You look very much the Latino,' she remarked help-lessly.

'I am English,' he declared. 'To the last drop of my blood.'

'You never used to deny your Brazilian side,' she whis-pered. 'You—'

'Well, now I do deny it!' Rocking her back with a fresh blast of his anger, he swung away from her, then violently back again, hard lines suddenly raking his lean face. 'Six years ago you rejected me because my *Englishness* did not appeal to you. You didn't want to move to England and play the banker's wife. You did not want to rear English children who would have their natural passions bred out of them.'

Like a machine gun he shot her with all the hateful words she had thrown at him six years ago.

'Finding out that my real father was a Brazilian does not alter the person I am inside, Cristina. I still *am* an Englishman who *thinks* like an Englishman.' Hard fingers made a tight, stabbing gesture at his head. 'And I promise you that I will go back to England and marry an Englishwoman, remain this English banker who will rear English banker children, while you—' he made a gesture of derision '—get your dearest wish.'

With that he bent to zip his bag up, cursed when he remembered his soap bag, still languishing in the bathroom, and strode that way, leaving Cristina standing there white-faced and shaken, stripped to the very bones by her own cruel lies.

A shudder raked her slender body, a hand jerking up to cover her mouth in guilt-ridden dismay at the cruelty she had used six years ago to make Luis walk away.

She had mocked his English upbringing, his public school accent and his stuffy banker family. She had scorned his offer of marriage and demanded to know where he had got the idea that what they had was anything but a temporary affair. Cringeing inside, she had listened to her own voice demolish everything they'd spent a whole year cherishing.

Then she had just walked away.

This time Luis was going to do it. And she could see in the hard set of his face as he strode back to his bag that this time he would not come back.

He zipped the bag up again, ignoring her as he straightened and turned for the door.

Oh, *Meu Dues*, she thought. He was going.

It hit like a thunderbolt. 'No,' she wrenched out, and moved like lightning, racing past him to stand with her back against the door. 'I need you to listen while I tell you something.'

His wide shoulders tensed—his back, his whole body. He did not look into her eyes and she knew—*knew*—he did not want to look at her ever again.

'Move out of the way, Cristina,' he instructed grimly.

'Please,' she begged him. 'You must understand before you go why I cannot marry you!'

Fury leapt in his eyes. He took a step towards her. 'If you say that to me one more time—'

'I lied to you Luis!' she cried out. 'Everything I said to you six years ago was just one big wicked lie! I never, ever wanted to hurt you. I have always loved you more than anything else in this world! But I am not what you need! Your mother said—'

'My mother?' he lanced at her. 'What the hell has she got to do with this?'

'Nothing.' She had not meant to say that. 'Sh-she loves you.'

'Great,' he snapped. 'So everyone loves me.' The bag dropped to the floor as he threw out his arms in an arc of blistering contempt. 'So what am I supposed to say to that life-changing statement, Cristina? Oh, that's okay, then. *Now* I don't mind if you walk all over me!'

'Don't shout at me!' she shouted, on a loud, anguished sob. 'I need to tell you something and it is hard for me!'

'Tell me what?' He was not going to make it easy for her. 'That you treat me like a football for my own good?'

'I was pregnant with your baby when you left me to go to your *papa*'s funeral!'

CHAPTER TEN

THE agonising confession left her lips at the same moment that the weather front moved in. Anton just froze where he stood as the sky blackened around him. Nothing moved on his face—nothing!

Christina was suffering from the opposite. She was shaking all over, her arms wrapping tightly around her body as if they were trying to hold it all in.

And she could not look at him. It hurt to look at him. As the first flash of lightning lit the room Luis spoke. 'Pregnant?' he repeated hoarsely. 'You were pregnant with our child and you didn't tell me?'

'I did not know then.' Staring fiercely at her bare feet, Cristina was fighting to hold back the tears now. 'I f-found out later—af-after you'd gone…'

It had all been so wonderfully perfect to her. She was in love with Luis and carrying his baby, and he was going to come back for her as soon as he could, and then they would—

'I wanted so much to tell you each time you called me on the telephone. But you were grieving for your *papa* and busy trying to walk in his shoes, so I decided to wait until you came back to Rio. But…'

The baby had not waited that long.

'I l-lost it, Before you came back for me…'

'How did you lose it?' he questioned huskily.

'I was working in the café when I got this—pain. The next thing I knew I was rushing to hospital in an ambulance. I was frightened and you were not there—'

Like a man who did not want anyone to see his expression, Anton spun his back to her, eyes closing as he listened to her trembling voice.

'I was in danger, they told me. The baby was not growing in the right place. And they said—they said that if they did not remove it I would—'

She stopped to swallow. It was too much. Anton spun round and attempted to take her in his arms. But Cristina didn't want that. She wanted—needed—to stand alone with this, because that was how she had dealt with it then. And it had all been so quick. One minute she was carrying Luis's beautiful baby, the next thing she knew she was—

She shrugged his hands away. 'W-when I woke up it was over,' she continued. 'They said there had been—complications. They had to remove—too much. There would be no more babies...'

'Dear God...' She heard him swallow.

'My—father arrived at my bedside.' Still she kept her eyes fixed on her bare feet. 'S-someone had contacted him when I w-was admitted. He...'

Stood over her like an angel of darkness and poured his shame and contempt over her. Accused her of sullying the Marques name.

'He w-wanted to know what use I was to him now that there would never be a grandson to inherit Santa Rosa. He...' She stopped to moisten her dry, trembling lips. 'He asked what kind of man would want to marry a barren woman.'

'Dear God,' Anton breathed. 'What kind of man was *he*, to say such a thing to you?'

'A desperate one,' Cristina answered. 'Santa Rosa was deep in debt even then. His only chance of saving it was to marry me off to some man willing to pay him well for the honour. I ran away when he first began parading his suitable candidates in front of me. That's when I met you, lived with you, became pregnant by you, and...'

She left the rest unsaid. Luis was Brazilian enough to know how things worked in the archaic corners of society. A nice young, protected virgin would win a high price on the marriage market. A spoiled one would earn much less.

A barren one was worth nothing.

The next crack of lightning lit the bedroom. Cristina folded her arms more tightly across her chest. 'The next time he came to the hospital he brought Vaasco with him,' she continued. 'Vaasco was willing to put a large injection of cash into Santa Rosa if I married him.'

'So you said yes, just like that?'

'No, I did not!' For the first time she lifted her eyes to him. He looked pale in the darkness of the room, shocked, appalled—revolted by her now? She looked away again. 'I s-sent them away,' she continued quietly. 'I n-needed time to be on my own, to grieve and to think. I had nowhere else to go so I returned to your apartment. There was a message from you waiting for me on the answering machine, telling me you were on your way to Rio. So I w-waited for you to come...' One of her hands unclipped itself from her arm and lifted to rub her trembling mouth before it dropped back down again. 'I was going to tell you what had happened, but we had that big row—'

'You needed to hurt me as you were hurting.'

'You were talking about marriage and babies.' Her voice choked on the memory. 'How do you think that made me feel, Luis? I was in love with you and I was hurting. I was in shock. Would you have preferred it if I had said yes to your marriage proposal and then said—By the way, Luis, there will be no children because I am barren, you see?'

'Yes, I would have preferred it,' he replied. 'I had a right to know. Do you think I would have walked away from you if you'd told me the truth?'

'I did not want to give you that choice.'

She heard his breath hiss from between his teeth. 'You blamed me.'

Cristina stared down at her feet and thought about it. Yes, she concluded, she had blamed him—for not being there when she needed him—but as for the rest...

Luis let out a sigh and moved right away from her. 'It's okay. Don't worry about it,' he muttered heavily. 'Right now I am blaming myself.'

'No.' Her head came up. 'I did not tell you this to make you feel guilty about it!'

'Then why did you tell me?'

'To make you see why I cannot marry you!'

'You married Ordoniz knowing you could not give him children. Why not me?' he bit out roughly.

'I did not care about him. I care about you.'

Anton pulled in an unsteady breath. 'The man was child-less, Cristina,' he delivered painfully. 'Surely he must have married you so that you could give him a son?'

'I am not that wicked!' For the first time since this little scene had begun she let her eyes make contact with his. 'Why do you always have to look for the bad in me?'

She was right; he did. Hell, I'm losing my head here, Anton thought. And he wanted to—

'Vaasco could not have children!' she threw at him. 'He could not have sex! He—the accident,' she added on a shiv-ering breath, 'the horse—it damaged him there. And he did *not* want me because I was young and for everything else I see twisting around in your head!' she threw at him. 'He wanted to punish me because I—I caused his accident, and...' She paused before asking warily, 'Has your mother explained what Vaasco was to her?'

'Oh, yes.' His mother had been totally honest with him—at last.

'Vaasco never forgave her,' Cristina said, then released a sudden cold laugh. 'He forgave Enrique Ramirez for his part in your *mamma*'s affair because he was a man, and "a man is allowed to sip the nectar if it is there to sip"— Vaasco's words exactly,' she explained. 'He also knew about you and me—my father had told him. He expected you to come back for me. He wanted to watch me hurt you when you did. He wanted you to be hurt in your *mamma*'s place, by seeing me married to him. He made me stay in Rio with him for a full year, w-waiting for you to come back.'

But he hadn't come back.

'You let him do this to you without putting up a fight?'

Her eyes were cold now. 'He bought me from my father in the same way that you have been trying to buy me. When you sell yourself you lose the right to think for yourself.'

Anton turned away from that coldly honest statement, a hand with decidedly shaky fingers going up to scrape through his hair, then ending up grabbing the back of his neck.

What now? he asked himself as he stood there trying to numb the shockwaves crashing into him. Cristina was right about him. He did always look for the bad in her. He had done it six years ago, when he had taken what she'd said to him without bothering to question why she was saying it. What kind of man did that make him?

He had even come back here to Brazil bent on seeking his revenge on her for what she'd done. He need not have bothered. Cristina had been punishing herself.

He found he was staring at the bed, with its humble picnic, and suddenly he felt the sting of tears attack the back of his throat as he began to see every single thing she had done since he came back into her life for what it really was.

An act of love for him that was so damn hopeless in her eyes she had to be tough afterwards—or how did she let him go?

He turned to look at Cristina next, standing there in his T-shirt and his bowtie and nothing else. His scent on her body, his kisses on her lips. His love was wrapped all around her if she would dare to let herself to feel it.

'Let's go back to bed,' he said.

She stared at him. 'Have you listened to anything I have said to you?'

'All of it.' He nodded. 'It doesn't change a single thing.'

'Oh, *meu Dues*,' she sighed, as it all flared up again. 'Luis, I know about Enrique's last will and testament!' she cried. 'I know why you need to marry quickly and produce a child! You have half-brothers you need to—'

'Don't talk about them,' he uttered. They did not belong here—not in this room with this situation and this woman who had sacrificed so much! Well, he was about to learn what it felt like to sacrifice something he wanted badly. Because from this moment on he had no half-brothers. How could he have when—?

God, he did not want to go there right now. He could not allow himself to if he was going to get through the rest of this.

'We have to talk about them,' Cristina insisted. 'The only way you can meet them is by marrying s-some woman who can give you a baby...'

Anton stiffened. She didn't know—not all of it anyway.

'Well, you cannot do that with me,' she went on. 'S-so you can go now and—and marry that h-horrible Kinsella Lane person,' she suggested with tremulous bite.

He laughed. It was bad of him to laugh with so much

anguish creasing the atmosphere, but that was what he did. Because here stood this beautiful, proud, *tragic* woman telling him to go—yet she was protecting that damn door as if her life depended on it!

He heeled his shoes off. For a moment he thought she was going to leap on him in a rage. 'Luis—!'

'That's me,' he acknowledged, and pulled his shirt off over his head.

She stamped a foot. Now, that's more like it, he thought as he began to undo his trousers.

'If you don't stop this I will—!'

He reached her so fast that it was all she could do to gasp out a protest as he clamped his hand over her mouth. 'Now, listen to me...' he said, bringing his head down so he could look right into those dark pools of tragedy. 'I am *not* going to stop loving you because you think that I should, and I am *not* going to walk away from this. I *am* going to marry you, whether you like it or not, and I *am* going to keep on loving you until I draw my last breath— so get used to it.'

After that he straightened up, took his hand from her mouth and lowered it to grasp both her arms, where they still linked defensively across her front. He used them to pull her over to the bed. It took him five seconds to get rid of the tray, another two to grab her again, then stretch out on the bed, pulling her down on top of him so she had no option but to unwrap her arms to support herself.

Her eyes were dark and her mouth small, and as he looked up at her he knew she had not given in to him yet.

'Sad little thing,' he murmured, and stroked a gentle finger across an unhappy cheek. 'Am I such a bad bet?'

She gave a sombre shake of her head, '*Arido,*' she whispered.

It came then. Six years of grief and misery pouring out of her as she lowered her face to his chest and wept.

Anton said no more. He did not attempt to stem the flow. He just held her. Held her and wished there was something he could do to make it all go away for her—but there wasn't.

Arido, he thought bleakly, and rolled with her, pulled the covers up over them, then curled his body around her as much as he could.

Of course he ended up kissing her out of it. How long was a man supposed to lie passive while the woman in his arms broke her heart all over him?

And he used words—husky, soft, honest words—like, *'Eu te amo.'* I love you. *'Nada matérias outras.'* Nothing else matters. *'Eu te amo. Eu te amo.'* Until words became warm, thick, tear-washed kisses, and kisses became—something else. It even shocked him how an overdose of heartache and anguish could generate the driving depths of passion they ended up sharing.

Anton still wasn't over it when he carefully slid from beneath her and stood up from the bed. She was asleep, coiled around the pillow he'd slipped into the place where his body had been. Turning away, he hunted down his discarded clothes and put them on again with a dry promise that this time they'd stay on. Then he let himself out of the room as quietly as he could do.

He needed some time alone to think.

Cristina came awake to find she was hugging the pillow. She sat up, blinking owlishly, trying to decide if the grey light she could see seeping into the room was the fading day or a new day just come.

She felt hot and sweaty, and every one of her muscles ached as if she hadn't moved them for hours and hours.

She had a cloudy recollection of the events that had led up to her falling into a deep sleep here in this bed, but in truth she did not want to think about them.

Luis's bag still sat on the ottoman, but a swift glance around the room told her that he was not here. She got up, discovered she was wearing his T-shirt again—though she did not recall when she'd pulled it back on after—

She sucked in a sharp breath, not wanting to go there—not yet anyway. Instead she crossed the room to look out of the window, then bit out a very unladylike curse.

It *was* daylight out there! She had slept the evening and the whole of the night away—plus most of the morning too!

Spinning around, she headed quickly for her own bedroom, where she showered and pulled on clean jeans and a fresh green T-shirt, then tried to soothe her fidgety nerves before she went to find Luis. Only to receive the shock of her life when she found a man—a complete stranger—dressed in a suit, wandering the hall with a clipboard.

'Good morning, *senhorita*,' he greeted her politely when he saw her standing there on the stairs, then just continued with what he was doing!

Anger began to fizz. 'Do you happen to know where Senhor Scott-Lee is?' she demanded.

'I think most of them are in the kitchen,' he replied absently as he wandered off into one of the reception rooms.

Most of them?

Cristina headed for the kitchen. On her way there she passed one of the women from the village, coming away from the kitchen carrying a mop and bucket. She dipped a shy hello at Cristina and, when asked what she was doing, said she was here to help Orraca with the household chores.

Since Cristina did most of those chores herself, she took the fact that someone had given this woman a mop and bucket and told her to go and clean something as a very personal slight.

Luis, of course. It just had to be him. She'd given in to a little weak weeping on his shoulder and now he thought he could—

Those thoughts ground to a stop at the sight that met her in the kitchen. For a few seconds she could not believe what she was seeing, and even thought of going out and coming in again. For there at her table sat Orraca, sharing what looked like a pot of tea served in the best china with none other than Luis's mother, who was looking lovely in a soft cambric shirt and pale blue linen trousers, her dark hair loosely looped at her slender nape.

'Ah, good morning, Cristina,' the lady herself greeted her warmly.

'Good—morning.' Good manners made her reply accordingly.

Mrs Scott-Lee smiled. 'I can see you are surprised to see me here, and I don't blame you,' she said. 'When my son wishes to move mountains, he moves mountains. Please—come and sit down and join us. Orraca and I were just reminiscing about the old times.'

'How—how long have you been here?'

'I arrived just half an hour ago. But Anton's team of experts were here at the crack of dawn.'

'Team—?'

'The men who are surveying the land edging the forest with the intention of acquiring a protection order for it.'

'Protection?' She was bewildered.

'*Sim.* Anton thinks it is best to do it officially, then you will not have to put up with greedy people like the Alagoas Consortium coming at you through the back door, so to speak. Come and sit down,' his *mamma* urged yet again.

'Orraca, another cup and saucer, if you would be so good, my dear...'

Orraca, Cristina saw to her utter amazement, meekly stood from the table and did as she was bade—when no one, but *no one*, told Orraca to do anything!

Cristina's eyes gave a flash. 'Where is Luis?' she demanded.

'In Sao Paulo, dealing with some other business. He said to tell you to eat a proper breakfast before you start shouting at me,' his mother relayed, dark eyes twinkling, and so thoroughly, unfairly disarming that Cristina found herself sitting down and accepting the cup of tea Orraca provided, along with one of her unreadable stares.

'I suppose you think it is okay to let strangers wander my home?' she said to the housekeeper.

'He is an architect.' Mrs Scott-Lee provided the reply. 'An expert in historical renovation. And he is so in love with your house, Cristina, he almost begged Anton to give him the commission. What do you usually eat for breakfast, *meu querida*?'

'She does not eat breakfast.' Orraca spoke for the first time. 'She does not eat lunch. Why do you think she is so thin? I am amazed your handsome son wants to marry such a—'

'I think we will have some hot toast with proper butter,' Luis's mother smoothly cut in. 'I usually deny myself butter,' she confided. 'Not good for the figure or the heart. But, since you make your own here, how am I supposed to resist it?'

Orraca moved off without another word to make the suggested toast, while Cristina tried a couple of calming breaths before she attempted to make sense of what was going on here.

'Senhora Scott-Lee—'

'Please call me Maria—everyone does—except for Anton, of course. If you prefer it you can call me Mother, as he does, though I always think it's such a stuffy name—very English.' She grimaced.

'He is English,' Cristina said.

'You think so?' His mother looked thoughtful. 'I suppose he must seem it to you.'

'Mrs—Maria…'

'Still, you haven't met his uncle Maximilian yet. Now, there is the quintessential Englishman—complete with bowler hat and umbrella in his prime. Now he prefers Harris tweed and a walking stick.'

'*Senhora*—'

'Ah, here is our toast. Orraca, I think I would like to steal you away from Santa Rosa. Would you like to live in London, do you think?'

As it began to dawn on Cristina that she was not going to be allowed to ask any questions as to what was going on here, she took a piece of toast, liberally spread with butter, bit into it, and sipped her tea while the other two women slipped into conversation about the advantages and disadvantages of living abroad. She silently seethed.

She was going to kill Luis when he put in an appearance. Who did he think he was? Taking over her home as if he owned it just because she had agreed to—

She stood up. It was the shock that made her do it.

But she had said it—hadn't she? She had lain in his arms and said *yes* to his marriage proposal—his proper marriage proposal, complete with—

'Cristina, what's wrong?' his mother asked sharply.

'I want to see Luis,' she insisted tautly. 'I demand to see Luis!'

'*Querida*, he isn't here…'

'I am not your darling, Mrs Scott-Lee,' Cristina replied.

'I am *viuva de* Ordoniz—the woman you travelled thousands of miles to stop from marrying your son!'

'That was yesterday.' Maria touched Cristina's hand in a gentle conciliatory gesture. 'Today I could not be happier for both of you—'

'Why should you be?' Cristina demanded.

'Ah, here are my two handsome young escorts.' She smiled with relief as Luis's two executives appeared at the kitchen door. 'I hope this means that Anton has returned?' she enquired hopefully.

'He went straight to the library—'

'*My* library?' Cristina swung on them.

'Er—yes.' They were startled. She did not blame them. If Luis had been there to see her face he would be taking a very wary step back by now.

'Please excuse me,' she said, with an icy politeness that did not reflect what she was feeling inside.

Polite? she thought as she walked out of the kitchen, having to sidle past the woman from the village who was mopping the hall floor. Then she caught sight of the architect person, carefully scraping at the plaster on the walls. It was like being invaded, she thought as she stalked past him across the hall and pushed open the library door. Luis was there, all right, standing by *her* desk, using *her* telephone, dressed in a sharp dark pinstripe suit and giving off the arrogant appearance that he ruled the world!

Her world.

Cristina slammed the door shut to get his attention. He swung around and snatched her breath away, because he looked so big and lean and alive and—

'What do you think you are playing at?' she scythed at him.

The smile that had been about to arrive on his lips disappeared before it made it. With smooth aplomb Anton concluded his call and replaced the receiver on its rest. Then he settled his hips against the desk and just looked at her while he decided how he was going to tackle this.

The tempting way was to provoke what he could already see was erupting. The safer way was to soothe the situation down.

He went for the irresistible. 'You've forgotten.'

'Forgotten what?'

'That in a week you and I will be getting married,' he provided. 'It is usual to—'

'*A week?* I didn't think it would be so soon!'

'I moved the date up. I told you I was going to do it last night, when we—'

'All right.' She held up a hand. 'We will begin this stupid conversation again!' She took in a deep, calming breath. 'Luis—there is a man wandering around *my* house, picking plaster off the walls.'

'An architect.' He nodded.

'I know what he is!' she snapped. 'Your mother kindly informed me of it. I want to know when it was exactly that I gave my permission for him to be here!'

'You didn't. I did.'

'And your permission came from where?'

He sent her one of those seductively appealing lazy grins. 'I'm not answering that. I daren't,' he confided.

She frowned and crossed her arms. 'I believe there is also a team of surveyors on my property?'

He nodded in confirmation. 'After we marry. Santa Rosa will be placed in a trust—or have you forgotten about that too?'

'A trust for whom?' she almost choked out.

'Whoever you decide will inherit it from you.' He shrugged. 'Since we won't be able to spend all our time here it seemed sensible to protect Santa Rosa as much as is possible. The surveyors will also be looking at the forest. The Government frowns on deforestation these days. In fact I am amazed a protection order was not placed on it years ago.'

There was so much sense in what he was saying that he could see she was struggling to find an argument—though she did find one.

'I would have liked to be consulted about all of this *before* Santa Rosa was invaded.'

'No time,' he said. 'You were asleep and I needed to get things moving. My mother—'

'*Why* is your mother here?'

'She's not welcome?'

'Of course she's welcome.' Cristina frowned. 'But I—'

'She wants to help you choose your wedding outfit. But if you would rather she—'

'Luis—I am not marrying you!'

'Not that again.' He sighed. 'Which door would you like me to try and leave by, so you can have a running start at barring my way?'

She flushed. And so she should, Anton thought, losing enthusiasm for the provoking game. He had known she would change her mind again the moment she opened her eyes this morning. He had known that the tragic creature he'd loved in every way he could last night had only been recharging her batteries before she went on the defensive again. He'd meant to stay out of her way—had planned to do that right up until the moment he'd stood over her this morning, watching her sleep with his pillow clutched in her arms, and something had hit him.

The sense of honour that Sebastian must have instilled in him—because he sure as hell hadn't got it from his real father. Cristina deserved to have her say, even if it did mean yet another battle.

'I'm going to tell you something I had vowed to keep to myself. But having you continually try to make me walk away from you, I've changed my mind.'

Her chin came up in defensive readiness. Anton thought about going over there and just kissing her into surrender, then grimly stuck to his guns and pushed himself into speech.

'When Ramirez tempted me out to Brazil to look for you he did it with just one clever sentence that insisted I ''make reparation'' to the woman I ran out on six years before, leaving her in dire straits.'

'But you didn't do that.'

'Did I not?' He looked grimly at her whitened face. 'I thought I hadn't. I thought that you should be making reparation to me for the way you kicked me out of your life— but look at you, Cristina.' He indicated brutally. 'Look at the prickly, self-defensive, half-empty shadow you've become of that wonderful, excitingly vital and light-hearted creature I knew six years ago.'

She went pale. Anton sighed. 'Would you have become this person if I'd stayed around and fought for what I wanted? No, you would not,' he declared without expecting a reply. 'You would not have let your father sell you to some no-good vengeful swine because you didn't care what happened to you. You would have been mine! And, on being mine, you would have been pulled by your beautiful hair out of your shock and your grief and made to see that you did not need to be anything other than the beautiful person you are—to be loved by me! However, I walked,' he breathed in contempt. 'Which makes the accusation Ramirez made against me true. Because I *do* owe you— for not being man enough to stop still long enough to think *why* you needed to lash out at me. I owe you, *querida*, for six long miserable years of existing in a vacuum breaking your poor heart over me!'

She walked out. Anton stood there staring at the door she'd shut behind her. His hand went up to wipe the angry pallor from his face. He didn't know why she had walked out, or what she was thinking. He didn't even know if he'd just made the biggest mistake by telling her that he had his own guilt to feed.

CHAPTER ELEVEN

ORRACA found Cristina in her bedroom, staring out through the window.

'Enrique Ramirez is the English gaucho's *papa*. His *mamma* has just told me,' she announced. 'Enrique is the man who saved your life when I foolishly let go of your hand. He pulled that horse away from you at great risk to himself, never mind that swine Ordoniz. If Ramirez wants you to marry his son, then do it. You owe him that.'

'Everyone seems to owe everyone something,' Cristina murmured.

'*Sim,*' Orraca agreed. 'But a debt only becomes a burden if you do not want to pay it. You want to pay the debt, child, but you are too surrounded here by bad ghosts that tell you to turn the debt into a burden. Get away from here, Cristina,' the old woman advised. 'Marry the son of Enrique Ramirez, spit in the eye of the bad spirits and see what life brings.'

'Happiness?' She turned a sad smile on this woman who had been in her life for as long as Cristina could recall.

'If he is man enough to pull you free from this place, like his *papa* pulled that horse free, then he is man enough to give you happiness.'

Maybe Orraca was right. Maybe it was time to stop communing with ghosts—time to stop pulling against Luis.

'His *mama* is waiting downstairs to take you to Sao Paulo,' Orraca said. 'Go with her, buy the prettiest wedding outfit you can find, and marry your English gaucho. If he

171

turns out to be no good you can always come back here and be miserable again.'

Cristina laughed. She couldn't help it at such sober advice. Orraca just shrugged and left the room again.

Fifteen minutes later, Cristina was sitting beside her future mother in law in a helicopter, flying to Sao Paulo.

Anton watched them go from one of the windows. She would not be coming back here before they married— though Cristina didn't know that yet, he reminded himself. Nor would she be seeing him again until they stood in front of the registrar and made their vows—if his mother got Cristina that far, that was.

He turned away from the window, a wry smile playing with the corners of his mouth. His mother was the best gentle bully he knew, but could she handle Cristina if she took fright again and decided to make a run for it?

He had Santa Rosa covered as a place to escape to, because he was staying right here until the morning they married in Rio. And Gabriel Valentim no longer held a reliable bolt-hole because the man was too much the romantic. Gabriel was so convinced that Cristina belonged with Anton that he had agreed to be his best man. And even Rodrigo Valentim had been convinced that he had Cristina's best interests at heart.

The lawyer had listened to everything Anton had said to him this morning in Sao Paulo, and carefully read the documents he'd placed in front of him which showed that if Cristina could not be happy in their marriage then Santa Rosa would always be here for her, safe and cared for by the trust he was setting up to protect it. Then he'd played his ace card and asked Rodrigo if he would give the bride away. Recalling the way the older man had filled up, Anton was prepared to trust that Rodrigo Valentim's home would not be a safe bolt-hole for Cristina to use either.

If all of those people managed to get Cristina to stand in front of the registrar, then it only left him with the prospect of a full blown face-to-face rejection in front of everyone in the Blue Room at his hotel in Rio.

Could he handle that?

Yes, he could handle it. He could handle anything—because this time he was not going to let Cristina down. And on that final thought, he turned his attention to the next grim task in hand.

Going to sit down behind the desk of the late Lorenco Marques, Luis put his mind into a different gear, then picked up the phone.

Two minutes later a cool, smooth, quietly refined voice greeted him pleasantly. 'Good afternoon, Senhor Scott-Lee. It is a pleasure to hear from you.'

'It's quite possible that you won't be saying that in a few seconds, Senhor Estes,' Anton replied. 'I am calling you to formally withdraw any claim I have on Enrique Ramirez's estate.'

There was a small silence. 'May I enquire as to why you've made this decision?'

'That's personal.'

'Your half-brothers—'

'Will survive without knowing me.'

'But will you survive without knowing them, *senhor*?'

The quick answer? Anton mused. 'Yes.' If he had to.

'You do understand that by doing this your share of your father's estate—'

'Ramirez was not my father.'

'A moot point we will leave to one side for now, if you will. As I was saying…You understand that your share in the estate will go to Cristina Marques?'

'Since you've already handed over a chunk of it to her

I think I've managed to get that, Senhor Estes,' Anton drawled. 'Was that ethical, by the way?'

'Was it ethical that you brought your mistress with you to Rio?' the lawyer returned.

Anton sat up straight. 'Explain that,' he commanded.

'I think you prefer to call her your secretary,' Senhor Estes said.

'So the money went to Cristina as a slap on the wrist for me? Is that what you mean?'

'Your—Enrique Ramirez expected you to mend your lusty ways not continue them.'

'I don't bed two women at the same time, Senhor Estes,' Anton said coldly. 'Unlike my—father, who seems to have bedded anything he happened to see in a skirt.'

'He was not the most discerning of men where his personal life was concerned,' the lawyer agreed. 'May I ask why you will not be marrying Cristina Marques?'

'But I am marrying Cristina,' Anton confirmed smoothly. 'On Saint Sebastian's day at two p.m. in the Blue Room at my hotel. You are welcome to attend, if you wish.'

'I will certainly consider it,' the other man said politely. 'Though I don't see the point if you are definitely pulling out of this.'

'I am.' Anton was adamant.

'Then you will understand that from that day forth all correspondence to do with Enrique Ramirez's estate will be forwarded to your wife?'

'Of course,' Anton agreed. 'Prefixed by my name, if you please, Senhor Estes, since I will be taking complete control of Cristina's business interests from that day forth.'

There was a pause, a long pause, then the merest hint of smile sounded in Senhor Estes's tone. 'Machismo still rules on the pampas, heh, Mr Scott-Lee?'

'Most certainly,' Anton confirmed.

'Then all correspondence from this office to your wife will be prefixed by your name,' the lawyer established.

'And, as I will be attending all meetings with or on be-half of my wife, may I ask if she will need to attend any meetings at your offices with regard to Enrique's estate?'

'That will of course, be up to your wife.'

'Thank you.'

'Please don't mention it,' the other man said, and there was a definite smile in his voice now. 'Before you go, Mr Scott-Lee, I am curious—do you know why your father took so personal an interest in Miss Marques?'

Anton tensed. 'I believe he saved her life once.'

'And a life once saved becomes the saviour's responsi-bility,' the lawyer confirmed. 'Enrique lived by that maxim where Cristina was concerned. He even found her a job working in a café-bar on the Copacabana when she ran away from home seven years ago—though I don't think that she knows this. It was purely coincidental, of course, that the café-bar was the place you used to frequent each evening on your way home from the bank. Fate lending a hand, do you think, Mr Scott-Lee?'

It did not take Anton two seconds to understand what Estes was really saying. Anger erupted, pushing him to his feet. 'Then where the hell was Ramirez when Cristina needed protecting from her father and that bastard Ordoniz?' he rasped.

'Enduring his first heart attack,' the lawyer came back. 'Where were you, Senhor Scott-Lee…?'

Anton was pacing. He had never thought he would be a pacer at his own wedding. He'd always teased his friends when they'd done this at their weddings. Now here he was—pacing.

She was late.

He glanced at his watch. Not very late, just a few minutes late—the bride's prerogative.

'Anton…' Gabriel touched him on the shoulder.

He swung round. One glance at the other man's face and he knew his worst prediction was about to come true.

'Where is she?' he demanded.

'Not far,' Gabriel quickly assured him. 'She's at the restaurant downstairs, by the pool. She wants to talk to you before she—'

The rest was spoken into fresh air.

Anton stepped outside and saw her instantly. She was sitting at a table staring at the ornamental pool—and he had to pause for a moment because she quite simply took his breath away. Her hair was down, rippling in glossy, loose spiral twists down her back, and she was wearing a simple short silk sheath dress in a shade of warm ocean-green that could have been hand-dyed to match the colour of his eyes.

Relief swept through him. A woman who bought a dress to match the colour of her lover's eyes had not been thinking of jilting him when she chose it. As he approached he even smiled when he caught sight of what she was wearing to tie her hair back from her face.

'Hi,' he said as he arrived beside her, touching her warm sun-kissed shoulder with his fingertips and bending to brush a kiss to her cheek.

'Hi,' she greeted him huskily.

Swinging out the chair next to hers, he turned it around, then straddled it.

Cristina glanced up and felt not just her heart but everything else take a warm, swooping dive inside her. He looked so very good to her hungry eyes, with his neat dark hair and warm golden skin, and a smile on his lips that made her vulnerable heart ache. He was wearing a pale cream silk-linen suit that did disturbing things for his broad-shouldered figure, and the silk shirt he wore beneath the jacket was an almost exact match to the colour of her dress.

'Now I know why my mother bought this shirt and insisted I wear it,' he said. Reaching out then, he flicked a finger at the cream ribbon she was wearing in her hair. 'And you've been filching my bow ties again.'

Cristina flushed and looked away. 'Don't tease,' she shook out.

A waiter appeared beside their table. Without hesitation Luis ordered two glasses of champagne. The waiter moved away—curious, Cristina could tell, because it had to be obvious that they were the bride and groom supposed to be getting married in the Blue Room right now, instead of sitting here. Luis was even wearing a creamy rosebud in his jacket lapel.

'Luis…' she whispered anxiously.

'Mmm?' he responded, in an intimately seductive way that brought some colour into her pale cheeks.

Leaning forward, he rested his arms across the back of the chair, then placed his chin on his arms. 'You look amazingly, beddably gorgeous, *meu querida*,' he told her softly. 'Will you come upstairs and marry me?'

Cristina sucked in a breath. 'Can you be serious for a moment?'

'Not today, no,' he refused.

'But I need to talk to you—'

'You could try looking at me when you say that, my darling. At the moment you are talking to your poor mangled fingers.'

Her chin shot up; her eyes flashed. 'Will you please listen to me for one moment without—'

'Listen to you try to kick me out of your life again? No way.' Anton shook his head.

'I don't want—'

'Then what do you want?' he asked, and the humour was starting to leave him, no matter what he'd said about refusing to be serious.

'I want to talk about what you really want,' she told him.

'I want you as my wife.'

The champagne arrived, delivered to the table with a flourish in two fluted glasses. 'With the compliments of the hotel, *senhor—senhora*.' The waiter smiled, then melted away.

'He thinks we are already married.' Cristina sighed.

'Optimistic of him—but then he doesn't know my bride's penchant for pulling my strings.'

'You're cross.'

'Getting there,' Anton agreed as he handed her a glass. 'Now, drink,' he commanded. 'You are going to need Dutch courage to sustain you when I become weary of this and decide to pick you up and throw you over my shoulder—and don't kid yourself I won't do it,' he added warningly. 'Because you know very well that I will.'

'This just isn't fair! If you had agreed to speak to me on the telephone we would not be sitting here at all!'

A sleek black eyebrow made a sardonic arch. 'You wanted to dump me by telephone this time?'

'I'm going to hit you in a minute.' She glared at him.

'Well, that would be a whole lot healthier than sitting here giving the impression that you are about to attend a wake,' Anton snapped, then uttered a sigh. 'You know that I love you, Cristina,' he declared wearily. 'I've tried to show you I do in every which way I can. But if you cannot find it in you to love me enough to want to spend the rest of your life with me, then I *will* accept that and let you go.'

'I don't feel like that.' Cristina even shivered at the thought of him letting her go. But her eyes were bleak as they stared into her champagne glass. 'You are being asked to sacrifice too much for me, Luis.'

'We aren't talking about me, now. We are talking about you and what you want.'

'I want more than anything for you to be happy.'

'And you believe that you are the best one to judge what will make me happy?' His tone alone mocked her ability to judge anything with any accuracy.

'Your half-brothers,' she said huskily. 'I cannot let you sacrifice the chance of meeting them because I cannot—'

'They are not an issue,' he interrupted. 'Seriously,' he added, at her impatient look, 'they are not an issue. You are the issue, Cristina. You know it and I know it, so get to the point.'

'I don't think that *I* can be truly happy again,' she admitted on a helpless rush. 'And that could make you unhappy—understand?'

'You could be right.' Anton was not going to pull his punches here, this was just too important, but he did reach out to gently move a stray twist of hair from her unhappy cheek. 'I know I can never fill that empty place you carry around inside you, and that does make me unhappy, but I would rather live with it than live without you.'

'And what about the empty place that you will carry around inside *you* because you can never conceive your own child with me?'

Anton heaved in a sigh and straightened his body. He spied his mother standing anxiously by, not far away, and knew she wanted to approach them, but he stopped her with a small frowning glance.

'I wish you had met Sebastian.' He turned back to Cristina. 'If you had met him you would know what a true father really is, and then you would not have needed to ask me that question. Sebastian was—special.'

'I know.' Cristina nodded. 'You used to talk a lot about him six years ago, w-when…'

'What you do not know is that Sebastian always knew that I was not his real son,' Anton told her, and watched her gaze flick to his in surprise. He held it there. 'Yet he loved me, Cristina, totally and unstintingly, from the moment I arrived in his world. My being someone else's son just did not matter to him. And if there is one thing I wish I could have changed in my relationship with him I wish I had known that he was not my blood father before he died, so I could have shown him how gut-wrenchingly *grateful* I feel for his loving me the way that he did.'

His voice had roughened with feeling—the same feeling that was showing on his face. Cristina wanted to reach out and soothe it away, but he had not finished.

'Well, I can do that,' he avowed. 'I can love someone else's child like that, because I had the best to show me how to do it. The point is, though, Cristina—can *you* do it? Can you take someone else's child into your life and allow it to fill that empty space inside you, as Sebastian allowed me to fill that empty place inside him?'

He was talking about adoption here. Filling their lives with other people's children and filling her with that dangerous thing called hope. Could she do it? Would it really be enough for him?

'But you *can* have your own child if you want to,' she persisted. 'It has to make a difference to how you feel! Maybe not now,' she conceded. 'But in years to come you might feel differently, and—'

'We don't live in the Dark Ages any more, when a man's only quest in life was to pass on his genes to the next generation,' he cut in. 'We've managed to evolve, look for other quests in life to chase—mine being getting a wedding ring on your finger, if you would only stop being so damn stubborn about this!'

'You really don't mind that we will have to adopt our children?'

'One, two, five—ten! Hell, Cristina, I don't care how many it takes to make you feel better about yourself! We could fill Santa Rosa with them if that's what you would like to do.'

'Or bring up a dozen little banker's children in England,' she added, with one of her impulsive little laughs.

The little laugh did it. Anton had had enough. That laugh told him he had her hooked, whether she wanted to be hooked or not. He stood up and swung the chair out of his way, then tugged his bride into his arms and kissed her—hard.

She fell into that kiss as she always did, without an ounce of control. By the time he pulled back she was wrapped to him, clinging and wanting more.

'Can we go and get married now?' he requested hopefully.

Cristina looked up at him, all dark, glowing eyes. 'I love you so much it frightens me,' she confided. 'But if you are absolutely sure this is what you want, Luis, then, yes.' She smiled. 'Let's go and get married.'

At last! Anton almost shouted it. Instead he contained the urge and drew her beneath his arm. As he turned them towards the restaurant exit his mother began to approach with one of her anxiously hopeful smiles. She received a kiss from her son, then one from her future daughter, and all three of them walked arm in arm back inside the hotel.

A very short half-hour later Anton turned to kiss his new wife. Then their small group of well-wishers crowded in and they were separated by everything but their clasped hands.

Cristina was flushed and happy. *He* was happy—and relieved that it was finally done.

Someone tapped him on the shoulder. He turned to find an immaculately dressed young man standing beside him—a young man Anton had seen before, right here in this hotel.

'My apologies for intruding, *senhor*,' the young man said. 'I have been instructed to pass this letter to you.'

The letter changed hands, then the young man bowed politely, turned, and walked out of the room.

Everyone else had gone silent. Anton smiled as he split the seal.

'What is it?' Cristina was suddenly at his elbow—clinging to it.

Without saying a word he handed her the envelope while he opened the single sheet of paper that had been inside. He could sense her puzzlement, her growing confusion.

'Looks good, hmm?' he prompted. 'Cristina Vitória de Marques Scott-Lee.'

'But it says care of you.' She frowned. 'I don't understand.'

Anton did. He handed her the letter. 'Wedding present,' he explained.

She read, then had to re-read what was written before it finally began to sink in. Then one of those pained little whimpers broke from her throat as she spun around.

'Rodrigo—' She held the letter out to her lawyer with trembling fingers. 'Please explain this to me!'

Rodrigo glanced at Anton, took the letter, glanced at it, then handed it back again. 'It's quite clear, *minha amiga*,' he said. 'On marrying Senhor Scott-Lee you became one of the three beneficiaries of the estate of the late Enrique

Ramirez. That makes you a very wealthy woman,' he added gravely.

'But how—why?' she demanded in complete bewilderment.

'By default,' the lawyer provided.

'I didn't want it,' Anton put in.

Cristina turned wide, horror-filled eyes on him. 'But, Luis, this belongs to you. *I* don't want it!'

'Don't say that,' he groaned. 'I've banked everything on you accepting it.'

Then he banded his arms around her so he could lift her off the ground and carry her away from the wedding group to a quiet corner of the room. Their faces were level—just how he liked it. He pressed small smiling kisses to her worried mouth as he walked.

'You are beautiful. I adore you. And you are going to be *such* a wealthy wife too.'

'Did you know this was going to happen?' she demanded, between the kisses.

'Of course.' He lowered her feet to the floor.

'Then why are you happy?'

'Because, *minha esposa bonita*, I get to have my cake and eat it.' He kissed her again.

'Talk sense to me!' Cristina snapped, prising their mouths apart.

'I never wanted Enrique's money, but I did want to meet my two half-brothers,' he informed her, more seriously.

'I still don't understand,' she sighed.

'It's simple—stop glaring at me. Enrique demanded certain—things from me before I could meet my half-brothers.'

'A wife and a baby,' she whispered bleakly.

'No, *querida*,' Anton said gently. 'He demanded I take *you* as my wife and *we* produce a baby—no, don't look sad again,' he chided. 'This is not a sad occasion, I promise you. Enrique was a cruel bastard, but I think he must have known that we would not be able to fulfil his demands. I hate having to do it, but I will even say that he planned things to conclude this way.'

Cristina crossed her arms. 'I wish I knew what this conclusion is that you keep walking circles around!'

'You and me finding each other, ending up here like this,' Anton explained. 'He wanted me to dance to his tune. He wanted me to fight tooth and nail to marry you, but he didn't want me to do that while still lying to myself that I was only marrying you to fulfil *his* wishes and not my own. And here is his cruelty, *cara*. He built a knockback into his plans to force me to face myself.' Anton grimaced. 'He didn't need to do that. I'd faced what I still felt for you within the first twenty-four hours of seeing you again.'

'The knockback was the baby I cannot give you.'

'I think he also knew that once I had met my half-brothers I would tell his lawyer where to put his money. So he made certain that I wouldn't have the option to refuse. Instead it would go to you, and I would be forced to take care of it.'

'I can take care of my own money.' Her chin came up.

Anton sent her a rueful smile. 'I hope not, Cristina. In fact I'm banking on you handing over full control of all your business interests to me.'

He took the letter from her and made her read the final paragraph.

You are invited to attend a meeting at the office of Estes and Associates at four p.m. on February fourteenth, to

*hear the final reading of the last will and testament of
Enrique Ramirez, in the presence of the other main beneficiaries.*

'Your half-brothers.'

'*If* they have jumped through the hoops I don't doubt
Enrique set for them, as he did for me.'

'Your brothers…'

It was beginning to dawn on her. He could see the light
beginning to glow in her eyes. 'You are going to attend the
meeting in my place, because you are so full of machismo,
so domineering and arrogant and…you love me for it,
hmm?'

Cristina laughed. Anton laughed. The watching wedding
group on the other side of the room gave a communal sigh
of relief.

Champagne corks popped. The day moved on in a slow
and easy romantic kind of way neither Anton or Cristina
were in rush to bring to an end.

Eventually it did, though, and they went to their suite
and to bed. Being officially man and wife added a delicious
new level to their loving. Later, Anton was in his usual
wide-awake relaxed sprawl while Cristina lay on top of him
like a second skin.

'Valentine's Day,' he murmured thoughtfully.

'Mmm?' Cristina really did not want to raise herself out
of the sated haze she was drifting in right now.

'February the fourteenth—Valentine's Day. I wonder
who the die-hard romantic is that picked that particular date
for me and my brothers to meet?'

'Your father?'

'Hmm, no.' He shook his head. 'I had several more
months left to fulfil his wishes. I have to assume—*hope*—
that having the date of the meeting brought forward like

this means that, like me, my brothers must have hit their required targets earlier than expected.'

'You did not hit your target. You defaulted,' some imp made Cristina remind him.

'But I made sure I hooked in the woman who was going to get my share of the booty.' He smiled. 'I'm a winner—always have been.'

'And arrogant.'

'That too.'

'I can still remove my permission for you to attend that meeting in my place.'

'But you won't.'

'No.' She cuddled closer. 'I wonder if your brothers will look like you?' she pondered curiously. 'Can you imagine not one but *three* tall, dark, arrogant men strutting around as if they own the world?' She affected a shudder.

'We will probably hate each other on sight.'

Cristina lifted up her head and touched a gentle finger to his mouth. 'You are worried about meeting them?'

Anton tried for a macho indifferent shrug, but ended up sighing out a much more honest, 'Yes... And hellishly excited about it too. In fact—' he moved, using an arm to haul her further up his body '—too excited. I need a diversion.'

'Sex is going to be a diversion?'

'Making love to my beautiful demanding wife,' he corrected. 'The best diversion there is...'

The World of Mills & Boon®

There's a Mills & Boon® series that's perfect for you. We publish ten series and, with new titles every month, you never have to wait long for your favourite to come along.

Blaze®

Scorching hot, sexy reads
4 new stories every month

By Request

Relive the romance with the best of the best
9 new stories every month

Cherish™

Romance to melt the heart every time
12 new stories every month

Desire™

Passionate and dramatic love stories
8 new stories every month